tender morsels

ALSO BY MARGO LANAGAN

White Time
Black Juice
Red Spikes

tender morsels

Margo Lanagan

Alfred A. Knopf

New York

THIS IS A BORZOI BOOK PUBLISHED BY ALFRED A. KNOPF

All rights reserved. Published in the United States by Alfred A. Knopf, an imprint of Random House Children's Books, a division of Random House, Inc., New York.

Knopf, Borzoi Books, and the colophon are registered trademarks of Random House, Inc.

Visit us on the Web! www.randomhouse.com/teens

Educators and librarians, for a variety of teaching tools, visit us at www.randomhouse.com/teachers

Library of Congress Cataloging-in-Publication Data
Lanagan, Margo.
Tender morsels / Margo Lanagan. — 1st ed.
    p.   cm.
Summary: A young woman who has endured unspeakable cruelties is magically granted a safe haven apart from the real world and allowed to raise her two daughters in this alternate reality, until the barrier between her world and the real one begins to break down.
ISBN 978-0-375-84811-7 (trade) — ISBN 978-0-375-94811-4 (lib. bdg.)
[1. Fantasy.] I. Title.
PZ7.L216Te 2009
[Fic]—dc22
2008004155

The text of this book is set in 11.5-point Goudy.

Printed in the United States of America
October 2008
10 9 8 7 6 5 4 3 2 1

First Edition

For my sisters, Susi, Jude, and Amanda

tender morsels

prologue

There are plenty would call her a slut for it. Me, I was just glad she had shown me. Now I could get this embarrassment off me. Now I knew what to do when it stuck out its dim one-eyed head.

She were a revelation, Hotty Annie. I had not known a girl could feel this too. Lucky girls; they can feel it and feel it and nothing need show on the outside; they have to act all hot like Annie did, talk smut and offer herself to the lads, before anyone can tell.

Well, we lay there in the remains of the hay cave, that we had collapsed around us with our energetics. We looked both of us like an unholy marriage of hedgehogs and goldilockses. I laughed and laughed with the relief of it, and she laughed at me and my laughter.

"By the Leddy," she said, "you have the kitment of a full man, you have, however short a stump you are the rest of you."

"I'm not so much shorter than you," I said, perfectly happy. She could not annoy me; no one could, this night. Shakestick

1

might come along and stripe our bums and fill our ears with shame and still I would be swimming in air. Let him try.

It was warm, perfect for nudding down, the air like warm satin sliding all over me. The last blue of evening, close around us, shielded us from eyes, and yet some stars winked there and were festive also and who could mind their watching? And moths flew soft and silver. The stars silvered them, I guessed, and the last light from the sky, and the slight light from Shake-stick's lamps as he hurried the last of the haystackers, other end of the field. Anyway, they were low like a mist, the moths, like a dancing mist, large and small like snow wafting on a breeze, as if the very air were so alive that it had burst into these crea-tures, taken wing and fluttered in all these different directions.

Everything made sense—this girl and me wrapping each other, and what had gone before. I could see, as I'd not seen heretofore, why the whole world was paired up man to woman like it was, buck to doe, bull to cow, cock to hen: for both their releases, to keep them present on the earth, instead of away suffering inside their own bodies and heads. Moth to moth too, eh? Moth to moth—look at them, floating and flirting, giving off their moth-signals, curling their feather antlers at each other's nearness.

"Gawd, Annie," I whispered. "What are you made of? Caves and volcanoes!"

"I am!" she said. "I am!" And she laughed, a careful laugh so as not to be heard outside this hay, yet full of delight and delights.

Our laughing wound down and we rested. We could rest a little longer, before Shakestick's deputies came along the field rounding us all up to go back to St. Onion's.

"Here," Annie said, and there was more kindness and gen-tleness than ever I heard in this girl's voice before; she was a brassy one, this one, all bawd and bluster. "Close your eyes." She closed them for me with her damp fingertips that smelt of her and of me, ripe with the thing we just done, the parts I just discovered.

"What?" I said. "What you going to do to me?" Not that I cared, not the littlest jot.

"Shh." With her smelling fingers she made a sign on my forehead, and another, and a third. She wrote and wrote.

"Makin your letters?" I said. "Writin your name on me?"

"Shh." She kept writing.

"You're very welcome to if you want."

"Dought, shut up or I'll whap you," she said but without heat; she were too concentrated on the marks she wasn't making.

And she put me to sleep that way, and in my dream I sat up and the hay fell away, and it was daylight, and the field was full of haymakers, but they were all to a man or woman short-stumps like me. In fact I was one of the taller among them and one of the more handsome. *Dought*, they were saying. *Where is Dought? We need his aid at the wagon. Oh, here he is!*

And they needed me to do much what Shakestick did— that is, to say how things would be done and choose who would do them from the crowd. Respect came at me from all sides. People soberly took me at my word and did as I said. And several girls' eyes gleamed and some of the older women's too, towards me. I could have said the word and they would have follered me into the hay tonight just like I follered Hotty Annie.

"Come back, Dought. Here comes Oul Shaky," says Annie in my ear. Darkness fell on the hayfield and she were pulling my pants up. Shakestick's anger blew and banged towards us. Everything was scramble and stack the last forkings of hay, and shouts and smacks of the head for a while. Then we were in the cart and able to rest, jammed in so close we might almost do the thing again and not be noticed.

"What was that," I murmured to Annie who I was half on the lap of, "what you done to me?"

"Well, if you don't know that, there's something wrong with you." She laughed.

"No, after. On my forehead. So that I went away."

"I don't know," she said. "I've begun to be full of that stuff, these last several months. Curious, int it. Did you like it?"

"Like it? If I could get there and live there I would be happy as a king in his treasure-house."

"Hmm," she said, "I have wondered that."

"Oh, I would be happy, all right, no doubting it."

"No, I've wondered if I could send a person there. I think mebbe I'll be able to, one day. Right now all I can do is show." She looked tired, and more serious than I had ever seen her. The road's stones and sprouts flowed behind her along the gaps between the cart-slats.

Beamer leaned in and goggled at me. "She will show anyone," he said. "You show her yours, she will show you hers, and even give yours a rub for you if you ask nice."

"You goose." Annie laughed and whacked at him. "We're not talking about that."

"Oh well, makes a change, then, don't it?" said Beamer mildly, and sat back to his place.

4

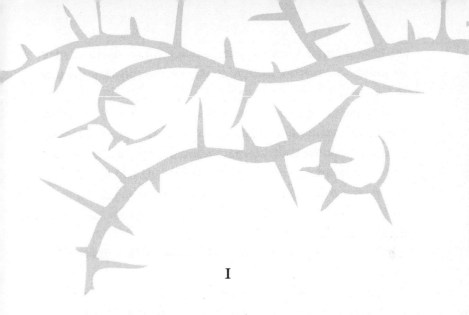

I

Liga's father fiddled with the fire, fiddled and fiddled. Then he stood up, very suddenly.

"I will fetch more wood."

What's he angry about? Liga wondered. Or worried, or something. He is being very odd.

Snow-light rushed in, chilling the house. Then he clamped the door closed and it was cozy again, cozy and empty of him. Liga took a deep private breath, then blew it out, slowly. Just these few moments would be her own.

But her next breath caught rough in her throat. She opened her eyes. Gray smoke was cauliflowering out of the fireplace, fogging the air. The smell! What unnamable rubbish had fallen in the fire?

She coughed so hard she must put aside the rush mat she was binding the edge of and give her whole body over to the coughing. Then pain caught her, low, and folded her just like a rush-stalk, it felt, in a line across her belly, crushing her innards. She could hardly get breath to cough. Sparks that were not from the fire jiggled and swam in her eyes—she could not *see* the fire for the smoke. She could not believe what she was feeling.

The pain eased just as abruptly. It let her get up. It gave her a moment to stagger to the door and open it, her insides dangerous, liquid, hot with surprise and readying to spasm again.

Her father was halfway back from the woodpile, his arms full. He bared his teeth at her, no less. "What you doing out?" White puffs came with the words. "Get back inside. Who said you could come out?"

"I cannot breathe in there." The cold air dived down her throat and she coughed again.

"Then go in and *don't* breathe! Shut the door—you're letting the smoke out. You're letting the heat." He dropped the wood in the snow.

"Has the chimney fallen in? Or what is it?" She wanted to step farther out and look.

But he sprang over the logs and ran at her. She was too surprised to fight him, and her insides were too delicate. The icicled edge of the thatch swept down across the heavy sky, and she was on the floor, the door slammed closed above her. It was dark after the snow-glare, the air thick with the billowing smoke. Outside, he shouted—she could not hear the words—and hurled his logs one by one at the door.

She pressed her nose and mouth into the crook of her elbow, but she had already gulped smoke. It sank through to her deepest insides, and there it clasped its thin black hands, all knuckles and nerves, and wrung them, and wrung them.

Time stretched and shrank. *She* seemed to stretch and shrink. The pain pressed her flat, the crashing of the wood. Da muttered out there, muttered *forever*; his muttering had begun before her thirteen years had, and she would never hear the

6

end of it; she must simply be here while it rose from blackness and sank again like a great fish into a lake, like a great water snake. Then Liga's belly tightened again, and all was gone except the red fireworks inside her. The smoke boiled against her eyes and fought in her throat.

The pains resolved themselves into a movement, of innards wanting to force out. When she next could, she crawled to the door and threw her fists, her shoulder, against it. Was he out there anymore? Had he run off and left her imprisoned? "Let me out or I will shit on the floor of your house!"

There was some activity out there, scraping of logs, thuds of them farther from the door. White light sliced into the smoke. Out Liga blazed, in a dirty smoke-cloud, clambering over the tumbled wood, pushing past him, pushing past his eager face.

But it was too late for the cold, clean air to save her; her insides had already come loose. She could not run or she would shake them out. Already they were drooling down her legs. She must clamp her thighs together to hold them in, and yet walk, and yet hurry, to the part of the forest edge they used for their excrements.

She did not achieve it. She fell to her knees in the snow. Inside her skirt, so much of her boiling self fell away that she felt quite undone below the waist, quite shapeless. No, look: sturdy hips. Look: a leg on either side. A blue-gray foot there, the other there. Gingerly, Liga sat back in a crouch to lift her numbing knees off the snow. The black trees towered in front of her, and the snow dazzled all around. She heaved and brought up nothing but spittle, but more of her was pushed out below by the heaving.

She crouched, panting. From her own noises she knew she had become some kind of animal; she had fallen as low as she could from the life she had had before Mam died. Everything had slid from there, out of prosperity, out of town, out of safety, when Mam went, and this was where of course it ended, with Liga an animal in the snow, tearing herself to pieces with the wrongness of everything.

With one last heave, her remaining insides dropped out of her. She knelt over their warmth, folded herself down, and waited to die.

But she did not die there. The snow pained against her forehead and her knees, and the fallen mass of her innards began to lose its heat in the tent of her skirt.

She tried to lift herself off it. At first her knees would not unbend, so she tipped herself forward onto her front . . . paws, they felt like, her front claws. And hoisted her bottom up from there.

"Oh, my Gracious Lady." Her voice sounded drunken and flat. Between pink footprints, her innards lay glossy and dark red. Her feet were purple, blotched yellow, weak and wet with melting pink snow.

She should go back to the house—that was all she knew. And so she labored towards it, top-heavy, slick-thighed, numb-footed, and hollow, glancing behind as if afraid the thing would follow her, along its own pink trail.

Da snatched the door open as soon as she touched it. He stood there, hands on hips. "What's a-matter with you?" The air around him was clear and warm; in the crook of his arm, the fire flowed brightly up around the new logs. Would he even let her in?

"Something," she said. "I lost. Something fell out."

"What do you mean, silly girl?" he said crossly. "You went for a shit and you had a shit, as you said."

"Something else," she said uneasily. His scorn, as usual, made her doubt her word, made her doubt her memory. Here he was, same as ever; here too was the house, all familiar, ready to go on just as it always did. Look, there was her weaving, put aside perfectly neatly. *Pick me up,* it snapped at her. *Continue with me; time is wasting!*

"Get in, get in!" her father growled. "You are letting out all the warmth, standing there like a lummock." And he flapped his hand at her, sweeping her in without touching her—and no, this was not what she wanted either. It was good to be warm, but dying outside in the snow would be less wretched than the indoor life again, in all its shuffles and snarls.

She washed and organized herself; really, she was quite similar to before, only somewhat softer and leakier and cramp-bothered. Her father kept his back to her, and hummed a tune under his breath. Slowly, slowly, she went about; slowly she began their meal, scraping the parsnip, pulling the dry-meat into its strands. Everything looked odd and felt odd in her hands, as if she had never done this before.

Her father, still humming, went out to relieve himself. He spent a good while doing it. Liga peeled the last onion they had and chopped it up fine and glistering, like salt-crystals or jewels, only with that good rich smell.

He strode back in, startling her and making her knife hover over the board. "Mekkin a stew, are ye? I'll melt ye some clean water." He was inflated, glowing. She felt him take the pot and go out again.

"Here we are!" He thundered in and swung towards the fireplace, hooked up the pot of snow, bullied the fire. "Nothing cozier on a winter night: a nice hot fire, a bit of stew!"

He stood and turned, pleased, hands on hips. Warily, she

glanced at his face, which beamed on her. All sense that she could judge things aright had left her; he would have to show her again, piece by piece, and she would have to sit very still and alert, and learn as well as she could.

Winter passed, night by long night and day by short day. Liga was kept busy following all her father's rules. These seemed to change by the hour. He railed at her for sitting quietly by the fire; he grew irritable when she busied herself about him. He roared at her for oversalting the smoke-meat; in cold silence, he added salt to it himself. He nagged and banged about that her bloods did not come; when they did, he cursed her and called her filthy. He banished her to the truckle bed; "What are you doing down there?" he said, outraged, when she went to it the next night.

The best was when he went into the town and left her; he had now forbidden her to be seen there, even in his own company. "Especially that," he said. "Especially that. We don't want people talking, how old you are now and all filled out like that into your bodice."

It was very dull there in the cottage alone, but it was better than the adventure of his presence, which, even when he was silent, put such a press on Liga's mind that sometimes she could not think at all; he made around himself a kind of frozen space into which she could only step wrongfooted.

At the very end of winter, Liga turned fourteen, and no one noticed but herself. Then spring exploded in its usual celebrations, fat with clumped blossom and bursting leaf, raucous with birdsong. In April, her bloods stopped, and Da grew by turns wilder in his tempers and more silent in his sulks.

"Bleed, girl, bleed!" he shouted at her one night, turning back to her after he had had at her and fallen away.

"I cannot *make it happen*," she said angrily.

"I *know* that, curse you!"

"I'd think you would be glad—you always say how dirty it is." And she crawled away to the truckle.

His head loomed at her over the edge of the big bed. "Are you really so stupid?" he said, as if astonished.

And she supposed she was, because she did not know what he meant. She stared up at him, at the shaggy shape of her looming ignorance. She thought he might spit on her, so long and intense was his silence. But he only jerked out of sight, with a scornful noise in his throat.

In late summer he brought home a preparation in a cloth, and boiled it up, and drew the foul-smelling liquid off the boilings into a cup. "Drink this," he said. "I have got it from a woman up town. She says it will give you strong bones."

Is there a problem, Liga wondered, with my weakling bones? There must be. She glanced stealthily at her arms on the table beside the dreadful tea, and waited unhappily for something to crack and crumble in her frame as she sat there, her mouth shriveling with the drink's bitterness.

The thought of her bones seemed to preoccupy him all that evening: he looked upon her with dislike, though she went about very carefully.

"I will go walking," she said, because she would be shouted at if she did not tell him. She said it from outside, already making for the trees.

"You will not," he said, and got up from the table. "You will not," he said again at the door.

Whyever not? her look said.

"You will stay by the house tonight." And he was gone back in, to gloom at the table.

"For what? There is nothing to do here!" she said, but not

loudly enough that he would hear and invent some nonsense work for her.

Right out to the edge of the clearing she walked, and circled there quietly, so that he would not hear where she was but would have to come out and look for her. This he did, twice, before he trusted her not to go farther.

Finally it was quite dark, and she had tired herself out with this form of taunting him, and with trying to read what he wanted and did not want. She heard him pull out the truckle with a great screech of the wood, and without thinking, in her disbelief and her relief that he would let her alone tonight, she went and stood at the cottage door. It was warm in there, and it smelled of his sweat and of the bones-tea.

"Sleep in that tonight," he said. He blew out the lamp and flung himself in the marriage bed. And though this should have been a relief to her, yet he had made of it somehow a humiliation, so that she crept away to the truckle and lay facing the wall and wondering what it was she had done, or which well-behaved daughter he had seen in the town today that made her so unsatisfactory by comparison.

Her own groan woke her in the middle of the night.

"What is it?" he said at her ear, clearly and instantly.

"My guts," she said.

"What of them?"

"They are twisting like laundry being squozen out."

"Thank the gods of all hearing," he said. "Thank the heavenly stars and the sun."

He lit the lamp and stood looking down as the pain tangled inside her on the bed, and drew itself tight. "Don't you worry, my honey," he said. "It will all be over soon."

"Yes, I am dying," she managed. "And right glad to die, too."

He laughed—laughed!

"And you so glad to see me gone."

"Ah, no," he said with satisfaction. "Ah, no." And he stilled her head under his hand—she could not tell whether it was from annoyance or affection. "I will make thee a hot cup." And he was up and humming, waking the fire.

"Don't make me one like last night's." The taste of it was still in her gullet, bitter, weedy. "That's what has killed me, that woman's poison. Strong bones, my arse."

He laughed that she had borrowed his way of talking. He went at the water-boiling with clanking gusto. She wished she might be well, to witness the spectacle of him doing this for her. Tremendously disappointed, she was, that she would die soon and not have pain-free time to look back on this and appreciate his kindness, to say to herself, *See, he was not such a bad man; look what he did.* She gasped and he set the door wide so that she could breathe better, and she marveled at his doing so, and at the blossomy, bosomy, rotting night, stirring outside in its blanket of summer warmth.

But in from that night kept sidling the thin black witch who was the pain. It lifted Liga and clasped her and made her dance against its iron, and dropped her, and wandered away—and then turned back, suddenly urgently interested again.

Liga clambered and slid from moment to moment through that night, waiting for the pain to reach the pitch where she would break apart and it would all be over. The very house was gone from around her—her very father was gone. He was a bee caught in her hair, singing. He was hands all over her, patting and laughing. "Thank that muddy old hag," he said. "It is just as she said, after all." Which made no more sense than anything else had, this night.

Dawn came, and he strode out to meet it and stand in the first light before the sun rose and sweated up the world again. With him gone—just then, right then—the crisscross of bands gave out that had held Liga to the iron-witch's ribs, and she felt, deep within, a movement of some significance. Whereupon she knew, like falling to the bottom of a well, 'Tis a babby! And then she fell through that well-bottom—which was thin and crumbly, and how had it ever held water?—into a second well: And that before, that was something of a babby too, come out in the snow.

Up she got, out of the truckle, and squatted beside it, holding on to its wooden edge. She was excited. She wanted to see it. It was coming. She would have a baby. Now the pain was not so much pain; it was more like machinery working, a body doing its job, something going right instead of wrong.

Down it worked its way in her. Her muscles knew, and squeezed it down, her own baby that would make her a mam and respectable, that would look to her for care and loving.

It turned some corner in her, through exquisite levels and points and presses of pain. She was weeping with the joy of the small arriving thing that knew nothing, that would be her companion and her plaything.

Now it was at the door of her—she would split like a berry-bead and spill out, baby and innards and all. She put her hand down there and felt the bulge, at once hard and soft. She was in between pains, and the house was scarcely big enough for her breath and her heat; the *world* was scarcely big enough.

"And are you done, then?"

Liga shook at his voice.

He came in, stamping off mud.

14

She tried to stop the baby, but it had been poised to rush out, and so it rushed out, with a quantity of wet noise.

He heard it too. "Is it out? Are you done?"

Clumsily she bent over it, and tried to see it without him seeing—she must claim just this first look.

She had been all prepared to love it, but there was not very much to love. She had never seen a baby so thin and wizened. Its face was just creases, thick with down. It had the finest, darkest, sourest lips, disapproving anciently, godlikely, distantly. It had the look of a lamb born badly, of a baby bird fallen from the nest—that doomed look, holy and lifeless, swollen-eyed, retreated too far into itself to be awakened.

She gathered up the baby in her two hands, its unliving heat. She turned, holding it as far out as the cord would let her. She didn't know why she was showing him, *offering* it to him— to him, of all people, and so tremblingly. Maybe she imagined he would mourn with her?

"Give it here," he said disgustedly, coming at her big and heavy, alive and full of will. He took the baby and went to turn away with it, but the cord dragged it off his hands.

She caught it. "It's still attached," she said. She was beginning to shake hard.

"Well, cut it, cut it!"

She thought he meant her to cut up the child. "It is already dead."

"Oh, you!" He swung from foot to foot in his exasperation. "Don't you look at it. Give it me. Don't you go getting moon-moody on me; don't imagine this is anything more than you bleed out every month." He took it again, more carefully this time, and tried to interpose his shoulder between her face and his hands.

The afterbirth came out, a great soft rag to her startled, wincing parts.

15

"Is that all of it?" he almost shouted, clawing for it, the child held like waste meat in his other hand, its head preoccupied with its ancient thoughts.

And then he was gone, taking everything dripping with him, and Liga was too glad to be rid of him to do more than kneel there, a drizzling mess, and stare at the fact that it was over, stare at the messed floor.

"Muddy Annie Bywell," she realized aloud, out of nowhere, a few nights later.

He was whetting his knife-blade before the fire, the pipe between his teeth with no leaf in it, just clamped there for habit.

"What of her?" he said, as easily as he ever said anything; the rhythm of the sharpening did not change.

" 'Thank that muddy old hag,' you said, that night. Did she give you that horrible tea? To bring out the babby?"

"She did," he said. He paused, wiped the blade on the rag across his knee, tested it, and pointed it at her, and at his own next words, as if that made them more true: "And well rid of it, we are."

"That's not what I'm saying," said Liga. "She knows, is what I'm saying. What we did." She did not even mean "what *you* did"; he had brought her as low as that.

"She knows nothing." He waved the knife and reapplied it to the stone. "And what she says, no one believes, so it is as good as no one knowing. Why else would I go to her? Think on it."

Liga thought. She could hardly imagine. "There are people who take what Annie says very serious, every word."

He gave a quick snort between sweeps of the blade. "Women and God-men, and who cares what they think?"

"How much did it cost?" she blurted.

He glowered at her. "A lot and don't ask. A *lot*."

With her fingertip, she drew around a knot in the tabletop quickly, several times. Then she folded her arms, glanced at him twice. "It might have been nice."

"What might of?"

"A babby. The babby."

"Ha!" *Sweep, sweep.* "You saw it. It were a monster."

" 'Twere not! Just undercooked, that's all."

"I told you not to go moony," he said around the pipe, concentrating on the edge's perfection. His face and front, his knees and shins, were orange slabs before the fire. His eye and his lower lip gleamed, and the knife's light danced on the wall.

"It might have been a granddaughter for you," she said, just to hear how that sounded.

"Why should I want one o' they? I never wanted a *daughter*." And he laughed as if she were someone else, someone not that very daughter sitting opposite him—someone who would laugh along with him. "I wanted *sons*," he said, with a flick of his eyes. "A man wants *sons*."

Of course he does, thought Liga, and that must be where his rages come from, that disappointment. But—

"A son," she said. "With a son you cannot do"—another flicked glance from him made her falter—"what you did on me. What you do."

He looked at her narrowly, then widened his eyes. "Naw," he said, as if explaining to a stupid person. "That is what you have a *wife* for."

He almost laughed, almost snorted, almost spat—all three at once—as if her stupidity were not to be believed. Then he returned to his knife, and sharpened on.

❖ ❖ ❖

Life went its dogged way after that. Liga worked and listened and reflected, and when her bloods came in November, for the second time since the night of the dead baby, she put Da's relief together with the memory of his looming head—*Are you really so stupid?*—together with the events of the summer, and she realized that one was a sign of the other. No-bloods was the sign of a baby coming; bloods were the sign of no-baby.

She bled again, three times. At the third, Da said, "Mebbe we have ruined you for babbies, wi' that mudwifery, wi' that tea." He was cheerful for several days.

But the next month, as winter loosened its grip on them, she knew it had happened again, from her tiredness and faint illness, from the feeling of significance budding low in her belly. And she knew also what she would do, to keep this baby, to see it safely born in its own time.

When the next rag-time came, she took her rags when she went out to check the snares. She killed the leveret that was snared, and the older buck rabbit, and bled them onto the rags. Then she tied the cloth to herself.

All the tight watchfulness went out of Da when he felt for her that night. He clicked his tongue, and "Curse you filthy things," he said, but she felt him ease, and when she rose early to go and wash the rags at the stream again, he gave a certain satisfied sigh in his half-sleep.

Four more moons went by. The breasts on her, plumped up by the baby—he liked those, she could tell, but she caught him looking her up and down sometimes when she straightened from tending the fire, looking her up and down and scowling.

She collected her bloods a sixth time. This could not go on, she knew; she had felt the baby twitching in there, at first tiny and sudden as midge-larvae in a backwater, as if with joy, as if in play—and then not so tiny, quite solid and decisive in its movements; she could feel herself swelling, not just in body but in *self*, in happiness, with the pleasure of having a secret from him, a secret that mattered. It could not last; nothing she wanted for herself ever lasted.

"Wait," he said from his bed next morning, and she knew it was over.

"What?" she said too carelessly, not like herself at all.

"Show me that."

"Show you what?"

"The rag of you. That you're washing out."

She held up the balled rag, the dark blotches on it.

"Bring it here."

She pretended disgust. "No, I'm to wash it!"

He held out his hand.

She went and put it in, and stood back a little.

If he had not seen from the dried, browning blood, her guilty face would have told him. "What's this?"

"What does it look like?" She lifted her chin.

"It looks like last month's blood. Is it last month's?"

"Of course not!" She saw her own hands bleeding the bird last night, the bird they had eaten for supper.

"It's none of it fresh. Show me yourself."

"I shall not." She clutched her skirt to her legs.

"Don't come outrage at me, you little sneaking."

He pounced at her out of the bed. He was so heavy, but so quick; it always surprised her. There were two or three thuds and flashes and a jerking of her head, and he had pinned her breathless to the wall and upped her skirts and was holding the fresh rag away from her.

"Not a drop." He dug the cloth into her and looked again. "Dry as a fecking bone."

19

He stood straight and looked in her face, satisfied, disgusted. Then he slapped her harder than he ever had. She lay still on the floor under the spinning air, thinking he had broken her face.

"They say a good beating sometimes shakes 'em loose!" he bellowed down at her. "They say a few kicks to the stomach!" He only gave her the one, but she was sure it had worked. She lay curled around her disaster while he flung himself about and shouted.

In time, he sank to the table, and muffledly said, "Where am I to get the money? . . . Feckun deceiving witch! . . . What were you thinking?"

"And when you've done all that, sew me up a new shirt with the cloth I got you." He stood at the door with his bag of kill that he was off to town to sell. There was a hare in it, or a good-sized coney or two, the way it swung. He had a plan now; he was not despairing as he had the last few weeks since he had discovered about the bab.

Liga bent to her sweeping. "I don't know how," she said coolly. She did not know why, but she wanted to make trouble, for him and for herself. It was like thinking she must put her hand into the fire, that the pains and the blisters would be gratifying somehow.

"Use the other. The other that's fallen apart. Undo it and spread out the pieces flat. Then cut around them, and sew the new cloth together like the old was."

"There'll be more to it than that, I'm sure."

"Have I got to clout you?" He lunged at her. "Tib Stoner's daughter that's *simple* can do it. What's up with you?"

"All up the top there." She pointed at his chest. "Where it's pinched like that. How do I do that?"

20

"You think I know?"

"Aagh," she breathed. "Just go, then."

"Do I look like a sempstress?" he shouted in her ear. "Do I look like your ma? Have I a skirt and a bosom and a big round arse?"

She turned and pushed him. "Go on."

"Push *me*?" He pushed her back—he was much bigger and stronger—and again, and again, until she was up against the chimneypiece, rolling her eyes, carefully not showing that her shoulder was smacked to bruises against the stone.

"Go on," she said. "Your ale is waiting. Osgood has peed in it special."

He hit her hard, the back of his hand to the back of her head. She dreamed some shouting as she fell.

She swam up from blackness into the noise of her blood pulsing, into the tight feeling of a bump to her forehead from the bench or the floor. He had gone; he was striding away, a small figure between the table- and bench-legs in a doorway full of trees beginning to color with autumn, and lowering sky.

"Oh," said Muddy Annie. "It's him again."

He stood in her doorway, all knotted up with emotions and posings. "I want to do business." He was trying to sound scornful of her, but he was afraid, not so much of her mudwifery, she knew, as of his having to resort to it.

"By the look of you," she said, "you have already done the business."

He shifted his feet and peered in. It was too dark and smoky in here for him to see her; it would be like the darkness speaking, not a person.

"On whoever-that-poor-girl-is-give-me-three-guesses."

"That's none of your affair."

"No, thank the Leddy. Look at the mix of you, all proud and afraid of yourself. All swaggering, and yet—"

"I have silver." He knew her well, this one. Knew how to stop her gabbing if he wanted.

She snorted, allowed herself one last little jibe: "Silver won't stop my mouth. Int no one else you can go to, is there? I can say what I please."

"Say what you please," he said. "Just give me my preparation."

She got up off the stump she used for a seat. "What will it be, a smoke or a decoction?"

"Make it both."

"Ooh. He knows what he wants, this one. How *much* silver?"

He showed her, in his palm. He moved his hand so that the sunlight beamed off the coin and dazzled her, dazzled away all her rudeness.

She went to work, and did not speak for a while. He stood and watched until she told him, "Sit aside of my light, on the bench out there. There's no need to watch me. Have I ever disappointed you?"

"I had to wait a good while for that tea to take, that you guv me." But he moved away.

She went to the doorway. He was just planting his arse in the sunniest spot. "And how long, pray, did you leave it, to come to me?"

He shrugged. "I didn't think it would come out at all. I was readying to visit here again by the time she started."

"This—*this*—is what you told me." She made the exact belly shape with her hands. He looked away. And so he should; and so he should. "Would that be about how far?"

"About." He tried for carelessness again. Go inside, he'd be thinking, and get on with it, so's I can pay you and leave. She could read him like a charcoal-man's palm.

"Then shut your whining. That's a lot of flesh to shift."

"Don't I know. You would of thought she was dying."

The mudwife cleared her throat, spat on the ground. "Silver," she reminded herself, and went inside.

When she was done, she tied up the burnings and the drinkings in two rags and took them to the door. There he was, sunning himself, smug as fat Goodwife Twyke that sat in the town square, cutting maids to pieces with her tongue under the ash tree there. Muddy Annie felt her own face screw up with dislike.

"This one is for the smoke," she said, "and this for the tea. Don't confuse them, or you'll kill her." And then what will you do with yourself, she wondered. Come to *me*? She chuckled. Or go at donkeys and goats? "You know my price," she said, collecting herself. "For the two."

He brought the money out and they exchanged, bags with one hand, coin with the other, so that they each had what they wanted.

"Silly girl," he said. For a moment Annie thought he meant herself, and was astonished, but then she saw the bitterness at his mouth as he watched her fold the coin away into her hand. Yes, there was a good weight of it. You could buy plenty with that, if you were not filling up your daughter with unwanted kin—two pair of good boots for the winter, maybe, or a month's ale at Keller's Whistle, or three at Osgood's if you could stomach his stuff.

She did not snort at him, though she could afford to now. She folded her arms and made a mouth and watched him go. Smoke *and* tea. He had left it even longer this time. That girl would have a fine wringing-out of it.

She remembered the wife, Aggie—she remembered her big with child, too, of the fecund old bugger. She could not recall the daughter, though, as more than a floss-headed, knee-high thing that she might easily be confusing with some other girl-child of the town.

A curse stirred deep in the mudwife, almost as if she were with child herself. She must be careful; she had a gift, and she must not allow anything to affect her too strongly, remember. That was why she lived out here, in this burrow, instead of in St. Olafred's town—so that people would not bother her so much, knocking and demanding and bringing her irritations on themselves.

He was gone now, that . . . Longfield, his name was, and Aggie Prentice his wife. Aggie had had him on the right road for a while there, in the town. Helping out in stables, he was, and she was housemaiding for someone. Who was that, now?

The mudwife went back into her burrow, which smelt of all the poisons she had mixed, and the spices that made them drinkable and breathable. Carefully she tied up her grains and fragments, and every time that little floss-child walked into her mind, she said, "No. Off with you, now," and got out Long-field's silver, and rubbed the coins together.

Liga finished sweeping. She chopped kindling, scrubbed out the porridge-pot, attended to the cheese-barrel and the bread-starter, milked the goat. Whenever she neared the end of one task, he was in her head, telling her the next, and sharply.

She applied herself to the shirt. She thought as she sewed that she was managing it quite well, but first, with the bunching, she sewed it too tightly and ran out of the lower cloth, and then she unthreaded it and sewed it so loosely that there was a good half-a-hand hanging over, and when she had undone that, the pieces were all holed and unclean along the edges from her efforts, and she sighed and walked away from them, and occupied herself with small tidyings and polishings and thoughtfulnesses that might please him should the shirt not be ready when he came back. She could hear him commenting all along, on the poor job she did of this and the clumsy way she accomplished that; sometimes she looked up almost in surprise that he was not here, he was so strong inside her, directing her.

She sat to sewing again, but made no better progress. At the end, she laid the shirt aside, frightened of the oncoming evening and the sight of the poor work, so much like the snarl that would be on his face when he saw it.

She heard a rumbling up on the road. She would not see the carriage pass from here, but she went to the door to listen, to the coachman's cries and the drumming of the horses' hooves and the expensive squeaking of the carriage's under-pinnings and the soft crashes and scrapes of leaves and twigs against the body of the thing on that narrow part of the road. She followed these noises with her eyes. Where might it be going? Away, away, that was all she knew; with people in it who never had to sew a shirt but only to wear one; who wore, day and night, clothing of such smooth stuff, made by such fine tailors, that Liga would never be allowed even to pick up the snippings from their workroom floor.

Now evening had come, just while she watched there. She hurried back into the house and built up the fire and began yet again on the shirtfront. She labored into the night, and achieved one side of the bunching, at least.

She yawned, cracked her knuckles, stood and stretched, and went to the door. "When is the old bugger coming, then?" she said to the goat that lifted its head from its folded forelimbs out there. Look, the moon was up and all, the trees scrambling black across the stars, empty of half their leaves but still concealing bird and road, and Da in his silent striding. Everything felt unlatched, and swung. Was he still in the village, or nearly home, in the trees there? Everything was waiting for him to appear and tell her what she had done wrong, and what she would be doing to make up for the shirt, and the bread not rising so well, and above all, the baby.

She could take the lamp up to the road, maybe, to see if he were coming. But wouldn't that enrage him too, that she had left the house? If he had drunk enough at Osgood's, he would be angry whatever she did: leave or stay, sew the shirt well or poorly. He would be enraged by Liga's very existing, and by her condition, and by his own stupidity for drinking all the mud-wife money he had gained with that hare or whatever.

She took herself off to bed. Footfalls and rustlings filled the night outside, and imagined shouts of him coming drunk through the wood, calling out to her from high along the road, or from the path, or, like an owl, from the nearer trees. He walked around and around the house all night, never quite reaching it but always threatening to. In the course of one dream, she decided she would get up and go out and sleep in a forest place where he could not find her, but she did not wake widely enough to follow this good plan.

Morning came, sweet as new milk spilling up the sky, all dew and birdsong and bee-buzz. Up came the sun and beamed through the open window and woke Liga in her truckle bed. Had he come and she not woken? No, the big bed above was flat and untroubled. Had he fallen the other side of it, in his drunken state? She climbed over and no, the floor was empty there. She sat on the bed and stared at the strangeness of it. Maybe some woman? she thought hopefully. That would set things to rights; it would have to. Maybe he would distract himself enough, and drink enough with that woman, to forget about Liga and allow the baby to happen?

At any rate, she would dress so as not to be too available to him when he came. She washed and clothed herself, and then went out into the sun. The day's hugeness lay before her. Something was wrong that he had left her alone so free, for so long.

She milked, attended the cheeses, ate a little milked-bread, and tidied after that. She sat to the shirt out in the sun and completed the gather on the second front-piece with such dispatch and neatness, she could not believe she had had so much grief from it yesterday. And then she went gathering greens near the marsh; she would check his snares as well, and maybe find something soup-worthy to please him for his dinner, or roast whatever was roastable, before he had a chance to sell and drink it. He would slap her, but she would eat meat.

But when she came back near sundown, he was still not returned. She was at a loss. She ought to go up to the village and find him, dig him out of Osgood's before he made a trouble of himself. For her own sake, she ought to locate him, see if he had broken himself somehow, or got himself put in the roundhouse. Before someone came by, smirking and gossiping all the way, to tell her; to say, *You are all he has, then, by way of family?* And to draw their own conclusions.

But instead, she propped the greens in water to keep them from wilting, and cleaned the snared rabbit kit and hung it, and neatened the shirt still further, and dreamed at the fireside.

She went to bed, and slept better that night than she had the previous. She woke to steady rain, though, and her cold duty. He would be so angry with her, that she had not fetched him sooner, before he spent all the coney-money. Or that she had not come and pleaded with whoever held him to release him, because he was all that kept her from starvation.

She put a sack across her shoulders to keep the worst of the rain off, and went up the path towards the world. Two nights without his shouting, two days; she was flying apart, without him to pack her into her corner and keep her there.

She found him in the ditch by the road, face down. The water all around him was thick with floating autumn leaves, and several were scattered on him, as if the forest were moving as quick as it could to conceal him. He had not drowned—his head was all caved in on one side, and when she turned him over she found an unmistakable hoofmark on his soft front.

She stood and she stared at him. What was she to do? She had not the strength to carry him. And where would she carry him to? What was the point of taking him anywhere? She must dig a grave for him. Right next to the ditch there—she could roll him into that. But to leave him, to fetch the spade—now that she had found him, could she walk away from him again? she wondered. Was that permitted? And so she stood undecided, taking in again and again the signs of the violence that had killed him, unable to trust her eyes.

Clack-*hoik*. Clack-*hoik*. Here came Lame Jans, who was a bit simple too. "What have you there, Liga Longfield?"

"It's my dad," she said. "Someone has run him down and left him."

"He don't look too good."

"Oh, he's gone." Da lay there, embarrassing with his head spilling along the drain-water, his face as if asleep where it was not smashed, one eye the littlest bit open, leaves in his hair like a girl dressed for a festival, a red leaf adhered to his head wound.

"Looks like he have been stompled by a horse."

"I would reckon." Something threatened to rise from Liga's insides. She squashed it down. What, you would cry for the old bugger? You would mourn?

But another part of her was all confusion. Without his voice and body to shape her, did she even exist? She had not the vaguest notion how to live on, alone. No, not alone—with this baby, this baby!

Jans shifted his stick on the road. "You'll be wanting him on your kitchen table," he said.

"You don't know what you're talking about," she snapped.

"For the washing. You know. To wash him all down for burying."

"Oh," she said, freshly mortified. She had thought she must smell of Da's handling somehow, or betray it in the way she moved, in her face; it must leak out of her eyes. That was why, she thought, Da had kept her from the town lately, because she could not be discreet. She would announce by her very presence what no one must find out.

"I will fetch Seb and Da to bring him to you," said Jans.

"That's very kind."

The rain hissed all around them, and dripped among the trees its many different notes.

Off Jans swung. When he was a flat, pale shadow behind several screens of rain, he turned. "You gorn home. They will bring him to you."

"I can't leave him—"

"You will just soak here. You will chill to your very bones."

He left her doubtful in the gray. And then, because *he* had said it, because it was instructions from someone else and not her own swinging will, she put the sack over her dad's face and

29

made off home, without its weight and warmth, the rain driving cold into her back as her punishment for not fetching him earlier, for being so uselessly alive, for everything.

All she did when she got home was move the cheese-pot off the table, sweep the breadcrumbs into her hand, throw them to sog in the grass outside. Then she roused the fire and sat in the corner chair, wondering at the changed shape of things. Such a weight had lifted off her, she was surprised not to be up there, floating among those rafters, breaking apart as steam does, or smoke. And people would come soon and make this house a different place, look upon it and see how neatly she had kept it, look at the marriage bed and the truckle and not know, not for certain, the dreadfulnesses that had happened there. Certainly they would not speak of that possibility, not while she was there, whatever they suspected. Other people knew how to be discreet, even if Liga didn't.

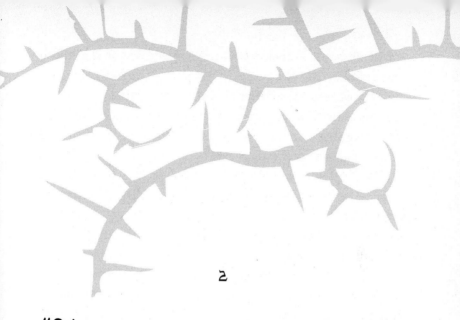

2

"You are lucky with the cool weather." Jans's mother pushed past Liga at the door, a look on her face as if this were all Liga's fault.

Four men carried Da in, in a cloth. Jans's father and the man Seb gave Liga the proper sober nod; the boys avoided her eye and affected to strain with the weight.

Jans came up after them, importantly. Behind him bustled two more women, one with a white-covered basket—that was Rosa, or Raisa, Liga knew—the other with such a bosom, it seemed to be what she must carry in her arms instead of a basket, her main burden. Liga could not remember that one's name.

"Little Liga!" The basket woman's feelings drove her forward. "Since your dear mother, Agnata! . . . Well—" Her embrace ended. "They're together now, the two lovebirds." And she adjusted her cap and looked away from Liga's puzzlement to Da's worn bootsoles. His feet had crossed themselves with the carrying, but now that Seb man put them side by side and he lay neatly on the cloth.

The visitors stood silent, but their selves filled the cottage air just as Liga had anticipated, bumping each other off-kilter with glance and shift and footscrape. The room was loud with unsaid things and awkwardness.

"Well, thank you," said Liga. "Very much," she added, but nobody heard it among the sighs and turnings of the relieved men.

"A good man lost to us, Gerten Longfield," said Jans's father to her on the way out.

Liga lowered her head in confusion—had Da been good, and she'd just not seen it? Could he have been good despite all of the—all of those twisted feelings he gave her? What did she know of goodness, of what constituted it?

"Shall I go for the God-man?" said Jans.

His mother shook her head and tutted. She might as well have said it aloud: *These is too poor to afford such burial, can you not see, boy?*

"Here, I have brought—" Raisa blumped her basket on the bench-end there and swept its cloth back from pots and rags.

"Oh, good," said Jans's mother. "I have plenty of practice laying out, but none of the makings anymore." For she had buried baby after baby—Jans was her only survivor.

"Has he another shirt?" said Goodwife Bosom, all solicitous.

"He has," Liga said, and she brought out the shirt she had sewn, and by the light of their silence she saw it for the slip-shouldered, cobbled-together thing it was. "Or there is the one—" And she brought out the pieces of the better one, which were worn through in places, patched to confusion in others, transparent as spiderweb in yet others.

"Oh, that will do better," said Raisa. "One of us can sew that up."

"It is very ragged," said Bosom.

"Still, he is only going into the ground in it, isn't he?"

They all looked at the man on the table. The shirt he had died in was the best of the three.

"What say we wash that one and dry it 'fore the fire? It needn't take long," said Jans's mother. "Here, Nance, you help me. Oh, his poor head."

"Liga, fill a bowl of clean water. I will put the bobs in it, and you can help wash him." Raisa was busy-busy, thinking and sighing and putting out pots and little sacks for the work.

Liga went out for a brief time into the day, which was so much like any other and yet quite, quite unlike. She breathed its clarity and its coolness as she dipped the bowl in the water-bucket and put the lid back; she admired the sodden brightness of the leaves. Then she returned to the fusty house, which now smelled of death-herbs she remembered from her mother's lay-ing out, as Raisa unstoppered things and muttered to herself what they were.

"Liga, you shall wash his legs and feet," said Jans's mother. "You should not have to see this head too closely."

"Very well." Liga was glad to be directed.

"Oo-er, he have something—" Bosom was loosening his trousers. She drew from the belt-pocket two small, soggy bun-dles of filth.

"They are amulets for something?" Raisa darted to Bosom's side, restrained herself from taking the objects from her. Jans's mother leaned over Da's head to peer at them. Liga's scalp crept, and then the rest of her skin. The baby was in her like a third bag of mudwifery, invisible to these women.

Bosom laid the things wet on the table like two dead mice, and timidly tweaked their folds apart.

"That," said Jans's mother heavily, "is the way Mud Annie wraps her devilments. I ought to know. I went to her often enough for help getting babbies."

"Erw," said Bosom at the wet black crumbs in one of the bundles. She sniffed them and made a face. "Some furrin spice."

"Oh, she puts all everything in it," said Jans's mother. "Some that's supposed to work and some that's just for dazzlement. I rekkernize that smell."

"It was not of good times for you," said Raisa, her head on one side in a sympathy that was just a touch pleased with itself.

"It was not."

"Did he have some ailment, Liga?" said Bosom.

Liga started. She had been scrubbing busily at Da's toes, which were all wood and black crevices and kicked yellow toenails. "I— No. Not that I know about."

"Might not have been such a thing as he would tell his daughter," said Raisa, and Bosom nodded to show she knew the kind of thing that might be.

Well, Liga also knew it, didn't she? Yes, there was some ailment, all right. *I cannot help myself*, he had groaned often enough in her ear. *A man must do it or he will go mad.* And then he would perform that madness on her.

It was then—and only Liga noticed it, she thought, because she was the youngest one and the unmarried one—that Jans's mother lifted the cloth off her father's marriage parts and washed them, with exactly the correct degree of detachment and efficiency. Look at it, Liga thought—not exactly looking, herself—so small and nothing, crinkled up there, and the bags below. How could I have ever felt him harmful, with just that

34

shrunken flop to hurt me with? Now that his mind is taken out of it, now that he's not directing it, it is all such scrags, such as you might trim from a plucked bird, nothing fearsome at all.

As for the rest of him, now that he had no will to move himself, no mind or voice, he was just so much meat, wasn't he, that they prepared for cooking in the ground, cooking away to nothing. He was just a slab of flesh lit coolly from the unshuttered window, with unpleasant glistens at the head end, of wet hair and wound and teeth.

"What will you do, girl? Who will you go to?" said Raisa.

"Yes, I have been wondering that," said Bosom. "It looks dire on your Longfield side, with your uncles gone to gypsies and that aunt of yours—where did she follow the man to? Middle Millet, was it?"

"And Prentices will not have you, I don't think," said Jans's mother, "seeing as they would not take you when your mam went. You might try them, though, now that he is dead, for it was your da they took exception to, mostly."

"She does have Longfield eyes, though, and the cast to her face," said Raisa. "They will not like that."

"If they know he is not alive to bother them for money, maybe . . . ," said Jans's mother.

They were all looking at Liga.

"You might try Rordal Prentice. Or his goodwife; she may have a heart for her granddaughter." But Bosom sounded doubtful.

"I don't know," said Liga. "I will have to think." And she made a vague movement on Da's shin with her cloth. The idea of her doing anything, or going anywhere, was entirely new to her. Everything up to now had been constructed on her father's purposes—her whole life and, she assumed, the world around it. She had had thoughts that were her own, now and then—

35

such as when that carriage had passed, up on the road—but she would never have been so daring as to call them wishes, and the notion of herself pursuing them, pursuing anything in her own name, was not one she had ever conceived of before.

"And very well, too," said Jans's mother to Bosom. "Give a girl time to grieve."

They contained Da into his clothes, and combed out his herb-washed hair. Hmm, Liga thought, he is better gentled by their hands than he has been for many a year; how odd that he must be dead for it.

It was a relief when they lit the vigil-lamps and went. They embraced her confidently on the doorstep before leaving. They were proper women, from real families, and they knew how to behave; she wished she knew how to be daughterly, instead of baffled and envious as she was.

When they had disappeared up the path, Liga stepped back inside. Her father lay in the candlelight, cleaned and dignified by their arrangements. He could not harm her now; he never could again. She might crow and dance around the table; she might cover his body with filth or flowers, or knock him clean off onto the floor, drag him outside, and chop him to bits with his own ax. She might kick the pieces about like pig-bladders—he would never rage at her or strike her again. He would never give her those nights' peculiar sufferings again, where she could not tell what he meant as consolation and what as punishment; what he intended and what he was doing in sleep or madness; what indeed she herself endured or nightmared—or *enjoyed*, yes, because apart from him, there was no one to hold or touch her, and sometimes her lonely skin would stubbornly respond, though her muscles and bones were tightly resistant against him, all fastened gates and barricades.

He had pressed and forced and pleaded, and in his frustration threatened her harm if she would not let him in.

She stood at his mended, misshapen head, all mix-feelinged and waiting, for the women's murmurings to clear from the room, for belief in the sight of his deadness to rise within her, for knowledge—of how to be, now, of what to do next—to arrive. He had run the world for her; it was a vast, un-navigable mystery without him.

In the end, she did none of the desecrations she had imagined. She decided she would not spend another night in the cottage with him, and she shut him up alone in there and took herself out through the cold rain, which was gentle now, not driving down as it had been that morning. There was an oak she knew, broad and bent and barely alive, that had made a little house of itself, as if just for a fifteen-year-old girl like Liga. She had spent other nights there when a morning's being shouted at felt like a fair price to pay to avoid a night's being fumbled by Da. She slept there tranquilly now, waking occasionally to the knowledge that the universe had changed shape for the better, although sometimes she could not recall exactly how.

Jans's mother came back the next day early, and the two younger men brought spades—she heard them jolly on the road and then subduing themselves as they neared the house and the body. Liga went out to greet them and to approve the grave-place they proposed, among the first trees behind the house, away from the dung-place.

Midmorning, Jans and his father came, having finished the milking, and Bosom and Raisa came too, and the men buried Da and the women watched silently, and then they sat and ate the foods that Bosom and Raisa had brought, and the visitors talked to each other quite easily so that nothing was expected of Liga. She sat, and ate soft cake, and had a sip of watered apple brandy, and wondered whether she ought to try to cry. When Mam had died, she had spouted tears like the town fountain and made noise and thrown herself about. But now it was as if she had no heart at all and no feelings, as if she were no more connected to Da than she was to that bottle there, or to Jans's father showing chewed cake as he talked cattle and weather with the man Seb.

"You must come to us if there is anything you need," said Jans's mother as they left, and Raisa and Bosom nodded too, very vigorously, and Raisa said, "Any advice, and when I can spare aught from my garden, I will bring it by."

Then they were gone rather swiftly, and Liga sensed from their swiftness that they had discussed her when they left the day before. It was improper for her to stay here alone, but Jans's house was not big enough, especially with Jans there—that would be even less proper. And the other two women, they must have other reasons not to want to take her in. It was not that Liga wanted to go to any one of them; still, there was a kind of shame in not being welcomed anywhere, in being of- fered nothing. But what had she expected? Da had made ene- mies of everybody; no one wanted dealings with that daughter of his, who hadn't a word to say for herself, only those sliding eyes and that creeping demeanor.

And how could she make herself useful? Did you see that piti- ful shirt? Doubtless her cooking is just as poor. I would not want to have to teach that one, so far behind, she is virtually a gypsy- girl. That was the sort of thing she imagined them saying, as she closed herself into the cottage and regarded the table's emptiness.

❖ ❖ ❖

Right through the autumn she managed to keep herself, without once having to trip to the town. Da had taught her, with his bossings and his beatings, to provide for him, and now that she was alone, she could provide—not too badly, either—for herself and her little wants. She laid up wood dutifully; there was the garden and the goat; there was the forest all around her, and the stream beside; and she had all the time in the world, and his remembered voice to guide her with its nagging, and his silence when she was busy and certain of herself. Every morning she woke in the truckle and sat up, and his wide bed was still empty and made neat, and she rejoiced that he was not in it.

"What have we here, then?"

She straightened from setting the snare, suddenly awkward about it.

There he was, watching, one of the boys who had helped carry Da home. He had gone from big boy to near-man in those few months. He was much larger now, and his face was bonier and had a nap on it of a blond beard beginning. He quite spoiled that thin spread of bright leaves, where the breeze fiddled and the sun considered this and that. "This is town land," he said.

The soft, heavy cords for the snares hung from Liga's hand.

"My father and I, we've got rights to cut here," he went on. "Have you rights to snare?"

She glanced down at the snare she had just arranged, which might deceive a coney but was all too obvious to a human eye. "These are my father's snares, in my father's places." Her voice, after his deep one, floated feather-light and ineffectual from her lips. *Chock . . . chock*, an ax said nearby, but not near enough.

"Ah, yes, your father," said the boy, half smiling. "May he rest easy. He had the right or maybe he didn't. What I'm asking is: *You*. Do *you* have dispensations?" The young man stood looking clever. Such a bulwark was a man with folded arms!

"I have to eat, same as him," she said.

"Then buy your own chicks and seeds and kits and raise them. That's what we all have to do—we can't just come and take what we want from town forest."

Blood-beats and confusion seeped up into her head.

"Anyway, you are eating plenty, by how you look," he said. "Look how fat you are, on the town's game. On ill-got game. Fat as yellow butter."

Her hand placed itself to her rounded-out middle.

The woodchopper's son saw it, saw the specific curve of her, and now her pinking face. Her wedding hand had shouted, *Look at my nakedness! I wear no ring!* and he had heard it clear as sneezing. His eyes came alight and he quickly doused that light. If she had had a ring—even of iron; even of carved wood, as some women wore whose men could not afford iron—all would have been different. She and the baby would have belonged to someone, someone who would protect them, and he would have seen that and not allowed his face to crawl so, with craftiness and disgust.

He looked her up and down as if she were a beast he was assessing the conformation of, in a market stall. The whole aspect and stance of him changed. He had the coin to buy her, the set of him said. Was she the kind he would buy?

She hurried away from him. If he followed her, could she still run? She had not run lately; she didn't know how much of an encumbrance the bab was now. Did she know this part of the wood better than he? Would that save her, if he was a good runner?

She could almost count the trees behind her and the gaps between them. Without looking back, she knew the moment when there were enough trees to close her from his sight if he stayed where he had stood. She risked a glance around and he was not there, was not following. Still she hurried on. She went well out of her way, to a thicket she knew where she could entirely hide herself. She lay there until nightfall, when they would have gone, the woodcutters. Then she returned to her father's house.

She checked the snare, next day. The stone was kicked aside, the cord pulled down, the overhanging branch snapped and dragging in the path the many coneys had beaten since last spring. Coney droppings lay across the wreckage. Had he fetched them from elsewhere and put them there, that boy? Was he as subtle, as nasty, as that?

She did not quite know what to make of it all. Would he tell his father that he'd met her, and would they talk about it, and would they go to the mayor? And *did* her father have dispensations, and were they hers now? Ought she to go to Jans's mother and ask? But if she had nothing and no rights, might not Jans's mother join the woodmen in moving the beadle or the constable or *someone* to cast her out, to put her on the road?

So little was different from yesterday morning—the sunlight and birds moved secretive among the branches; the wind wagged the last yellow leaves very soothingly. But Liga was not soothed; she stood, struck still with anxiety there, her hand on the bab—which was like live coals inside her, heavy and hot—and she felt her ignorance sorely.

Nothing came of the encounter with the woodman's son, though: not through the remainder of autumn; not into winter, either. Liga kept herself secret, and sometimes, without aid of any village life, she had a thin time, but always at her thinnest, some skinny fish took her bait under the stream's ice, or she chose the right snow to dig at and found some bit of growth that would boil up flavorsome, or some small hibernating thing sent up a curl of sleep-breath against the sunlight. She all but hibernated herself, eking out her firewood and her squirrel-store of nuts, harboring her small warmth in the truckle, dragged close to the tiny fire.

Her baby came steaming into the world one deep-winter night. Straightaway Liga saw what had been wrong with the other one—its head too big for its body, its pointed chin. This one had cheeks; it had limbs like baby-limbs, not like an old man's, all shrunken and delicate. And this, look: it was a girl, like her. He is outnumbered now, she thought deliriously. We will combine against him! We will get what we want!

When she had dealt with the mess of the birthing, she laid the wrapped baby on the table. All stiff and light-bodied and leaky, she sat on bunched rags on the bench and examined it by the candle.

All the expressions that are possible crossed its face, as if its thoughts were wise and limitless one moment, daft and animal the next. And Liga too was pulled towards awe, that this little girl-thing gave off such an air of being entitled, and then towards pity at its abjectness and its frailty and—how soft it was, the surface of it, and so warm! She could not believe the tiny makings of its mouth, or its perfected eyelashes, its ears like uncrumpling buds, all down and tenderness. She was full of the joy of her father being gone—that she could sit like this all night if she wanted, not bothered or harangued, without a remark from any other person, and watch this creature busy with its morsel of life, its scrap of sleep, its breaths light as moth-wings lifting its narrow red chest.

Sleep nudged at her eyelids before she had looked her fill, and she took up the baby and brought it into the truckle bed with her, for still she did not like to go to the marriage bed. She never would; she had thought several times to break that bed up for fuel, except that her mother had died in it too, hadn't she? It was all she had of her mam, however loud sounded the the snores and creaks of her father's memory.

The baby squeaked sometime in the night, and Liga woke from the darkest, softest sleep, wondering muzzily as she surfaced what kind of rat or vermin had got in and how soon Da would wake too, and crash about, chasing and killing it. And then she realized—oh, he was gone, gone forever! And this, this being tucked against her that clawed the dimness, with its thin throat learning to push out that miniature voice, this was—

She brought out a breast, pleased to employ it for the first time in its proper usage, instead of endure its being fumbled from behind as he muttered her mam's name in her ear. The baby mouthed and nodded bemused against it awhile, and then its instinct fastened it to the nipple, and after some noises so much like relish and surprise that Liga could not help but laugh—a soundless laugh, through her nose, such as would not frighten a bab—it more or less settled to what it must do.

She lay there in the grainy dark with the little animal at her, its fist on her breast as if holding it steady for the sucking, as if it had organized the world this way and were only taking its due. How charming it was, and how lucky was Liga, to be thus organized by a being so harmless, and so clear in its needs, and those needs calculated so exactly to what she could give!

Spring blew in, not quite expected. Fistfuls of pale leaves spurted from the oak branches; buds like candle-flames glowed along other tree-limbs; snow sagged away, leaving wet black ground; and bulb-fingers probed up there, all hopeful curiosity. The earth's lungs, coated in green ooze and thaw, breathed out blossom-scent and sour rot and fungus-must, wet and warm and aware, where before the air had been cold and blind, remote as the moon.

Liga went out and stood in the first surprising morning of that breeze, all milky and with her baby in her arms. Her hair blew out long, hardly tied up anymore, she had so neglected it; its dull yellow strands smelled of smoke and bed across her face.

The baby blinked and wondered against her chest, waved its aimless arms, frowned in the sun-dapples. Liga could almost imagine this was her own first time outside too, her first spring, the world was so quiet and light without her father, and there was nothing in it that she was obliged to fear.

The first she heard of the lads was their voices up at the road. There was a burst of rough laughter as they rounded the hill—three of them, maybe more. Then they quietened, suddenly, as if hushed by someone.

She knew that laughter. It was the noise of boys showing off for each other, boys with heavy voices and eyes that didn't properly look at you. She'd a distant memory of that noise, in the market in town, as she walked with her mother. *Come,* said Mam. *We'll walk through the cloth hall while they pass.*

"Come," said Liga now, and picked the baby up out of the truckle, and stood listening.

They were coming down the path to the house. They could not keep silent; there were too many of them, and some wanted to show the others that they didn't care to be hushed; they slapped their feet down and grunted. One of them hawked and spat. Another hissed a remonstration, and was snarled at.

Liga crept to the chimneypiece, fast, silent. She took out the loose stone and the key from behind it, and crossed to the wooden store-chest. She opened it, laid the baby on the cloths inside, closed it, locked it. She hid the key and there they were, clear of the trees—five of them, all large except for that runtish boy cockily leading. The woodchopper's son was there. That foreigner's boy was there. She remembered asking Mam, of his even darker father, *Why has he all sooted up his face?* And Mam had shushed her.

This she saw as she dragged the door closed. On seeing her, they started to run. That little one shot towards her, but she got it done, she dropped the latch just as he banged into the door from the other side. She gasped and jumped back. Coldly she thought, You should have run for the trees.

They threw themselves at the door. Terrible things they were shouting. They were not sensible; they were in a kind of frenzy. Nothing would stop them, not door, not latch, not wall. She understood not to shout back or to cry out in fear—they would enjoy her shouting; it would whip them up worse. She sat silent beside the chest in the corner, trying to disappear.

Their heads came to the window, and shouted there and joked and crooned; their laughter bounded about in what was once her home, which had been cozy and safe until just a little while ago but now was spindly as a birdcage, fragile as a fey-lamp on its dried stalk under a bush. She had never felt the house to be fragile before, not even in the wildest storm, but now it seemed made of leaf-matter or smoke, and the boys' arms waved in the window like May-ribbons loose from their pole.

They pulled out the windowframe. They started to break pieces off around the window. Liga put her hand on the wooden chest. "I will come back for you," she said to the child inside, and she climbed up into the chimney. She thought of herself going nimbly up and out the top—she had done it before—dropping off the edge of the soft thatch, running, losing them in the forest, listening to them disperse, disappointed; instead, she found her shoulders wedged, and no way to turn them so as to fit through. She looked up and saw the chimney-cover and a wink of sky.

The boys thudded into her house. Their voices funneled up to her. She reset a slipping toe and a stone came loose and carried soot down to the dead hearth.

"She's up the chimney!"

"Can you see? Is she out the top?"

A voice came suddenly loud up the chimney. "I can see. I can see right up her. Right up the crease of her. Come, sweet one, bring down that little purse to me! I shall count every coin you have in it!"

"Light a fire! Smoke her out!"

"She'll be the stubborn sort; she'll die up there of smoke rather than tumble down."

"We'll have her then, then."

"You want a roast, go and buy your feck-meat from Sweetbread & Sons."

"Fox, you go up. You're littlest."

"Yes, Fox! You're perfect for the job!"

"Wi' this new shirt? My mam would kill me."

"Take it off, man!"

"May as well be nekkid now as later, eh?"

"Must I?"

"Go on! We'll let you have first go of her."

In the silence, Liga pushed her shoulders up against the obstruction, turned, pushed. Soot went dancing down.

"She have not gotten out the top yet, have she?"

"Shut up and listen!"

They shut up.

"Look up there, Fox."

"I can hear her in there," said Fox. "I can hear her breathing. She is trapped."

Liga took the sleeping baby out of the chest, out of the house. She carried her with care and pain to the stream and laid her on the bank there and waded in, and washed and washed her cringing parts, her torn. She took off her dress and washed herself—all of herself—rinsed out her hair, rubbed the smell of them off her, soaked her clothes and squeezed them out and dressed herself in their limpness.

She carried the baby into the forest. The day was closing, the sun gone from casting its excessive light on everything. But then, eye after eye, the stars came out. The moon's fat face rose and hung in the treetops, staring.

Liga only walked, only walked away. Slowly, because to walk was to hurt, she put the distance, step by step, between herself and her father's house, where all her troubles had happened. No matter now that Mam had died in that bed. At least Da had called on Mam's memory as he misused it. But that strangers should come, and with no awareness of its sacredness, one by one, have of Liga there, and think that that was the place to do such things—well, Mam must be truly dead and gone, and not watching from anywhere; clearly she was of no help to Liga now.

Liga came to a part of the night where the path ended and the ground dropped away to rocks far below, and a different level of forest. It seemed like the answer to her; it seemed fated, a kindness. She would throw the little one first, and then there would be nothing left for her in this world, and she would be able to cast her own self off.

But she found when she tried that she could neither throw the baby nor hold it over the emptiness and let it go.

I will tuck her in my shawl, she thought, so that we are smashed dead together. And she did tuck the baby in, and tied it tight against her.

But then she thought, If I die and she doesn't, think of her, mouthing my dead breast, crying under the weight of me, perhaps broken and in pain. And she could neither step nor leap from the precipice.

"I could kill her against that tree first." She said the outlandish words aloud. She had brained many a coney and kid; she would know exactly how. "Against this rock right here. To make sure."

She untied the baby from herself. She lifted her out of her wrappings, shutting off her own nostrils from the scent— warm; a little sharp, like vinegar. She held her up and the child slept on, her wise mouth expectant of nothing, not caring if she continued or no. The little heart coursed along there, under the heel of Liga's hand.

Liga gave a great living sigh, and sat on the ground, and laid the baby on her knees. So soft was its cheek that Liga's finger-skin could not feel it; she leaned in to breathe of the milky breath, and watch the eyes moving under their dozy lids. So beautiful and unsullied; how had the bab known to lie quiet all that time in the house? Surely it was best to end her before life broke and dirtied her. If Mam had only ended me! she thought. I was well-grown and walking, not a bab like this, but she might have strangled me with a snare-cord, or cut my throat. She might have taken me with her. And if she had—

Liga stood up—I would not be holding this sweet, soft thing out here, with the breeze coming up from below and tickling the downy hair on her brow, the last soft movement before I let the rocks have her, let the rocks break her—

With a sob, she let the baby go. Her hands snapped to fists at her chest, her eyes closed, her face averted itself from what she was doing.

Two ragged breaths she took and released before she would look. But when she did— "Ah!"

For the baby had not dropped. It hung there against the stars, held up by nothing at all, its head sunk to one side, perfectly asleep.

And it commenced to glow. All around it, needles of light spread out against the night sky.

Liga stepped back. "Go, little one! Die! This is no place for you!"

But the baby would not drop, and the light spread around it, and from the brightening center flung out loops and arcs of crinkled light like loosened swaddling.

At the sight of these, at the thought that they might encircle the baby and take it from her sight, Liga stepped to the edge again, and reached and took the baby out of the air into her shaking arms.

On the sky, though, where it had hung, there hung another baby, or at least the shape of one drawn in the brightest of the light, as if when she took down the child Liga had peeled a layer off the night's skin, exposing the stuff behind that the skin protected the world from. She could barely look at it—it had some kind of burn or chill about it—but she glimpsed within the baby-shape other shapes turning, moving, plumping and contracting; the vague attempts at form of whatever force had suspended her bab, had intervened and cut the connection between her act and its consequence. A vast power had had to be channeled—she was awed and hotly ashamed that it must—through this small aperture so as to be tolerable to Liga's senses, so as to handle the mortal scrap of her child without harming it, so as not to break either of them with its strangeness and strength.

What are your babbies' names? it said, direct into her mind.

Babbies? Babbies more than this one? Should Liga have named that stain in the snow? That little blue personage so quickly handed over to Da? "I have not given this one a name, not as yet," Liga said. "I had not really thought of it."

No name? it thought at her, astonished, and perhaps also offended. She had not known that she was accountable to such a thing.

"Because, you see, we never— I have not taken her into the town," said Liga. "I have not met anyone with her. There has been no need for a name; she is the only other person in the world with me. She is 'babby,' or 'my little one.' "

There will be need, though, the moonish matter thought, flesh or cloth or whatever it was. *To distinguish the one from the other.*

Part of it burst and laughed, the lightest, shortest bit of delight. From the bursting it thrust a luminous limb, much like a baby's arm in shape, if not in movement. Whether the hand was tiny or vast Liga could not tell, but on its palm an immense clear jewel lay and glinted.

Liga was frightened to take it, but she was more afraid that the light, that the flesh, of the child-thing would touch her and burn her, or worse. So she took the stone, neither hot nor cold as it was, neither painful nor pleasurable nor yet entirely inert, into her own ordinary hand.

A second limb of light, opposite and yet not opposite the

first, erupted from the mass, bringing another jewel, but a black one this time, which when Liga took it showed through its heart a gleam of this moon-child's light, turned red by the gem's internals.

"But what am I to use these for?" said Liga. "People will ask how I came by them. They will string me up for thieving. They will cut off my hands."

Paff, said the moon-baby. *This is not for selling. This is for planting. Plant the clear stone by the northern end of your doorstep, then the red by the southern. Then sleep, child. Rest your sore heart and your insulted frame, and begin again tomorrow.*

"But how shall I get home? I am quite lost here."

A globe of light the size and shape, perhaps, of a ripe plum broke from the moon-child, moved towards the trees, and waited there at their fringe. Liga followed, and the globe went in among them, along the path she had arrived by. The moon-bab emitted something like a laugh, something like a sigh; it hovered there behind her at the cliff-edge, laboring to contain its glory. She glanced back many times as she went, watching the moon-child shrink and reappear among the accumulating trees, until at last they obscured it altogether.

3

The moon-plum dipped and skated ahead, lighting every crease and pock and root of the path, sinking to show the muddy places, bobbing higher to point out low-hanging branches. Liga began to recognize some of these branches, some of these knolls. Her spirits should be cast down, she thought, at coming back here when she had vowed to leave the place forever. But her returning seemed hardly related at all to her leaving, so distressed had she been and so calm was she now, and so companioned by the light of this plum-thing so confidently leading her.

Besides, she was tired from all her wandering, and injured and weak from the day's events, so for a long while's walking she did not have the spirit to think or feel anything whatever, let alone resist following the little moon-lamp. Had it led her back over the precipice or into the depths of the marsh, she would have gone there without question, without happiness, without terror.

But it returned her instead to her father's house. She stood in the trees and watched it approach the broken cottage, and spill a small puddle of light at one end—the northern end—of the doorstep. The resistance to following, the fear she ought to feel, sat just the other side of her numb exhaustion.

Near falling with tiredness, Liga walked past the folded-asleep goat and up the path. She knelt, laid her baby daughter down, dug a hole a handsbreadth deep, put the clear stone at the bottom, and pushed the earth back in. As she tamped the dirt flat, the light slithered across the step and pooled at the southern end, and she crossed the step and, grimly obedient, set to planting the ruby there.

But when she was done, she could not bring herself to walk in through the gaping door of the cottage; it would be too much like entering the mouth of a laughing ogre, or rushing into the arms of a nightmare.

She walked back into the wood, found a dry, grassy place, and lay down there. "I must name you, that creature said," she told the baby, untying her own dress-front. "Ah, it is too much for me now. I will name you in the morning." She put the child to the breast, where it seemed to suck all the moisture straight from Liga's mouth, and she thought she would not sleep for thirst. But the moment she laid her head in the grass and the forest shadows, she was gone away into sleep—not hungry, not thirsty, not mourning or enraged or frightened, but as comfortable as she could be, insensible.

She woke into a body so whole and healed, it was as if yesterday's horrors had not happened. Her fair-skinned daughter lay asleep beside her, a glimmer of milk on her lip.

"Branza," she whispered. "I will call you Branza, after all things white and clean and nourishing."

She stood, and picked the child up, and set off towards the

cottage, putting her mind to the tasks that must await her in the ruin.

But when she stepped into the clearing, everything was changed. The house, which had always slumped to one side as if held up only by the force of her father's anger, sat square and solid on the grass. The torn-out windowframe had been reset in the wall, the trampled wattle shutters woven anew. The door bore none of the boot-marks and splinters she had glimpsed by the light of the moon-plum the night before; it did not gape, but was held just a little way open with a rounded knuckle of wood. At the southern end of the doorstep, a red-leafed bush grew to the height of Liga's knees; at the northern end stood a green bush of the same size and circularity. The roof-thatch had no holes or thin places, and the chimney had lost its inclination towards the west.

"What is this, Branza?" she whispered, in fear of what she saw. This was the house her father might have made them had he had the money and the heart to fix the roof and straighten the frame—had he been, in fact, *not* her father, but a different man.

She stood on the step and pushed open the door. "Oh, my Gracious."

The polished-earth floor spread out before her, unscarred, unscraped, untrod by booted feet, her little rush mats rewoven here and there on it. The marriage bed was gone, as was Liga's truckle; now the bed was set in the wall—a fresh-made bed for a single person, she could see from here, with the curtain, of new calicut, tied back with a clean band to a proper hook in the wall. Near the head of that bed stood a cradle very like one she had once seen outside the cabinet-man's workshop, which her mam had stopped and admired, and in that cradle new linen rested soft as a cloud, and a canopy shaded it. Slowly she approached, expecting it to fade like a dream-object before her eyes. Timidly she touched it, and gasped at how smoothly, how heavily, how soundlessly it swung. Feeling most impudent, she laid the baby Branza there, and covered her with the soft woolen blanket. Again, slowly, she walked about the room, noting the instances of repair and renewal—a fresh-carved spoon where the old one had worn almost to a stub; a new lamp for the one that those boys had knocked from the table and broken. Everything was clean, as if swept and wiped by a woman just now left the house to shake out her cloth; it was all as new and neat as a bride's house with every gift on display.

"Who has done this?" She still spoke in a whisper. She was afraid some person would hear, and step in from outside, and say, *I did, and it is mine; be off from here.*

She went to the door and looked out fearfully, but that woman—that owner, that cottage-wife—was not there, only the two jewel-bushes, the red and the green, one with a tree-sparrow in it, hopping and fidgeting. And as she stood there worrying, the house laughed, a minor squeaking rumble of its timbers, a twitch of its fabrics and a titter and click of its shutters. Laughing at her, it was, but hardly unkindly. Like a shaft of moon-plum light, it came to her, the realization: this was hers, all hers, the work and gift of the moon-baby.

"I do not deserve this!" But she heard the words miss the mark. The forces behind these events, these gifts, had stars and seasons to move, oceans to summon, continents to lay waste. They did not take account of such small things as Liga's deserving or Liga's not. To them in their vastness, she must look as blameless as her baby. This was a mere blink of their eye, a grain of purest luck fallen from a winnowing of such size that it was not given her to see the sense or benefit of it. She could only marvel at her good fortune; she could only tend the child who *did* deserve this fresh house, this clean world, and hope that no one noticed the injured and besmutted mother, or called her out and required her to justify herself.

Her first week in the renewed cottage was a time of such unalloyed luxury and peace that when the thought occurred to Liga that she might go into the town, she was sure her mind had been addled by her new, soft way of life. But why should she not? She frowned and went outside, and sat in the sun and tried to recall why she had stayed here in the house for so long, for she knew she had had good reason.

Mostly, she remembered when she put her mind to it, she had been afraid of meeting those young men. Any one of them would be bad enough, but what if two came along at once, or more? Might they not follow her, and pin her up against a wall, and fondle her or worse? And who would come to her aid should she have the courage to cry out?

That had been her main fear, but underpinning it were the habits of all the years since Mam died. *We don't need anyone,* her father had often said, so often that she hardly heard the words anymore. *We can look after ourselves with no aid nor interference from no one.* Year by year, he had grown less sociable and harsher to others until, during the last round of the seasons before he died, Liga had seen exactly three people besides themselves: a pretties-seller at whom he had shouted, like a madman, *I will set the dogs on ye!* although he had no dog, until the poor man had fled—Liga had only glimpsed a flash of his legs, a basket with a swatch of ribbons flapping; Lame Jans up on the road near where Liga sometimes hid on the chance that something of the world would wander by; and a hunter whom she saw, like foliage-mottle moving without benefit of wind, among the trees below Prospect Hill.

Then, when Da had died, those women had visited, and Liga had not wanted to encounter any more such as them, with their needling eyes—and no man, either, taking care to look away, that the sight of her did not taint him or make him laugh, or whatever it was they feared.

What was more, with the passing months her belly and then her baby had become very evident, and anyone who met her would have wanted an accounting of either of those. Liga had given up most conversation when her father started his fondling of her, and she no longer had a very great sense of what she could say, words she might use, to describe her own circumstances.

So she mustered all these things in her mind against the flarings of curiosity that afflicted her, against the growing conviction that the town promised interests and pleasantries she had missed in her solitary life at the cottage. She tried to feel reluctance—she tried to hear her father remonstrating in her mind's ear—yet as she climbed the path to the road next morning, with Branza in a cloth on her back and some rushwork in a basket on her hip, her step was light, and her heart would not listen to her memory's dark warnings. I can always turn and come back, she scolded herself. At the first sign of trouble, I can hurry right back here.

Everything was as it should be on the road, with the wheelruts and the hoofclefts gleaming with the night's rainshowers, the oak with the cut branches that looked like a popeyed old scawcraw, and the scattering of wildflowers either side. Slowly, Liga walked towards the town. *If I ever see your face there . . . ,* her father had said. *If I ever hear of you turning up there . . .* He had seemed to be talking of quite another girl, someone saucy and brave. Liga had been offended that he did not recognize how meek and obedient she mostly was.

She rounded the bend, and there at Marta's Font was stooped to drink who else but Jans's mother. Liga was about to retreat into cover, then turn and run back home, when the woman heard her step and straightened, dashing water-drops from her chin. "Liga!" she laughed. "What luck to meet you. How are you keeping, and your little one?"

"Ah . . . we are well, thank you." Liga searched the woman's face for unkindness, for smugness, for disapproval.

"Is that her there? Let me see the lovely!"

"Oh." Liga turned around doubtfully as the woman approached.

Jans's mother barely touched Branza's cloth to lift it from the baby's face. "Aaah, look at that! Curled up sweet as a chick in the egg, aren't you, little Branza? She's the image of you, Liga; it is like you have guv birth to yourself. I remember you from a babby in Agnata's arms, sleeping just so."

"How—" But looking the woman full in the face, Liga felt the oddness of asking her, *How do you know my babby's name?* "How . . . is Jans?" she asked instead, in a frayed voice.

"Jans is well, and Stella, too, and all my grandchildren. She has another on the way at midsummer, you know, and she says to me she thinks it's another pair, if you can believe that!" Birds caroled in the forest as if echoing the woman's laughter. "She's drowning in children, that woman, making up for all my missings. I'm a happy old grumma, I am."

"It's good to hear," said Liga—because it *was* good, if very puzzling. Stella? Could she mean Merchant Oliver's Stella, that beauty? How had she married Lame Jans? And when? They had not been wed when Da died, so how had she managed to drown in children in those few months? Liga had only just had time to bring forth the one she carried.

Jans's mother took cheerful leave of her, and Liga, wanting to seem purposeful, set off as if she intended to continue along the road. And then, so occupied was she with going over and over their conversation and looking at all corners of its senselessness that she kept up the briskness of her walking without thinking about it, and before she knew it, she was at the outskirts of St. Olafred's.

But they were not quite the outskirts as she knew them. Farrower's pig farm was here, but it was pin-neat, with all the fences fixed right, and it was not Farrower and his sneering daughters moving about there, but strangers, of rosy complexion, their hair a light brown. Neatly clothed they were, if poorly, with nothing unhemmed or holed. One of the girls, too far away to call out, raised an arm in greeting, and Liga nodded, and the girl turned back to her work.

And then, look at the town itself. It was like a grandmother's teeth, half the houses missing. She took a few steps in through the gate, to look at the first one gone from its row. That was that Jinny Salter's house; Jinny, who had said to her one time, *Don't put yourself near me, poacher's girl. I don't mix with your like.* And had flounced away, and her flouncing friends with her, leaving Liga alone and hot with puzzled shame. She stood now and touched with her toe the edge of the grassy rectangle, nicely mown and with a seat there for taking the sun, that lay in place of Salters' house.

She took a little courage from this and walked on, still fearing to meet those lads. *Bring that little purse to me*, they crowed in her memory, and *Look, she loves it. She can bare keep her cries in, of lust and loving it.* She moved Branza around to her front—for the baby's protection or for her own, she did not know which.

But the town was much quieter than she remembered from coming here on market days with Mam, and later with Da before he turned bad. There were more of those pink-faced, brown-haired people that had been at Farrower's. They shook their rugs out their windows or stepped out of their doors and greeted her, and she thought, Who used to live there? Did I ever know? And it came clear to her gradually that these families, these pleasant strangers, had come to replace all the people of the town who were unfamiliar, or whom she had not liked.

She came to what had used to be Blackman Hogback's house, and it was now a broad parkland, grassed and flowered, with arbors and fountains and people strolling, and an Eelsister conversing over the convent hedge with one of the rosy ladies. Timorously, Liga went across the lawn—which should be walled, should be Hogback's mansion, guarded by Hogback's servants. A climbing rose clung to a lattice, bursting with pink and white blossoms, and she sniffed a flower and she felt the smooth petals between her fingers and she watched a bee fill its pannier-baskets with pollen, and everything was real, scented and textured as it ought to be—thorned, too; she might easily prick her finger to bleeding with that thorn if she wanted to prove how real.

She walked on, up to the market square. There she exchanged some of her rush-matting for a length of lawny cloth just the right softness, she thought, for the making of some garment for Branza. She traded more for a little smoke-meat, and two figs in syrup, and a tiny package of violet-sugar, for the color and scent as much as for the usefulness. Market stalls she had once been afraid to approach for their bluff or noisy sellers were now fronted by these calm, kind-faced, brown-haired people, who were ready to explain their wares to her if she asked, but refrained from pressing her too insistently to buy.

She walked about some more, and when Branza grew fretful, she sat in the sunshine in the grassy place where the Fox family's house had once stood, and fed her. Sukie Taylor, whom Liga remembered playing with once or twice in their childhoods, came up then, and sat by Liga and cooed and admired Branza's health and beauty.

"That is a fine piece of broidery about your cuffs there, Sukie," ventured Liga, when Sukie's chatter ran out.

"You like it? It is my mother's work," said Sukie carelessly. "I can sew a seam all right, but for finework I always have Mam take it over. She tries to teach me, but I can never settle to the finicky parts."

"I should love to sew such stuff," murmured Liga, touching the tiny flowers' knotted centers.

"You should ask my mam—she despairs of ever teaching Nettie and me!" laughed Sukie.

"In return for . . . some rushwork, maybe? Maybe she would think to teach me?" This felt most audacious, emerging from Liga, but no stranger than most of what had already happened that day.

"I would think she would pay *you*, almost, to have someone to teach! I would think she would walk out past Marta's Font and find your house and sit upon your doorstep, needle at the ready, for you to show your face! You should come up now—she is marketing today—and offer your interest."

"I saw her there, but I have never really spoken to her, so—"

"I shall take you—when Branza has had her sup. Look at

61

her, little Miss Sleepy-cheeks. She is surely the prettiest bab I have ever seen, you lucky girl."

Lucky indeed Liga felt, walking home that day with figs and sugar and good smoke-meat in her basket, and her first lesson with Mistress Taylor set for next afternoon. It was all very different from the noise and bustle and nastiness she had expected to weather in the town; it was very odd to have conjured a headful of terrors and carried them into St. Olafred's, only to discover them all to be unfounded.

She held her baby close against her breast as she walked along. "How lovely, Branza! Such a different place! How long can it last, do you think? Is it to be ours forever?"

Several weeks later, Liga woke, went out in the early dawn while Branza slept, and admitted, as she stood in the first sun, with the dew chilling her feet, that this feeling low in her belly, these washes of illness she had been putting down to the shocks of the changed world, this distaste for smoky air and for pan-fats—she had had them often enough, and she knew what came of them: babies. She was carrying another baby.

She had woken in this place feeling so well, and had been so intent on exploring and adjusting; she had assumed—it had not occurred to her to think otherwise—that the moon-baby's bringing her here had erased not only the boys who had insulted her so, and their houses and their families with them, but also the insult itself, the very event. She had certainly put it out of her mind, and if she did think of it, it seemed distant, and unattached to emotions of any particular strength, as if it had happened to some other girl she barely knew and did not care greatly about.

But no, it had happened to her, and here was the consequence, growing inside her: a child of one of those boys—she might never know which—or perhaps some monstrous amalgamation of them all, some terrible mongrel. It might come out and look at her and laugh; it might speak straightaway in one of their rough voices, and say the things that they had said. She stood in a slant of weak sunshine and rubbed her arms hard against the cold.

From the cottage, from the lovely cradle, came Branza's tiny whimpering and shifting. Liga stepped across the cold grass to the house, sick at heart. But Branza, after all, was no monster; why, she was the prettiest bab that ever Sukie Taylor had seen, and plenty other people besides! The monstrousness of her begetting did not show in her. Certainly, it was never referred to in St. Olafred's—it was as if Liga's father had been scrubbed from people's memories, just as all her other enemies had been banished from the town. Perhaps it would be the same for this second child, seeing as all the fathers, all their houses, were gone? What was there for people to remember?

She looked from the red-leafed bush by the doorstep to the green. Both had thickened and flourished in the short time since she had planted them, and now several buds were swelling, of red blooms on the red bush, of white ones on the green. She inspected these now, as she did every day, impatient for them to burst into some bloom she could recognize.

There will be need, though, the moon-baby had said, for a name, *to distinguish the one from the other*. Branza had thought it was talking about those others, the dead babies, but it must have known; it must have seen the very first glimmer of this new baby happening, arising from that afternoon's ordeal.

And then, in disgust and disappointment at her own condition, she clicked her tongue and went inside, and rescued Branza from the complexities of bed-linen that had fallen across the little one's head. She lifted her out of the cradle and kissed the baby's pearly-skinned face, which fretted and squinted and sucked a fist and looked smokily about—they were going to be blue, those eyes, like Liga's own and her da's and her own long-lost mam's.

"Another one of you!" she said severely, startling Branza's fist from her face, which stared, then creased to cry. Liga laughed and put her to the breast. "There you go, you poor sook-a-bed."

She went to the shutter to let more light in. She gazed out at the forest as her milk began to ache and tingle and flow, as the cold air trickled in over her from the window. She stroked the round white cheek next to the round white breast, and marveled at the firm connection between the two, and the goodness that flowed from one to the other.

That happy summer mellowed to a rich, bright autumn, and Liga made many visits to the town, to market and to visit Goodwife Taylor to learn seamstressing and finer needlework. Wife Taylor was kinder and more patient than Liga remembered her from previous days—indeed, she barely remembered the goodwife at all, it had been so long since she had been in that house with Mam and played with Sukie.

The baby grew inside Liga, and as with Branza, it was as if everyone knew, but nobody minded, or held against Liga, the manner of the baby's getting. Wife Taylor put Liga to hemming little linens for the cradle and showed her how to cut the cloth of small nightgowns and bonnets. "These is perfect for learning on," she said. "No great long seams to labor up, and if you go awry, it's little enough bother to unstitch them." And the goodwife worked on the yoke of one shift a perfect little rose of red silk. "I will learn you how to do this too," she said, filling in a cushiony crimson petal, "so as you can have pretty things around you, spring blooms all through the wintertime, and leaves, and life."

Whatever Liga did seemed acceptable, and people smiled on her and were polite and kind to her, whether she behaved quietly and shyly or, on brighter days, ventured conversation herself.

She never invited any person to the cottage, nor did anyone visit unasked; it had never been a welcoming place, and now that it was all repaired and presentable, Liga was content to have it welcome only her and Branza while she accustomed herself to her new existence. Besides, she never quite lost, through all the pleasantness and convenience, the sense that the real holder of her house—maybe the happy-kind-patient Liga who belonged in this happy place, who *deserved* to belong here in place of this chance arrival, with her sullied body and clumsy mind—might knock at her door at any moment and claim the cottage back, and send her on her way. *Look,* she would say, *you have only made a wrong turning; that is your cot along there, see? Through the trees. Look, your da is there, hands on hips, wondering where you have been all this time! Run along and take your punishment, girl. With your girl-bab and your big belly, you've many a night's shouting and slapping coming to you.*

Months passed, and the nights began to nip in, and harvesttime came and went and left Liga her winter's grain and nuts and preserves, and the leaves began their changing, and still no town-man came and ousted her, and still no one asked her to justify herself, or put any question to her for the purpose of shaming her. She kept herself busy, her head down always at some task when she was not feeding Branza or sleeping. If there was no way left to manage the house or garden or pantry, she applied herself most diligently to her needle and whatever piece Wife Taylor had her working. However long this good fortune lasted, she must prove to whoever had given it, to whoever might be watching her, that she was worthy of it, that she would make the best use of her time here that could possibly be made.

When first the new baby was born, Liga thought the eyes were only a little bruised from birthing, perhaps; she thought the skin might clear and lighten with a few days' life, as Branza's rashes had come and gone. They changed so fast, babies. They coughed and their lips turned blue, but they ceased and smiled pink as hedge-roses the next moment. They were like shrews or wrens that rushed through life on a different scheme of time; a person could only stand, in her huge body with its slow heart, and watch in amazement.

And in amusement too, for this child, unlike the first, was easily stirred to rages. The slightest discomfort set her asquirm, and if it was not remedied, off she would go, inconsolable, outraged. Sometimes it was as if some scandalous situation reminded itself to her as she fed, and she would detach herself from the breast, and look up at Liga in horror, and redden. If not very quickly replaced on the nipple, she would begin to wail, and she protested herself to exhaustion then, her limbs stiff and straining, her little sense unreachable through soothing words or the close embrace of her mother.

"What kind of creature are you?" said Liga one of the early nights, when some owl or dream had woken the baby in this way. "You would think you had all the world's sorrows in you!" She had made a light to see if something was perhaps gnawing on the child, some rodent or insect—she could not think what.

But nothing could she find and still her daughter lay, angrily crimson against the bedclothes, shuddering the breaths into herself between screams that tore the sleep from Liga's mind in ragged strips. Branza slept on, undisturbed, in her bed. Such a difference between that one's peaceful, pearly slumber and this one's red rage! She scooped up the child and kissed the hot face; the clenched-closed eyes that still leaked tears; the tiny mouth, with its leaf of tongue, from which such noise emerged! "I think you should be Urdda—little red one. Look at you— you are quite the wrong color." And she kissed the mottled stomach, a squall deafening one ear. "Shush, child! Shush, Urdda, before you start to bleed out of your skin!"

Her rages aside, if anything Urdda grew darker with time. It happened so day-to-day that Liga did not notice; it was only when Branza crawled to the bab as it lay there on a cloth on the grass and Liga looked up from the little night-shift she was sewing and saw them side by side that she realized, no, it was not the fall of any shadow on the littler one, it was the cast of her skin.

And the young men came down the path in Liga's memory, and the foreign man's son was among them. How unconnected this seemed with the two tiny maids on the cloth there! They seemed to bear no relation whatever, the two events, the two small play-acts, one to the other, despite their being clearly both parts of the same story.

Or if there was a connection it was not one that mattered, not here in this house and this place. Here things were just as they were; they were not made something else by the work of fathers and gossips. Branza gave Liga only joy that Da was dead and his daughters living. And in the same way, Urdda, with no man nearby claiming or denying her, remarking either way on her, was her own darkening self alone, her gleaming eyes awakening, more and more thought and life growing behind them. It might have been different had she been a boy-child and had Liga to handle his little spout and be reminded of those others, those weapons such spouts could become. But instead, here they were, the three of them, each with her parts that could hurt no one, that could force themselves on no woman, folded neat away between her thighs.

Four years passed, and not without incident, for the infancy and childhood of two girls, making a mother out of their mam and sisters out of each other, is one incident after another, each as momentous as the last.

The two bushes grown from the jewels attained the height of Liga herself, and then stood and thickened there on either side of the cottage door, tended by Liga, and as they grew capable by Branza and Urdda also, and flowering each spring: the northern bush with large, waxy-petaled flowers so white they almost burned the eye, the southern with red blooms of the same shape, and equally dazzling. In spring and summer Liga was always anxious that some person would happen by the cottage, for the flowers were so conspicuous and yet she did not know the name of them, having never seen their like on her walks with Mam as a child. She felt sure any visitor would want to know their identity and origin, and though she was confident as time went on that she would be able to answer, *Oh, I don't know—aren't they strange? They have always been here, that is all I know,* she was uneasy that the very question would attract the wrong attention, and lead to some power realizing, *Oh no, she is too happy, Liga Longfield. How have we let her languish here so many moons?* And the bushes would puff away like blown dandelion clocks, and the house would lean and sag, and fill with her father's thumping and shouting.

Though she tended the bushes dutifully and a little fearfully, to all her other occupations she brought the kind of joy that other women, in that other world, might reserve for Bear Day or the dance on Midsummer Night, or for a daughter's making a good marriage. Her girls she watched in wonder: their growth and increasing sureness of movement; the world's pouring of itself into their gradually, constantly, confidently realizing minds; their readiness to smile and laugh and draw Liga's own smiles and laughter out from the deep place where they had run away and hidden in the years since Mam. The girls were two flames at which she warmed herself to humanness, having long been something else—stone, perhaps; dried-out wood. Their perfect trust that the happy times would continue—she watched it and she sipped it as some small birds sip nectar, and she began, if not to perfectly trust it herself, at least to hope more strongly, at least to look beyond the beauties of the immediate season to the plans and practicalities demanded by the next—or the next several years, maybe? Maybe.

Branza and Urdda themselves—she could not have asked for finer children, or for two more different from each other. Even the contrast in their appearance amused her: Branza all white-golden tranquility, standing straight and observant; Urdda always moving, bent to run or spring, her black hair flying; her words, her nonsense words, her songs, unreeling from her mouth like strings of colored pennants. "Angel girl" was Liga's fondname for Branza, while Urdda was "my little wild animal." Branza was the sort to crouch by a stream for all the time it took the fish and waterbirds and other creatures to forget her; Urdda was the kind to run up and fling her dress to the shore and her self into the water, shouting. They maddened each other, as all sisters do, yet neither would have known what to do in a world without the other. Liga fed them, bathed and clothed them, told them stories, sang them to sleep and learned their songs, kissed them and accepted their kisses, held them and was held by them and soothed by their hands' touch. Sometimes she cried from it, and sometimes she thought she would die of it, of the luck and the joy of having been given these two little animals to grow and to love, and to be grown by, and to be loved by.

"Come help me, Urdda!" Branza shook her sleeping sister's shoulder. "There is something I want to try."

Urdda curled tighter away from her and grunted.

"I need you." Her sister poked her with all the authority of a five-year-old over a sister of four. "I need a person with two arms."

"Use Mam's," said Urdda indistinctly.

"Mam is busy sewing. Come on, you will like it."

At last Urdda crawled out of the bed, and they dressed and sat to their sopmilk, and then Branza took two stale bread-ends and off they went. It was not far, only to a clearing a little way from the house where Branza came to see deer sometimes.

"Now, stand," Branza instructed, "like this." And she stood with her arms stretched out from her sides.

Crossly, still not properly awake, Urdda did as she was told.

"No, here, in the sunshine. Keep very still. Put your hands flatter. Yes." She broke off a piece of bread crust and put it on the back of Urdda's hand.

"What are you doing?"

"Shh. They will not come if they hear us squabbling."

Patiently she moved up Urdda's arm, laying crumbs all the way. Then, to the great amusement of both of them, she placed crumbs on top of Urdda's head, and then moved on to the other shoulder and along the other arm. A finch flew down and landed on the first hand. "Do not move," Branza whispered. "I want to see you quite covered." And she withdrew into the forest shadows in sight of Urdda, and stood there and watched, pale and excited.

Already several birds had come—they must know this place; Branza must have fed them here before. The air began to fill with the light, dusty sound of their wings, and the pips and peeps of their calls. They landed and landed, and Urdda's arms rocked at each landing. When the first bird arrived on her head, she managed not to cry out, but she made such faces at the catching of their claws in her hair, at the small blows of their pecking on her scalp, that she saw Branza cover her mouth to keep the laughter in, off there among the trees.

The birds were bright in the sun, and the busyness of them flaunted and flapped the sunlight so that Urdda felt radiant with them, as if they were a kind of fire flaming across the top of her. What a grand idea this was! She could see why Branza had needed her; on her own she could only have organized bread along one arm. Of *course* it was better to have a whole person given over to birds this way, for them to perch on and feed off.

At the same time, Urdda wanted more than anything to laugh aloud, to shake herself and explode the birds away and run. She would not, but the desire to do so itched in her bones and made her stretched arms wobble under the combined weight of the birds.

She stood straight and still, not frightening a single bird away, and Branza, hands clasped, watched her from the wood-edge until the birds had pecked up all the crumbs from Urdda's person, and all the spilt crumbs and pieces from the grass around her feet, and one by one had flown off, leaving widening breaks in the flaring line of sunlight. Two sparrows must sit and preen awhile once they had fed, but when they were done they, too, darted away, and then Branza ran out of the trees in delight and satisfaction, waving the other bread-end. "Now me!" she said. "That was quite wonderful!"

4

Once I left St. Onion's, life were both kind and cruel to me. First chance I had, I grew myself a fine beard, for very early I tired of being mistook for a child, however much advantage I could get from it in terms of irresponsibilities, and I never shaved nor trimmed it, but grew it until it was well longer than myself eventually, and my head-hairs to match it, right down to the ground. Luxuriant they were to begin with, and dark, and I tell you the ladies could not keep their hands off them for a time there, however slight and warped were the body they hid.

I never managed a trade or profession, but I had some luck at cards, and in fine company, due to the oddity of my small stature and the inscrutability of my features to most men's eyes. There were a certain type of rich feller liked to use me much as a doll is used, to dress me up in tiny clothes and have me pop up around his house, spreading scandal and scampery. And many a year passed in this merry type of employment.

But I put all of my eggs in one basket with one lord, and off he went and died, didn't he? And what I thought I had coming to me through him, his family felt I ought not to gain—for certainly I had done as he said very well, and their names were all muddied about the place most satisfactory. I got barely a worm-squidge out of them. By dint of being inscrutable, though, I built and built that squidge up, to the point where it all exploded around me in a mess of thieves and cheaters—myself included, I don't deny that—and bills for liquors I and my fellows had drunk but not paid for, meals unremunerated that we had long since shat out.

I took myself to the country very quietly upon this disaster. I had heard a while before that Hotty Annie were doing her worst out of some hedge nearby St. Olafred's somewhere, and now that I were so downcast about my fortunes, I aimed for there.

And a cheerful town I found it, though a little overdecorated with flags and shields of rampant black bears. The guard were not nearly so toothful and clawsome, though, and on the way up the street I were teased and flirted with by some most robustious young women of the laundry trade; they slapped their work very promising on the slabs along that lane. Should my fortunes turn, there will be good pickings along that lane, I thought. Heavens, I might find a lass so amiable, so amused by me, she would turn me her tuffet gratis, out of no more than curiosity. One never knew one's luck in a strange town, I had found.

"Annie Awmblow?" said the wool-hag in Olafred's market, and chewed the inside of her cheeks awhile. "I non't know that name."

"She were a bit touched, as I remember," I says. "Had something of a talent as a charmer."

"Ah!" Her friend, who had several more teeth but was none the prettier for it—oh, I was spoiled from my time of fine living, when pretty women were provided me as natural as bed and board—her friend leaned over and said, "A charmer called Annie? That will be Muddy Annie Bywell and no other, roun this districk."

"He says Awmblow," says the first.

"She may've married," pointed out the second. "Even witches marry, you know."

"She may," I said, "though she were not exactly the marrying type, if I recall her right."

"Well, if it is her, she is widdered now. She lives by herself out by Gypsy Siding somewhere," said the first hag.

"Yes," said the second. "Find the muddiest spot upcreek of the willows and strike east up the hill from there."

"Aye," laughed the other. "You will smell her, and her preparations."

I followed their directions, and indeed there were a right mire a little way along from the willows, and there were also whisper-ribbons hanging out the trees' summer leafage, and crotch-stones if you looked for them, and these told me someone were practicing mudwifery hereabouts.

"Annie!" I struck up through the trees. "Annie Bywell that was Awmblow! I of come to visit you—your old friend."

She came to the door—was it a door? Was more like the mouth of a weasel-hole. Gawd knew I would not like to go in there to look—or to sniff any deeper, blimey.

Oh dear oh dear oh dear. Of course I must have been almost as old as she, but Gracious the Lady knew my years had treated me better than hers had. She had bugger-all teeth left, and so her face had shrunk into itself that I remembered as so full and handsome—how jealous I'd been of her strong jaw! And now I had the stronger.

"You rekkernize me?" I said, and I struck a pose, the kind

of lackerdee-day thing that makes the ladies think I am a good sort, to get amusement out of my stature instead of embarrassment.

"Ach." She shows off her teeth, such as they are. "Collaby Dought the Short-stump, and no less. Behind and under all that hair like a fall of snow."

"This is what twoscore years will do to a man, Annie." I gathered my beard forward and stroked the full length of it. "But you were short as me once, I remember. Do you remember that, Annie-Belle?"

"I do well," she said, and clacked her tongue or her gums or her throat or Gawd-help-me. "Things were desprit back in them days."

"*You* were desprit," I said. "You would jump on anything that moved, and a few things that didn't."

"I weren't desprit. I were bored. Bored, bored. Bored of coal-scuttles and thin porridge and cat-soup and chilblings and blankets made of paper. A bit of pokelee-thumpelee were something to sparkle up my day." She sucks on some bit of mouth—a toothache, maybe. "And yours too, I recall."

"Indeed," I say, although "sparkle" is not the word. I was mad in love with this oul witch when she were young and a looker, the way a man always is, they say, with the first one as lets him have at her hind end. It was nothing to her, of course. She grew up out of me—she just grew past me and there were other, bigger beggars for her to fry, including the biggest of all. "Do you hear from God-man Shakestick lately?"

"No, he likely finds it difficult to send word to me from where he is burning, much I'm sure as he'd like to."

"He died?" The very thought made me cheerful. Well I remembered the sting of that stick of his, and the bruises rising. "That's a blessing, then."

"Except I had him paying by the end, so my livelihood took a beating. Still, change from my bottom. What you wanting, Collaby? I'm guessing it's not a leg-over unless you of fallen on *very* hard times. Although, as I remember, you were of a decent size down there, anyway." Her laugh was all rattles and wheezes, like one of them bear-flags flapping on a wall. "Could of hired yourself out and made a fortune by now, a certain class of lady. But you hadn't no sense of enterprise ever, did you, my duck? Just a moper-around and 'poor me, poor me.' Take a seat out here and I will bring you a drink. Tea or dandwin?"

"Make it tea," I said. "I can't abide dandwin."

And I sat and swang my legs and sulked awhile that she had seen me so quickly, that she knew me so well and all that story of me, because it were her story too.

"So what piece of poor luck have you fell on, stumpet?" Annie put down two cups between us.

"It is too dull to go into," I said. "But some thief from Middle Millet have took my moneys for a ride—all I had—and I've no way to make it back, having burnt some bridges to get it in the first place."

"Is always about coin," she said, "isn't it? 'At's what the sun and the moon is there to remind us, with their roundness and their flatness." This had a worn sound, like words she dragged out for one customer after another.

"Exactly, so dull. Every day coming up and going down, like someone's fortunes. Like someone's bottom above a laundry-girl, so reg'lar."

She woke up and laughed at that.

"All I can hope," I went on, "is that *my* fortune will wax again. Ack-sherly, I was thinking you could help me in that."

"Ah, here it comes, Collaby's scheme." She arranged her lips for listening.

"I have never forgot that day at haytime, after we had done romping, you and me, and you performed that thing to my forehead and I seen—you remember, I told you all about it?"

"You told me and told me! Jumpin alongside me like a flea in a hotpan."

"And you said you could get me there, to that place, if you just had but a little more powers, and I could probably stay there, or at least come and go as I pleased."

"Hmm."

"So I am wondering, did you come by them powers? Did they grow as you grew? So that now that would be possible?"

"No, they did not. Especially they did not if you have throwed away all your money and are expecting actual sorcery for no cost. I am not such a Gormless Gussie as that."

"You are not," I agreed, "but I thought you had some kind of a heart."

"Oh, I'm all heart, where is not whiskers," she says, very dry. "But a woman must think to her own welfares. What do I get out of your proposition? A headache and half my bits and bobs used up—and you gone? But I have had you gone for most of my life, at no particular cost. You are going to have to plague me something dreadfully to make that a factor to decide me. Which, seeing you were never that offensive—to me at least, even if you made of yourself a pig and a pain to others—I am not thinking you're capable of it. I reckon I could still best you if it came to an out-in-out battle. There's other things I can re-sort to, even if these old strings should give out." Or wires, she might have called those scrawny muscles, standing out from her sticks of arms.

She looked down at me. I tried to see in that saggy bag of face the little strumpet that bounced on me that day in the hay when I was in heaven, when it all was new and life turned to fey-tales for a moment. Certainly she did not look on me so superior then. We were eye to eye, snuck away together from the God-man's toil and picnickery. That were years before she were sucked in by his power and purse.

"Have you done such, then, for people as *do* have money?"

"Of course I have," she said.

"You dint look me in the eye to say that, Annie. I don't believe you have."

Now she looked, though—all put out, too. I were going in the right direction.

"Why can I not be in the nature of an experiment?" I said.

"And you would be, too, it has been so long since I done anything proper, and never have I gone so big as that."

"And you don't reckon you could?"

"I don't— Well, I . . . You see, Collaby, experiments is not what is done, this field of endeavor. The misadventures might end up too serious."

"More serious than being sought by murderers a man owes money to?"

She looked at me sidelong. "To be sure," she says. "The worst could come of that is your murder, is it not? Which would all happen in this world, no? Whereas *twixting* worlds, sending someone *across* to his own heaven, well . . ."

I waited on her. "Well, what?"

"Well, it's not as if you're askin for a poultice made up, or a love potion. I don't even have all the preparations I would need. We are talking about a visit to High Oaks Cross when the market is on."

"It needn't be done today. Sooner is better, but I can wait if I know you are putting something together for me."

"That is big of you. Right gen'rous. How 'bout if I am still out of pocket, though? Some of the items I would need is quite expensive."

"Point me at them, Annie, and I will obtain them for you. Or the pocket to pay for them. Such lesser amounts is no bother to me."

"Oh, so your fingers is light *and* little, is it?" All eyebrows, she peered around her cup at them.

"And the next man, you can charge *him* a fine price, and get all your costs back and some over."

She mouthed out her lips awhile, like a girt catfish's, right down to some of the moustachios.

"I will leave it with ye, shall I?" I said soberly. "I know you have the power; it is just the will you must summon."

"Oh, must I?" She mumbled her mouth and moved her ragged dress on her knees. "Must I just."

"You worked it so close in your youth, Annie," I said. "Are you not itching to use the fullness of what you hold inside of you?"

"I don't know." She looks down into the forest. "I have itched, I suppose."

"You see?"

"But there was no living in it. There is a living in the herbs, you see, and in reading hands."

"Is it in my hand?" I laughed, holding it out. "Look there and see if you're going to do it."

She eyed my palm, but did not touch it. She read it quick as a kestrel reads a hillside, and looked away. "Dought," she said, and her voice had lost all its front and bravery, "it looks good for you. Right up to the end, it looks good."

"Right up to anyone's end is good!" I laughed. "Nobody wants to end, whether their life were good or ill."

"I've seen plenty that wanted to go before time took 'em. They come to me for the wherewithal."

"Well, anyway." I swigged the last of the tea and jumped off the bench. "You think, Annie, how the thing might be accomplished, and I will be your white rabbit. I will come back tomorrow."

She looked down at me. Everyone had grown into giants around me, all the orphans I used to be equal with. Here she was, sitting, and me standing, and she must still lower her eyes, when I used to poke her looking almost straight into them.

"There might be many you can promise this to," I said. "You might make your fortune sending people to the place of their dreams. Come, Annie"—I stepped towards her, pulling out my last card, which with women is always His Majesty of Hearts—"for the sake of times at St. Onion's. Poorhouse rubbish together, we were. 'Tis a binding that never unravels."

"There are dangers, Dought. You cannot imagine. I am not sure of them all myself."

"Mebbe not. Get it wrong with me, that you may right it with others, and become a rich woman in a house on the hill."

Still she regarded me, all uncertainty. If I'd looked more pleading, my eyes would have fell right out my head onto the dirt there.

"Leave me think," she said. "You nuisance, coming here with your Onion's-talk. Why should I want to recall all that?"

"It's what we're made on, Annie. We cannot deny."

"Go on."

"I'll go on." I patted her gray-clothed knee. "I'll come back tomorrow."

"Next day. I've a batch to mix tomorrow and don't want disturbing." She said this to the forest wall over my head.

"Very well," I said, and I was gone, leaving her thoughts, I was sure, bubbling like broth over a cookfire.

"There was a woman said I ought never to do this," Annie said. "I met her at High Oaks Cross when I were deeper in the telling game. Come all the way from Rockerly, she did. Miss Fancy-pants."

We were by a stream, because running water was required. The air was ripe with the things she had laid out, which were all gray and dusty, except the fresh mother-in-law ear, which were green-gray and hairy. She were not done yet. She were busy with the bits as she went on.

"I said to her, *Why is it guv me, then, if I'm not to use it?* But she says, *Ooh, not all as has wombs is good for mothering.* And coming from Onion's, I took her point; some o' those old besoms, you wouldn't wish 'em on the Devil as an enemy, leave alone a mam. A little fire, Collaby, is what we're needing now." She tossed me a tinderbox. "When it is going, await my word to put these on." And she prodded at a bundle of sticks with dried buds falling off and through them.

Well, the magic-making went on such a long time, I were on the point of complaining. Remember, she is doing you a favor, Collaby, I told myself any number of times. I'd had to flit away in the night when the men of my main creditor, Ashbert, caught me up at Osgood's inn, so I was all twitchy. The whole world seemed in pursuit of me, and all I wanted was an end to the fleeing.

"And now," Annie would say. She would glance at the sky as if she were wishing away rain. "Everything that is bitter." And this plant and that powder would go up in an awful stink, and I would have to breathe the smoke of that. Or, "A spot o' signage is in order now," and she would sit me down and draw her mysteries on my brow, which I was hopeful would bring on glimpses such as I had enjoyed at haying that time, but no, it was just *rasp, rasp, rasp*, and her hand this time smelt of that distinct repulsiveness women have when they are past childering, overlaid with this herb and that mineral dust. "And now for the mershon," she would say, and then make me go down and dunk myself three times in the freezing stream while she stood and muttered her stuff on the bank.

I grew miserable and bored of it, and still she came up with new trials. I began to think a beating of Ashbert's boys would be preferable. However close to death it brought me, at least it would be quick. Certainly an end to this and a nap in a sunny place where my clothes could dry out were seeming most immediately attractive.

"Ha!" She checked the sky again and grinned at me, her face all folds of leather. "Look at it, Dought!"

"At what?" I grumped.

"There." She pointed up into the flying smoke.

It seemed to me I saw only a smudge such as is often in my eye when I have the leisure to look awhile at the sky. It took a time of squinting to the sides of it that it became a crinkle, a star-ish shape of gray pleats hanging over us, around a puncture mark.

Now Annie was beetling about with this and with that, all excited. She sent up smokes, and some of them obscured the mark and others brought it to more darkness, until I was quite used to and bored by the horrible hovering thing, and unconvinced. I could not see how this had to do with the vision she had showed me as we lay in the hay, which had been of a world where nobody loomed or towered. Many maids there had been,

83

my size, and men of a spirited disposition, my kind, who would join me in whatever prank or party I might devise. It had been all color and dancing there, not this shadow growing on the air, not the cold water dripping off me and making me sniffle, not one foul smell upon the other until my nose was so dizzy it could only discern the outermost edges of the nastinesses.

"Here we go, Collaby," she finally said, and *there* was that little gamester I knew, bright and naughty as ever in the stance and glancing of her. "I will leg you up to it." She linked her hands into a stirrup and bent down to me.

"What? What am I to do?" I put my hand on her shoulder and my foot in the stirrup, suddenly all boredom gone and my knees locking with fright.

"Go on up to it. Your world is waiting, what I drew on you."

"Up there?" She had hoisted me, and the thing was over me like a lowered bum, like a lowered cloud ready to release its storm. Oh, it was no ordinary cloud; I could feel the concentration of it, its compressed lightnings all unable to burst out.

"Push into it!" she cried. "Dig! Quick, afore my skirt catches in the fire!"

I joined my hands as a God-man prayeth, and pushed the point of them up into the gray. " 'Tis quite hard, Annie; it does not feel inclined to yield."

"It will yield, it will yield. Just you push, just you force it. It is yours, I tell you, on the other side."

What a substance it was, particularly when my fingertips broke through. Nasty washes of sensation passed down me; Annie felt them too, I could tell by her shaking. "Cawn, Dought, my toes are crisping here." And she straightened further. Her head was against the edge of the phantasm, all misty there. She had forced my arms through into cold, cold! Cold water had broken out the bottom of the world above and was dropping and soaking me.

"Blemme, woman, you are putting me through into an ocean, to drown there!"

"'Tis not salt," she said, smacking her lips. "It is lake or pond or stream or summut."

"Some fish is brushing me, aak!"

But she forced me up with my feet, and I was so stiff with fear that I did not think to bend my knees. My head went through; it felt as if all my hair and beard were tearing out on the way. All the forest sounds turned to the *gloomp* and *glop* of bubbles through water, and the push of it. Light, there was light up there! And a great plant—not a fish, a broad plant with leaves flat as eel-tails—trailed overhead of me in the stream-current, in the frothing mud.

Two strong pushes and Annie had skinned me alive, but I was through. My feet could kick and they kicked upward, with stars swimming all around me in the ribbons of eel-weed.

Up I gasped, through to the glorious air, and there I was, being cradled on the water-top and spun under the trees, the bank empty of Annie back there, but the trees the same, the sky.

Best get out of here, I thought, before I hit that rocky, rushy part downstream, and bang my magical brains out.

So I whumped and galumped my way to the bank. It were all pretty steepish there, but I gripped up handfuls of the grasses and dandlin-daisies and pulled myself out, and some of the daisies out the ground, but there was plenty more, no?

Then, as I sprawled there, wondering how this was any different and where was all my new friends, something happened to the grippage in my hand, and when I opened it, not

85

dandlin-daisies but shining coins new-minted of the king's currency lay there.

"What is this marvel?"

I turned the coins, I bit them, I weighed them in my palm. I plucked, all frightened, a dandlin-head off its stalk. It melted to gleaming gold on my wet hand and lay there, valuable.

I quite lost my senses for a little while. I yelped and leaped about, picking flower after flower, watching them change, pocketing them so that they clinked at my belt. I tore off handfuls of the blooms; danced about, raining gold on myself. "I am a king!" I shouted. "I am a prince and a wizard! I shall fill my bath with gold and wash my beautiful beard in it! I shall eat gold for dinner and drink golden wine!"

Then I calmed and busied myself. I filled my belt and pockets, I did, until I had to pull the belt in a notch so's not to lose the heavy thing, and restrain myself so's not to burst the pocket-stitching. That were well enough to get me out of the hole I'd dug myself with Ashbert, not to mention going back to Middle Millet and maybe even to Rockerly town, and paying back the men I'd borried from there and restoring my good name. Then I would buy myself a house and a horse and carriage and some suits of clothes, and so much else besides! I had never had money to dream beyond that, it had all been scribbling-scrabbling here and there, clawing up coppers like sifting spilled grains from dirt. How I laughed and sang and exclaimed, for there were no one else around here, neither short-stump nor long.

When my belt and pockets were full, I set off along a path uphill, wishing to find the people of my own size that Annie had shown me, and to see what manner of merchant or spank-house or kellerman they had here that I could impress and make use of with my new wealth.

✳   ✳   ✳

Branza held out the leaf of row-cabbage. At last the hare, very slowly, approached her with its rocking stride, almost like limping. It paused and breathed before her, its yellow eyes looking at everything, its velvety lips nibbling the air. It reached across very delicately, not at all jaunty as a hare should be but quite humble, and nibbled the edge of the leaf, and in the quietness its teeth broke the flesh of the leaf, and crushed and crushed it with a sound like panting.

Branza tried to stay as still as a cabbage. Her body swayed very slightly and her insides rushed and thumped with excitement, her breath gusting, her eyelashes swishing as she blinked. Her body was like a storm gathered into itself over the hare, putting out a very narrow, silent finger of lightning. She crouched huge and dangerous, brimful of her five human years and growing all the time, and the hare had seemingly forgotten what a thunderous presence she was, had come and put its delicate furred self, its veiny ears that would tear like rags, its jittery bones, at her mercy.

Urdda could not do this sort of thing so well; she was too restless a person. Branza sat in her patience like a rock lodged in a stream-bed, and the frail animals came to her. It was gratifying that there were creatures smaller and frailer and quieter than herself, the quietest and most timid of her family. She had tried all her years to understand them, to listen as they listened, and now she sat and felt around her the forest and all its dangers for hares, all its possibilities for being leaped on and swooped on and devoured.

There went the hare, into cover with a bound, at that step, at those steps: Urdda's little runnings behind Branza, and a heavier tread on the path skirting the clearing. Branza was startled up herself, her heart thumping on the hare's behalf.

She only had to glimpse the man on the path—hardly bigger than herself, but very old and wrinkled and fierce, with much too much silvering hair and beard—and she knew to run, silently, to Urdda, to crouch behind the holly-bush there, her finger on her sister's lips.

Urdda thought it was a game—her eyes brightened and rolled with the fun of it. "What is it?" she murmured around Branza's finger.

But Branza touched her own lips, stilled by unaccountable dread as, over Urdda's innocent shoulder, she watched the littlee-man go by.

5

Before long I came to a road, and there beside it was a spring and cup exceeding like the one near to St. Olafred's. I drank, and very sweet it was, and then I set off towards what I hoped would be the town, but all brought down to a useful size, so that I would have no need to make a joke of myself, hoisting myself like a toddler into giant chairs, poking my nose above market tables and ahoying to be served.

The road took all the turns and had all the boggy and broken bits that I remembered from walking so glumly into St. Olafred's a few days ago. Were it not for the weight of gold in my belt and pockets, I would have thought I was in the same old world. And then I came around the last bend and there was the pig farm, same size, and the giant-sized huts all clustered against the same towering town wall, and as I came up I saw the pig-farmer out by his house, not the same twisty-faced misery as before, but just as big a lummock, it looked.

The town guard, also, were beanstalks as usual. They looked at me, though, with more than curiousness this time, and they walked forward into my way. Maybe they smelt the gold on me.

"What may I do for you today, youngfellers?" I says, a bit testy at having to look up to them still, and a bit uncertain because I could see, behind them, people coming and going, and none of them short-stumps.

"You don't belong here, Mister Collaby Dought," says one.

This nettled me. "Mebbe not," I says. "Where is all the little people at, that I was promised?"

The other spoke, but his voice and manner were exactly the same as the first's; they must be twinned. "You ought go back where you came from."

I looked upon them close; something were not right about them, about their identicality. They met my eye quite without enmity or any other active feeling.

"I will look about somewhat first, if it please you," I said.

"You shouldn't dally here," one said.

But they did not stop me walking around them, and they did not come after me as I sauntered up the street.

Half the houses seemed to be missing, and the street were a lot less busy than the true town's. The people were all, to a man and woman, your standard tallness, with no one my height bar the children ten years or under. They did not stare, though, as the real townspeople had done; instead, some of them walked out of their way, to mutter at me as I passed, "Mister Dought, go to your home now," or, "You're not welcome in this place, sir." But no one shouted and no one impeded me. No one even gave me a dark look.

I kept my courage all the way to the market square. There I found a mam selling plums, and these smelt so good I asked her for three of them.

"And what do you have in trade for them?" she says.

"Ho-ho! What do I have? I will show you what I have." I took out a gold coin and waved it at her.

She took it from me, and on the instant it turned to dandlin-head again. "I can give you nothing for a weed-head, I think."

"Then I shall just take what I like, shall I?" And I picked up a plum in each hand, looking for her surprise and ire.

But there was none. I might of been some misbehaving boy that she never expected better from, she was so serene.

I were about to eat one of the plums, but they lost their texture as I lifted them, and there I was, holding two plum-sized rubies instead. "What is this?" I said. "What is a man to eat in this place?"

She shrugged and turned away from me.

I put one ruby back to become a plum again. Taking the other, I went to the bread-stall next to the plums, and took hold of one of the floured baps there, which immediately heavied into a little loaf of gold, dusted with gold dust. "Shaish!"

"Put that back, sir," says the bakewife kindly. "It will do you no good."

"I don't know," I said. "I have a small fortune here in my hand."

"As you please. But off you go, now."

I walked about the market some more, but now I had one hand full of gold and the other of jewel and no more free to fondle things, and I could not see how I was to eat anything without it turning to metal or stone in my mouth and choking me. And these people kept muttering to me—all of them in the same sort of voice, very civil and low:

"Come along, now, don't linger."

"Go back to your true world, sir; this is no place for you."

"You ought shift yourself, Mister Dought."

I left the market and walked down through the town, hoping for an alehouse, or hoping to find the place that I had seen, when I first walked up St. Olafred's looking for Annie, that had had the woman at the door with the right sharp look about her for a bawd. Well, I found those places, but someone in their joy-killing had razed both buildings, and cleared all the rubble away and grassed the ground over, so a fellow might drink nothing but dew there—if it did not turn to diamonds on his tongue—and play with nothing but himself.

"Well, that's a fine spoiling of my sport," I said there in the sun. "I know, I know," I added to the goodwife who was veering towards me from the lane beyond, " 'Get thee home, Mister Dought; there's nothing for your sort here.' I shall go, I shall go, in my own good time."

"There is no good time for you here, sir. You are injuring this place every moment you tarry." And the smug cow passes me onto the road.

I went after her, and I tucked my ruby against myself with one elbow, and I caught hold of the woman's bum through her skirt, right there in the street, with who knew how many to witness!

She went very still.

"I was just seeing were there real flesh in there," I says, "or only a wooden frame." I let her go, and she walked on as if I had not touched her. No one shouted at me; no one looked askance. I ran after her again. "I'm reckoning I could have you here in the street and no one would stop me. Am I right?" And I grasped her bum-cheek again.

She turned on me such a face! If I had managed up a fist, it would have withered on me right then and there. It was not that she were cold, or angry, or scornful; it was that she were *not a woman*. She were not even a *person*. Her eyes were white as skylit windows; the wind whistled through her earholes, through her hollow head. I let her go. To be sure, where is the fun of outraging someone if they are *not* a someone, if they do not feel the outrage; if there is no rule to break, no punishment to risk? You might as well fondle a tree, or poke yourself into a hole in the wall.

Well, I was hungry now, ragingly so, and all this muttery and mistaking were depressing my spirits, so I hied me out of the town and back down the road and to the waterside where I had come to this horrible place. I found the torn and trampled place where I had jubilated before, and walked upstream of that to where I thought was the place where Annie had mag-icked me.

"Now, did you think to mark it, the place where you came up, Collaby Dolt? I think you did not! Well, serve you right, then, to be laden down with valuable coin, and stuck in a place where you cannot use it." My arm ached from carrying the golden bap, and my head thudded with all the newness of things. I stamped out into the water near to where I thought I had come up, squitching and squertching about among the eel-weed and the unidentifieds in the mud. But of course, I had been out of my depth when I emerged, and the deeper I got, the stronger the stream's pull was on me.

I tried several ways, starting upstream of the place and letting the current take me down to the stream-bottom to feel with my hands or feet, the weight of the bap and coins advantaging me to help me sink, but then, of course, being impediment should I perchance wish to breathe. And of course I could see nothing for my swirling hair, for the swirling eel-tails, for the mud I clawed and toed up from the bottom.

"Curse and crangle it!" I bellowed in the end, floundering

half drowned in the shallows. "Where are you? Let me through!" And I stamped as hard as I could, and I frothed up the water around me with my fists full of gold and jewel, and flung my hair all about in my rage.

Then there came a horrid deep blurt of bubble, up from the bottom, and oh, didn't underfoot feel uncanny, sagging and pushing my slipping feet together into the sag. I have done something to the geologics, I thought. I have unsettled an earthquake. And then the water slid cold up my chest and my neck and, "I am going to dr—argle-argle-aaaah!"

Down I went through the mud swirl, the pond-bottom tightening around my ankles like a monster's mouth. It lipped and tongued and sucked me in, and the light and the swirling weeds disappeared, and my breath had all gone out of me on that one scream I had given. Then the mouth clamped my neck, and my head were the only cold wet part, and the rest of me were being crushed and munched, and I must not breathe or I'd drown. So I did not. The thing's lips sucked my face and head. A crowd of golden stars fizzed across my mud-squelched eyes. My skull were gripped hard enough to crack, hard enough to peel my scalp off.

"Ow! . . . Uff!"

I were sitting in the stream-edge with a bumful of bruise-beginnings from the rock bed, and the pleated thing were wheeling gray in the sky above me, and there were Annie turning all surprised, pipe in one hand and pipe-makings in the other, on the point of sitting on a tree-stump and smoking, after her morning's labors hoisting me through into Drowningland.

"Already?" she says, astonished.

"What d'you mean, 'already'?" I upped my sodden self and stamped out the water. "*Hours* I have spent in that place." I laid the bap and ruby in the mud at my feet and squeezed some water out of my hairs.

"Hours? You're nonsense. I have just kissed your toes goodbye, no more than an instant ago."

"Well, *hours*, I'm telling you. I've come back laden with what took *hours* of gathering."

She came down the bank, poking the air with her pipe-stem. "Time must go different there, then."

"I suppose it must." I was most uncomfortable, all wet and bumped and weighted by coinage round the middle, and I did not enjoy being contradicted or mused over.

"That's not supposed to happen." She frowned at me, watched me not-caring awhile, then walked back up to her stump. "Well." She started arranging her leaf-bits. "What can I *possibly* have done wrong, after all that work?" She sighed and she sucked there, and fiddled with pipery. "Well," she eventually'd, "you are back now, and what is done is done."

The both of us examined the air where the wheely-thing had been, but all there was was sky, empty but for breezes.

"So, did you have a time there, with your stumpesses?" She cackled at me. "I'm surprised you still have your pants on." She pulled on a mask of sympathy. "You must be very tired, Collaby, with your heavening, poor lad."

"No such," I says. "There were not a single one of us, of anyone I saw. It were the same as here, with everyone towering over me, girt lumps the lot of 'em."

"That does not match," said Annie. "That's not what you seen before, is it? They were all littlees you saw in the hay, you said. A world o' them. Did you imagine us bigguns your servants, mebbe, or some such downstruck types?"

"Nobody were downstruck there. They were all with telling

95

me what to do. 'Get out of here, Mister Dought,' they all said—yes, and every last soul knew who I was, some down to my name!"

"Oh dear. Oh dear." She took the unlit pipe from her mouth. "That sounds very bad, Dought. I dislike the sound of that *very* much."

I picked up the bap and stone and walked my damp self up the bank to her. My pockets jingled, and my belt felt like to fall off me.

"But I may have good news, Annie." I handed her the bap. "Just hold this for a little," I said, "to see if it lasts in this world. I seen gold change back to flowers in that missus's hand. Maybe I've brought back nothing of worth."

"Oh!" She held the heavy lump as if it might burn her, turned it over, turned it again. It stayed gold in her hand, though smudged now with her mud, and with a leaf-scrap adhered to it. I held the ruby out to her. She gasped and put her pipe and stuff on the ground, and took the stone in her other hand, and moved it in a sunbeam so that it shot color about. She stared from gold to jewel as if they were two eyes hypnotizing her. "You have made your fortune, Dought!"

"Annie, I have made mine, and yours, and plenty left over." I showed her inside the belt with the coins nestling like gold-backed insects, gleaming outrageously all around my middle.

She jumped up and away from me. She darted back and laid the treasures on the stump, careful, as if they might explode. She trembled behind her clutched hands, staring at me, her eyes filling. And then she was off in some kind of mudwife mad-dance, stamping and choking and waving those string-and-wire stick-arms she had threatened me with just a few days ago. I laughed to see her, and to see the bap still gold on the wood, and feel the coins still weighty at my waist. First, I would get Ashbert off my tail. He was ready to stave my head in if he saw me, though. I would get me a *servant*, and I would send my *servant*—a good big brute of a servant at that—with the payment, and I would not sully myself with company such as Ashbert's again. I would move in entirely higher circles. I would be like a soaring eagle, tiny in that man's eyes, not with insignificance but with unreachable height above him and with wealth.

Annie came laughing and weeping back to me, where I was smiling and piling the coins upon the stump.

"Put it away, put it away!" she whispered.

"It is yours, though, Annie!"

She shook her head and the tears fell and flew. "It is too . . . much . . . money!" she said. "How does a person spend such coins? They are too big for me! They shine too bright! I would faint, presenting them. People would follow me home to rob me! I could not *carry*," she almost pleaded, "the copper I would get in change, did I spend one—it would tear through my pocket and fall all over."

Oh, she was old, so old, and she had never known much of the ways of the world. That was mudwifery for you—sitting to one side and catching the odd copper fallen out of people's ill-luck. "Let me organize it for you, Annie. Do you want a house built, or would you rather buy the fanciest one extant in town? I can arrange either for you—just you say what you want me to do."

She gasped some more and looked around, at the rubbish of her magic-making, the ends and ashes of all the ingredients, the expense of which, I knew, was greater than any she had met before. I held out her pipe-bits to her and she looked at them as if they were challenging her to a punchfight. Then she took them and sat on the grass, and carefully made up the pipe and lit it, and surrounded her head with smoke.

"Just," she croaked in the middle of the smoke-cloud, "a little cot is all I've ever wanted—just something a little better than I have. Not even that! I never thought to want! There was never any hope of such!"

And then she was weeping into her hands for all her years of hardship, from St. Onion's days to this. And then she had thrown her pipe aside and was up on her knees. She came at me on her knees like a pilgrim—it was alarming to see—and she kissed my hand, clutching its stubbiness in her long gray fingers.

This was not at all what I had been after when I came to her for aid. I'd been thinking of some brisk and cheerful transaction—as between men, is what I likely had in mind. She were twisting me all up, pouring her emotions out on me. I could see that such wealth was going to be more complicated than I had thought.

Branza walked a dream-forest, wearing a shift with two pockets. A tiny Urdda chattered in the one, a tiny Mam sewed silently at the bottom of the other, and from their fragility an air of dread spread among the trees, thick as water.

He was on his way, the littlee-man she had pushed out of her mind this morning. She could feel him coming, though she saw nothing yet: all the birds, sensible birds, had fled; all the leaves hung very still. Branza stood aside from the path.

Here he came, with his unnatural walk. He was no bigger than when she first saw him, but his very stumpiness terrified her, his child-legs carrying all that intent, his big-baby head with all the hair, with all the beard, sprouted from his harmful intentions.

He drew level with her and stopped. He could smell her; he could smell how frightened she was, hear her heartbeat. Urdda was silent in her pocket, under her hand, but Mam worked on, and she was knitting now, and her needles gave off tiny, busy clickings.

The littlee-man's face worked with delight and hatred. His head slowly turned, macabre on his hidden neck—perhaps he had no neck, but only the hairs tethering the ball of his head to his doll-body.

She could not even *think* of running. What would be the point? She stood among the trees—there was something chapped and scabby, something charred about their bark. Her hands, over her pockets, shielded the tiny Urdda, warned the traitorous knitting Mam. The man's head turned slower and slower, teasing her with its slowness, letting her terror build. He was not smiling, yet he gave off a strong sense of glee.

Then she was pinned and screaming in the dark, struggling as he muttered in her ear.

"Branza, Branza!" Mam cried from her pocket, from her shoulder, from outside the dream, and Branza rushed awake and clung to her. Urdda reached out of her sleep beside her, patted her sister heavily as Branza wept, then slipped back away into her own busy dreams.

Well, I thought I were set for life then, I had so much gold. But then I found that human wants are like an evil fart; they will swell to fill every corner of whatever wealth is available.

I were sensible, I thought: I did not give to beggars nor splash the money about too wantonly. I bought three fine houses: one for Annie in St. Olafred's, one for myself in Broadharbour, and another for myself near Annie's so I could visit now and then and instruct her further in how to be wealthy—

for she had no more idea of handling money than a slug has of flying. But I did not dress outrageous, only sober and high-class; and I did not squander on parties, or on devilments beyond the odd *very* fancy fancy-woman; I did not lose my senses and marry or breed up a big puddle of expensive children or nothing; I lent money to no one except those I knew to be trustworthy in meeting my terms and rewarding me later.

Still, it ran out—well, not completely, but two years on and my pants-seat were looking a bit thin to the wind; I could feel the whistling. And then one of my trustworthies come along and admitted to me that it were, matter of fact, his feckless *son's* venture that he had had me backing, not his trustworthy own, and sure and he'd have the sixty crown to me just as soon as he'd earned it off his tin mine, but with the tin mine, see, things were not going so wonderful there as they had done the past many years, and, well . . .

Which it ended up, very suddenly everything went to shit and there was one, just *one*, card game involved where I had done all I could to ensure that I would recoup the part of my fortune I needed to meet those hanging off my hems for payment, but even that were not enough. So, as I say, very suddenly I found myself fleeing Broadharbour for the country, with Pinchman Brady and his boys on my tail, and despite my feinting and dodgery, they managed to follow me to St. Olafred's, and before I knew it I was skedaddling down the town with Brady's boy Canard after me on his great long legs like a spider's, and me thinking, What the bishop's knickers am I going to do about this?

And there must be something after all in bishopry, or at least in godding, for as I were running down that twitchel behind Eelsisters' convent it comes to me, in a kind of slow flash, if you know what I mean—the kind of very clear thinking a person is capable of in a very tight spot, a more or less ultimate spot. Between one step and the next I seen again Muddy Annie brooding and looking shady as we walk through her town house that I'm about to organize the buying of, our footsteps echoing in the big empty rooms.

You could always go through a second time, she says, *and fetch more money. Now that it have been punchered, the . . . the rind of it, like. I could not exactly advise it, but there is nothing in your way, only my qualms.*

So there I stopped, right in that twitchel. Canard turned in at the top and shouted triumph. And I stamped my foot and I said, "Let me through, let me through!"

"You hoping for the nuns to save you?" says Canard, running down at me.

Nothing gave underfoot, stamp as I may. "Through! Lemme through!" I danced like a kitten on top of a stove.

The bugger was laughing, stopped in the lane right before me and laughing, close enough to grab me but now taking his time, enjoying the sight of the little stamping stumpet.

Then he laughed no more, but stepped back in a fright. I glanced behind me—what was he falling back from? Nothing there. And then I heard it, like the flap of a bird-wing above me, and there it was, the wheeling star, the fold between the worlds. *Sproing!* I was up there, dived up into it like an arrow with my joined hands, like a prayer darting up to the heavens: Thank you, bishopry and nunnery and goddery! Off I go! And the wheel-thing sucked me up into the water.

Well, it was just as nasty as last time, the sensations, like being swallered by a very thin and muscular snake. I forced up through the water—not half as deep this time, thank the Pieman in the Sky—and tried to pull my beard after me, but it was all snagged and snaffled in the bottom. I could stand straight, and well out of the water from my tailbone up, but I could not get free of the mud. And there—I just got the one horrible glimpse before the muddy water slopped back over—was my beautiful beard, grasped in Canard's fingers, which had forced through the star-fold, coming after me.

The snake's belly did not want to let him through, though. I pulled and pulled, thinking my entire manhood would be torn out of my chin by the roots, but all that must have happened were, the hairs must have slipped some through his fingers, for he did not come through follering.

I kept to pulling, wishing, oh!, for a stone to whack at Canard's fingers and make him relinquish me, whereupon I was sure he would slip back away. I cried out for someone to rescue me—I should not care how much they lectured me the while—but no one came to my calls. So on I fought—'twere like dragging an oxcart by my beard, I tell you, so-o-o slow and hard. The water, bit by bit, grew shallower—ah, but I turned and what did I see but the bobbles of Canard's knuckles coming up the surface? Gawd, I were pulling him through, though I did not want him here—perhaps I could just get him partway, stand on his head, and drown him?

I were too panicked to consider if this would help my cause or harm it, if I would manage to get back *myself*, were he jammed dead in the hole between worlds. I were too busy eyeing that clump o' daisies there, near the bank. If I reached those and held them, I'd have coin to quiet him—quiet them all. So, all made of leaden pain, I clawed my way up the shallows.

Well, I had paused to thrash a little in my frustration, and Canard's force were dragging me back down somewhat, when I saw to my surprise and relief, lifting my hand, several pearls underneath it, smeared with mud. A broken blob of frog-spawn floated at my fingertips also, slipping away as Canard hauled me. I made a snatch at this and lo! the little jellies turned to hard sweet lovely shining pearls in my magic hand. Fast as foxes, I pulled out my pocket and began stowing the things, and reaching for more—maybe pearls would do; maybe pearls would be sufficient to gold! I remembered pearls being a fine price when my fancy-girl's fancy turned to them that time as I were wooing her. And that were Broadharbour—here in at landlocked St. Olafred's, they'd be thought marvelous indeed.

I had only a whisker of hope there before Canard, the nuisance, gave a tremendous jerk to my poor beard, and just like a hooked fish I was brought back to the depths, where he wanted me.

Not as far as his grasping fist, though. Besides, I had seen the pearls, and there is nothing like a gem or precious metal to give a man strength. So up I got, and against all his force and no longer caring should I lose my beard and all my chin-skin with it, I leaped and strove and raged back towards the bank. He were terrible strong, though—Pinchman's boys were all big, on top of which, all men are bigger than me, and stronger. I were cursing my size and being trapped in a situation where my wiles were bugger-all use to me, and calling out for someone to come: Where are folk ever when you want them? When you don't, they are always in your face with their prating and whinnying! And my pocket were dropped and all the pearls were rolling out of it, beyond my reach and sinking. I were desperate, I can tell you. I flung myself about like a dying trout on a streambank, only a degree more noisier.

The sisters were walking home from the town. They had been baking that morning with Wife Wilegoose, and Branza carried in her basket three of the pies they had made, the three very finest and most perfect, still warm and covered with a cloth. Down the hill they went, and along the path that skirted the highest floodmark of the marsh-edge.

They were about halfway along it when a roar, at once enraged and pleading, chopped through the forest peace. "What is that?" said Branza. "Someone's bull escaped and is trapped somehow?"

They walked on more slowly. The roar came again. "I think it is a *person*," said Urdda, veering off the path towards the sound.

Branza stopped dead and held her basket to her chest. "Urdda, come back!"

"Who can it be?" Urdda darted off through the trees to find out, then ran out onto bushier, more open ground. Branza made a small, anguished sound. She did not know who it might be; she did not *want* to know; she was afraid of the sound.

"Come!" Urdda's voice was tiny with distance. "Branza, look! Come and look!"

Branza hurried down towards the marsh. She worked her way around the marsh-edge, muttering and stumbling over roots and dead branches to the place where there was a break in the bushes. She looked out across the tussocky waters. Urdda had run far out on the bank, quite unafraid. "Come back, you silly girl!" Branza cried.

The roaring thing—it was not a bull—was trapped, certainly. The mound of it was so mired, it barely moved when it struggled. It seemed bound to the water with many fine threads, as if the water surface itself were a net and the creature were trying fruitlessly to push up through it.

With horror, Branza saw the eyes. They seemed the size of ladle bowls, they were so wide with rage and terror, and they were fixed on Urdda through the whitish webbing that held the creature to the marsh-water. The noise came again, bub-bling the water under the net, and there was an edge of begging desperation in its horrors, so that Branza, however great her fear, could not quite turn and run from it.

She stood, panting, and gradually the creature seemed not so large, was not so new and frightening. It had a large head, but it was not far out in the marsh, and judging from the rip-ples, the body was quite small.

"Come, Branza! We must rescue it!" Urdda knotted up her shift and stepped out into the marsh.

"No, wait!" cried Branza weakly.

But Urdda forged on. Whimpering, Branza found a place to put the pies where they would not be found too soon by ants, and tied up her skirt and waded after her sister. The thing lay quiet under its bindings, its eyes glowing between lids that were like worn leather. It had a short, wide nose hovering just above the water. It was the sort of face Branza did not want to see the mouth of.

Oh, how hideous: that was its *hair*, that white web, from its own wide, round head, slicked out across its floating wet shirt.

"It *is* a person, Branza!" said Urdda, very pleased. The per-son muttered as she investigated. "His hands are pushing in the mud," she said, "holding him up to breathe."

His great eyes rolled at them, and he bubbled and growled as Urdda felt all down him.

"Oh, it is his chin-hair!" she cried. "A piece of it is caught in the mud!" And she knelt, shift and all, and took a breath and submerged herself, groping about in the brown water.

"Urdda, come up, come up!" Branza patted at the water, at the floating cloth of Urdda's shift, not liking to be left alone with this person's glaring eyes.

Urdda bobbed up. "There is no log or stone," she said.

"Nothing weighing down the beardy hair. It is growing from the bottom, and my fingers cannot even dent that. It is hard clay."

The little man's eyes danced and rolled, clenched closed and goggled open. His braced arms weakened and shook underneath him.

Urdda tried to uproot the beard, but the marsh-bottom would not give it up. The man's face was at her elbow, his furious bubbles bursting against her armpit.

Urdda took from her belt the little knife she had made herself, of flint bedded in a stout stick. "I will cut him free," she announced, "before he drowns himself in his floundering." And she ducked underwater again.

Both of them exploded up at once. Urdda, though only six, was still a touch taller than this strange man. He was not afraid of her, though. He pushed her hard, back into the water. "You great *goose*!" Branza heard him say—he had a strange way of speaking. "What business have you?"

Urdda spluttered and rose, and the man launched himself at her. She pushed him away, but his hard little fists beat at her elbows. "Cut off my manhood, would you, that I have groomed and grown since I were a bare sprout?"

"It was stuck in the mud!" cried Urdda.

"She was saving your life, ungrateful man!" said Branza, hating him, hating him— "Oh!" she said suddenly, recognizing. "It is that littlee-man!" But of course, Urdda had not seen him that time, from behind the holly-bush.

The man gasped and sank back a moment, as if Branza had stabbed him in the vitals. Then he was scrambling towards her throat, his voice gone to a shriek. "Littlee, you call me? Outrageous orphan! Whore-mouth! You shall never speak again!"

The two girls fought and dragged the littlee through the

water, trying to flee him, trying to detach themselves, until all three of them, mud-slopped and disheveled, reached the shore.

"Look at the fool you've made of me!" the littlee-man howled. "The stunted, chopped thing! I have never met such cruelty, you bold-faced brindle-cow!"

He sat in the mud and wept, his beard-end in his hands. Branza could just see how it should have been, how it should come to a soft point there instead of being crisply sliced off by Urdda's knife.

"Surely it will grow again?" she said gently.

His eyes blazed at her through his tears. "This part, that was the first to protrude from my innocent chin? You ought to be shaven clean yourself, you clumsy offal-bag. All that floss scraped off the top of your clunk-empty head! *Then* we would see what would grow again. Fur or fine fuzz, mebbe, or mebbe nothing at all! Bald as a doorknob, you might be. You are certainly about as bright!" Then the chopped end of his beard caught his eye again. He pressed the hairs to his lips and the tears ran down his leathery face.

"But we couldn't let you stay stuck in the water!" said Urdda.

"Stupid, stupid . . . ," he sobbed.

"Come along, Urdda," said Branza. "We will go now, seeing as he is in no danger."

"Just you do that, you lump. Stab a man through the heart and then walk off and leave him bleed."

But something in the marsh-edge caught his eye. He dropped his beard, took out his pocket, and went to scrabble in the mud there, snatching up what looked like frog-eggs and pushing them, gleaming, away into the cloth, dropping some in his haste.

"What have you got there?" Urdda squatted cheerfully

107

beside him and picked up one of the white things. "My, that's pretty—oh!"

"Ha!" The littlee-man snatched the muddied frog's egg from her. "You ain't got the magic, have you, you lump? All you get is a bit of jelly. I get *this*!" He waved the thing in her face so that she must pull her head back to see it. "And *these*!" He plucked up several more eggs from where they were floating on the ripples. He rolled them together in his hand, and when he opened it, a white bead the size of a pea sat there. "You got a use for this? I thought not, iggerent. No one here knows the worth of money. And no one here has this magic—which stays good on a trade where *I* come from, whether I give it to merchant or mudwife, woodman or woman-of-the-night, so there!"

"Money?" said Urdda. "I've heard Mam use that word, for stories."

"I bet you have, little slutter-tart. I'll bet you have."

"Come away, Urdda," said Branza, hating his sneering tone. "He is free now; we can leave him be."

"But I want to know, yet. How did you come to be caught so?" Urdda pointed into the marsh.

Where does she get such curiosity? Branza wondered. How can she care one way or the other about this worn-out boot of a man and his unpleasantness?

"None of your bee-wax," he said.

"What *are* you?" said Urdda, fascinated. "Are you a bad man, such as fireside stories have? Should we run away from you?"

"Oh, no," said the littlee-man smoothly. "I am Saint Collaby himself, and you should always come to my aid when you find me in trouble, on pain of the God-man paddling your bottom."

What is he *talking* about? thought Branza, exasperated.

"Who put you in the marsh, then," said Urdda, "and tied your beard there, if you are not bad?"

"You'd never understand." The dwarf picked up another clump of eggs and watched them shrink and gleam on his palm. "Not the permutations nor the torchurous exigencies." He clicked the beads into the cloth with the others. Then he fetched out his muddy pocket-string and tied up the cloth. "I am done here," he said. "I am off home to go shopping. You can sit and goggle all you like."

"Aren't you going to thank us," said Branza icily, "for saving you?"

He turned and she flinched, not knowing what to expect from him. "Oh, yes," he sneered, offering a smart salute that flicked mud at both the girls. "A thousand thanks for chopping off my manhood; pardon me that I do not stoop to kiss your filthy feet, whore-daughters."

He hoisted his little sack, walked around a flattish rock, stamped his foot and was gone, seemingly into the ground.

Urdda laughed! And now she was running after him!

"No!" Branza followed, terrified her sister would also disappear behind the rock.

"He's gone into nowhere and nothing." Wonderingly, Urdda patted the moss, peering under the rock's little overhang. Then she lifted her face, finely spattered with mud, to Branza, all alight still. "Where can he have gone? Has he changed into the ground, a part of the ground?"

"He's gone to a place of monsters just like him," said Branza tightly. "Where he belongs and we most certainly do not."

Urdda stood up from the rock. The shore was empty. Only the scrapes and scrabble-marks in the mud showed that anything had happened; only her own wetness and muddiness, and the stubborn set to Branza's shoulders as she picked up the pie-basket.

"Are there such places?" Urdda skipped after her sister.

"He had to come from somewhere," grumped Branza, "and he had to go."

"And more like him live there?" Now Urdda was dancing backwards, watching Branza's mouth. "That shout out whatever pops in their heads, and are ugly, and hit out at people?"

"I don't know. Have I ever been?"

"You *might* have. You might have, and not told me!" Urdda laughed at that enchanting thought, and danced on beside Branza. "But wouldn't you love to follow him and *see* that place?"

"I would not want to be *anywhere* that horrid littlee is."

"I would love to go there! Do you think *Mam* has ever been? Has she ever seen that man, do you suppose?" Urdda's blood itched in her veins.

"She has never said so," said Branza.

"But then—" Urdda hopped after her steady sister. "There may be a lot of things that Mam has seen and never spoken of, to us. She is tremendously old."

Branza cast an alarmed look over her shoulder.

"Well, we ought to ask her," Urdda said.

"We ought *not*," said Branza.

"Whyever not?"

"Because if she has not seen him . . . well, I shouldn't think she would *want* to know of someone like that."

"Why wouldn't she, you daftun?"

Branza pushed on through the bushes; the twiggy noises against the basket's weave were like her irritation come alive. "She just wouldn't. I'm sure she wouldn't."

"*How* are you sure?"

"I just am. Because I am seven summers old. When you are seven, you will know some things too."

"I will?" Urdda ceased her hopping and conjecturing. She slowed and walked along beside her sister, hoping by her similar gravity and sensibleness to attract the knowledge down upon herself.

Next morning, Urdda went to the marsh alone, took off her shift, and waded out into the water, feeling with her toes for that bristly bit of beard-hair she must have left in the hard clay floor. It must have caught when he magicked himself here, she thought yet again. There must be some little door, some tiny opening, some mended place between here and wherever he had come from.

Urdda looked up into the great careless sky, with mare's-tails curling in it like peals of laughter made visible. Was there a whole other region down there with its own skies and marshes, a whole other world?

She searched and searched for some object or dimple or unusual sensation underfoot. She searched until her teeth chattered and she could no more feel her feet, let alone the shapes beneath them. But all she found this time was squish and squash, fish-nibble and eel-whip and the flowering of mud up around her middle. *A-dark,* said a frog to her; *pok!* said a fish; and a crane smoothed the air with its passing wing.

Suddenly impatient, she waded back to shore. Several flat rocks lay there, all very like the one the littlee-man had disappeared behind. She stamped all around them. "Pardon me I don't kiss your feet, hoar-daughters," she said several times, in case it was the words that had made him disappear. "Hoar-daughters. *Hoar*-daughters." She stamped and stamped behind each stone.

She tired of stamping. She stared at the ordinariness around her. She could stand here and listen to her own world breathing, with all its catches and coughs, all the many thoughts passing cold and busy under its surface. But she could not pass through to that other one. She could only watch and wait, and hope the littlee-man would come through again, and not disappear as fast this time, so that she could see how he did it, how he came and went, and follow him.

6

$\mathcal{I}$t is a great honor to be made a Bear. Only the best of young men gets it in this town, the strongest and the handsomest. You may not be Bear if you are already wed, but usually you have had girls interested in you, and you may have shown some interest yourself.

Which is why I thought some sort of mistake had been made this spring, that I was here. Because I had hardly lifted my eyes from my misery this last year and more, losing our mam just after New-Year, and then our da of grief from losing her. *You must get some joy of life*, Uncle had been saying. *Dance, boy; drink! Steal some kisses! Sow some oats! What do you think you have all that youth and health for?* But *No*, I'd said, and *No*. And when he wanted to garland me and drink to me for my eighteenth year I would not let him, for I could not see what there was to celebrate in that.

I would not be surprised if Uncle had prevailed on someone in the council to make me Bear, however much he insisted not.

Or perhaps they felt enough pity themselves, seeing my long face about the town, my earnest work in the wool hall and among the shepherds and flocks on the Mount, among the merchants and wool-hags and weavers in the market square.

That young Davit Ramstrong, he needs taking out of himself, they might have said around their meeting-table.

Someone would have made a face. *I don't know. These Bears, they is supposed to be everything that is spring. You know: strong, wild, mebbe a little dangerous, fulla juice and roar. Do you think—*

Have you seen the size of the boy?

But he handles it so clumsy. And he wouldn't know what to do with a woman, which way up to turn her. He is still moodling after his mother, that one.

All the more reason. He can learn it on the trot, on Bear Day. I know a few girls as will teach him a thing.

And a grimace and a shrug, and the thing was done, and now here I was, stuck with it, honored and shamed both.

There in the cold room, dressing with me, Fuller, Wolfhunt, and Stow made a lot of noise to cover the quiet inside us, the awe, putting on the stiff skins.

"Can we not wear them over our own clothes?" Stow had said. "These trousers scratch like mad, the stitching."

"You sop," Wolfhunt's dad had said. "You will die of heat in there as it is, running. Also, the maids like to know there is nothing but yourself in the skin. The maids and the maids' mothers. No one wants a glimpse of breeches or smock. Flesh is the thing. Muscle and sweat." And he went at Wolf's face with the oil-and-soot, so energetic that Wolf squawked. "Shut your mewing," he laughed. "How can I be proud of a boy that mews?"

"Hmph," said Stow. "They have a very particular pong."

He sniffed the shoulder of the costume. "All those stinking dads and granddads, eh?"

"Of Bear!" cried Wolf's dad. "Of Bear and privilege! Of good usage! This is my happiest day!" He kissed Wolf smack on the forehead and got a blackened mouth from it.

Wolf looked bashful. "Do my hands, you great softun. Good and heavy, so I can mark many and well."

Uncle tied my skin shirt at the back. Except for the bonnet, I couldn't take these clothes off myself. I was supposed to be a man, but I felt like a bab again, having its bib tied.

Uncle was the only quiet man here. *I am thinking of Whin,* he had said to me this morning, standing there as I woke, the milk-bowl steaming in his hands.

I know, I said. I had my da in mind, too. My da in the deep winter, declined to bedriddenness, a terrible sight—so thin and so pale and old, it would make you weep to see—it made me. *I shall never see light again,* he told us when the winter storms drew in. *No, Davit, Aran, protest all you like. I am going down the long tunnel now, the one that don't surface again.*

Well, turn around, you donkey! I had thought at him, but did I say it? No, I was too struck at the heart of. And now of course I wished I had, or Aran had; I wished we had nagged and begged and shamed him into staying.

The wind whistled in at the window. "Smells of snow," I said. Spring was undecided this year about coming; all the trees were nubby with leaf buds, and still the weather flurried and near froze.

" 'Twill be a light dusting, if it falls at all," said Uncle, "and you'll be warm enough with your exertions."

"Even if all your skins fall off, you'll be warm," said Stow. "Piled there under all them women. Even if it snows a blizzard."

Ah, Gawd. Even since the council had told the names of the chosen, without a whiff of bearskin or a touch of soot, I had seen the girls seeing me. It was uncomfortable; I could not meet their eyes and read that question there; that wondering, that measuring of me and of theirselves against me. Before this, no one had noticed my growing, I had been so quiet and then had been singled out for such ill-luck. With the weight and color of my miseries, no one had noticed me bulking out, lengthening, it went so gradual. I was become a man under everyone's noses, even to my own surprise, a little. And now everyone was looking; I saw the flicker of it at the edge of everything. The girl-groups fell silent as I passed, and whispered behind me. *You can have your pick!* Norse had hissed to me, who would never be Bear, he was such a bean-stick and a whiner.

Have my pick? It bewildered me, the very idea. Da had not *picked* Mam, nor Uncle *picked* Aunt Nica, as from an array of pears on a tree. Although both women widowed them and left them almost limbless from the loss, so perhaps their method of wife-choosing would not bring me happiness either.

"So here we are," said Wolf's dad. He scrubbed at one eye with the heel of his hand and stepped back and took us in, Stow and Wolf now with their tall bear-bonnets on, Fuller watching his dad color his bear-feet with soot. "The finest of our town."

"Oh, we are," said Stow. He would always be sure. He never had thought he would *not* be here this day. *There* was a man would pick his wife from a row of them, all lined up and giggling.

Uncle swallowed and blinked away dew to see me here, among these. He clapped my furry arm and his touch was a dead thump, thick with feeling. I smiled at him, glad he were there, glad he were glad.

"Oh, the teeth on you," he said, his voice gone all partial, and clapped me again.

Out we went through the room of the old Bears, who were cheering and weeping and some of them drinking already to warm their stiff bones against the oncoming weather.

Hogback Elder blessed us in his foreign speech from his throne-ish armchair; and then the God-man in his disapproving way, tall and starven-looking and dressed black as a moon-shadow; and finally the mayor spoke something we could understand, how we were fine young men and would remember this day all our lives and such. We stood quiet for it, and the olds behind us restlessly quiet too.

Then the words were done.

"Go on up, boys," said Stow's dad softly.

Fuller whooped, and *then* it was on, *then* everyone knew, and like a hit of brawn-liquor it came alive in my stomach: Bear Day. It was ours and no one else's—not these olds', not our friends' or brothers', but we four only's. I was not myself anymore; I was one of the four Bears. I cannot tell you the relief.

Up the tower steps we ran, out into the sunshine and across to the wall. As soon as they saw us, men shouted below, and women screamed, and the rest of the crowd turned up their faces. It were the women screaming that gave us our power: the sound hit my ears painful as knife-edges, but in my stomach it was like fat meat and clean ale, filling me for my day's wild work.

We roared and clawed the air and ran back and forth along the battlement. We all but threw ourselves off the top, leaning out fierce and threatening. Every child does this, boy or girl, in play. But we were not playing; we were the real bears that children wanted to be, to terrify the world and bring spring.

I don't remember getting down to the streets, I was so ahead of myself, so gone from myself. But I did, and then there were simple rules to follow. The ones that came at me, young and old alike, I picked them up, planted a black kiss on them, put them to the side, and ran on, roaring. The girls that cringed and shrieked and ran, I pursued. I brought them down, smeared them with my face, gave them a good dose of my hand's soot-and-grease, messed them right up. Children that were offered me, terrified as I were terrified once when held up by my mam—for them I softened my roaring to a growl, and streaked them lightly on their cheeks, thumb and forefinger in a single pinch. I uttered no word to anyone. If any women broke the rule and fled indoors, I'd license and permission to follow her in, smudge and disarrange her house, and break one thing—pottery I found to be the most satisfying—unless she offered me her cheek.

I could feel it in me, the force of spring. I could see the excitement and the fear of the maidens, the fervor of wives wishing for a babby, putting themselves in my way. I could see the men, too, pushing their wives and women forward and their daughters, and laughing a particular laughter, with a jealous note in it—I could hear that. I had never laughed that laugh myself, but now I saw the reason for it: they wanted to be so tall and furred and wild as me, so disguised, and turn the season, and be so free. It had never quite made sense before.

My path crossed with Stow's. One of his cheeks was clean, but the soot around that eye kept him monstrous. We ran together for a while, taking courage one from the other, combining to chase down some of the fleeter girls.

"Eeyaagh! Ooraaaarrgh!"

We ran through quarters I had never been, down every alley, kissing old women pressed against their doorposts, laughing; following clumps of girls, their flying skirts, their blue running feet.

"I've a rod on me like a pike," Stow panted as we cut along the lane by Wellbrook. "I hate to think if my skin falls off."

Did I want to know such? I did not. "It won't fall," I said. "These are cut and sewn and tied for a full day's worth of rough running. We are prisoners in them."

"They are hot, though, ain't they? Might be a relief to lose them. And some of these wives, the look in their eyes, they'd sit theirselves upon you on sight, hunh?"

"Maybe," I said. "Here, you run along straight. I will go down the twitten and head those washergirls off."

"Good man! Sharp thinking!" He was gone, and I was in the twitten, Hogback's wall at one ear, the Eelsisters' hedge at the other, their sunny lawn glittering through.

I was all slime inside my skins; sweat was drabbling from under my bonnet. How long had we run? And we must run, and kiss and roar and paw and smash, until we were stopped—we'd be derided if we fell down for long among the women. We must spread ourselves thin—everyone must be touched and marked. A Bear moved fast so as not to be recognized, so as not to be himself, to stay a stranger and a bear.

And then either the twitten grew long or my running slowed without my deciding, for it were very difficult on a sudden. The sunny lawn streaked aslant one way and another through the hedge of Eelsisters', from one step to the next. The flagstones went soft underfoot, like sucking bog; my feet would not spring back as they should. It was all falling away—the narrow hot shadowy air of the twitten, the damp paving, the square of bright grass within the cloister, with a sister there, stitching—and I was running fast and furious into the air. What was I to do? I could not stop; I would fall and shatter. In terror I brought my feet up under me and *jumped*—against what, I could not tell you; against some solid bit of nothing. I spread my arms and flew, like swimming on cold air, and the town dropped and tilted, and I could see more country than I had knowledge of—I could see how the forest and hills were disposed; how each town snuggled against its glitter of water; how the roads crept about around them, flung from one to the other like a boat-rope or a goat-tether. Oh, I thought, there is a system about all we do and live—look at it. There is a pattern. Everything fits here, even the fact that Stow has his rod about this strange day while I do not; while it is nothing of that kind for me. The pattern is bigger than my own body, certainly bigger than the manhood of me; 'tis seasonal and circular; births and deaths happen, and lives, so many lives, overlap each other, full of lessons and habits and accidents—and those is just our cozy matters, people's, small and colorful, in the midst of everything we do not know, which goes on around us regardless—

The cool air turned cold and flapped my skins, turned icy, with a smack of snow. I did not go high as the clouds, but nearly, and then I tipped and slid and wheeled, and there was the town again, complete upon its hill. I could see quite sharply that there was not a person in its streets; the whole place was shuttered up, indeed as if against a bear that had wandered down from the hills all hungry from its winter sleep. This seemed all part of the pattern, though I can hardly explain why. I was not alarmed, though I had plenty reason to be, you would think. But I was not thinking. Being a Bear had done with my thinking, just this while.

Now a different season was spread all around the town; the green bloom had gone off everything, the green air, and all was snow and wet black branches, and evening of a different day, closing blue and fast. I flew lower, but it was snow-cold there and began straightaway to numb me. *Rise, rise to where it's warmer*, thought my frozen mind.

But already I had reached the treetops and was falling. I snapped and tangled through the shocked branches. And then *thump!* I was sunk over my spinning head in the soft snow, breathless, and with snow aching against my teeth.

I sat up and spat. I seemed to be able to breathe again, to move my arms, my legs. I could not find anything broken. Even my fur bonnet seemed to be straight on my head.

I should take this skin off, I thought mazily. I should turn it around so the fur warms me on the inside.

But when I stood to begin doing that—how I would of, I do not know, seeing it were all tied behind—I saw through the trees a red-gold light, so instead I made towards that, my bare feet turning to numb lumps in the snow. This was dangerous cold—it bit me in the throat, and ran its fingers all about under my costume, stealing the heat out of me fast.

'Twas a little house that the light shone from, sweet under a cap of snow, with shuttered windows so snug they showed only a few seams of light between their wattles. I did not try to peep in; I went straight to the round-topped door to beg those inside to admit me and save my life.

Knock, knock, knock. My hands surprised me, they felt so clawed and furred, so lumpish with the cold, but only my own man-fists came up to knock. The sweat had frozen the soot to them.

121

The door opened to nothing—no, to a little one, a dark girl only a third my height. She screamed and was gone.

I put my head in and she screamed again—had I thought, I would have taken off my bonnet first.

"It will surely eat us!" the dark girl cried.

It was a mother and two daughters. Both little girls had shrunk to the mother; she was freeing her arms first from one and then from the other.

"Calm yourselves, you sillies!" she said, and laughed towards me, a little embarrassed. "It is only a bear. Why would a bear eat you?"

"In the story, he does," said the other girl, a touch taller than the first, and golden-haired. "He eats the bad hunter."

"I will not hurt you," I said, but my voice came out growls into the room, though it were words in my head and on my lips, wherever they were. Frightened, I tried again. "I am only half perished from cold, and would warm myself."

The girls hid more behind their mother, but she walked forward away from them. Straight to me, she came, and I towered over her, but she looked up into my eyes, clear-faced and audacious. What relief that was after all the girls today, their sly glances or their terror or that strange excitement Bear Day gives them.

"Are you a heaven bear?" this woman said.

That made no sense. Maybe she spoke a different language. Nothing seemed to be as it ought.

I lowered myself to all fours, to a sensible height before her. My costume had changed and thickened; my bonnet had extended as a mask down my face. "What have happened to me?" I said in confusion, trying to look at myself—but my eyes had changed too, and the mind that translated what they saw.

I felt the mam's tiny touch on the top of my head. From her

and around her were all the smells of warmth, of home, of women. Fire and food, cloth and cleanliness. In my own house—my father's house, but only me and Aran in it—no matter how I swept and scrubbed, all it smelt of was grief yet. I did not know what to do with it to make it a home again.

"Come in from the night cold, Bear," said this woman. "Sit by our fire here, but not close; don't singe that lovely coat."

I went to the fire, and clumsily I crouched there. The two little ones watched me fearfully. The mother smiled on them, and then on me again.

"Your husband," I said. "Is he out hunting, then?"

"That's right," she said. "It's better in here than out in the snow."

"He must be hungry," said the paler child. "Hunger must have woke him. You should be sleeping, Bear."

"He is deciding which one of us is best to eat," hissed the darker girl—with some relish, I thought.

"Bring him the littler of those tar-midgins, Urdda," said the mother to her.

The girl went to a basket and lifted the cloth off two snowy feathered mounds. One of these she brought out and laid on the floor in front of me. She was so fearful and yet so excited in her demeanor—and so small!—that all of a sudden I remembered my own grumma from when I was little, laughing and catching me in her arms and saying, "Ooh, I will eat you up, I will!" and growling and mouthing the side of my neck.

But the bird distracted me. I was not hungry, yet when I saw it there, I could not stand the sight of the plush breast intact when I knew what goodness lay inside; I tore it in half and crunched it in my teeth and, feathers and splintered bones and all, both halves went down and were delicious. I licked the blood from every crease of my hands.

And then I sat and sighed, the fire's warmth now deep in the fur of my back.

The darker girl, Urdda, approached me again, and in wonder lifted my hand, then lowered it. "So heavy," she gasped, and lifted it again, and higher, and put it on the top of her head, and stood around to face her mam and laughed.

Then the paler girl came and got under the other hand likewise, and there they were, like two gateposts or arm-ends of a throne, laughing at their mother, and she smiling back. "A bear and two gooses," she said.

I had never had maids or maids' mams trust me before. Everyone I knew thought children a great bother, and girl-children the worst because they screamed so high and painful sometimes.

But these ones did not scream, because they were not unhappy, or frightened any longer. Now the dark one—"Take care, now, Urdda; do not hurt him," says her mam—had put my hand aside and climbed onto my knee. And then they were one on each knee, as on a pair of ponies. Very small they were, with the dandlin-fluff of one's hair and the smoke of the other's dancing about at my chin. The darker one, she turned and touched my face, plucking away a white feather, pushing apart my lips to view my teeth.

"He is terrible cold and wet, Mother," she said.

"Fetch the brush, why don't you," said the mother, getting up, "and brush that wet and mud out of his fur."

Which they proceeded to do. The two of them made some careful bargaining as to who was brave enough to do the belly and who the face and who the back, and then they took their turns, busy and attentive around me. The mother spun all the while. "Gentle," she said now and then, when they grew spirited in their brushing. I was too preoccupied, myself, to mind how rough they got. The feeling of being a man inside a bear inside their brushing had my whole skin and brain busy. They were brushing a bear into existence from my matter—I began to sense and then to see that I had claws, that I had paws, as they did their delicate work upon them.

"His tongue has been very good at getting out the blood," said Miss Urdda, very businesslike.

"But there is older dirt," said the pale girl at my back, whose name I had not heard yet, "and around here is quite matted. Hurry with the brush, sister." So imperious she was that I laughed, and they looked at me and I tried to explain. They smiled at the little whinings that came out of me.

"He sounds very contented," said the pale one, and while the other went on brushing, she leaned on me and put her arms forward over my shoulders and hummed into my fur, waiting her turn. "Such a lump. Such a girt lump. Such a *quantity*, and every bit and big of him alive."

All and all, it was an evening sweet and strange; there was no other to compare it to, as I had never had another beast combed out of my being before. It was the kind of thing a person might dream, the senselessness of it and yet the realness, although it persisted much longer, and it made more sense moment to moment than a dream often does.

When the brushing was done and the little ones had climbed into their bed—which was a most ingenious thing, set into the wall behind a curtain of green tapis—the mam came to me and stroked my head and told me, "You stay right here at the fire, Bear, and sleep in the warm." Before I could see her go to her own bed, I had fallen into sleep, as if into a sack of warm fleeces. I slept warm all night, not waking, not worried, no dream or notion troubling my mind.

Before dawn I was roused by the mother's being up, first

stirring the fire and then going to punch down bread dough on the table. Her face was settled not into most wives' dissatisfaction or distant stare, but into a serenity that reminded me very much of my own mam's before she fell ill. The usual cares did not press on this woman as they did others, so she had plumped up into her own shape the way a perfect apple grows that is unrubbed by a branch, or a perfect carrot that does not encounter a stone in the loam below.

"Go back to sleep, Bear." Her voice fitted in with the crackle of the fire, with the creak and rush of the wind in the trees outside. "There'll be your bread soon enough, and some honey, too, I have left."

My great stomach growled and a kind of whine, a kind of groan, escaped my bear throat, my long mouth and nose. I stretched myself out in the warmth and my eyes closed upon my view of her, on the winking of the lamp-flame.

When morning properly came, it was a sunny one. I went to the door, but although I could see my own blackened hands working upon the latch, I could not seem to place them right to unfasten it.

"What are you up to out there, Bear?" It was the little dark one, Urdda, using her mother's tones. She drew aside the bed-curtain and ran to me. She pushed my hands away and had the door unlatched before I could see how she did it.

I would have thanked her, but the cold day rushed in then, and the sunlight on the snow was like the trump and thump of a soldier-band to me. I ran out, and I breathed the cold and rolled in the new-fallen snow and ran about, and by the time I turned to call to the little one, "Join me!" I was not even there anymore, in the place where the house was, but in some other part of the forest's vast palace with its snow-broidered tree-pillars and its ice chandeliers and its little musicians, the very first-most spring birds come back from the winter bird-place, flitting from here to there above me and singing fiercely in their spots of sun.

All that day I spent in bear-business, which was very simple and very wonderful. Certain soft underbarks I found excellent to eat, and certain types of tree were the exact right roughness to bliss me when rubbed against the itch that bothered me low on my back. I thought of nothing; all I did was look, and heed the tumbling of scents through my sensitive nose, and accustom myself to the new way of hearing, and propel my new body through the forest. I enjoyed myself, no doubt of it, but I hardly realized I was enjoying, it was all so fast and instinctual.

But when evening drew in, I found myself to be more like my old self, and felt how very abruptly I had left the woman and little Urdda and her sister that morning, and I realized that I required some kind of cave to return to for the night, and I did not have that cave, had not discovered that cave in the course of my disporting myself this day.

So, all shamefaced, I found my way back, and I tapped very gently upon the door, and when the little dark girl ran to answer and embrace me, I kept very still and good, and when she allowed me, I entered and prostrated myself before the mother, feeling as if I were too enormous for this pin-neat house; I could not get myself low enough to match what I was endeavoring to say.

Well, the mother laughed, of course. "Get up, you great furthing. Get off my feet," she said. And the two girls, they were already upon me, climbing on my back and sliding off my rump, hardly heavier than raindrops. And there followed an evening that was equal parts laughter and gentleness, while the two explored and groomed me and used me as their plaything, and the mother, too, felt sure enough of me to lean before the fire into the fur-backed armchair of me, and touch and remark on the length of my claws, the conformation of my face, the sweetness of my ears, given the bulk and wildness of me.

And I—who had not been touched so curiously since my mam cared for me in my own childhood, who had not been embraced except by my own grieving uncle and aunt since my da went into the ground—I was enchanted. It seemed much preferable, even if I could not speak, to be a bear. There was so much more sensation in being animal. The scents of these three, for instance, were so distinct, though they were clearly a family: the dark girl more savory and the golden-haired one more honeylike and the woman sweetest of all—I could not place what flower it was she recalled to me, or perhaps what sweetmeat. The three scents together, they busied and dizzied the air around, and I were continually snuffling at it, reading their flashes of mood and interest.

And their resting against me and clambering on me—I drank up the weight and warmth of it like an ale or a cup of hot wine, it had been so long and I could have it so blamelessly and without embarrassment. I didn't know what her husband might think, walking in and finding his wife and daughters disposed around a bear, but certainly it would not be the same as if a visiting man were at the center of things. I were so comfortable, though, I would have been happy for him to walk in and slay me with bow or pike; even that would have been worth this enjoyment.

Who would *not* stay in such a place, being bear by day and as good as man by night, with such a beauteous family to welcome him whenever he appeared? And so I stayed, from that midwinter through into spring. It did not occur to me to leave, so I did not seek ways to do so, and none presented themselves to me unbidden, either.

Such children I had never known, so happy, unbowed, and unbeaten. Free as the forest they were growing, but they were by no means wild. The fair girl, Branza, was as kind and dutiful and diligent a daughter as any man could wish for. Urdda had bite and spark for all of them rolled into one, but when she had tired herself with her running and her outbursts of temper, it was clear how gratefully she rested with the other two, and enjoyed both to command and to amuse them.

And the mam, well, she worked some kind of slow-growing magic on me. At first I could not admit to its happening, expecting at any time the arrival, in person or even in their conversation, of a da, of a husband. He must be a dusky type—Franitch, maybe—that Urdda took after, while Branza had the fairness of her mother. Perhaps the fear of him was why I avoided people; he might at any time be thrown up out their midst, to show me exactly the man I could never hope to match, and claim these women from me.

At any rate, he did not come and he did not come, and there was no talk of him either, from girls or mam. I never saw him; neither did I see another man or woman, although there were signs of them: a road that I came to know and avoid, the sounds of a smithy one day as I patrolled my borders. I did not need other people; I did not want them; my days were brimful and overspilling with what I had.

And alongside the smoke-tendril of hope that then crept up in my heart there grew—I allowed myself to see it—a beauty in the mam that swelled and goldened as the leaves budded and burst upon the trees. She was a fine woman, strong and lean with always moving energetically from task to task, with lifting her lovely daughters to console or converse with them, with striding from cottage to town with cloths and rush-work, and town to cottage with foods and necessities.

My love of her went undercover of some muzzier bear-instinct. In my clearer moments, I longed to sit and question her: *What life have you come from? What is your name?* And: *May I stay? May I be bear with you always? May I keep you company, and you me?* For I was content to while away my days bear-ing in the forest, if I might always return and rest my eyes on her movements, so sure and steady among the flicker and dance of her daughters, and my nose in the air of her, in the atmosphere, and my ears in her lullabies, in her fey-tales and other stories, in the prayer-whispers she offered up when she had put her daughters to bed, when she were going herself to her night's rest.

One sun-dappled spring afternoon, Branza and Urdda had fallen to sleep across each other, like thrown cloths in the grassy shade. I found them at the end of my morning's explorations and pleasures and duties in the woods, when I was ready again to lounge and play.

I sat and watched them and tried to remember children, girl-children, of my old home-place—more clothed and fearful girl-children, because so many more dangers beset and surrounded them. But I could not remember clearly—I could not think very clearly of that old place at all.

But I could hear, and what I could hear was the slapping of laundry down at the stream. Someone was awake and working. And singing, singing a song I thought I knew, from that home-place. Her singing lifted me and called me down through the trees, trying to work out the puzzle of it; there was something about being a bear that took the sense out of words put to song, and at the same time made them bewitching, made me think, At any moment I will recognize this and it will all rush back, the memory, the life before.

There she was, with the stream around her like mirrors begging to be broken, like sumptuous silks and linens longing to be rolled in and creased and besmirched by kings and queens. And before I knew it, I had plunged in and was wallowing, biting fish of foam, tackling them to the round-stoned stream-bottom, leaping up with them and tossing the heavy water out of my head of fur.

And her song was gone, the mother's, and she was laughing at me. "That's the way of it, Bear!" she cried. "Show the water who is lord here!" Which I did, great clumsy me, beating it with my paws and plungings and quite wettening the woman with my splashes.

When I saw that I had done this, I came to her quietly, trying not to huff and splutter so. I nosed her elbow, which I hoped she would take for apology. Then I went up onto the bank and found myself a stretch of sunny grass. I lay down where I could doze to the sound of her singing and slapping, and wake to the sight of her.

When I was all but dry, she was done with her washing; she had spread all the cloths and garments on the grass and the bushes nearby. But I did not want her to go, and I sat up and said so.

She stood hands on hips and smiled. "Oh, you are awake now," she said, "now that all the hard work is done?"

I went to her and stood on all fours, my forehead against her front very lightly so as not to overbalance her. She was nothing; she was a wisp of beauty, her muscles fine as tassels of silk. I could destroy her with a swipe of my paw.

131

She dug her hands into my head-fur and scrumbled around my ears the way she knew I liked—they all knew. She laughed when I told her not to stop, and she did not stop, not for a long while. And then she did, and I sat back with such satisfaction that she had to laugh again. Our heads were at the same height. She stepped up to me, and at the sight of her little nude face so beloved I lifted my paw, which was bigger than that face and that whole head behind it, and I touched her cheek with what would have been my palm, had I been a man and sensitive, but on a bear was thick pads rough as sawn wood-ends, and I could feel nothing through it, not even the warmth of her.

I tried—I tried as I had with the daughters, tried to dredge up the person-ness in myself, to see into the person of her. She was not like anyone I could remember—any woman, any man. She searched my eyes all the while. I hoped she saw in them, inside this confident, clumsy bear, that vestigial man and his confusions.

She put her hands to my face, light and cool against my sun-warmed skin, and she explored it all over right out to my mane, as if she were thinking to model me in clay and needed to memorize my shape exactly. Her breath was a sweet cloud around my head, and I, who was heavier than six of her, almost fainted from breathing it.

I closed my eyes. *She is a wife*, I told myself. *Or she has been a wife. Is she missing him? Has he died, or has he simply gone to seek his fortune?* My paw had long fallen from her face; she stood between my hind limbs and I did not touch or look at her—the slip of her, the damp, clothe-wrinkled tininess— only felt her delicate searching of my strange features, my wild face. *Bring out the man of me*, I pleaded with her in my vague bear-mind. *Reach in and bring him out of this head. Let him talk to you.*

She scratched and scratched me under my chin. "You big soft thing," she whispered. "Feel the size of your head. I could not lift even that."

I licked her forehead. She tasted salty, and the simpler bear-part of me told me she would be good to eat. She laughed and stood back a little, touching the lick, her hands so finely made with all those fingers, maneuverable each one, her face— how *would* someone carve such a thing, catch all those live surfaces bending and folding and breathing, the movement in that mouth, those eyelashes soft as feathered moth-horns?

"Come, then," she said, and started up the slope. "Can you chop wood? Then you can help me."

I can, I can, I said to her in my mind. I could remember the feel of it, stretching up, bringing down the ax; I could remember the rhythm of it, and the sweat. But I was useless to her in this body; I was a strayed-in wild thing, that she could walk away from me like this, back to her kind and their separate life. I followed her, sad at heart, but still I must follow her, and so I followed.

And still they must follow *me*, her daughters, when they were rested and the evening had cooled and freshened their energies. "Shoo with you, you bouncers!" their mother had said when they'd eaten their suppers. "Run and play with Bear, and let me settle things here."

So we had run, and we were running still. Quite a way we had gone—they would have to climb aboard me and ride home at the end of this; I was right out beyond their borders, though those were not near as extensive as my own.

"Come back, beauteous bear!" cried Urdda. I could scarcely credit that in my lumbering I moved faster through the forest than those darting, fine-limbed girls could move. "You will fill your coat with burrs and thorns and there'll be such brushing to do, bad thing!"

How sweet it was to be scolded by such a tiny. I turned and I could glimpse her, or at least the shakings of leaves that marked her, and Branza coming after her, below me on the hill. Just a little farther and I will turn, I thought, and I will let them catch me, and then carry them back to their cottage, and their mother will welcome us all.

But then I ran out across a brief clearer part of land, and the grassy ground gave under my feet, and I was turning and tumbling. A painful snap sounded through my head, through my body. I saw, each so fast upon the last that I had no time to register the separate sights: a mass of twiggy forest hazed with near-spring green; the blocks and laneways of a town rushing upward; tiny Fuller in his bear-suit chasing screaming, laughing girls; and finally, an Eelsister in a sunny cloister—flying over her, I saw that she was embroidering a dandelion clock upon her linen. Then the slate smacked up at me and I was running out the end of the twitten, and Stow was there among the laundry-slabs, shouting, "Where did they go, the sneaky witches!"

I had turned to warn Urdda and Branza before I realized he was speaking of town girls. "I did not see them," I said.

But I did *remember* them: the girls' blue-white heels; the skirts above and the set of the body that was Washerwife Bean's daughter fleeing, the last of them; her happy screams of moments, of months, ago.

"This way!" cried Stow, and I followed him at a run. My body was thin and fleet, and the loose, hard costume rubbed at me. "Quick, Ramstrong!" he called back over his shoulder—and cannoned into just the whirl of washergirls he was after as they took the corner, faces all vivid with surprise and the glee of being girls and free today, powerful together.

They knocked us down, there were so many of them. Stow cried out in ecstasy and welcome, I in fear, these great ruddy girls kissing me when I was already so disheveled in my mind. The Bean girl wiped my face with hers, cheek and cheek both sides, to get the most black onto herself. Another took my charcoaled hand and put it into her blouse, to her damp hot breast with its unmistakable nipple, and it was the first time I had touched such a thing since I was too young to care about anything more than the milk in it. Who was it, that I might avoid her hereafter, her and her bold ways? They bussed and buffeted and rolled us, and then they leaped off, screaming:

"It's the bakers, the bakers!"

"Here is your comeuppance, beast!"

I rolled to my feet. At the end of the laneway, four pink faces jostled, white caps above and white smocks below.

"For your life, Ramstrong!" Stow caught my furred sleeve and hauled me up.

I ran hard. I was not as tired as I ought to be. I was strong from those months' rest; I was fresh, and full of honey and milk and grass and pigeon and pine-bark and all the berries yesterday, and from carrying about the bulk of a bear. I led Stow and the flour-men both a merry dance, down along the wall and up through the mills, ducking the wheels, jumping the courses, kissing the millwives and brushing the cheeks of their babbies all the way.

I tried to lose Stow, but he kept up for a while, and he found, curse him, a moment where there were no maids about, to tell me, "I went orf like a fountain back there."

I affected to be busy calculating the best way on from Springwater Cross.

"Among those laundry-girls," he insisted. "I tell you, I have right messed the insides of my bear-pants. Thank heaven they are not of cloth and show the dampness through."

"Into the Thatchlanes," I said. "The ways are good and tangled there. We can dodge and confuse them."

"Good man," he puffed.

I ran from him, from the state of his trousers. I led him fast and complicated and I lost him well enough that he called after me, piteously, "Ramstrong, don't leave me to them!"

When I turned next he'd been overtaken, swallowed into the bakers' white bodies and a cloud of flour going up, the whole gang of them so intent on him that I could run on.

That Bear Day made me: that chase, my strength, and the tricks I played, the feints I ran. I ran near to sundown, and half the town gave up on me because they wanted to begin the drinking-and-dancing part of the day, and when I finally gave myself up to the bakers—I had to walk out and find them, mind you; they never caught up with me—as many mouths cursed me as admired me. My fellow Bears could not believe that I was still upright in my skins. I was a new man in their eyes; they did not understand how I had kept on. They were somewhat afraid of me, I think.

But more important, as I was ambling, now quite tired, up the shining cobbles of the Rise—there where the cloth merchants begin, though they were all shuttered up for the day—there was leaning in a doorway of the silent street a serious girl, that I did not see until I was almost in kissing distance of her. Whereupon she saw in my eyes, which had had no chance to cover themselves, my true self, tired and frightened, and I saw her in hers, thoughtful and alone.

"You look thirsty," she said without a smile or a flirt or a change in her look, as if every day a bear walked up her street that needed tending. "Come inside," she said, "and I will give you a cup."

And this was Todda Threadgould, the girl that became the woman that became my wife, and bore me my three children.

But that gets ahead of the story, for that first time I hardly saw her. I followed her in and I sat, itching and trickling sweat and glum, in her shadowed kitchen. I gulped two cups of water and sipped another, knowing that I was back in the world, the world where I was man and orphan. Todda did not bother me with questions or conversations, but only watched me. *I think you were far gone*, she said to me later. *I think I caught you just in time, and brang you back from the brink.*

I could feel it: Branza and Urdda, peeping and piping in the woods behind me, turning to shreds of imagination, and their mother invisible beyond them, busy about her house. Clearly I had not been there; clearly some kind of brain-spasm had given me that time and that place; clearly Todda was right and I had had some kind of insanity, and had nearly been lost to normal life.

But with the shock of my recovery, and the grime and the skin-scraping, and the squealing and the laundress-breast and the chasing and confusion, it seemed to me to have been a much stronger pleasure to be mad, to be bear and solitary in the wild, than it was to be man and celebrated in the town. I could not see why I had been ejected from that existence, and I wanted nothing more than to fly back to it, and leave this place of gab and gossip and ale and embarrassment forever.

Well, I tried. Before I despaired and decided to notice Todda putting herself in my way, and to woo and wed her that high summer of my nineteenth year, many a time I went to the twitten and lingered there, hoping. I walked down it; tried running; tried to get up the same sweated panic that had drove me the first time; tried to discern, as I ran, the exact point where it had happened, where my feet had left the ground and I had taken flight.

Taken flight, I would end up thinking, standing out on Laundry Lane, heavy with my own weight and my disappointment. You are daft as Inge Minsoll under the Square Ash, with the birds that flitter around her face that only she can see, that she talks to. Taken flight! Tell it to Stow or Fuller and see how they look at you. Tell it even to Uncle and see how he worries for your senses.

And I'd search back up the sunny lane and—there was something, wasn't there? Why did I feel like this if there was nothing—like the rope of a tuggawar pulled one way by one gang and another by another? The sunny lane—there'd be bees there in the hedge-blossom, or a bird would fuss and squawk, and dart across to the top of Hogback's wall. Once a young rat ran from a wall-corner to under Eelsisters' hedge. And there'd be the slapping sounds of laundry up and down the lane, and laughter from those bold girls; it would turn your ears blue if you listened hard enough, which I did not.

The last time I went to the twitten, I examined it closer, trying to find some clue, some magic piece in the hedge or the paving or the cracks of Hogback's wall. What I was looking for, I didn't know—some mark or soft bit or smell of the other place—but I spent a good while at it, the sunny stone soothing me and the dapply leaf-light laying its patterns across my mind.

Until somewhere through my puzzlement I heard cloth and breath, and up I looked and there was the Eelmother in her gray gown, neckless like that seal that was brought on a cart from Broadharbour last winter, her face bunched up and whiskery.

"Get along with you," she says.

"Pardon, mum?" I scrambled to my feet.

"What do you think you're doing with your lurking?"

"I was looking for something."

"And I know what it was. I have seen enough of lads like you. How are my women to go about their devotions with such as you sniffing and fumbling themselves in the lane outside?"

My face filled up hot, bang, in an instant. "There were *none* of that!"

"What *is* it you were looking for, then?" She put her seal-head to one side. Through the hedge, I could see she was standing on a little ladder, the ladder the gardener must use when cutting the hedge-top flat.

And even as I stood there, unable to answer, I remembered, clearly, running up into the sky in my bear-suit. It was too strange to put into words and be believed. The Mother would think I was even madder than she already did.

"Scat," she said, disgusted. "Take yourself off. We've enough on our platters without your likes loitering on our borders. Go find some unholy woman to give your sly eye to. Go down the laundries, why don't you? There's bosoms and buttocks pushing out all over there, for your gratification."

I'd been about to head that way indeed, not for the girls, of course, but only because it were the closest end of the twitten, but when she said that, I couldn't, of course; I must instead walk right under her whiskery scorn, uphill. At the top I turned, and she was still looking, with something in the lean of her that said, *I have all the day, Mister Filthy Mind, to see you off; if you want to take your time, I can match you.*

And I walked out of her sight quickly, feeling sick that I

139

was so misread when I only was looking for something that had been there before—it *had*! I could feel the lift of it; I could see the town shrinking below. I had not been doing anything smutty or sly. Just the thought of her conceiving that—or the Sister conceiving it that first saw me and went and fetched her—and the blood was in my face again, throbbing shame.

7

"Come back! Come back!" Urdda broke from the trees and ran helter-skelter after Bear.

"Wait, Urdda! Don't leave me behind!" cried Branza.

Bear stumbled, he tumbled; he was gone from Urdda's sight. And then there was a flash, like lightning, but lightning that did not end, and Urdda fell back, and Branza ran up behind her, exclaiming, and pulled her out of the light and away from an edge of thin grass, beyond which was nothing for a long way down to treetops, which seethed and swelled like shineless water there.

The sisters clutched each other. "You nearly fell, Urdda! You would be dead!" Branza's teeth chattered with the surprise of it.

"What has happened to Bear?" Urdda tried to see through the glaring light to its source. It churned and bulged; its edges confused themselves among sunset-lit clouds. Was it a thing, or a hole with light pouring out?

"Look, ears and a—oh, I cannot see it properly," said Urdda. "I thought for a bit it was Bear-shaped."

"I too! But no, it is much too big, don't you think? And more ferocious-looking."

The hovering presence, as well as light, shed a kind of sound, almost too high-pitched to hear, and a kind of mood, genial and strange.

"Let us just go in among the trees a little way," said Urdda, still trying to see the creature's full shape.

"Yes, this way."

Branza led, which was most unlike her. Surefooted, she hurried along the path, and then, as Urdda followed, she stepped to one side, pushed her way into the undergrowth, and dropped out of sight, straight down.

"Branza!"

Had she fallen in a rabbit hole? Or off another cliff, a hidden one? Frightened, Urdda scrambled after her. The moon-thing came too, as if it were joined to her with a ribbon or cord.

By its light she found Branza curled up on the ground, as deeply asleep as if it were midnight and she were snug in their own bed.

Urdda knelt by her. The ground was softest moss, thick and deep; it caught the warmth of her knees and held it around them. "Oh my." She sank upon it, next to her sister. "How did you see this, in this dimness? Did you know all the time where we were, and not tell me?"

Branza did not answer. If she had, Urdda would not have heard her, for sleep came up from the moss like spores, and she breathed it in, and it drew her down into its warm heart and held her there.

✤ ✤ ✤

"Yes," said Liga when they reached home next morning and told her their adventure. "I have seen that light."

"You have?" said Urdda. "And you never told us?" What kind of mother kept such a thing to herself?

"I have been to that precipice and spoken with that moon-babby."

"*Babby?*" said Urdda. "That was no bab, unless it was the babby of a *monster*. It was huge, Mam! Big as this cottage."

"Oh, Urdda, it was not!" laughed Branza. "It was the size of Bear himself, maybe a tadge bigger."

"Well, whatever size," said Liga, "you do not need to be frightened of it, Branza; it means you nothing but good. See how it stopped you falling?"

"It did not stop Bear," Branza pointed out.

"Yes, it did," said Urdda. "It *was* Bear, magicked so that he floated and was safe." She nodded, and nodded some more at her mam, hoping to reassure herself by convincing someone else.

"You have not seen Bear this morning?" said Liga.

"We looked, didn't we, Branza? To see if he *had* fallen, you know. Certainly we could not see him from above. And no, we didn't meet him, all that long way home. We could have ridden him if we had, couldn't we? We would have been home so much sooner. Truly, you have not been worried about us, Mam?"

"I did wonder. But I knew you were out there with Bear. I knew you would come to no harm. And neither *did* you." She picked a scrap of moss from Branza's golden hair. "Tell me again, Urdda, how he ran off the cliff."

Urdda described it again, and Liga listened, so attentively that Urdda did not have to enlarge or embroider the story to keep her from picking up needle or broom.

"And you did not . . . Did you think to reach out and touch the moon-bear?"

"Touch him?" Branza made a face. "He would have burnt our fingers off! Or froze them, maybe. Or . . . it might have hurt."

"Or it might not. It might have brought him back to his usual self, just to . . ." Liga made the gesture herself, her face hopeful and thoughtful: "Just to take his paw, you know, and pull him to you, as when you make him dance with you."

"Well, we did not," said Urdda bluntly to her mother's far-away face. "Branza was too frighted."

"Oh, I did not see *you* grabbing him when he reached for us."

"Reached for you?" said Liga sharply.

"He did not reach. He did this." Urdda swiped the air nonchalantly. "Near us. As if just to play or something. Or to wave a fly away."

"Or to knock us off the cliff-top," said Branza dryly. "Which is when you said, 'Let us go in the trees.'"

"And *you* agreed quick-smart, and ran straight off."

"Oh, do not quarrel about it." Liga gathered their two damp, tired bodies to her. "We are all upset to have lost Bear."

"Yes, we are." Branza laid her head gratefully on her mother's shoulder.

"Where do you think he has gone to, Mam?" said Urdda.

Liga thought on it, holding them, swinging them a little. "I do not know," she said. "I cannot tell you. I cannot imagine." And gradually she stilled, and gazed at the floor as if standing on a precipice herself, searching the forest below for the tiniest glimpse of tiny, tiny Bear. Urdda had been on the point of asking, *Have you also seen that littlee-man, down by the marsh?* But that look of her mother's, as if the surfaces of things hardly mattered against what she saw in her mind, against what she regretted that she saw, kept the daughter silent.

Midafternoons or evenings were when he would arrive. As the year warmed, they had left the cottage door open to breezes, and he would be an event, nearly filling the doorway, all muddy fur and fishy or clovery breath. If the girls were there, they would run to him and make a great fuss, remarking on his state and delighting in putting him to rights. And there was always a point, when they had groomed and arranged him, at which he would make his way to Liga, and nudge her with his head if she was busy, with her back to him; or lower his head and tickle her bare feet with breath, seeming to ask her blessing for being there among them.

It took Liga a long time to stop expecting him. She would hear the girls' voices coming through the wood, and she had to school her feelings not to lift into amusement and anticipation, but only to be happy to see her two daughters squabbling or laughing—slender, smooth-limbed, unshadowed by Bear.

It is just that he was so large, she thought, so that he leaves a large emptiness behind him. But it was not his largeness she missed—or not only that. Every way that he had disposed that size around them, or at the center of them—accepting his role as toy or bed or amiable furnishings; snoring on the hearth or across the cottage step in the springtime; friendly and foolish one moment, gentlemanly the next, solemn and vastly noble the next—had improved and enlarged their lives. Liga found— as she laundered at the stream and glanced up at shadows that were not Bear; as she tidied after the evening meal and Branza and Urdda ran out into the last light, just the two of them, speeding around until they dizzied themselves, with no Bear to clamber on or instruct or reduce to rumbling contentment with scratchings of his head and back—how easily she had accustomed herself to him: to his size, to his maleness, to his easy acceptance of all their embraces. She could lie across her own bed, but it did not have the shape and warmth of Bear; she could be prone on a sunlit knoll of fine grass that almost, *almost* gave the feeling of Bear's fur if she closed her eyes and imagined hard, yet it did not sigh and shift beneath her, or make Bear's digestive mumbles and squeaks. He was with them no longer, she must always, at some point, admit, and once she had admitted it she would go out and gather up a daughter, all bones and flying hair, and tumble her Bear-like on the grass and growl, or sit by the fire on one of the wooden stools and wrap her arms around her own self as she gazed into the flames.

Urdda stamped back and forth along the cliff-top, beating at the edge with a long, stout stick.

"Show yourself to me!" she muttered. "Whatever you were, magic Bear or star fallen out the sky. Come and glow at me." *Thud, thump,* she went with her stick.

The world below was all dark billows of hill and tree, and sunlit birds' backs as they flew. The breeze teased everything. Urdda's dark curls stroked her cheeks and forehead. All was movement, yet nothing was happening.

"It was *not* a dream," she insisted to the sky. "We followed Bear! He jumped off here and flew away, and then there you were. Both of us saw you—even Branza, who didn't want to. And Mam, she knew—she never once said we must be making up stories, or touched by the sun, or what."

Thump. A spray of dirt flew out from the cliff-edge and fell away. Why would nothing do as she told it? The drifty clouds followed their own breeze; the sky dreamed; in the great hard world, sticks stuck out and scraped you, stones tripped you, trees stood silent and required you to find your way among them. Everything ignored Urdda, no matter how angry she grew.

"I have not brought Branza today!" she called into the emptiness. "I believe in you! You can show yourself and I will not be frightened. Come on, bright thing, whoever you were!"

The silence streamed at her in its disguise of hissing leaves and bird-cry. "Blast and bother you," she whispered. "Where in the name of that hairy bad-man are you?"

She stood very close to the edge, shut her eyes, and imagined the space before her: the maw of it, the yawn. It had been nearly dark when Bear disappeared—not the red-dark of sunlit eyelids like this, but proper thickening dusk, full of evening creatures, the thrill of their fleeing paws. She had run up that path with Branza's whimpers in her ears and Bear's mass ahead, and she had seen him lope off into the stars just as if the ground continued. And she would have, *would* have followed, had not that bear-thing, that moon-thing, come beaming at them and said— What had it said? No, there had been no voice, no words. Only it had made her think how tired she was, and how she ought to look to Branza's safety, and to her own. If it had not got in the way, she would have run right off after Bear into . . . wherever. Into that place of light. Into the place that caught you if you fell from a cliff-top, and stopped you dashing to pieces on those rocks down there.

Still she swayed on the cliff, trying to pull the magic up from her memory, to infuse this afternoon with whatever had obtained that other evening to make impossible things possible. She thought about the moon-bear; she pretended, with all her heart and imagination, that the hot light on her eyelids

147

was of the bright thing, that all around this blob of heat that was moonbear-lit Urdda, evening was breezing, full of owls and owl-prey, bats and bat-beetles on the wing. So strongly did she want this, she convinced herself she had made it so; that the moon-thing had heard her plea and come to fetch her, just as it had fetched Bear. Slowly she walked, backward down the slope, eyes closed, feet feeling, holding the real gravel and hot ground entwined with the moonish thoughts, the cool-night-air imaginings.

She ran forward now, up the same slope, ignoring the memory of Branza's voice—*Oh, Urdda, do stop! Stop and he will come back to us, all by himself*—running into the red darkness. Bear lumbered there, hot with light, red with heat. "I'm coming too!" Urdda cried. "Wait for me!" Squeezing her eyes tighter shut, she ran out into the air after him.

There, you see? It had worked. See how dark it really was, and the stars! And here—she was in Bear's claws, or teeth; he had picked her up in some awkward way. Oh, but—curse and cross it—there was the moon-bear, away off there so far, hovering out of Urdda's reach like a glowing cheese-round in the sky, blotting out so many stars with its busy light.

But this time it thought nothing at her; it only shrank and steadied and became the ordinary moon, pouring down its flat silver light, coating Urdda in the disappointing stuff. This was a tree she had been caught in, not bear-claws; she had not flown, but only fallen, like the lump she was, down a slope that had not been there when she had peered down over the cliff-edge, into a tree that most definitely had not been here—she would have noted it in the bright afternoon; she would have been careful to avoid it. She had knocked her head on something and slept for a time, to wake now with her skin all hot and sunstruck inside the chill shell of the night breeze, her flesh bruised and stiff, and the moon above her not come to fetch her at all, not even looking at Urdda with its big blind eye, but lighting, as it lit up everything without discrimination or favor, the sloping path she must follow back up to the dreary world.

"Daft girl," said Liga fondly. She ran fingers light as a drift of pollen over the bruise on Urdda's brow. "Girls were not meant to fly. Where are your feathers? Where are your wings?"

"Bear didn't have feathers, nor wings, and yet he flew." Urdda sat quiet and good in the washpool in the moony dark, and Liga rinsed the dust and sweat off her slowly, carefully, and with some curiosity. This washing made Urdda feel she ought to be a little ill, or just soft, as Branza was, who loved all touches and kindness and was never impatient with them.

"I don't think Bear flew at all," said Liga, squeezing a clothful of water over Urdda's dusty hair.

"No, nor do I," said Branza. "Bear changed into a moon-bear and magicked us to sleep."

"And then what?" said Urdda. "Where did he go then? And why can we not go there too?"

"Why would you want to?" said Branza.

"Because *Bear* is there, that is why! And other people and things, surely." Urdda caught Branza's warning glance and shrugged. "All the wonderful things Mam tells of in her bed-stories."

"But all the dreadful things too," said Branza darkly. "Evil warlocks and greedies and those horrid horses with the eyes like carriage-lamps. Why would you want to go to a place like that?"

"Because it is there! Because you *can*—or you must be able

to somehow, if Bear went, and—" She twitched at another meaningful stare from her sister. "*I* would want to see it, anyway. You don't have to come. I think a person should see everything there is to see."

"Perhaps," said Liga. "Perhaps an older person. I think you belong here with me, the both of you, for a good while yet. And by the growing of mysterious trees and the plumping-out of pieces of cliff-faces to catch you, I would say some powerful person agrees with me."

Liga chose a market day, when there would be more people about. She took the girls to the Whistle to visit Keller's daughter Ada so that she would be alone. Slowly she walked up the town. Everything was reassuringly the same as usual—goodwives going about their business, greeting her here and there—and around and among them the mysterious affairs of men went on, which seemed to involve standing in confident attitudes together and talking earnestly when they were not driving carts or toiling in smithies and workshops. If she drew near any talkers, she knew, they would gently recoil, and glance at her and nod without greeting her, not interrupting their talk.

She had considered these men. She hardly knew any by name; most had been replaced by the light-brown-haired folk, and somehow she could not approach those ones; they existed to be strangers, to make the town amiable and bustling with their numbers. She thought, but vaguely and glancingly, about her own purposes—they were to look into someone's eyes as she had looked into Bear's and see thoughts shifting there; to reach out and touch the skin of someone who had lived a little, as she herself had—skin that was not the pearls and peaches of her daughters' faces; that was roughened somewhat, maybe flecked with a scar, and under which she might sense, as she had sensed perhaps with Bear, something of her own uncertainty, her own hopefulness. This was what she thought she wanted.

She had settled—so lightly and timidly that it could hardly be called settling—on Joseph the Lathe, who worked behind his father Tomas in the woodshop in the eastern lanes. Joseph was diligent, kind-faced; he was golden-haired like herself. She walked across the market square, her head thudding with nervous blood. Nobody seemed to notice that she carried this emotion among them, so inappropriate to the place, though her face felt rigid with it. The feeling tottered and tangled inside her, and she had to rest on a bench against the pot-man's shop wall. Fear, it was—the relief of recognizing it made her sag. She had not felt real fear in a long time—the pulsing of it, the discomfort of her innards. And why was she afraid? Da was gone, dead forever. All the young men who might harm her were gone. She was here, in this place that had never done her any damage and never would. It had given her everything she wanted, these seven years; why should it not deliver her this, a loving connection with some kind man?

Up she got, still frightened but more determined now, and she went into the lanes and found the woodshop. Tomas was not at his lathe by the door. Oh, good, she thought, they are gone out and there is nothing I can do. But there was Joseph, working deeper in the shop, as always. Well, see how it is all arranged for you? she told herself anxiously. The lane was quiet, though people passed at both ends of it.

"Good morning," she said, standing in the doorway. How could a person be clumsy, just standing? And yet she felt she was, as clumsy as one of those blocks of boxwood being seasoned there, unshaped, indelicate.

Joseph lifted his kind face. "Good morning, miss," he said in his quiet way.

"May I watch awhile?"

"Of course you may." And he went to his work again.

She brought forward one of the stools with the turned legs, that stood against the wall. She had plainer ones at home. Were she married to a woodworker, she might have him make any number of fancy things for her house.

But where would that house be? She settled quietly on the stool, watching Joseph's profile. Would he join her in the forest, or would she move to the town, into the house with his parents and his brothers and sisters? Either place was outlandish; a marriage, a wedding with herself as bride, was outlandish. How did girls move such concentrated beings, bent over their work, towards marriage? How was the thing done?

"Where is your father today?" she asked him.

"Out at the woodmen's camp, selecting," he said.

There, see? No one would return and thwart her if this was what she wanted. Liga watched the work, the wood-dust flying and the shavings spiraling off; a bowl refining itself in his hands; the hands themselves. How was a girl to distract them from such usefulness; to attract them to herself, to her own hands, to her face? And she felt the scratchy-wood pads of Bear's paw against her cheek, and she saw his eyes full of wonder and puzzlement, and she heard the breath in his big bear-lungs.

"Tell me, Joseph," she said. "Do you have a . . . sweetheart? Do you have a girl?"

"I do not," he said to the bowl, in a manner that neither

rebuffed her nor drew her on, so that she gained nothing from the question beyond the information. Well, that was something, was it not?

"Do you wish for one?" Oh, how bald that sounded. "Sometimes?" she added, to soften it; and then, "Ever?" quite at a loss.

He gave her a look. There was something of a smile in it— was he laughing at her, at her clumsiness, at the effort this took? There was—oh, she did not know anymore how to read anyone's face but her daughters'! She was not fit to be outside her home, she was such a poor judge of people.

"You don't?" I sound pitiful, she thought. And so sad!

He gave her a second look, as unreadable as the first. He had heard her, then. Did he perhaps have no opinion yet? But look at those hands; they were a man's hands. And look at that face, the jaw fully squared and glittering with stubble. Was he too shy to answer, then? She had chosen him for his shyness, she reminded herself; she had known he would not be sure enough of himself to harm her. Perhaps she had known she would have to put the thought into his head, that he was too timid to think it himself.

So, holding her breath, she reached out and rested the backs of her fingers against Joseph's cheek.

His skin was warm; the scratch of stubble along his jawline matched the sparkle of it in the sunlight on his chin and around his mouth.

He moved the bowl fractionally so that it was not against the lathe; he removed his foot from the wooden pedal under the workbench and the spinning lathe slowed. Liga took back her hand, frightened.

Joseph sat unperturbed, the bowl in his hands, his wrists resting against the workbench. And then he would have returned to the work—Liga saw his thigh tense to replace his foot on the pedal—had she not said, "Joseph?"

His thigh relaxed, but still he looked down at the lathe—he was not impatient to start again, but . . .

She glanced up and down the empty laneway. She took hold of Joseph's elbow in one hand and the bowl in the other, and she lifted his arm from the bench and unbent it, and laid hand and bowl in her own lap. She took the bowl from him and placed it back on the workbench. The unresisting hand lay in her lap—a man's hand, a strange animal. She fitted her own hand into the palm, lifted it, and slid her other hand underneath. Joseph's was warm; it was furred here and there with wood-dust that fell onto her skirt; the back was covered with strong, short hairs, bowed like eyelashes, springy. Did the hand grip her in return, or had she pushed the fingers into place herself, around her wrist?

"Sometimes I find myself lonely," she said towards the hand. "I thought you might also feel this, if you are grown now, if there is no girl."

She lifted her face, and there was Joseph's. But his eyes did not hold the thoughts, the troubles, or the desires Liga had hoped to see. Instead, the young man's customary kindness had unfixed itself somehow, was interrupted with a flickering in the pupils, so that instead of black depths there ran a glimpse of sky, a glimpse of frost, grainy gray streaks blowing across a pale blankness.

"Joseph!" she whispered in fright. "Master Lathe!"

And his eyes were all kindness again. "Miss?" he said.

"My name is Liga," she said.

"Yes." His hand lay warm in hers. It seemed to Liga that he looked upon her much as he had been looking at the bowl as it came into being against the lathe.

"What was that?" She was hot with fear. "What happened to you just now? To your eyes?"

"You asked too much of me, Liga." He lowered his eyes, but she had seen the sky rushing in them again. "I was not made for it."

"For what?" She hardly wanted to ask.

"To . . . to feel anything for myself. Lonely or no."

Liga was stiff with terror. The wind, the frost, and worst of all, the vast emptiness she had seen behind his eyes translated itself into his voice. If she could see them now, they would be blank as the moon. But he had used her name, *Liga*. He had known her better than Joseph the Lathe ought to, better than Ada Keller or Wife Taylor or anyone in this town or country did, better maybe even than she knew herself. To her very depths, with all her secrets, she was known by everyone here, by everything.

Joseph kept his gaze on their hands, but the light from his eyes stuttered in her lap. The world was flimsy around her; it rippled like embroidery on a curtain, and beyond the curtain was chaos, and a light that might blind her.

Trembling in the trembling world, she took up the wooden bowl and thrust it into his hand. His fingers closed on it, firm and limber, and he smiled at Liga. His pupils were dark again, but he did not seem relieved, or even properly aware of what had just passed; he was only his kind self, the same as ever. He turned back to the lathe and set it spinning again.

Rain was falling quite hard outside the woodshop door, where the sun had beamed down from a clear sky moments before. Two men passed and hailed Joseph, and he nodded and kept on working. They walked by without a glance at Liga.

She jumped up, knocking the stool over. Joseph did not even start. She could snatch the bowl from him, she suspected, and fling it out onto the wet cobbles, take up that mallet there and smash his creation to pieces, and he would only take up the next block of rough wood and begin again.

She hurried out of the shop, into the gasping-cold rain. The two men were walking away, their soaked backs to her. The sky was black and churning; wives exclaimed at upstairs windows, pulling in curtains, slamming shutters.

Liga ran, taking the beating of the rain as her punishment, icy arrows in her stupid head, cold lashes across her shoulders. *None of it is real,* she thought, *not this rain, not these slippery streets, not these houses, that wife hurrying, that carter leading his soaking horse.* She boiled with embarrassment and with fear; she must push him out of her memory, Joseph the Lathe, with his warm hand and his white eyes. She must run away from him hard, through the lashing rain, and find as soon as possible her Branza, her Urdda—her little daughters, the only true people in this world besides herself.

Time passed, and Liga was a score and ten years old, Branza fifteen summers beautiful, and Urdda fourteen years lively. Life was good for the women in the cottage; Liga toiled every day to make it so, to keep it so, to deserve it. Since she had sat in the woodshop and seen how fragile was their safety, she had been unable to rest; she might have been broidering the very forest, the very weather, into existence; she might have been stitching the seam where earth meets sky, so assiduously did she apply herself, and so constantly. The anxiety she had stirred that sunny-rainy day was now bound into her bones the way blood is, the way muscles are tethered in; in order to feel any joy, she must always be paying, always be showing how seriously she took this place she had been given, how willing she was to pretend it was all true.

Branza, with her soft heart, must have intuited something of the strain of this, for she had been visited many times in those years by nightmares. Liga would wake to Branza's shouts of rage and fear in the darkness, or to the sounds of the girl kicking and muttering in her bed. Liga learned not to touch or shake her, for then Branza dreamed she was under attack, and woke thrashing and screaming in panic. "Branza, Branza, wake yourself! It is only a dream!" Liga would exclaim, wringing her hands by the girls' bed over the two daughters, one fast asleep and the other fighting the covers, fighting the invisible enemy.

And when she was roused and the lamp lit to chase away her terror, Branza would lie and stare at her mother, her eyes fixed open so that she would not fall back into the dream. Liga would have to talk about daylight things, or bring the basket of rabbit-kits or the lately born kid from the fireside for Branza to cradle, to distract the girl, to soften her face out of its fearful expression.

"Who is he? What is he like? And where does he come from?" Liga would ask Branza in daylight, for all she could manage to gather on the subject of the nightmares was that they were always about a man, always the same man.

But Branza would not be drawn to describe him. However brightly the sun shone, however charming the animal in her arms, however delicious the honeyed fig her mother had just divided among the three of them, Liga's questions only reduced her to silence, to head-shaking, to shudders at the memory of her assailant. And Liga feared—for she did not know how magic worked, only that it was powerful, and fragile, and unpredictable—that her own undeservingness had visited the nightmares on Branza, that her daughter was being attacked in the night by a version of the man who had made Liga's nights a misery as she grew from girl to woman.

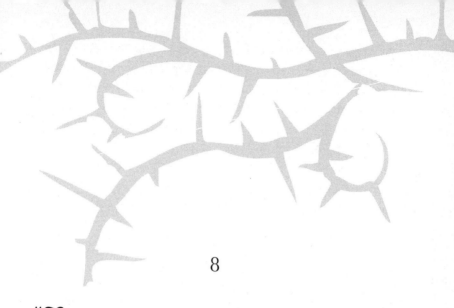

8

"Take these baskets," said Liga, "and the mats we made—the prettier ones—and the whitest of the cheeses, maybe three of those. Go into town, to Wife Gruen."

"Wife Gruen?" Branza was crouched in the sunlit doorway, watching the birds come to the breakfast crumbs she had scattered on the path.

"Yes, ask her to take the cheeses for two dress-lengths of that fine lawn, in the blue I admired the other day. I have made up my mind. And give Wife Wilegoose the matting for some of her beans, and whatever she gives you of her herb-garden."

"Come, Urdda, while the morning is still cool," Branza said.

Urdda laughed. "Hark at you. Branza has a sweet spot for Rollo Gruen, Mam, can you tell?"

"I do not." Branza bridled—or pretended to.

"Indeed she has," said Urdda. "I have seen her smiling and swinging her basket while he passed time of day with her under the Square Ash."

"You know nothing! I've a sweet spot for no one!" Branza came into the cottage and snatched up her comb, then stood to the full willowy height of her fifteen years, haughtily combing.

Urdda snorted. "No one but every bunny and babcock that hops out of the wood. Oh, and Rollo Gruen. Look at her, preening herself for him."

"Hush, you, snippet," said Liga. "You are only jealous you don't have such a way with wild creatures."

"As long as I can catch one for our dinner, that's as close as I need be."

Branza's tamed pigeon that she had rescued from the foxes suddenly resettled its wings on the chair-back where it was perched, and all three women laughed. "That's telling you!" said Liga. "What an outrage, to talk of dinner."

"Anyway, I think she has intentions on that Gruen boy, Mam. With what you have told us of weddings, I think she is wanting that fine dress and the feast, and then snuggerling off to bed with that Rollo, with their matching hair. Oh, such golden-head children they will have!"

Branza flicked Urdda with a hair-ribbon like a little shining whip. "Drink up your breakfast and let us go and get our dress-lengths. We can walk up by the heath, if you want, to make it an adventure."

And this they did, taking the hillier way, through the dark furze. In one or two places, great stones had been set, some balanced on others, but in time they had been tumbled, either by people who no longer knew their use or by strong weathers or movements of the ground, and now they lay long and sodden asleep, half buried in the bushes.

The wind goaded and worried the girls, and blew up their excitement so that they ran, Urdda ahead with the baskets and mats, Branza following more carefully with the cheeses. They were so noisy that they thought they were the only ones shouting, but then Branza called, "Urdda, wait!" and Urdda paused, and then they heard another voice, farther and with quite a different tone.

Urdda spun to face the sound. Branza turned more slowly in the path.

Beyond one of the fallen stones beat the tips of two huge wings. The noise came to the sisters on a snatch of wind, with another dire exclamation from the invisible person below, the invisible man.

Urdda set off fast through the bushes. Grumbling fearfully, Branza went back down the path. She stood by the rushwork Urdda had dropped onto a bush, eyeing the cleft her sister was making through the spiny branches. She took a few steps after her, holding the cheeses close, as if they were eggs in a fragile nest or the young of some furred thing.

When Branza next looked up, Urdda was prancing on top of a slab, the wind lifting her hair and flapping her skirts, snatching away her voice as she shouted back to Branza. She looks so happy there, thought Branza uncomfortably. I must make sure she is more modest when we reach Gruens' or Rollo will certainly like her better, for her courage and liveliness.

She put up her cheeses-basket and clambered onto the stone. "Oh," she said, "how magnificent!"

An enormous eagle strove on the slope below—a bird bigger than any Branza had ever seen, a giant of a bird, red-brown above and splendid bright white below.

"Look who he has, though!" cried Urdda, and Branza, frowning, saw that the powerful claws, the color of storm clouds but with an added cruel sheen, held not a large hare or lesser bird, but a person, a person whose size looked unequal to resisting the bird's force, but whose jerking and shouting brought the bird again and again to the ground, where it would reaffirm its grip on him, that small man seemingly made of torn leather and long white hair.

"Curse him!" said Branza. "I suppose we must help if we can."

"I should think so!" Urdda leaped like a freed rabbit from the stone and ran, heedless of furze-needles, towards the struggling bird, the shouting man.

With a soft moan, Branza sat down and dropped from the slab to follow her. *Flap harder!* she said to the bird in her mind. *Carry him off where we cannot reach him, where we cannot follow! Come on, you great strong thing!*

They ran underneath the burdened bird. Neither had been so close to such an eagle before—so near its relentless eye, the purposeful work of its wings, and the noise of its effort, that angry whipping of the air.

The littlee-man was like a dragging, blowing snaggle of hair from a thornbush or a fence-post, but with more weight in it, weight of flesh and feeling. "Help me, for the sake of all that's living! Its claws are in my back! It is tearing the very vitals out of me!"

"Struggle!" cried Urdda, demonstrating. "Wriggle! Wrest yourself out of its grasp."

"I cannot! It is disemboweling me!"

As Urdda ran on after the bird, Branza stooped for a stone. She straightened and threw it, hitting the man himself. The stone dropped onto Urdda's shoulder, so that both of them shouted in surprise.

"Not me, you gulping gosling!" screeched the man. His arms punched at nothing, and his legs kicked under his straggling cloak of hair. "Throw at the bird!"

Branza's second stone hit the bird hard in the breast, and if a beast can stagger on air, it staggered. It dropped somewhat. Now Urdda could jump and brush with her very fingertips the wispiest ends of the littlee-man's trailing hair.

"Higher! Higher!" His arms and legs now reached straight down for her. "And you!" he cried to Branza. "Keep with your stones! Knock the damned thing out of the sky!"

Branza threw and threw, and Urdda cast up a number of stones too, and dodged the falling ones.

"Aim for its head, sister!" Urdda called, but Branza had not a good enough eye to do so, and had best luck with the stones she pitched at the bird's body. Also she managed to bruise the leading edge of one wing, and with her next hit she made the bird plunge to a point where Urdda, well positioned, caught good hold of the littlee-man's beard and some head-hair.

"Aagh! You are pulling it out at the roots! Aagh!" For Branza had run up and taken handfuls of hair, too, and the two girls were trying to pull him down so as to catch his higher hair, and eventually the body of him.

"Stop flailing!" Urdda commanded. "How are we to get a grip on you?"

"You're hurting me, you vicious, common monsters! Gather more so you are not pulling only on three hairs apiece! Have you no sense?"

"We are pulling on what we can reach," said Urdda. "But it's too strong." She gasped as the bird tried to surge up and away, and managed indeed, momentarily, to lift her and her sister's feet clear of the heath.

"You are not heavy enough!" he said despairingly. "Oh, who would have thought, two such thumping great lumps! Anchor yourselves with these fallen stones, why don't you? Wedge your great flat feet under them!" The girls' toes were dragging through the furze—three of their four shoes were dropped or caught in the bushes. "Do something!"

"Do something yourself!" Urdda swung herself up higher on the littlee-man's hair. "Reach up behind you and pummel the thing. Dig in with your fingers so it thinks you are gutting it as it flies!"

"What, while I'm gutted myself? Shall I pluck it and stuff it with sage and onions and cook it on a spit while I'm up here, you stupid? I can barely move while it takes out my bowels!"

All the while, the bird's wing tips flicked and stung the girls' faces, and the wing-wind beat around them.

Urdda clambered up over the man's screaming form—and collected a panicked kick for her troubles that nearly knocked her away. She caught hold of the scaly bird-leg, which was like bone and iron bar both, and forced her fingers hard into the thing's hot feathered belly.

The bird squawked, and dropped the littlee-man with Branza still attached to him, and at the shock of the space below her and the sight of the rushing heath, Urdda let go the leg and dropped too. The loosed bird leaped away, suddenly small. Urdda rolled to a stop in harsh grasses and gravel.

Up she jumped straightaway to see whether her sister too had fallen on soft ground, or was she brained on one of the big stones. But there she was, red-faced and fighting tooth and nail with the nasty little man, the pair of them floundering and falling in the furze like downed birds themselves.

"Get off her!" Urdda ran at them and tore the littlee-man from where he clawed and bit at Branza, whose arms were tight across her chest and face, protecting herself.

"She has ruined my good jacket with her haulings, the careless witch!" All the man's fear seemed to have transformed into violent rage. "Do you know how much this cost me? Do you know how many times I've had to come to your benighted nowhere of a land to fetch the necessary?" *Thump, thump!* He went at Urdda with his fists, tiny and strong.

Branza stood back, stunned. "I never touched his coat!" she said, outraged, to Urdda, not daring to put her arms down yet.

"Get away off me!" Urdda pushed at the man. "We have saved your life, and more than once, and if this is all the gratitude you can show—"

"Gratitude? For having half my fine manhood torn out, and my face with it? For having my jacket rent and ruined? Look at it! It is all holes!"

"That's bird-claws that did that. Go and bring that bird to account, if you dare. Go on, shoo!" And Urdda went after him so angrily and loudly, and so big now—nearly twice as tall as he—that he stumbled back and some of the rage went out of him, became fear again. He fell harmlessly on his bottom. He more swam than ran away, his shouts turned to mutterings: "Blue-fannied broom-pushers! What use are they to a man? You could never get past *their* claws and beaks to give them the what's-tuppence!"

Urdda finished shaking her fists and shouting after him, and turned back to her sister. "Has he cut you at all?"

"Only these hurt the worst." Branza showed her some welts risen under her ear where the dwarf had clawed her. "Is there blood?"

"Not a drop, but they are very red and nasty."

"I feel as if he has hit me all over. But for a time there, I was giving him every bit as good as he gave me."

"He was all affrighted, I think." Urdda watched her sister seek out the bruised places. "He did to you what he ought to have tried on the bird."

165

"Those little arms," said Branza, with a shaky laugh. "He hadn't a chance at me, hardly, whirling them about, little stumps of things." She looked around distractedly. "Where can my shoes be? Where is our basket?"

They calmed themselves as they walked up to the town, and then, in their purchasing of lawn and obtaining of beans and cut herbs, and in Urdda's teasing of Branza about Rollo Gruen, they almost forgot their good work of that morning, saving the littlee-man from certain death.

But on their way home, in the forest, just before Hallow Top where the big stones lay, to Branza's dismay and Urdda's amusement, they came upon the little nasty again, crouched to one side of the path in the bloodied disarray of his hair and torn clothes. He had gathered such piles of shining objects, it was going to take all his nuggety strength to carry them.

"My!" said Urdda. "This is the treasure in all those tales of Mam's, Branza, remember? And *these*—look, remember these? I asked her, and these are called pearls."

"You said you wouldn't tell about him!" said Branza.

"And I did not tell, but I found out these were pearls, and they are very precious in some parts of the world, Mam says. This man is one of those greedy men from the tales."

The littlee-man looked up suspiciously from counting silver coin. "Why'n't you follow that bee there and buzz off from here?"

"His manners have not improved, have they, sister? For being so close to being pecked apart and stuffed down the craws of eaglets."

"Come away, Urdda," said Branza. "He is a foul man, and cruel, and he will not improve with being told it."

"Yes indeed, liller smoocha-pooch, I am foul and cruel. Let

your friend take you back to Niceland, or Sweetland, or Lovey-dove Land, where you belong. Or sisters, is it, did you say? Don't look like it. Poked of different dads, I'd say. Slut-mothered, and no doubt of such matter themselves, eh?" He spat into the bushes. "You don't know what I'm saying, do you, so iggenrent you are? I could flap out my old man, no doubt, and you'd think it was a turnip or some such."

The littlee-man's face fell as Urdda bent and selected a large ruby from the pile of treasure. "So, what do you call this color of treasure, greedy man?" She polished it on her sleeve. But then she gasped, and almost dropped it. The red stone turned over in her hand, and stood up on twig legs, and shook out a beak at one end and a tilting tail at the other. It plumped up, wriggled, flew from her hand a robin, and scolded them from a beech-branch nearby. "Did you see that, Branza?"

"Get you your filthy, common sow-trotters off my property, you minx!" The littlee-man leaped to his feet.

"But how is it you can turn birds to treasure," said Urdda, "and frog-eggs to pearls? I should like to be able to do such things."

"Get away! Stand you back from all of it or you'll render it rubbish, you waster-space!"

But Urdda stood firm. "Where do you come from, sir?"

"I come"—the littlee-man stalked towards her in a way that might have been menacing, had he been full-sized—"from Smelly-bumhole Land. You may call me Mister Odiferous. Up through the arse of the world I come here, and when I'm finished I will squeeze myself back out it. Now, take your lips and flap them somewhere else, useless hussy."

Urdda laughed uncertainly. "Half your words I cannot understand, sir, through your accent and their strangeness."

"You can tell they are not nice, though," said Branza. "Come, Urdda, let's leave him."

But before Urdda could obey, the wood beyond the littlee-man shook with a deep growling.

Branza and Urdda froze; the littlee-man fell to the ground, crawled back to his jewel-hoard, and threw himself over as much of it as his small body would cover. Then, from the trees, a smell, all wildness, poured, and a shadow that stood high, bellowing, steep-shouldered, fur-footed, round-eared, sprouting claws and teeth.

Urdda was gusted back to her sister on the breath of it. "Oh, Bear!" she cried. They clutched each other, Urdda in delight and Branza in terror at the beast that was not playful at all, that was no man's friend.

"Mercy!" screamed the littlee, hugging his jewels, trying to scrape them all together under his smallness.

"He is like a *doll* there," whispered Urdda. "He is like a *puppet,* so small next to Bear."

The bear bent and flicked the littlee-man off the treasure-pile.

"Take them, take them!" The littlee-man rolled and sprang up. "I can always find more! Take the fortune of them, all of them, and bless you, fine creature. You deserve, surely, to be bedecked and arrayed, oh king of beasts—"

But the bear had drunk up all the man-smell from the stones and coin, and now it stepped after the littlee, jingling the heaps apart and into each other with its uncaring feet.

"No, sir, I beg you!" he screamed. "There is nothing of me but a scrap of leather! Please, my lord, have these!" He was behind the girls, and pushing them forward. "So plump, so tender! Full of juice and fat! They will make a fine meal for you!

168

They will fill your belly twice over each one, not like dry old me!"

The two girls stood, still as landforms or dead things. Urdda gazed up adoring at the giant. Branza was locked against her sister, her face pressed into Urdda's neck. Only the little man shrieked and made prey-noises. Urdda could smell him; he smelled of fear and blood.

The bear's black paw came down. The wind of it swiped Urdda and Branza. Then the littlee-man was on the grass, the kicked jewels around him. His rags were torn away from his arm and belly, which all but fell apart into slices, they were clawed so deeply by the bear. His face also was cut open, and through the torn cheek Urdda saw two of his yellowed teeth before blood coated them and filled the cut. He gazed up from where the blow had thrown him, as if trying to make sense of the sky and the sensations of his body. And then he was a thing on the ground, a man no more.

Branza heard the silence and lifted her head. Her fright grew much stronger, but stiller, at the sight of the littlee-thing lying there. A worm of his blood trickled out into the grass, nosing to left and right.

The bear, breathing calmly, bent to him, its paws crushing the grass-stalks on either side. It commenced to eat him, and Urdda held Branza tighter at the sight, for fear of her sister gasping or screaming, and bringing the same fate on the both of them. The littlee-man swung as does a bird in the mouth of a hunting dog; he appeared not to mind any of the eating, to still be thinking about what had happened, to still be realizing. And then he had no face to realize with, and the bear was cracking his small skull in its jaws and licking out the contents with a very particular noise, all cupped close and rasping, and the littlee-man's hair was all over the bear's face and front like a spiderweb. Then he was nothing but pieces on the ground, cloth-rags and flesh-rags both, and bones, eyeholes in the red grass, and stains and shreds around the mouth of the bear, and patches in the clearing, memories of the noises.

The bear belched softly, swung its head towards the sisters and away again, then rose and walked on its bloodied paws in among the trees a little way, where it sat and began to groom itself.

Urdda and Branza, stiff with watching, watched still the tongue, like a pale creature, dancing in the shadows there. The teeth whitened again with its cleaning; the claws emerged yellow-gray.

A flight of tiny birds sprang up around them from the treasure-pile and flew out, some green-tufted, some ruby-throated, some gold-winged. In the grass the shine went off the gold and silver coins, and only flowers of dandelion and white-maiden lay, smelling of the sap of their torn stalks.

"A beast turning upon a person," said Urdda, thrilled. "Just as in a story, Branza!"

"I can hardly believe it, he is so gentle with us," breathed Branza.

"Nor can I! So savage!" The littlee-man twitched and swung and cracked in Urdda's memory. In the trees, the bear huffed and tongued his paws.

The first thing Branza must do, as soon as she could move, was hide the bits and bones of the littlee-man.

"Help me, Urdda." She pulled up a grass-clump to start her excavation. "Collect up the scraps of him and bring them here."

Urdda looked as if it were the first time she had seen them. "Whatever for?"

"Mam must not see him, even in pieces."

"Why not, though?"

"She will want to know who he was and what he wanted."

"Why then, we will tell her."

"We will not," said Branza, digging. "She must not see."

"What has got into you?" Urdda said distractedly, and wandered bearwards.

"Urdda, no!" Branza sat back on her heels and clicked her tongue. "Let her be eaten, then," she said to herself crossly, "for not helping me." And she rose and ran to where an oak-bough hung low, from which she could take leaves to use as gloves and wrappings so that she would not have to touch the little nasty's wetnesses.

After placing several pieces of him in the ground, she checked again, and there was Urdda in the forest fringe, leaning towards the bear and pleading with him. He took scant notice of her, but only busied himself cleaning the blood and fibers of the littlee-man from his fur. Branza could hear Urdda's tone—insistent, high, the tone she achieved just before Branza or Mam either smacked her or gave in to her pleading. "He will swipe you too, Urdda," Branza sang under her breath, shaking her head as Mam sometimes did, knowing better. Then a leaf unstuck from where it had been folded in the grave, and a littlee eyehole stared up, and she hurried to fetch other pieces and leaves to cover it.

"Here we are," Urdda said. She and the bear loomed at the edge of Branza's sight. He was on all fours, his head low and his expression almost chastened. Urdda had gathered some littlee-hairs off his chest and face, and carried them like sewing-silks loosed from a skein, floating out behind her. "Look, he is all cleaned up to present himself to Mam."

She bundled the hairs and dropped them into the littlee-grave, and stood with her hand in the bear's mane while Branza filled the hole in and replanted the grass she had pulled up. It did not look quite natural there; nor did the stamped earth around it.

"If we are out with Mam, we must avoid this place a little while, until this weathers in," Branza said.

Urdda lifted an eyebrow, as if Branza were mad. The bear beside her raised his nose from the soil, snuffed the air for Branza's scent, and pushed his nose into the palm of her earthy hand.

"You carry the basket, Urdda, at least until we reach the stream and I can wash." Branza scratched the bear between the ears while Urdda fetched the basket. "I am rather glad you ate that littlee-man, yes I am," she murmured to him. "I am quite pleased that we do not have to worry about meeting him again. I did not like him at all."

The bear made a contented noise, and rubbed his great soft cheek against her side.

Liga, well pleased, carried two gutted fish home, a heavy silver meal. Soon the girls would stride in from town with the fine herbs and long-beans that only Wilegoose could grow, and they would all be full tonight.

There they were now, on the other side of the cottage. She could hear their happy voices—but a little clearer, sounding more self-conscious than usual. Had they brought someone back? The Gruen boy, maybe? How ought she to behave with *him*? she wondered. Would he expect to eat with them? Would there be enough fish? How much did dream-people eat at a sitting?

She forgot fish and food at the sight of the shadow with her daughters—low, broad, rippling-edged. Too deeply delighted even to tremble or laugh, she stood feasting on the sight of his shape in the dusk, his amiable all-fours ambling.

"Mam, look who has come back!"

They brought him to her, and doubt sang down Liga like light along a knife-edge. His walk was different; she tried to discern in what way. And—it was like a cloak of mist or dust—a tawniness clouded his face and shoulders. His face was the wrong face: rounder, younger, blander. Worst of all, he did not seem to recognize her.

"It is not the same bear." Liga walked to the bench by the cottage door and laid the fish there.

"Are there more than one, then?" said Branza.

"Fool-girl! Just as there are many deer, many foxes, many swallows, there are bears all through the world."

Branza and Urdda both looked startled, and Liga heard the bitterness in her voice. It is only, she thought, that I thought you brought *my* bear, and life lit up for a moment. And now it is returned to its usual dimness, which truly I had thought was bright enough for me.

"But he came with us willingly," said Urdda. "He seemed to know us and to want to come with us."

The bear sniffed at Liga, her face and shoulders. Was he larger than the other? How long ago that was—why, it must be seven summers! Or was it eight?

She took his head in her hands to still him. She looked into his fine eyes, which were dark as the other's, deep as the other's, but not the other's. "Do you know that other bear?" she said.

He shook his head, but it seemed he was only shaking off Liga's hands.

She knelt before him. "Does he still live?" she said.

He looked back into her eyes. Was he trying to answer?

173

Was he answering yes or no? She could not tell, she could not tell.

"Will he come again? Do you know him?"

The tawny bear made a small strangled noise in his throat.

Branza threw her arm across the bear's neck, the white limb almost disappearing into his fur. "What does it matter, Mam? How we have missed having visits from a bear, any bear! Surely this one knows how to play, just as well as the other did?"

The bear made a shy movement with his great head; he swung away from Liga and lay on his side at Urdda's feet. Branza fell too, into his stomach fur, laughing. "See?"

A piece of other-world knowledge rose from Liga's bones: they were too old for such games, her girls now. Branza was of marriageable age and Urdda was nearing it, too old to tumble about with animals, especially this stranger, who seemed to Liga to luxuriate too much in the game. Improper, it was. She remembered women scolding, and talking about girls in scolding voices. If it had not been that she and her daughters were alone here, with no one to fill them with shame or to have any opinion of them at all, she would have scolded them herself. She could feel the inclination for it. She could hear other women's words readying themselves in her mouth.

Instead, with a forced smile, she took the fish inside, and desolately she laid their now less satisfying weight across the green leaf-patterned platter on the table. The laughter of her daughters sounded in the little house; the fishes gleamed. She eyed their silver skins, the blush of their clean flesh. What had she hoped for? What did she want? Only to be seen and known and some way understood, as she had been by that first bear. Well, it seemed she would not be, now, though minutes ago it had been as likely as not.

Could she even remember that other bear? Had he really come to her at the laundry-rock that day, and touched her face so lightly, and tried to speak to her? She was sure he had tried to speak! Seven summers ago, it had been—was she recalling it right, or had she dreamt it?

Branza's golden head bobbed laughing at the window; then bear-fur flowed past; then Urdda ran after the other two, laughing also. Then only the boughs of the green forest filled the window-square, dimming with evening around the little house.

Urdda set out early. She took nothing with her, only her own sharp eyes; only her thoughts, busy as a beehive. Through the cool of the morning, she hurried to the stained place in the grass; to the grave, still with Branza's hand- and footprints on it; to the crushed place where the bear had sat; to the forest from which the bear had approached unseen as she and Branza argued with the littlee-man.

She retraced the beast's path easily; he was big, and had brushed and broken things; he had been hungry and had torn this bush and grubbed up this plant and that. The light grew, and Urdda's confidence and happiness grew with it—and her own hunger, because she had brought no food. A few mushrooms she found, and she drank from the stream where she crossed it, and that must keep her going; she would not stop and return—she was too curious.

At last she came to a cave-mouth, and a single set of bear-prints leaving it. For a moment, she stood in satisfaction; then she bent low and walked in.

She had thought she could see all of the cave from the mouth, but, stepping in carefully so as not to mess the tracks, she found a passageway leading off into darkness to one side;

the paw-prints emerged from there. She had to bend her knees to move along it without scraping herself on the rock overhead. She felt her way forward until she could no longer see her hands, the darkness was so complete.

More and more slowly she moved, feeling all around. The smell of bear—of all his vegetable foods become animal inside him over the winter, become meat and fur—was strong, and she breathed it in hard.

At the end of the passage, she put out her hands. A rough rock-wall stopped them. She established the shape of the tunnel-end; she could stand straight here. It was so dark that she could not see her splayed fingers on the wall; already she was halfway to invisible in this world. She pressed her hands to the rock, full of hope.

When a girl of fourteen wants a thing—when she has wanted it all her conscious life; when she senses it near and bends all her hope, and all her will, and all her power to it—sometimes, *sometimes*, her self and her desires will be of such material that worlds will move for her. Or parts of worlds, their skins particularly, will soften to her pressure, and break in a thousand small and undramatic ways, so that she may reach through, so that what seemed a wall reveals itself to be only the thought of a wall, or a wall constructed of bricks of smoke, mortared with mist. There is a smell to such workings, and Urdda smelled it here and now at the rim of the bear-scent, as if someone had held a flaming brand near that bear-fur so that it began to singe and smoke and reek.

The wall of the cave was rock, and one version of Urdda's hands found it resistant, but another version pressed through, into an altogether spongier substance, the smell searing her nostrils.

She was up to her elbows in the wall. So this *was* possible;

so it was possible for *her*! She stood still a moment, accommodating the relief, trying to control her excitement. She had her four arms out, two of the hands exploring cracks and chinks, the other two reaching, reaching—she could see them, could she not? She could imagine them in sunlight. There was no doubt in her mind—she had not paused in doubt. She was only gathering her breath to move, to move forward, to move through to whatever other place would have her.

The membrane between the worlds was not wet and not dry, not cold and not warm; it was thick as a castle wall, and all give to the touch, and all blur to her eyes. She pushed her knee, her toe and shin through it; she pushed it aside with her hands; she grasped it and pulled herself through.

Sunlight burst on her. She glimpsed a sunny wall. Then something roared in her ear, and snatched her up, and kissed her scratchingly on the cheek, and rubbed her face with roughness. And she was pushed against the wall, coughing through her scorched throat, and he was running away down the narrow lane—a man clothed all in furs, with a tall fur bonnet on his head, his bare hairy legs and arms all roughly covered with black slime.

9

"*I* am alarmed now," said Branza when evening came.

"Alarmed?" Liga looked up from her finework with a smile. "This is our little wild adventuress you speak of."

The bear bulked at Branza's side in the doorway. *Did you eat her while I slept?* she wanted to ask him. *Did you have her for your breakfast?* But he had been with Branza all day and had never stopped browsing. He had even caught himself three fish in the stream while she rested from her searchings on the bank, her throat sore from calling her sister's name. And if he had devoured Urdda, he had left no piece behind of her, as he had of the littlee, for Branza to bury.

"How long should I wait, then, to worry?" Branza asked.

"Oh, a little longer. Are you hungry, of your wanderings?"

"Very." Branza shook off her shoes and stepped inside. The bear huffed and followed.

"No! Not you! Outside!" Liga cried, and flew at him, and flapped her hands.

"Mam! That's not kind."

"He smells bad, this one."

"Oh, nonsense. He smells of bear, and perhaps a little of fish."

"Well, that is bad enough. Yes, sit there on that step. Very well, you may lay your *head* in the door, but no more of you."

Branza laughed. "Oh, look how low you have brought him!" For the bear had rolled his eyes at her mother, very crestfallen.

"Well, he may sulk all he wishes," said Liga. "Spread a cloth, Branza, and we will have our supper."

When the bread and cheese and the salad were laid out, Branza recounted, with building anxiety, her day's searching. She had been to the old house-in-the-tree where she and Urdda used to play, on the off-chance that Urdda, unable to sleep, had gone there in the night and dozed off. She had scoured Hallow Top, behind every fallen stone and in every clump of furze. She had asked about the town, but no market-woman, and none of the pig-people outside the gates, had set eyes on Urdda.

"I will go up that cliff-top tomorrow," she said. "I know sometimes she haunts up there."

"Oh, you think?" Liga's voice was full of doubt. "That's a long way."

"And perhaps below it. Perhaps she has fallen. She might have tried to fly again."

Liga laughed. "Oh, Branza, she has fourteen summers now; she would not be so foolish!"

Branza sighed. "Well, I must do something. To sit here and stitch while she does not come—I don't know how you can do it. I am so cross with her one moment, and so frightened the next!"

Liga swallowed a mouthful of cheese and bread and patted

Branza's hand across the table. "All will be well," she said comfortably. "You will see."

But all was not well. Or at least, all continued well *except* that Urdda did not return. Branza went out in the mornings with Bear at her side and a place in mind that Urdda might have taken it into her head to visit, or to build a hidey-hole in and pretend to live in for a few days. It had been something they used to do together, she and Branza; Branza was offended not to be told, although both girls had had solitary games all their lives, as well as games they played together.

All day Branza would search cave and cottage, marsh and heath and town lane. As the days, as the weeks, went on, she sometimes paused, to rest and to weep discouragement and grief into Bear's fur; she would not burden Mam with it and threaten her eternal hopefulness, but she must release it somehow: Urdda might never come back, she feared. The forest was vast; no one in all their lifetime could explore every nook and crevice of it. And the stream was long, and in places pooled very deep. And the marsh—who knew what lay under that sheet of silver lumped with reedy islets, arrowed with the wakes of ducks? And Urdda might be in none of these places, for Branza remembered well that littlee-man stamping his foot and being gone behind the rock when there was nowhere for him to go. She remembered Bear—that first Bear—running off into nothing, into moonlight and enchantment. She remembered—the memory was like a red-hot iron against her heart—Urdda saying she had tried to fly after him; Urdda diving and diving at the marsh-edge, hunting for the beard-tuft. *Wouldn't you love to go there?* Urdda exclaimed in Branza's memory, wounding her sister again and again. She might not be in all the vastness here, in wood or water or town; she might be stepped through, stamped through, flown through finally to that place she had always wanted to go to—to the land of littlees, to the land of magicked Bears who consorted with children and mams.

As the weeks passed, as the months passed, Liga's greeting changed in tone, so subtly that only Branza could have noticed it. She always asked the same bright question: "And where have you been today?" But with time, the note that expected good news of Urdda, and then the note that even associated Branza and Bear's wanderings with her younger daughter—both those notes faded.

"And I saw no sign of Urdda," Branza would sometimes say dully at the end of her account of her travels, unable to believe that her mam could so forget, could care so little about, the reason Branza exhausted herself each day.

"Oh? Oh. No," Liga might say, remembering, then straightaway dismissing it. "These are fine cresses you found. You say the bear led you to them? I almost like him for that." And she cast a fond look at the beast's head in the doorway.

But Liga could not entirely forgive this bear for not being the other, that first one. He seemed stupid by comparison, and ordinary in his looks—not splendid at all.

"Scat! Scat with your eyes!" she said, shooing him away while Branza dressed.

"He is but a bear, mother," laughed her daughter, dropping her shift over her head. It fell to conceal that troubling body of hers, with the hips now, and the breasts beginning, and the fuzz of golden hair between the thighs.

"I don't like his look," said Liga. "There is something altogether unbeastly about him."

As the year passed and the weight of grief lessened somewhat on Branza and allowed in some playfulness, Liga was less and less inclined to let the girl out of her sight with the bear. She was so innocent! Liga was glad when the weather chilled and Branza ceased to swim with him, for she had been as good as naked in her soaked shift, laughing as he plunged about her, his excitement so evident that Liga was compelled to call Branza in.

"You should not let him nuzzle you so," Liga said, watching the two of them on the matting before the hearth that autumn, and she could neither bring herself to talk about men and their lusts and their ways (he was a *bear*, for goodness' sake, not a man!), and thus let Branza take charge of her own modesty, nor quite ignore the play of them, their positions and alignments and contacts. She seemed condemned to sit worried, and purse her lips at the beast, and invent errands for her daughter so that she would not rest too long in the bear's embrace or grow too accustomed to it, or too fond of the sensations.

Finally winter came. The beast began to spend almost all his days upon the hearthrug. One afternoon he came in muddy, though, and when Liga and Branza returned to find him filling the cottage with muddy-bear stink, and the walls and ceiling spattered with the mud he had shaken off, Liga decided they were done with him.

"Out! Out with you!" she cried, and flicked him about the face with her cleaning rag to move him up off the mat. "Look at the pig-mess you have made here! Go and find a cave and hibernate there, like a respectable bear!"

Branza would have protested against Liga's sending Bear away, but the mud-spattered room, and the hours that would be required to clean it, outweighed the sympathy she felt for him. She watched her tiny mother banish him—it was like a kitten terrorizing a wolfhound: the spitting fierceness of the one, the cringing mass of the other—and she knew that he had brought this banishment on himself, and that she would have no success if she tried to defend him.

He visited once or twice more, and then she did not see him again until the spring. When she met him then, out in the woods alone, he manifested great excitement, and she was so happy to see him that she allowed him to lick and whiffle as he pleased awhile, until he combined a lick and a pawing of her shift in such a way that he got out one of her breasts. Despite her laughing protests and her pushings, he held her body to the tree he had herded her against, and he licked and licked at the rosy nipple as if it were honey leaking from a cracked pot, until Branza hardly knew what to think, with the heat and strength of the sensations, and the horror of their newness. Other parts of her responded that were quite far from the nipple itself and yet were connected by some cord of sensation like a string through a wooden puppet.

Before long, though, her fright became too strong and her laughter turned to shouts and her pushings to slaps upon the bear's nose. She saw what it took him to wrench himself away—it was against every instinct in his body. His teeth showed for a moment, and the danger of him.

Branza hurried away, hurried home to her mam, pausing at the stream to wash the bear-lick from her chest, the bear-smell from her hands. She was torn. Should she tell Mam and wonder with her what Bear might have been about, or should she not say a word? By the time she reached the cottage, the latter intention had become the stronger.

When she next saw Bear he was calmer, and careful with her, but as the summer swelled, he grew more confident, and there was a game that he began, which was of chasings, just as first-Bear had played with Branza and Urdda when they were little, so that Branza played her part with a will, with nostalgia and a certain amount of poignant enjoyment on Urdda's behalf.

But the game changed, with only the two of them playing. Bear would run into a thicket, say, and Branza, giving chase, would plunge in after him, but the thorn-branches would catch her, or spring back into a screen behind her, and then it would be up to Bear to rescue her. At first she thought him very attentive and even gentlemanly, with his anxiety that she be scratched as little as possible; but the third time he led her into such a trap, she knew it was no longer accident, and there was something in his enfolding of her that was not solicitous, that was not gentlemanly at all. And after he engulfed her in a cave once, when she had followed him in without thinking, she had quite a time fighting herself free of the grunting bulk of him, of his terrifying strength, of the urges that had him in their grip quite as tightly and irrationally as he had her in his.

"Where is the bear?" Liga straightened from her work in the garden when Branza came home, and Branza wished she had straightened her hair and clothing better before walking out of the forest.

"I have smacked him and sent him away," said Branza. "He was annoying me."

"He will come back." Liga bent again to the glossy beginnings of her chard crop. "Tomorrow, you will see. He will skulk up that path and give you that moon-eye look, and you will forgive him, as you always do."

Which was so. That year progressed more uncomfortably than the last, with Liga more eagle-eyed and Bear more calculating about his behavior, and Branza between them only wanting peace, but compelled to apologize one for the other, excitement and repulsion pushing her towards and away from Bear; love, loyalty, and rebellion fighting each other in her mam's direction.

Winter descended again, and Bear knew not even to try entering the cottage now, though he lingered in the cottage clearing, particularly in fine weather. And then he went away entirely, to sleep out the winter somewhere. And so there were some peaceful months, with Liga happier and Branza less confused, as the snow lay thick over the cottage with the two of them as harmonious inside it as twins inside a womb.

Branza more or less forgot him, and when she walked out in the early spring, she was not even thinking of bears. But then she happened on one—a new, smaller bear than the ones she had known, standing in the stream, waiting for the salmon to jump. Did this bear come from the same place as the others? was her first thought. And her second, more wistful, was: Did Urdda step through from the Bear-world, from the littlee-world, with this one? Is she somewhere nearby?

The bear caught a fine salmon, and lumbered across the stream to Branza, and settled to consuming the fish almost at her feet. There was nothing in the bear's actions bespeaking any desire but to feed itself. And when it lifted its head from the part-eaten fish, there was nothing in its eyes but eye-color, and Branza saw that this was a much simpler animal, much more the kind of creature she was used to tending and observing, like the birds and fawns and kid-goats.

"Good morning," she murmured, and she fondled the bear's ears, and it continued with its meal.

But when it had cleaned one side of the salmon's flesh from its bones, and just as it was pawing it over to begin on the other side, noises from behind Branza made the bear lift its great head. There in the trees stood Bear, second-Bear, whom Branza had not seen since the dozy days of late autumn. There was still something slow about him now, something clumsy, but what struck her more—and with a shiver like the one she had felt on first sight of the littlee-man all those years ago—was his difference from this new bear, his air of intention, the smell of the unknown about him and the unexpected, when every other creature she knew besides Liga and Urdda was entirely predictable. And she knew on the instant of seeing him that the new bear was a she-bear, and that second-Bear would want her as his mate.

He blundered out of the forest towards them. With a huff, the she-bear was gone; Branza heard her splash across the stream, but did not watch her go. For Bear was running at Branza through the mazement from his winter sleep, and his dulled, complicated eyes were on her, and his black lip was lifted. His teeth were weapons; he had torn the littlee apart with them. Could he possibly mean to do the same to her?

She sat in disbelief, watching death bowl towards her; she had never felt such hostility from any wild thing. She had never felt so soft and fragile, so much like meat, the person inside so negligible.

Right upon the moment he might have damaged her, the realization, the recognition, brightened his eyes, and he propped, and slid a little with his own speed, and sat bewildered, enclouding her in his dreadful breath, months stale from hibernation.

"Bear!" she said softly, her heartbeat shaking her voice. "What are you about?"

He swung his head, searching the air for a scent. He found it, high up, and he stood. He followed it so certainly that she almost saw the braided spangles of it in the air, leading him to splash thoughtlessly, clumsily across the stream. Halfway, he issued a roar, a cry, a question; then suddenly he was climbing the far bank, and with a wriggle of his massy dark bottom he was gone after the she-bear, and nothing was left of the two encounters but the half-eaten fish, and the blood pounding in Branza's chest and head, and out into all her extremities.

Branza hurried back to the cottage after meeting the two bears, too shocked at the danger she had been in to ponder it very clearly, and wanting only the comfort of home, the murmur and industry of her mam, the requirements of the garden and house, and the straightforwardness of familiar creatures.

There she calmed herself for the rest of the day, but in the night she heard again Bear's cry, and there was something in the announcement of it, in the plaintiveness, that made her lie awake awhile and wonder.

In the morning, she said to Liga, "I saw Bear yesterday. Did you hear him in the night?"

"Not at all. Was he prowling around here?"

"No, off in the hills somewhere. I thought I might go out and find him again today."

"Oh?" Liga had been easy in the sunshine, but now she reached for her finework and examined it closely, deciding where to begin. "Perhaps it would be best to wait. Till he is in the mood to be civilized."

"Perhaps."

But Branza went anyway. She went many times in the following days, in search of the two bears, but they had traveled quite a distance, and she found that only by beginning just before dawn could she reach, with any hope of arriving home again by nightfall, the hill where Bear had herded the she-bear and was keeping her.

And the day that she did this, as soon as she sighted him

187

she wished she had not. For Bear, out in the hilltop meadow, was engaged in mounting the she-bear. Branza, having journeyed so far, felt she must stay; such a mixture of revulsion and hilarity filled her, along with her customary clear-eyed curiosity about the ways of animals, that she felt she must watch.

Sometimes bears are very cursory in their mating, but this was not one of those times. For nigh on an hour, Bear bullied the she-bear from behind, forcing her to collapsement in the sunlit grasses. Did she endure the coupling or enjoy it? Were the sounds she made protests, or pleasure-noises? Bear himself seemed alone above her, pursuing what it was he was pursuing, his rump working above hers, his paws on her shoulders, an expression on his huge furred face of ineffable seriousness and stupidity.

At the end, tremors ran through him and the she-bear made a gruff noise behind the grass, behind the wild blooms, white and mauve and yellow, of the meadow. He lay on her awhile, as on a sunny boulder to absorb the heat; then he pushed himself upright from her and withdrew from her his member, surprisingly thin, long, and drooping, which drooped further in the fresh spring breeze.

Branza must have made some tiny laugh or exclamation, for direct upon extracting himself, Bear turned and saw her. Straightaway his face regained its most speaking look. He towered over the prone she-bear, and the member on him stiffened again and gleamed with tightness and the wetness from inside his mate, and seemed almost to emit light against the hairy darkness of his belly and groin.

He spoke, and though his speech was wordless, there was no mistaking his pride and triumph, his pleasure that Branza had been audience to the mating. He plunged towards her— the ridiculous pipe-thing, the nozzle of him, wagging under his belly, and there was no mistaking that he desired to have of Branza in just the manner he had had of the she-bear.

But Branza was gone. The forest streaked and flicked past her as she fled; root and earth, pebble and moss-clump propelled her away. Down the hill she ran, back the way she had come. Bear's crying and crashing diminished behind her.

When Bear had been inaudible for a good long spell, Branza flung herself down on the next stretch of open grass in a strange fit of laughter at what she had seen, at what she had done; at the thought of herself skittering away terrified, with the lust-blinded Bear falling through the forest behind her. At first she covered her mouth to hold the laughter in, and rolled in the grass trying to contain it, but in the end she could not, and shouts and hoots escaped her, frightening away birds and ground-creatures.

I sound like Urdda, she thought. She felt a flash of understanding for her full-throated, passionate sister before that old grief, that two-year-old grief, smothered the laughter. She swayed, smiling and troubled in the sunshine. I know so little of anything! she thought. Affairs of the springtime forest rustled and hummed about her; a pair of hawks flew an arc across the sky above her; she could sit entirely still here and become just one among many splashes of sunshine and shadow. I love it all, she thought, but I understand none of it. And then there are these terrors: littlees and strange bears. What is the meaning of them? Will I ever be rid of them?

Bear came to the cottage many days later, and there was nothing in his demeanor to say that he remembered what had passed between himself and Branza when they last met, either to please or embarrass him.

But now he seemed to know how much he might venture

with her, and he was careful not to overstep the bounds. Several times that year she played his game, and followed him into cave or covert and allowed him to embrace her, but he knew to do no more than hold her, and perhaps lick her face or neck once or twice, and perhaps rub his cheek against hers. And she would stand or lean or lie against him and sense again how little she knew, and puzzle over things he had done before, excitements he had had and annoyances he had given her. She did not know whether she was afraid of him trying them again or desirous of it; did she want to feel the press of that wand of his against her, or did she want never to see evidence of it again?

And so the third year passed in a kind of wariness, in a kind of accommodation, with Liga always hovering nearby, wanting an accounting of things. Which Branza gave her, trimming and crimping her tale without even thinking anymore, in accordance with what Liga wanted to hear.

Bear disappeared for the winter, reappeared in the spring on a distant hill. Branza saw him wrestling a smaller he-bear under the leafless trees, with a she-bear tearing bark nearby as if quite unconscious of the two. She went home and waited, and eventually Bear presented himself, with a quiet, preening air about him, and a scar across his nose to show for his triumphs.

Shortly on his return he attempted his chasing game, but Branza felt it was too early in the season to be safe to play it, besides which the day was too inviting, too fresh. It had been a long stuffy winter in the cottage, and she only wanted to keep striding in the open air. So when Bear disappeared into his cave, she stood at the cave-mouth, calling, but not minding that he did not emerge, the sun was so warm and pleasant. And then she went up the nearest hill to gaze out beyond the folds of heath and forest to the far mountains, but never letting the cave-mouth disappear from view so that she would not miss Bear should he come out and start the chase again.

But he did not come out of the cave at all. Finally, she descended the hill. "Come out, Bear," she called. "We'll have none of that today, none of your nonsense! Out you come!" She stepped into the cave and felt her way along to the end of the tunnel, and all around. He was not there. She knew how quickly he could move; he could not have escaped past her, she was certain. But there was no sound of his breathing or his claws in that cave, only Branza's small and distressed lungs; only her shoes making their little dull scrapes on the earthen floor.

She returned to the cave-mouth for air, for spring air. All of a sudden, she needed the smells of snowmelt and raw earth and new greenery after that warm, still, gravelike place; needed to sense life moving in the air she breathed, in the breeze against her skin, pressing her skirts to her uncertain legs.

Urdda touched her face and looked at her blackened fingers. I am filthy, she thought dazedly. He has filthed me all up.

Screams and laughter sounded up the lane. Two girls ran in at the bottom, brawny girls, bare-armed and hoisting their skirts. They were in a fit of laughter and fear, and they bumped and scrambled past, hardly sparing Urdda a glance, and their faces were streaked and smudged with black, just as Urdda's must be. And their eyes—

I am there! she thought, watching the skirts of them, watching their dirty foot-soles as they ran away. I am in the other place, with the vivid people, with—

And then he was there again, the black-legged man in the skin costume, but he had neither run into the lane from above or below, nor flung himself through that hedge there— Oh, no, he was a *different* skin-dressed man, black-haired where the other had been reddy-brown.

"Blemme!" he said, and patted his clothing, and touched his tall fur hat. "You!" He panted some. "You're the sister, Urdda!"

"How do you know me? You're not from our village."

"Well, I am and I amn't," he puffed. "I been running," he said. "We were chasing." He gave her a sharp look. "You broke your sister's heart, you know. Branza's."

"She doesn't even know I'm gone yet!"

"Daft girl, it's three winters. Haven't ye—"

Wild shouts and women's screams sounded from somewhere. The boy looked up and down the narrow lane. "It's still the Day, my gracious. It's still the Day. How? The Day I left? Or a different Day, years on?"

"What day?"

"Day o' the Bear, of course. Why do you think I am all skinned up like this?"

People skittered to a halt at the bottom of the lane. "Bear!" one shouted. Urdda had never seen such an assortment of strangers, wearing such faces.

"The same Day," said the young man, sounding astonished. "Tad still has that cut to his forehead."

"Ooh, who's the lucky girl?" said one of the lads.

"No sneakin off with your lady-love, Bear!" trilled a smudged girl. "You're all-of-ours today!"

The boy jumped to his feet and ran at them, roaring.

Urdda was hot on his heels. What was this? If a game, it was exactly the kind of game she liked, the running noisy kind it was such work to enlist Mam and Branza in. Look at them all—grown people, running, shouting, filthy, the laughter falling out of them loud and unmeasured! Look at their warped faces as they glanced behind for the chasing bear, big-eyed and big-mouthed with terror and excitement!

She recognized the street, with its rock slabs—and this wide way, too, up and down the hill. This is my own town, she thought, hanging back while the bear-boy threw himself into the crowd, catching hold of girls and women and kissing them and smearing them with his black. But look, so many more houses! So many more people! And smells! Farmish smells and rubbish smells and— There was so much strength and color in everything, so much noise and movement, Urdda felt almost like Branza, wanting things calm and still so she could examine them properly.

But with a shout, the boy was on his way again. Urdda joined the smudged girls thronging behind him who were safe from his attack, she gathered, because they were already marked and messed. Some of the girls she thought she recognized—was Tippy Dearborn so little as that, last time Urdda saw her?—but most were big, loud lasses, like none she had ever consorted with in her life.

"He gets up a good sprint, this bear!" laughed one behind her.

"You'd think he'd be flagging," puffed another. "*I* am flagging, and *he's* been going hours now."

"It's magic!" A third girl ran up past Urdda. "They get strength from it, all the maid-kisses. Remember that feller Ramstrong, who went all day and into the night that time?"

"Bring them bakers on, I say, and let's move to the dancing!"

"Come on, Maddie. Pick up your skirts—no one minds today!"

The town raced by them in spurts and stops, known and yet not known to Urdda—some windows shuttered blank, others garlanded and with elderwives and grumpas leaning grinning in them. In the streets, children sat on parents' shoulders, some screaming terror, others delighted and beckoning the bear-boy. Pomade and body-dirt; hay, sweat, onion, and a bitter, yeastish smell—by turns each person's odor teased Urdda's nostrils. Everything was so thick and rich, she hardly knew whether to cringe or scream or shout for joy herself.

The chase ended in the ash-tree square, when a pack of men dressed as bakers leaped from a lane and brought the bear-boy down. They beat him with flour-bags, and all around had floury masks added to their smudged faces, and the girls cheered and shouted and celebrated. A man with an ax came, and through the mist of flying flour Urdda saw him make as if shaving the bear-boy's furred chest.

"Teasel! Teasel!" the big girls chanted. The boy flexed his muscles and roared.

"You is tamed now," shouted the ax-man. "You can stop with your noise, for you are man again. No more grabbin of girls; no more smudgery. Come civilized up to Keller's, and fill your belly with man-food and ale."

One of the girls rushed in and planted a kiss on the boy's mouth, then stood a moment leering at her friends with her floured face, her tongue startlingly red, her red hands rubbing the boy's chest- and belly-fur.

"Aye, you shameless!" The ax-man laughed and pushed her back into the cheering crowd.

Urdda followed the crowd to Keller's Whistle. The street there was strong with the bitterness she had smelt on some men's breath as she passed, and the house itself was crowded all about with laughing people. Two other bear-boys were there to greet the Teasel boy, their faces, like the women's, disquieting with black grease, and flour caked in their hair. Men clapped all

194

three boys on the back, thrust cups into their hands, clanked their own cups with them, and drank the foaming stuff that smelled so sour.

Urdda went unnoticed in that milling and mixing of people, trying to recognize girls she knew but frustrated by the face-paint. The men were easier, not being so marked, but here again there were differences. In general, they were fresher faced; some that she knew to have full beards were only just beginning to show down on chin and cheeks; some whose hair she knew to be silver-streaked were still fully golden-headed, or chestnut, or black. She was on the point of greeting one or two, but she was not sure that in fact she *did* know them in their present incarnations, and she would rather fill her eyes with sights and her ears with sounds, as a cat laps up a bowl of cream, and venture nothing herself yet.

Soon it was evening. The alehouse windows burned red and gold, and the festivities went on both within and without. Urdda continued to wander, seeking things she had not seen before—quarrels and sly looks and rude guffaws, and people fondling each other in corners. She returned and peered in the alehouse windows, and tried to follow the words being sung in there and find the face of that boy Teasel, which always was very red and busy with singing and the drinking of ale.

"How long will they be in there?" Urdda asked a woman near her who was selling white-dusted cakes from a basket.

"All night and well into tomorrer, I should think," said the woman. "Fancy a cake? I've jammed or plain."

"I have no money," said Urdda, for she had watched this woman transacting. Had she had the coppers, she would have counted them out correctly.

She walked away. She was not going to stay here all night. She was not even sure she did want to speak to that Teasel boy;

he looked quite wild and ill from the ale-drinking, and some people falling out the alehouse doors had been in no state to do more than slump in doorways and snore; or stagger away, singing or complaining. She was tired herself, with all the excitement and unfamiliarity, and the noise and the lamplit fragments of faces had the senselessness of a dream, and not an entirely pleasant dream at that.

She did the sensible thing: she set off for her home. Down the town she went, and the sound of her own footfalls emerged from the ebbing rousty noises behind her, and the hot glare of the alehouse faded to the cool of moonlight. The main street, with all its extra houses, channeled her down to the gate like a tunnel—a tunnel with a starry ceiling—and the town gate stood open at the bottom, giving onto the passing road. Two guards lounged there: strangers to her, one with a pipe lit, both of them with eyes.

"Who is us?" said one, approaching her from the gate-shadow. "A bitty maid trotting out on her own i' the night?"

"Where might you be headed, missy?" said the other from within his cloud of smoke.

"To my home, sir. I live out beyond the Font."

"Ah, is a gypsy lass," said the closer man. "I am surprised you is alone."

"We ought escort the maid, mebbe," said the other, shifting and waving smoke away. "She look to be quite pretty under the Bear-black."

"No, thank you," said Urdda. "I know the way very well."

"You hear that, Lorrit?" There was a note in the closer man's voice that Urdda could not interpret. "Your services are not required."

"Good night," Urdda said. Without slowing her step, she walked under the arch of the gate and out to the road.

"My services?" said the pipe-smoker disbelievingly. The other guard chuckled.

Outside the town, everything was more or less as she expected, in its shadows and cool night-forest smells and night-bird noises. Urdda made a good pace, pausing for a drink at Marta's Font. I hope Branza has left some bread for me, she thought, and not fed it all to the birds.

At first she walked right past the path that led down to the cottage. When she realized her mistake at the next bend and retraced her steps, she found that the tunnel into the forest was not nearly as easy to distinguish as it ought to be, although the rough stone steps down the slope were much the same.

Down she went. Twigs caught at her clothing, vines at her hair, and spiderwebs—not an anchor-rope here and there, but whole curtains and entrapments of webs, speckled with black-wrapped remnants of insects—masked and gripped her face, or required to be torn apart for her to make her way. But she was Urdda, not Branza; she plucked the webs from her face and hands and persisted.

She pushed the last overgrowings aside, stumbled into the clearing, and stopped. A little scream escaped her, very like something Branza might have uttered from one of her bad dreams. And then, in disbelief, in the strange noonish-moonish light, she walked forward through the wild grasses, dead and dried and risen into waves now that their burden of winter snow had melted from them. She bent to the wreckage of Liga's rose-arbor—the climbing rose uprooted, black and leafless, its knuckles in the lattice as if it were still in the act of tearing the arbor down. There was no sign of the garden's neat rows; it was a wilderness of bare ground with scraps of gone-to-seed herbs, with caved-in gourd-shells scattered about and rabbit-scrapes dug where once turnip-tops had swelled.

Sidling along the path, turning to left and right, gasping shocked breaths and exclaiming them softly out again, Urdda at last fetched up against the cottage step. It was the same step, without a doubt; she crouched and examined with desperate hands its pits and cracks, the hollow worn in the middle. But the ground to either side was bare of white-blooming bush and of red, and the doorway had no door, nor even a lintel, but gave straight onto the stars above, and below onto a mound of rotting thatch lumped with roof-beams that must have fallen years ago. The walls had melted under the rains and snows to stumps of things, with wattle sticking out, bleached and uneven, at the top.

"Where is Mam?" whispered Urdda. "Branza! Where have they got to?"

All appearances gave them to be dead and gone, but that could not be true. Urdda had left them alive and breathing in their beds that very morning. She had stepped over the paw of the snoring bear on just this step! She lowered herself to sit on the stone—she was cold, now that she had stopped walking and struggling through the forest—and stared at the ruin around her, the wasteland. And when that had exhausted her by not assembling into any kind of sense, she raised her gaze to the familiar stars, and to the cheese-round moon, rough-faced and impersonal, coasting along the cloud-streaks above the black trees.

"I tell you, they is not the same standard of Bears anymore," I said to Todda, pulling our door to and taking little Anders' hand.

"Says you, Bear of Bears." She smiled at me, organizing her shawl around the bundle that was Ousel.

"Says me. Even four year ago, we had better lads. Bigger

and of better mettle. All the high posts and offices of this town, Bears occupy now, and is respectable. Not one o' those four last night was respectable. They puked and bellowed and sauced Ada Keller so, her da had to put her away and do all the bringing himself. The whole day is supposed to be about civilizing men, not freeing them to paw and offend the women. It has all got bent out of its purpose."

"'Tis the lure of the boats. It is that Outman boy that turned a sailor, and brought back his coin, and strutted in his uniform. That glamorized them all, and off the good lads went."

"I know," I said gloomily. Anders were toddling too slow, so I picked him up and put him on my shoulders.

We walked across town to my brother Aran's house, where his wife's mam, Sella, had yet to see our new Ousel. We had a fine breakfast and morning there, most of the town still slumbering around us after the night's and yesterday's excesses. I was a touch faded myself, but I had taken care not to get in such a state as some so as I could be some use to Todda in the night, should Ousel cry and Anders forsake his bed at the same time. Which, of course, he had done. *Come, little lad.* I had peeled him off his mam so she could nurse the new one. *I've a story for you.* And I told it him in that voice, halfway between song and murmur, that settled the boy's eyelashes upon his cheeks again. *I cannot do that near so fast as you,* says Tod. *There is something about your rumblingness casts the spell, no?*

No, says I. *You make your stories too interesting, that is their problem.*

Anyway, here we were, making our way back home, through the mess and desertion of St. Olafred's after Bear Day. Todda led Anders; I had Ousel in my arms. The pennants on the turret of the castle still snapped their reared, snarling bears in the wind, and hunters' houses had bear-heads on their steps,

199

or hung on their doors, that protected their women from molestation on the Day, and there was some girl's ribbon trodden to the cobbles, and some man's pint-mug sat with drunken precision on a windowsill, that would have to be returned to Osgood's at some time.

I saw her as we crossed the High Street, standing like a lost lamb in the covered market, watching us but affecting not to. "Who is that?" I says to my Todda, even as I felt, I know that person, from life before my marriage, from life before Todda.

"I've never seen her before. Mebbe she's been visiting for the Day."

The way the girl stood, it was like a bee in my brain. Where do I know her? No, I have never seen her before! But—

Most uncharacteristic, I made towards her, away from Todda and Anders. Todda cleared her throat, slight but pointedly, behind me, but even then I must have known the face glowering at me, with the pin-drops of rain flying and falling across it.

Then I were in the market and there was no rain between us, and still she met my eye, in a way that would have been insolent in a town girl, but in this one—

All on a sudden, I knew the reason, and I clutched babby Ousel to me, because the first effect on me was to make me turn limp and nearly drop the boy to the slates.

"It's little Urdda!"

Her face cleared of some of its frowning, but still she were puzzled, I could tell.

"But all growed up. Grown to a young lady now. How old would you be, fifteen? But in the space of four years—how is that? You were but a little sprout then."

"I am fourteen summers, sir," she said.

"You do not know me," I said. "Forgive me. Of course not.

200

My name, sweet child, is Davit Ramstrong. I am a woolman and a citizen of this town of St. Olafred's."

"Oh, so it *is* the same town. But I have not met you, sir?" said Urdda.

"Indeed you have, my slip," I said. "But I were in bear form, in the place we met. Often we have sported, you and your sister Branza and your lovely mother and I. You will remember chasing me, I think, when I run off into the sky and never returned? Off that cliff there?"

She searched my whole face carefully. "You? You are Bear?" I could see her in there, the little one I knew inside this taller, less certain girl. Todda and Anders were behind me, watching, listening. I could hear my wife's calm breathing.

"I *was* Bear—for one day here and for some months in your place. The time must run different in the two places. Which is why you can be so much older now. But how do you come to be here, Urdda? What brought you?"

"I brought myself," she said unsteadily, glancing at Todda beyond my shoulder, and around me at my boy. "I followed the trail of a bear, a different bear; I pushed through the wall of a cave."

"Davit?" said Todda behind me.

"This is Urdda, wife. Remember I have told you? The day we met, that whole tale."

"Urdda is the younger daughter? Of . . . of . . . Liga, was her name?"

The girl's eyes brightened further. "You know my mam?" she said, and her voice was fraught.

My good wife went straight to her, bless her, and took her hand where it gripped her shawl. "I know *of* her, Urdda, that only."

"Do you know of where she is? Where I might find her?"

Oh, I had never heard that little sparkling girl so woeful. Todda turned to me and a glance full of doubt and pity passed between us.

"How long have you been here, girl?" I said, gentle as I could.

"I arrived . . . last evening," she managed, on either side of a gulped breath.

"And where have you slept? *Have* you slept," says Todda, "or only wandered?"

"I went out to the cottage."

"The cottage? There is no cottage left!" I said.

She nodded. "I made myself a kind of nest," she whispered. "Of grasses."

"And slept in the wildwood?" said Todda. "Girl, you were lucky not to be took by bears or gypsies! Davit, I think we must have this girl to our home with us. I shudder to think what will happen to her, do we not accommodate her. You must be the only man of this town knows her provenance—and no one else will believe her, but they will take any story you give them as to her origins. Who have you spoke to already, girl?"

"The guards at the gate. That Bear. Laundry-girls. A woman selling cakes outside the alehouse."

Todda touched her own cheek at the horror of it. "Come," she said. "There's the nook next the babbies' room; you shall have that to sleep in. Oh, that dreadful cottage!"

"You must have had a bad fright, seeing it for the first time," I said, following them out the market, "were you expecting it to be as you remembered."

"Oh, I did," she said, her poor mouth trembling between tears and a smile. "I did not know what to think—and still I don't."

And nor did I, as I followed the three of them, Anders now

on Todda's hip, watching the new acquaintance curiously. "I had begun to think I had dreamt you all," I said, "and my time as Bear among you. And now you have stepped out the dream, all tall and real. This will require some thinking."

So *that* bear is gone too, Branza finally admitted. First, first-Bear goes, then Urdda, and now this second Bear. Well, was he so much of a loss? Not compared to Urdda, certainly, or to first-Bear, an altogether kinder, nobler beast. She thought, though, of lying against the second one—the bulk and warmth of him, and his willingness to accommodate her there in her doubts and wonderings, his enjoyment of the little amount she allowed him. It was indeed a less worrying world without him, but it was lesser in other ways as well.

"I have not seen the bear with you in several days," said Liga. "In . . . in many more than several, now I think of it."

"No," said Branza calmly, as if it hardly mattered. "I have not met him hereabouts. He may be following some lady-friend up to the higher hills. Who knows? I have seen many bears about, this season. I am sure he will be back as usual."

But she knew she would not see him again, and she did not. And Liga, whether she noticed or no, never mentioned his absence again, never referred to his former presence, so that he vanished entirely from every part of Branza's world except for the store-chest of her memory. There he stayed, among all the objects bright and dark, and she pondered him as she pondered them, growing womanwards.

10

"What we ought to do," said Goodwife Ramstrong at her loom the next morning, "is visit on Leddy Annie Bywell."

"We ought?" Urdda was walking baby Ousel up and down, keeping him quiet while the goodwife worked. She searched the baby's cloudy bluish eyes by the light at the window.

"Muddy Annie, she used to be," said Todda.

"A mudwife? As in a story?"

Todda laughed. "Just so. But she does no herbing or mudding since she made her fortune; just sits up in that fine house and doesn't come out to say boo. But maybe she has heard of this land of yours. I know Ramstrong is searching out Teasel Wurledge this morning, to have his story from him. But Leddy Bywell is one you and I can approach. She might know what machinations brought you here, and how to reverse them."

"Reverse them? But I don't want to go *back*," said Urdda. "Not yet, at least. I want to look about here—this place is full of all kinds of odd things that we do not have at home." She

204

was much more reconciled to her new situation since sleeping a night in a comfortable bed.

"Odd is not of necessity good," said Todda gently. "Odd is not always kind."

"But odd is always odd, the same," said Urdda. "I cannot just turn around and go back to Mam and Branza—I've hardly anything to tell them yet!"

"Well," said Todda, "when you have. It's as well to know what you might do, then, and what is closed to you. Where you stand, you know, in relation to your circumstances and your family's in that other place. I will go up with you, when Anders wakes."

"This one is slipping to sleep." Urdda swayed, rocking Ousel. "I might visit her myself and not disturb your working."

Todda raised her eyebrows. "You may not move quite so freely as that, here in the real world. Not alone."

"Why not? I ran all about the streets on my own, day-before-yesterday, after that Mister Wurledge, and I saw plenty a girl doing the same."

"Yes, but that were Bear Day," said Todda. "That were the one day of the year you might do that. The rest o' the time, you must go out at least with another girl, if not a grown woman is better. That's in part why we were so worried for you, standing out in the market on your own."

"That's tiresome, though. Especially for girls who have not sisters—what do they do?"

"They go with their mothers. Or with friends. Or they bide at home. Who would want to go out alone? What would people say to you?"

"Well, what *would* they say?"

"Why, they would shout things. Boys, you know. They

would call you bold and a trollop. You might get things thrown at you, you know. A little stone, or a flick of mud on your clean dress."

"Truly?"

"Truly. You would be asking for that."

"*I* would not be asking."

"Just by going out alone, I am saying, is asking."

"That is terrible! We have no such strictnesses at home."

"Your home," said Todda with the thump of a treadle, "sounds like a very, very wonderful place."

I found Wurledge at his home abed—'twas nearly noon!—still sleeping off the Day's effects.

"For saints' sake, come in!" His grumping reached me at the door. "Don't stand there, shouting and bashing!" I had knocked the timidest of knocks—he must still be in quite a state of sensitivity.

When he saw me at his chamber door, he came up a little politer. "Mister Ramstrong! Feller Bear, now!" He elbowed himself up, swang his feet off his pallet. He had washed himself, at least, or *been* washed, of the state I had last seen him. He pulled his shirt into place around himself and pressed his sleep-cocked hair down. "What kin I do for you?"

"Only speak," I said. "Only tell me whatever you got up to, Bear Day."

"I'n't never laid a finger on Henny Jenkins, whatever Applin says. I were out cold under Keller's table by then. Never heard a whisker about it till yestiddy."

"Hmm," says I. It did not look as if he were going to stand and come out to talk civilized to me, so I crouched in the doorway, one shoulder to the post. "It is not that distasteful business I am about."

"Well, that's a relief. Ev'one else has their trews tied in a Franitch blood-knot over it, I cannot think why. 'Tis not like she ha'n't had a hand up her before, and more."

He expected me to laugh at that. This is what we have come to, the Bears we are putting up these days. "No, it is another matter. It is the matter of a lost girl my wife and I are accommodating."

Out of his what-the-feck-have-that-to-do-with-me look came another, more realizing. "Ha!" he said. "I'm guessing her name is Urdda."

I did not even like the sound of it from his mouth, but I must find out the worst, and waste no time about it. "She tells me you spent three years away, in the course of Bear Day."

"That is what I was thinking, when I talked to her. Now I am beginning to realize it were likely some kind of . . . of vision I had, or fever-dream, brought on by overexcitement, and thirst, and that costume, which—you know what it's like, Ramstrong, man: you're stewing in the thing! It boiled my brain, I'm thinking."

"Where did this Urdda girl come from, then?" says I, as patiently as I could. "You know her name; you called her by it on sight, yet you had never set eyes on the girl in this world, because she had never been here. By process of reasoning, she and I have pinned you down to a Bear that got there and immediately ate up some little nuisance of a man that were bothering the girls."

"Feck me! It did happen, then? But how could it, all that time and yet I pops back into the twitten there the same moment I jumped out? Only the maid was there before me. I don't understand how *that* works."

"Three years. So you're a man of twenty now."

"So it seems!" He rubbed his raspy chin in high amusement. "Though everyone still treats me as a Bear-age lad."

I had to work to keep my voice polite. "So how did you occupy yourself, those three years?" I said it so softly, it were sinister.

He heard all that. He looked like a lad that a landlord had told: *I saw the whole thing from my upper window, you and your gang-boys emptying my best tree of apples.* The guilt and the effort to look innocent were painted on his face, bright as pox-spots. "What you mean?" he said. "What have she told you? She were not even there!"

"Except when you ate that dwarfish man."

"Except then."

"Which were hardly nothing, are you telling me?"

"Well . . ."

"Which makes me wonder: how did you fill the rest o' the time? Did you eat anyone else?" What a question to have to ask a person!

"No, I did not! I only et *him* because I had been asleep all winter and were half mad with hunger. After that I were calmer, and found barks, you know, and honeys, and all what a bear *should* eat."

I was dizzy a moment with the memory of it, the jealousy I felt of him—three years in that place when I'd only had a matter of months. I'd a whiff of that bark, with a bear-appetite behind my nose, the forest my playground, and the cottage awaiting me, end of every day.

"But you associated with them—the girl's sister, Branza, and the mother?" I said, keeping the wretchedness out of my voice as far as I could at the thought.

He glanced at wall and floor. Across his face—I realized I must stay calm, feeling how intently I watched, how ready I was to leap up and lam the lad, any excuse he gave me—

amusement passed again, then something shady and sly, then careful concealment.

"Yes, I 'associated.' Am I to believe you of been to this place too, Mister Ramstrong?" he says smoothly.

"I have visited," says I.

"You will know what temptations they have set up for us, then, them two fine women unguarded by any man, and friendly toords beasts as you please. You is a married man now, but you was not when you were Bear; you surely cannot have not noticed that they was fine and shapely women."

"They were but bits of girls," I said sharp, "when I was there."

His eyebrows rose, and he chewed like a sheep on cud for a while. "Oh, then," he said softly, almost to himself. "Did you have of that mam, then? I did not think she liked bears."

"'Have of'?" I was on him with a fistful of his nightshirt. "What is this 'having of'? What have you gone and done?"

"Nothing, nothing! I never touched her! She come to *me*, that Branza, she did! Always flinging herself on me and rubbing up. She wanted it more than I did!"

I threw him away, like the piece of rubbish he was. He gave a bab-whimper and rearranged his shirt to cover his man-parts again, should I take it into my head to tear the things off with my bare hands.

"Tell me true," I says, each word like a quarrystone falling out the wall on his head. "Did you despoil that girl?"

Guilts twitched his eyes. I hung over him very much like a bear, and he cowered very much like bear-prey.

"Did you?" I pushed his chest, and the air whooshed out his lungs.

He shook his head and held his shirtfront, all terror now,

gasping. "I did not. I tell you true, Ramstrong, I would of liked to; you know how she smells! But she were a modest girl; all she would do were lie with me sometimes, without no touch-and-pokery. Three year I were there; if I had not expended myself on the she-bears of that world, I would of gone mad at the sight o' the girl."

I turned from him to stop myself doing worse to him. *The she-bears of that world.* Oh my gracious!

"She thought I was a bear, you know; she would swim with me, in her wet shift, clear to the eye as if she wore nothing at all. Where were a man supposed to look?"

"Away!" I said. "A man, a civilized man, is supposed to turn away, and walk away, not sit and slobber over the sight of a girl's nakedness, shown him in all innocence!"

"I never slobbered!" he said; then, "I never did," more doubtfully, sulkily.

I stood at the door with my back to him, trying to be calm. *The she-bears of that world!* Three years, for heaven sakes. *All she would do were lie with me sometimes!* You are only enraged, Ramstrong, because this accords too close with what you felt toords the mam there yourself. And you are jealous, of what you might have made of three years in that cottage, when this girt clod had that luck himself.

"Well, you have not harmed them," I said. "That is the main thing. And I am not the only man of St. Olafred's has found himself to be a bear in that place, which is what I came here to establish."

"You are not." He still sounded sulky. He looked like what he was: a child admonished, hairy legs, broad chest, and prickly chin notwithstanding.

"One more thing, though," said I—and he managed to cringe using just his head. "When I come back from there, I spent some time trying to return to it; to find that cottage again, that land. You may be tempted the same."

"As I said, I thought it a dream. Now that I know it were not, mebbe I shall be tempted, should things go bad for me here. I had a very pleasant time there."

"You will give me your word"—I turned fully to face him—"that if you discover a way—"

"I will tell you it?" he says with a crafty grin, which falls off his face like a hallows-mask when he catches my expression.

"You will give me your *word*," I says, stepping towards him, "that you will lay a finger on neither Branza nor her mam."

"I don't *have* fingers there," he says, resentful. "I have paws. If the leddies don't mind my pawing, I don't see why I should not paw them."

"Content yourself with beasts when you are there," I say. "I will have your solemn promise not to ruin that girl Branza, however affectionate she treats you."

He shrugged, the insolent lump. "Should she come and sit on me, I would not be pushing her off. And you might not be there to stop me."

My arm were so ready to hit him, it shivered in its socket. He blinked and flinched at that, though he were eye to eye with me. "Your word, Teasel Wurledge," I says very low.

He set his lips closed. I held his gaze, and he wavered; then he said, "I do not see why I should promise you anything."

Because I am an honest woolman and respected, and you is the dregs our Bear Day is reduced to. Because I were Bear before you and always will be. Because I am a steady citizen, married and with sons of my own, and you are a feckless drunkard what soiled the skins with your vomit. I might say all this and he would still look at me the same way.

" 'Tis true," I said even lower, "for what would your word be worth?"

Then I was gone from that fartsome, crumpled, ale-smelly room, before I undignified myself by landing a blow upon a poor ignorant beast.

Branza had long ago given up hope that she would find Urdda in her wanderings. She had long ago stopped expecting, cheerfully or uneasily, that second-Bear would surprise her in the near forest or on a far hill, in playful guise or terrifying. Still she wandered, though; still she strode the countryside. For a full round of the seasons, she went out alone—sometimes for only an hour; sometimes for a day, and a night in the wild, and a day's returning.

"Do you not feel lonely out there?" said Liga when Branza came home one evening, spilling autumn cold from her skirts and hair into the tranquil, fire-warmed air of the cottage. "Why do you not go up the town for a change, and visit with people, and have some conversation?"

"People are not nearly so varied as animals," said Branza, pulling off her boots by the door, "in their habits and shapes. They are not even varied as birds, leave alone all the other kinds. The town is always the town, doing the town's things over and over."

"I like that," said Liga. "I like to know what to expect. And that everyone is so friendly. Besides," she added, "I thought you had interests there."

"Interests?" Branza came to sit by the fire and stretched out her bare white feet towards the flames.

"I thought someone of the Gruen family interested you once."

"Oh, Mam. *Once. Years* ago."

"Why did nothing come of that, daughter? Or might something yet?"

Branza spread and wagged her chilled toes. "Do you wish it would?"

Liga made two more swift stitches in the seam she was sewing. "I should not like you to die unmarried."

"Why not? You yourself seem perfectly happy in that state."

"Yes, but—"

Branza turned to await the rest of the sentence, but Liga only stared into the fire, her eyes too dark to tell the black part from the colored. Branza rubbed Liga's shin. "Don't worry about me, Mam."

"I should like to have some grandchildren someday," said Liga simply, waking from her stare and sewing again.

And now that Urdda is gone—Liga's unspoken words hung in the air—*it falls to you, my angel child.*

Branza shook her head as if a fly were bothering her. Rollo Gruen belonged to her childhood; to the time before she knew she could lose her sister. He belonged, in fact, to the time so close upon the day she had lost her that Branza's curiosity about him and Urdda's disappearing had mingled in Branza's memory. She could not entertain the tentative sweetness of the one without calling up the pain of the other. And then there had been the second Bear, beside whom Rollo Gruen seemed so slender and simple; she had the sense that she could move the man around like a taw in a game of bobstones, and somehow he no longer interested her after Urdda left and after Bear. She would rather find herself a glade, or a seat by a pool, and position herself stonelike so that the forest ignored her as it did stones, included her and perched upon her as it did stones, so that the smallest and rarest and most timorous of birds came down to drink in her presence, or the wobblingest fawn took shelter against her unaccountable warmth. She would rather walk and walk until it was no longer clear whether she was shaping her stride to the landscape or whether the slopes and gravels, sheep-paths and tussocky meadows were in fact becoming, rising and declining, and giving way to one another in response to her own step.

"Why, do *you* feel lonely, Mam?" she said. "Do *you* feel left behind and old-maidish?"

Liga looked to the fire again, but not so hollowly this time. "Perhaps just a tadge," she said quite comfortably. "But always I think, 'Tis better to be safe than sorry. And safe is what I am here, in this house, and in this life."

The two of them looked on that safety as it enacted itself in the flames, spriting from log to log, runneling blue and orange up to the fire's peak.

"I don't know. Children?" said Branza dreamily. "I don't know very much about children."

"Children are delightful." Liga reached out and tousled Branza's hair, which was still damp and cold. "You would love them."

"This is a new house to me," said Urdda when they arrived at Lady Annie Bywell's. "Merchant Tenner lives *there* and the Ginnis boys live *there*—I recognize that horse-head finial—but this one, this is new-built."

"It has been here as long as the others," said Todda mildly. "And the Ginnises moved higher uphill many years ago, to Alder Park. They own more greenery than the late Blackman Hogback and the Eelsisters combined." She rapped with the iron doorknocker.

Urdda stepped back to examine the house again. All but

one of the windows were shuttered, and that lace-curtained one had the same sense of eyes behind it as all windows had in this town. At home, people let themselves be seen, waved greetings to you through the windows, or pushed them open and spoke to passersby. There was none of this lace business, none of this secretive peering. Was this Lady Bywell looking down at her now? Urdda restrained herself from waving or poking out her tongue.

Finally, a slow shuffling sounded from inside. Adjustments were made on the other side of the door, and then it opened. A woman small of stature stood there, in a neat-laced cap and a satin dress, with a sweetly embroidered slipper-toe peeping out below. Though she was dressed like a lady, her face was lined and brown, as if she had been out in the weather all her life, and the hand that held the door, for all its rings, had the same hard-worked look. She did not speak, only took in the sight of Urdda and Anders and Todda, holding Ousel, from bottom to top to bottom again, with glistening gray eyes.

"Leddy Annie?" said Todda. "My name is Todda, wife of Davit Ramstrong. These is my boys, and this is my guest, Urdda. I wonder if we might prevail on you for some o' your time and wisdom?"

"Wisdom?" said the lady flatly, but she opened the door wider and stood back for them to enter. All this very slowly, though, as if she were as unsure as Urdda of the etiquettes.

She waved them into a darkened sitting room on the right, into which they could not go far for fear of colliding with some chair or curio-case of the crowd of them there. The lady followed them in. Then she went to the window, slowly and laboriously looped back a curtain, and opened a single shutter to admit some light. She sat herself in a velvet chair in that light, sending up from it so much dust that she and the chair both might have been afloat on a cloud.

She regarded them each in turn, uncertainly. She exchanged a look with Anders, as if she felt herself to be on the same footing as he.

"We have come to ask your assistance," said Todda. "Urdda has arrived among us from a place very like St. Olafred's, but not exactly the same. My husband, Ramstrong, spent time in that place accidentally, one Bear Day. And there is another lad had considerable time there—near three years, while but a moment passed here—this last Day of the Bear."

As Todda spoke, the lady's hands locked into a cluster of knuckles and ring-stones in her lap. The littlee-man might make *that* stone out of a gold-barred finch, and *that* one out of a red-throat, Urdda thought.

The rings rearranged themselves and the fingers shook, whether from age, or the weight of the rings, or the lady's fright at the sight of the visitors. "I cannot help you," she said huskily. "Collaby is away. My assistant. My helpmeet." With the word "helpmeet" came into view her fine ivory dentures, even-edged and gleaming.

Collaby? thought Urdda. I've heard that name.

"Do you know the place I speak of, though?" said Todda. Anders stood by her, a proprietary hand on her knee, looking from face to face as each spoke.

The dust and the silence hung. "I do know of that place," the lady said reluctantly.

"Is it a difficult place to get to?" said Todda.

The lady reorganized one hand over the other, then the other over the one. Her skin sounded papery against itself, and the metal of her rings clicked against the stones. "Ah," she murmured, "it is all too easy now-a-day."

"It is? How should such as our Urdda get there, then, as already belongs there?"

The lady looked up at Todda through silvering frizzles of eyebrows. "I would ask you to wait," she said. "Until my man returns. Lord Dought, you know."

"Will that likely be this morning?" said Todda.

"I do not know when it will be."

"Within a week? A month? A year, even?"

"I do not know. He comes and he goes as he pleases. He do not keep a reg'lar calendar."

The lady lowered her gray eyes. The rings clicked and scraped some more. The dust sank in the air around her.

"I believe I know your man Dought, Leddy Annie," said Wife Ramstrong. "He is a smaller man, is he not? With a fine head of silver hair, and a beard he mingles with it over his shoulders?"

Why, the littlee-man! Urdda thought. Collaby—of course! *Saint* Collaby, that was what he called himself! They *were* finch, then, those rings of the lady's, and red-throat. *These stay good on a trade, where I come from,* he had said.

"I saw him just the other day, I think," said Todda, "did I not, on the Chambers steps? He has set himself to besting Hogback Younger now, I believe. Lord Dought is a great recourser to the law," she added with a smile towards Urdda.

"I . . . I am very sorry," said Urdda in a fright. "But I must inform you, my lady, that Mister Collaby, Lord Dought, is no more."

The little old lady's face came up, crossed by surprise; then wariness that Urdda might be tricking her somehow; then rage that she might, and fear that she might not. And behind all this, Urdda saw Lady Bywell waking, as if from a long preoccupation or misery; waking into this dust-cloaked room, into this life, into this situation.

"Urdda-girl," said Todda anxiously, "how did you come by such news?"

"He was killed by a bear. By that Teasel Wurledge boy as a bear. In that place, near to my home. And most of him eaten up. I saw it myself," said Urdda. "And my sister too."

"Your *sister* was et?" gasped the lady.

"No, my sister saw him eaten. She buried what was left."

"Buried?" This seemed to frighten her even more. "Oh greshus, no. This is no good at all." Lady Annie brought her hands to her face. They were like claws—or twigs, with the rings like galls swollen on them.

Todda gave baby Ousel to Urdda and went and knelt before the widow, laying her hands on the woman's arms. "Leddy Annie, what should we do for you in your bereavement? Do you use a God-man? Do you want a service read?"

"I have no one," the lady barely said. "I use no one but Dought. I am all alone in this fortune, in this house, in this town. He took such joy in his riches, while I"—she opened her eyes and looked at Urdda without seeing her—"I really could not care, when it comes to it. I never quite accustomed myself. I am only here because he told me I ought."

Wife Ramstrong rustled to her feet. "We should help Leddy Annie to bed, Urdda. She needs to rest from her grief."

"You are from that land," Lady Annie now said with intensity to Urdda. "You saw him often there?"

"I saw him twice."

"Was he a lord there?"

"Indeed, no. He was a nuisance and a thief."

"Urdda!" said Todda. "That is not kind, at this time."

But Lady Annie laughed, and wept. "Of course he was! A nuisance, a thief. He were probably stealing from the *bear*, some trout or honeycomb, that he killed him. An Onion's boy

218

to the end. Oh! Life is so long, and too hard, and then it ends so cruel and sudden!"

"I will take her upstairs, Urdda, before she is any further upset," said Todda. "Anders, you stay here with Urdda. I will not be long."

Anders moved solemnly from beside his mother's chair to beside Urdda's, and stood watching as Lady Annie quavered and clung on his mother's arm. When the two women had gone, he turned to Urdda. "We made the leddy cry," he said.

"I know. That was not very nice of us, was it?"

He shook his head, then checked his dozing brother. Then he went and sat in his mother's chair and swung his legs awhile, listening to the voices and the footfalls of the women on the stairs. Then there was quiet for a time, and then for more of a time, and he sighed and said pointedly to the ceiling, "She said it would not be *long*."

"Oh, there will be lots to do up there to make the lady comfortable, I am sure. Dressing her in her nightgown and bed-bonnet; putting her rings into a jewel box; stirring up the fire so the room is warm. Your mam might even have to make her some draft or tisane, you know, to help her sleep."

"Oh," said Anders desolately.

"I'm sure she would not mind us looking about this room, if we are careful not to disarrange anything. We would have to go very softly, though, and not make any fingermarks in the dust."

And so they were engaged in a slow, whispering tour of the furnitures and ornaments when Wife Ramstrong returned to the parlor.

"Oh, Anders, you must not touch," she said in the doorway.

"We are only walking about and looking," said Urdda. "Is Leddy Annie sleeping now?"

"Well, she is settled somewhat. She wants—" Todda took a

few steps into the parlor. "She would like *you* to sit by her, Urdda. 'The foreign girl,' she says, because you knew Lord Dought in that other place. She says you will be a consolation."

"I will?"

Todda took Ousel from Urdda's arms. "I think the poor thing had no friends but that dwarf-man," she said softly. "And he—well, I know he were not well-liked in this town, although his wealth brought him the kinds of friends that can be bought. But he were all this leddy had, and she says he did right by her. So her loss, you can imagine . . ."

Anders had appeared at Urdda's elbow. She rather wished he could come and sit with her upstairs, he was so grave and curious a child. "How long should I stay?" she said.

"Midafternoon, we will call in again. She has a woman bring her evening meal; perhaps then she will be comfortable to be left alone."

All day, then! Well, this was unexpected; Urdda had thought she would have a day with Wife Ramstrong, a day like yesterday, full of questions and surprises and the wants and games and squeakings of children.

Instead, she was ushered to a chair at the lady's bedside, and Todda rustled away with Anders and Ousel, and Urdda sat alone in the great cloth-swathed room, with the dust swirling through the solitary sunbeam that angled from window to floor, as Lady Annie sank away into sleep, curled like a child in the big bed.

But Urdda's mind would not stay still for long; even sitting alone in a bedchamber was exciting for her. Here she was, in the place she had suspected of existing ever since she had seen that littlee-man dancing vivid and enraged on the stream-bank, ever since Bear—Ramstrong-Bear, not that other silly—had flown into the nothingness off the cliff. And it was just as rich and peculiar as she had hoped and wondered. The people—Todda, who explained so well all the rules she must follow; Ramstrong, who discussed her situation so gently and at such concerned length; even little Anders—everyone had such depths and flavors; everyone had histories of their own and with each other! When she heard snatches of other people's conversations in the town, though she could recognize every word, she was rarely the wiser as to what they conversed about, their talk was so much a reference to bygone events she had not witnessed, people she had not met. This was the wildest, most curious-making thing—the size and suddenness of her own ignorance.

She sat long enough for Lady Annie's soft breathing to infect her with sleepiness. She got up from her chair then, and added a neat-cut log from the bucket to the fire, and yawned and stretched while it took. She picked up one of the lady's rings from the night table—one with a milky greenish stone—and held it awhile; it warmed, but did not spring to life as the robin had from the red stone in Collaby's treasure-pile. Then she sat in the window, pushing the lace aside so that she could see more clearly down the street into the town. Several people passed, or came out onto their steps and spoke to each other. Urdda kept the lace across the window whenever someone walked near, but when the street was empty she moved it aside and strained her eyes to see the orchardwoman waving her arms down in the market square, ordering her children about, or to see the wagons crossing in the distance.

She wondered what Mam and Branza were doing now. But then she remembered Teasel's talk of three winters having passed since she left home, and the wondering evaporated into confusion.

"Are you there?" a frail voice said from the bed.

"Yes, I'm here, Lady Annie." Urdda crossed the dim room to her side.

The lady's eyes shone like two little lamps. "What were your name again, girlie?"

"Urdda, mum."

"Urdda *what,* child? What is your other name, your father's?"

"Well, we have determined that it is likely Longfield. But I have never had a father, mum."

"Longfield? I hope not, for your sake. You don't want to be any relation to that no-good." She scrutinized the girl. "You haven't got the look of him, I don't think."

"Do you know him?"

"I knew enough of him to know I dint want to know more. He is dead now, and nobody misses him."

"Well, it seems we lived in a house that matches a ruined one here, that he used to occupy."

"Oh, I know the place. I used to live just up from there myself, 'fore I came into my money. So tell me, foreign girl, how did you transmit yourself, there to here?"

"I found the spot where that Teasel-Wurledge-bear came through, and I wished it strongly, and I pushed."

The lady looked very hard at Urdda. Then she relinquished her thoughts and sat forward, out of the pillows. "I done a terrible thing," she said.

She was not at all like a lady, with her hair all wisped like that and without her teeth. She was like a beggar-woman who had fallen by accident into this scramble of fine bed-linen, with a fabulous bed-bonnet landed by chance on her head.

"She told me not to," she continued, "but I went ahead and did it, and I made a mess I could not tidy."

It sounded as if her mind were still quite disarranged, but she spoke clearly—if a little whuffingly from her toothlessness—and her gaze was steady and bright.

"Who told you?" said Urdda gently. "What kind of mess?"

"That lady at High Oaks Cross," Lady Annie said, as if surely Urdda must remember. "She said, *You have powers; what are you doing with them? No harm, I hope.* And in the course of talking to her, I told her of that thing where I could make signs upon people and they would see their heart's desire. I arksed her, could I ever send them there, could I ever move them toords it? And she says, *Mebbe, but best not to. You can never know the consequences of such transmissions.*"

She sat, childlike again, and looked fearfully at those possible consequences, her face folded tiny around her toothlessness. Then she noticed her own mouth, and she reached to the night table where Wife Ramstrong had placed her teeth, and she clomped and clacked them into place.

"But you did?" said Urdda when the teeth were settled. "Against her saying?"

Lady Annie folded her ringless hands in her lap and glanced about as if someone might leap out from behind the hangings to scold her. "I sent Collaby there."

"*You* sent the littlee-man? I thought he got there by his own power."

"His own? Collaby had no powers."

"He didn't?" A tiny fist crushed frog-eggs to a shining pearl in Urdda's memory.

"No, his stumpetiness was the only thing odd about him. He wanted use of *my* powers. And once we had punchered through, he went reckless back and forth despite my warning him—because what could I warn him of? *You can never know the consequences,* said that lady, and I did not. When he described the place, it were nothing like the place I'd thought I were sending him. All them tall people? It must be someone else's place of their heart's desire, I thought. And I were afraid of what I'd gone and done, and I never did no more that kind of thing. Now you are here, and I'm wondering, is it yours, then?" She looked keenly at Urdda across the crumpled linens.

"Is what mine?"

"That place what you come from. Is it the place of your heart's desire?"

What could she mean? "I always wanted to come here," said Urdda blankly.

Lady Annie sagged.

"All people do at home is smile and smile, and be kind. They have no opinions, and never want to go anywhere or do anything new. It is terribly dull."

"Bugger. If it *were* your place, see, now that you are here, the punches Collaby made through would all be gone. That whole world would be gone, once you'd stepped out of it. But you don't reckon it were yours?"

"I don't know what you mean, 'place of your heart's desires.' And worlds 'belonging' to people. Are you saying that I lived in a world that . . . a world of someone's *mind*? That someone dreamed of?"

"Something like that."

"But . . ." Urdda held her head to keep the thought from popping it like a soap bubble. "Why am I real, then? Why am I not dream-stuff? Why don't I melt to nothing now that I am not in the dream?"

Lady Annie spread her wrinkled paws helplessly. "I don't know, my poppet. The state I am in, you might well *be* dream-stuff, sitting there and us talking so reasonable."

"I should perhaps find this lady, the one you met, that told

224

you not to do . . . what you did. She might be able to explain what has happened."

"Oh, I am sure she would. And be very cross with me too, she would." Lady Annie eyed the bed-linen next to her as if she would like to crawl under it and lie very still and hidden there.

"What was her name?"

"I think it were Miss Prance." Lady Annie bit her lip. "It were so long ago, and I got to calling her Miss Fancy-pants for a long time, I were so cross with her for spoiling what might have been my fun and profit. But Prance, or something very like."

"And she was at High Oaks Cross?"

"Yebbut she had come from farther, all the way from Rockerly, on some business, terribly important, oh-so-important. I were just a midge in her ear, an accidental dung-bundle she stepped in, that she must get off her shoe. She done that and left me by the roadside in my smell. Well, thank you, Miss Fancy, Miss Prancy. Off she goes down the road, in a hat that is like some foreign bird come alighted on her head and froze mid-flap. And would of cost a fortune to me, them days. Now I have so much treasure, courtesy of Dought, I could wear a new hat every day if I wanted, the rest of my years, with whatever bird, or a marmot or a satin rose or a gentleman's *boot* on it. And no one would laugh at me, were I to walk out to market in it, I am that rich," finished Lady Annie.

But then she looked out from her memories to Urdda's listening face, and all the puff and outrage left her. "Open the curtains wider, girl—Urdda. Urdda was your name. I can hardly see your face in here."

She watched from the bed as Urdda went to the window

and returned. "So, you is fetched up with Davit Ramstrong, have you? That is lucky, that you fell in their arms."

"They're very kind."

"Did she say that her man had *been* there, that goodwife, to where you come from?"

"Yes. For several months, when I was little. But he went through on Bear Day, so he was in the form of a bear."

"But a *different* bear et Dought?"

"That's right. Teasel Wurledge."

"Oh my Gawd. So many to-ings and fro-ings. None of it is good." Lady Annie sucked on her lips awhile, and then some impulse made her fling back the bedcovers and lower her feet to the bed-box. "Come," she said. "Bring me that house-gown and them slippers. Let us go and see if I am ruined."

She took a lit candle and handed one to Urdda. Then she led her down to the cellar, through a house that echoed around them as if all the rooms behind all the doors were empty. The kitchen alone was finely equipped, although the tarnish on the pans suggested that they had not been used in some time.

Three strongboxes big as coffins squatted in the cellar. Lady Annie set her candle on one of them, took a key from a chain around her neck, and unlocked another. "Help me open the lid," she said. "All that metal strapping weighs it down fearsome."

Urdda put down her candle and helped lift it open. Inside was just such treasure as the littlee-man had died protecting: bright coins, silver and gold; pearls such as he made from frog-eggs; and here and there a bird-stone, veined or mottled or a clear single color.

"Good," said Lady Annie. "That much is established, then: it were not your heaven. But what were you doing in someone else's heaven-place? When did *you* sneak in?"

"I always lived there."

The lady perched on the rim of the chest, picked up a smooth chunk of turquoise, and tossed it from hand to hand as she thought. "Oh dear, oh dear," she said. "What a horrible mess I have made."

"Mister Dought must have traveled there many times, to gather this much treasure." Urdda turned to the other two strongboxes. "Are they full of treasure too?"

"To the brim," said the lady glumly. "He were very naughty. And of course he fetched as much or more for himself." She let the turquoise fall with a *chink* into the treasure-chest, then brightened and sprang up. "Anyway, what I was about to say— help me lower this without losing my fingers—is, I were on the point of offering you a position, for I cannot have you burdening the Ramstrong purse when it were me—or Collaby empowered by me—that made it possible for you to travel here."

She stooped to lock the box, then straightened and took up her candle again. "Can you cook?"

"I can cook."

"Do you know about ladies, and how they comport themselves?"

"Not really. Only a little, from stories. But I can discover. Goodwife Ramstrong knows a great deal, and she also knows some women who work for that man Hogback, and other merchants."

"Good, good." Lady Annie had begun climbing the cellar stairs; her eyes were now level with Urdda's. "I will tell that sluttern what comes and does for me to take her slops and go. You shall light my candles for me every night. You shall draw the curtains, and open them of a morning. You shall bring me my bloom-tea upon a tray, like a lady, and cook me little lovely-things to tease my tastebuds. I shall have a lady's maid as

227

befits my station, just as Collaby always said and I refused it. We shall play at ladies together; we will stroll about the town, a lady and her companion. You shall have bed and board and . . . some money. How much is sensible? More than that cook, because you will be doing more."

"I . . . I do not know how much. I will have to ask Todda," said Urdda breathlessly.

"Yes, she will know. Now let us go and choose you some quarters from the many rooms I have, all knocking about empty, and think about how we will furnish it for you."

Urdda retrieved her own candle and followed the lady's brisk figure up the stairs.

In the spring after second-Bear left, Branza came upon two wolf-cubs, starving and staggering in the forest.

She brought them back to the cottage. "I cannot think what has happened to their mother," she said, opening her apron to show them to Liga. "Will they take goat's milk, do you think, or will it kill them?"

"It must be better for them than nothing," said Liga.

Branza went to their care with her usual diligence. Both cubs grew well at first, increasing in energy and playfulness and then in bulk and strength. Branza asked of a shepherd how he commanded his dogs so that she could tame her new charges to sit and lie when told, and behave themselves in and about the cottage, and come to her call or whistle when they were farther afield. But no sooner were they of an age to reliably trot at Branza's heels when they were not stalking and pouncing on one another, than the larger, girl-cub caught a fever from playing too long in swamp-water, and after a night's shivering and burning, she died.

"Oh, little one," said Branza to the brother as he pawed the earth in which she was digging the wolf-grave, "now you will be like me, won't you? Always missing someone, sister or sweetheart or bear."

She fetched the dead wolflet and laid her in the ground, and the brother went down there too, and sniffed all around her as if to assure himself she was positioned right. When he was satisfied, Branza lifted him out, and he sat, quite sober and respectful-seeming, as she pushed the earth in, and covered the she-wolf, and patted the grave flat.

For several days he did not understand that his sister was gone. Branza took great care to engage him in play just as much as the dead wolf had used to, and at the times when the brother and sister would have rested together she carried him about in her arms, or had him in her lap as she sat holding wool for Liga to wind, or only resting herself, noting the weathers as they passed across the window.

And from that time, the two spent every hour together. The wolf slept in the house, even when he grew full-sized, on the floor beside Branza's bed where she could reach down and touch him whenever night thoughts woke her, or bad dreams. And during the day he companioned her, whether she gathered or gardened, laundered or fished, snared, strode the hills and heaths, or wandered singing in the forest. He even sang himself, after a fashion, if Branza prompted him right, and in this, as in everything he did, he delighted her.

He was welcomed as she was when they went into the town. He would submit to pats on the head and scratches on the belly most willingly, and even would suffer some of the smaller children to ride on his back a few steps, held on by their bigger brothers or sisters. Branza was careful to keep him obedient when the market was on, and Wife Sweetbread sometimes gave her a piece of this or that meat to reward him with.

Others remarked on his fine coat and intelligent face, or greeted him as if he were as much a person as Branza herself—which indeed she grew to think of him as.

Liga, too, approved him. *Most suitable friend,* she called him, *for my angel child,* but only when she thought Branza was out of hearing. She too enjoyed to command and reward him, and to have him draped over her feet as she sat working in the sunshine at the doorway in autumn and spring.

Wolf was not nearly as close a spirit or as complex a companion as Urdda, Branza thought, but he was warmth and consolation. He was not nearly as mysterious and alluring as second-Bear had been, but then he was not nearly so troubling either. He had his touch of wildness, his fondness for howling to his fellows on still nights under a full moon, but in the main he stayed content to brighten their cottage, their days, their world, with his extra ration of beauty and youth; to come to their call and play when life grew overly quiet; to prompt them for touches and attention when either of them was tempted to regard herself as lonely.

Urdda reached the top of the tower before Annie did, and crossed to the castle wall. The icy air was not quite as still here as it had been below; its pauseless breath chilled Urdda's neck and hands and ankles, and made her eyes water.

St. Olafred's was almost silent below, everyone huddled at their hearths except the smith, from whose cozy shop echoed up his hammerings, like a dulled bell. The forest around was a vision of lifelessness, leaflessness—a black mist barely moved by the breeze—and snow rimmed the view, painted thickly on the distant heights.

Urdda's gaze fell, as it always did eventually, to the southwest beyond the town, to a curl of smoke there. Well she knew that it was from the wildfolk's fire at Gypsy Siding, yet her heart still wanted to believe that Mam and Branza were out there in the cottage among the trees; that the smoke was from the cottage chimney; that she'd only to run down the town and out along the road past the Font to join them there and tell them of her new life: of Annie and her customers, their ills and remedies; of Ramstrong and Todda and their families. Most of all, she wanted to tell about, and thus relive, the carriage ride she had taken with Annie to Broadharbour at summer's end to see the ocean's hugeness and flatness and wildness at the edges; to help Annie choose fabrics (such fabrics!) for her winter clothing; to buy herbs and dried creatures, ground horn and such, for Annie's mud-makings, which she had got up the spirit to begin again; to order furniture and cartage. To exchange, in fact, as much of Annie's wealth from the strongboxes, in as many different places as possible, for items of real and lasting value.

So I can bring you there, Mam, Urdda might say, shedding her shawl with the heat of the soup, with the heat of the cottage fire. *You and Branza both. As soon as I have got all her wealth exchanged, she's promised me, we will make some effort towards bringing you there.*

Annie muttered and puffed at the top of the stairwell. "Blemme, that's warming," she said, emerging. "Ooh, and just as well!" She pulled her cloak closer at the neck. "We mustn't stay too long up here. We shall freeze to the stones like a pair o' gargoyles."

She came and stood close at Urdda's side, pushing her chin into the breeze. "Gawd, there's a joyless prospect." Her sharp eyes in their nests of wrinkles took in the leaden sky, the mournful forest, the snow-white line, irregular, dividing them. "Look at that miserable streak of gypsy-smoke," she said. "They will be down there in their dark little dugouts of houses. I nearly starved out there myself, a winter or two. We must take them down a side of bacon, the next week or so. And some roots, and cabbages. Mebbe some wool blankets. They shared their scraps of food with me once or twice."

She shifted her teeth and noticed Urdda watching her. "I had forgot those people," she said with some embarrassment, "since I got my wealth. I had sat up here in the town like the leddy I am, like the only person in the world, until you come along. You nuisance." She poked Urdda's arm with her crooked twig of a finger. "Making me *do* things. Making me *see* things again."

11

Up from the millrace I chased those slutty girls—me, Bullock Oxman, as before would never meet a girl's eye. "I am Bullock!" I roared. "And I am Bear! Aargle-argle-argh!" Spirit of the spring, I roared and ran after them.

They crowded and screamed and funneled and flooded up Laundress Lane, around the well and the slap-rocks, their mad noise racketing off the walls. I caught the skirt of one and kissed both her cheeks black. "Eeh, you devil bear!" she cried. But I'd run on before her slap could connect.

Some went straight, but several swerved off up that cut-through to Murther Lane, behind the convent there. All I needed was for one to stumble there and they would all fall in a pile and I'd be the top one, slapping soot on them all.

And joy! even better!—there were Filip and Noer in the lane-top, rushing down, Noer in his hat that was a mask too, and covered his eyes.

"Eee!" went the girls, and turned back; then "Eee!" again, seeing the me-Bear blocking the lane-bottom. And wild they were, finding themselves trapped. Dodge and peer, shove and scream—it was like uncovering a nest full of rat-babbies all squeerming and squeaking.

I spread my arms to catch as many of them as I could.

As I pitched myself forward, there came a flash, as if someone had struck my mind with a shoe-hammer made of silver, or of ice, or . . . Then, as Filip and Noer cannoned in from above and pushed the whole ruck back, it came again; the flash, the blow, the cold and silveriness.

"D'ye have to shout in my ear?" screeked the maid in front of me, though I had no memory of shouting. And then, as we were still pushed and staggering, first Noer "Yowp!" and then close upon him Filip "Yowp!" they both said, like dogs clipped by the wheel of a wagon. And the juice of fear ran hot all through me, the juice of discombobulement from that strange silvery shock. What had it been? Stop a moment and let me think.

But there's no stopping of a Bear Day, not till the bakers stop you. We had to run ourselves to rags, dint we? And then Noer, half blinded by his mask-hat, blundered pretty much straight into their arms—out the end of Mittenhead I seen them *blonk!* him with a flour-bag and the white go everywhere. I were free to run on, though I almost wished it were me that had been blonked, I was so hot and weary.

'Twasn't long till another brace of them come after me. I put up a good last spurt of running, but in the end, of course, there was the *thwap* at the back of my neck, and the world shot white ahead of me. My nose was rubbed into cobbles and my head was rolled upon them, and Pader the pastry-man were bouncing the breath out of my ribs.

Then there was drinking, vast drinking, at the Whistle,

and I thought of nothing but shouting the next jibe at Noer and laughing, and singing all the verses of "The Thin Soldier," with the rude bits especially loud, and cooling the tip of my nose in the good white foam that quilted Keller's ale so thickly, which underneath was as golden and smooth as honey, as cold and bitter and pure as the Eelmother herself.

Then it was along to the mayor-hall for the feast we rolled. Oh my! There was foods I had never had in my life. There was shellfish brought all the way from Broadharbour that were like spindles and coin-cases that you hammered open for their white meat. So sweet! Sweet and rich, with sauces such as my tongue were startled and bewitched by.

Somewhere there, with the band playing and the wines also, somewhere in the tantara and the rataplan of the whole thing, I fell to sleep. Well, it were hardly surprising; I had been running most of the day, I had been overexcited beyond sleep for two nights before that; it was only to be expected. The feast went on, but it were a dream-feast, mixed up with the shine and flash of rushing cobblestones, the beam and stretch of faces afeared and thrilled, the whole day's memories tipped and stirred, blurred and misshaped in the mixing-bowl of sleep.

Next I knew, someone reamed out the inside of my head with a burst of noise and light, that was the curtains being rattled back from a window vicious with spring sunshine, each pane packed over-fully with warped and bubbled clouds.

I was in a strange room, a back bedchamber of the Whistle, and not one of the plain ones either. All us Bears were here: Dench with his hat and bear-shirt cast off, hairy chest aglisten; Filip and Noer still furred, Noer's eyeholes goggling but the eyes within them scrounched tight closed.

"Shaish, it smells like bear-farts and beer in here," shouted

Keller's sister, blocking out some of the window-light with the bosom of her, with the big arse, her hammy arms propped upon the arse-edges.

"It'll smell worse in a moment when I've brought up all my innards." Dench had his arm across his eyes like a saint in the throes of conversion.

Keller's sister laughed like thunder and thundered away.

"I hurt all over," said Filip softly, unmoving, his eyes closed.

I creaked up into a sit, and my hat came up with me. I grappled with it, my arms sogged and tingling from lying so long stretched above my head in sleep, but it would not come off. I pulled it harder, and a different which-way—I wanted more than anything to get air into my damp, flatted hair and to have a good scratch—but blowed if I could make it even wobble. Then I had to stop or I would have brought up my shellfish into my furry lap. Oog, I did not like to think of those shellfish now, their rich flesh and the sauces—oh, no.

"Have they stitched our bear-bonnets on us in the night?" I grumbled. "Have they glued them?"

Dench, hatless, gawped at me. Filip reached up and patted his bonnet. "Oh, I am still wearing it?"

"Stop griping and shouting, all of ye," muttered Noer into his blanket.

"By the Greshus Leddy, you are right." Filip's eyes came open. "I cannut remove it."

"Undo my strings." I turned my back to him.

"They are undone, Bullock," he says. "Don't you remember? Baker Sansom loosened us all last night. *Best Bears there of ever been*, he said."

"Take it offer me, then," I said to Filip. "I couldn't shift it in the night."

There was tugging at both sides of my back. "Yes, it is affixed to ye somehow."

"Pull it harder," I say. "Like a bandage off a wound."

Which he does. Which the pain was like nothing I've known before, and the shout I gave was similar incoherent.

"Jay-sus *feck*, Bullock!" Noer lifted his face a moment, horrible white and creased from his bed.

"What of they *done?*" I said, near weeping, and the grog spun in my head and my eyes bobbed on it like corks. "Oh, they have sewn it into my very bones!"

Filip, behind me, was interested. I could feel his breath; thank gracious I couldn't smell it, the state my stomach was in. "There is no glue," he said. "Put yourself to the light more, man. No, there is no glue and no stitching. It is only . . . joined. It looks just like you are part-skinned, that I would just have to pull a little and it would peel away from you beneath, like the skin off a sheep or something. But I pull and it does not come away."

His hat bobbed and tapped at my shoulder. I took hold of it and tugged. "Hwoor, stop," he said. "That is awful. They have done it to me too."

And now Noer had half sat up and looked ready to shoot flames out the red eyes of his mask. "What is *with* you, for gossake?" And he wrenched at his hat-mask and just about pulled his own head off, then lowered himself very carefully back to the blanket, a hand clapped over his mouth.

Dench laughed at him. "I don't know what is wrong with you that you can't undress yourselfs." He stood up, and off fell his bear-pants. He swung himself about in the fresh air from the window. "Bears that can't get bare. I never heard the like!"

"Netherless"—Filip plucked at his shirt—"it seems to be so."

Dench stepped over Noer's legs and picked up his folded trews from a carved chest. He pulled them on, watching Noer work on his hat and me on *my* skin trews, which were stuck just as fast as the rest.

"It makes no sense," said Filip. "You cannot pull it free, yet where'er you slip your hand in, you can *feel* it free and loose— there is my skin, all sweated, and there, separate, is the bearskin. Flap, flap."

I followed his lead and yes, I could push my fingers in all around the hat, but as soon as my finger moved on, the skin would be tight to my head again. "This is frightening me." I put my face in my hands. "How much of this is the drink? This is just the kind of dream I were having on all that fine wine."

Dench, reaching for his shirt, let fly a trumpeting fart. "There, pick the dreams out of that."

I flung myself across Filip on the bed and buried my face in the quilt.

Filip cursed. "Phoargh, Dench, what have you et?"

"I know," Dench said, pleased. "Who would have thought such a feast would ingender such foulness?"

"I will sleep some more," I said. "Mebbe when I wake again, I'll be unstuck."

But no one heard me; Filip had gone from under me and was wrestling Dench on the floor and on Noer, who begged them to stop or be sicked upon, they were doing such violence to his stomach.

I did manage to sleep, and for quite some time, going by the light when I woke. Noer sat on the far edge of the bed, looking glum.

"You are still a bear," I said. I was awake now; I was coldly sure of that.

"I am," he said. "And so are you, and so is Filip. Forever-more."

"It cannot be," I said, and commenced pulling at my sleeves and hat.

"Well, it is." He was bored of the whole question. "Not soap nor hot oil nor solvent poultice can break the seal. See?" There were welts and scratches all up and down his back-skin from the trying. "It is not glue holding it to us," he said. "It is some force more sinister. I tell you, we were about to be cursed as dark-arts-men when we went abroad this morning, and people saw what happened to us. The God-man were bent on it. It were only Filip's quick tongue that saved us. We were the victims of someone, he says, not practitioners ourselves. We are just helpless innocents, like someone slipped a potion to or something."

I stopped trying to peel off the skins; it was making me ill again. "But who, though? Who would *want* to?"

"No one can guess. Some spellmistress as wants babbies of a Bear, is the conjecture. Others tried saying we had brought it on ourselves, wearing the skins past midnight. But everyone remembers Blaze sitting in the square just a year or two ago, spinning tales in his furs all next day, and he shed them no difficulty."

Our eyes met for the first time.

"Is this real?" I said very softly.

"Oh, I'm afraid so, Bullock."

We sighed, me flat, him hunched over.

"I cannot think why this has happened," I said.

"I don't care why or what for. I just want my face back," said Noer dully.

"Yes indeed, it is worst for you. Bad enough the head, without around the eyes too. It does not itch, at least, or pain."

"No, it is just clamped there. As if we are in harness for something. Or in prison, in chains."

"We can move about, at least."

"You will find that is not such a blessing when you see the way folk look at you. Why do you think I am back here? I am enjoying this fine room to the last possible minute before the kellermistress is too unsettled by us and gives us the boot, out into the stares and the people crossing theirselves."

We both took in the rich bed-curtains; the carvings on the chair-backs; the fine rug, with Noer's blanket twisted and clumped on it like a battle-corpse.

"It can't be forever." I moved my finger around inside the bear-hat.

"They are working on Filip. Any moment they will burst in the door and say they have found the method."

But the door stayed fast in its hole, and no sound came from beyond it.

The three of us shifted on Leddy Bywell's step, listening for sounds from the other side.

"I hear she is terrible to look upon," I said under my breath.

"I don't care if she look like cat's meat," said Filip, "as long as she gets this skin off."

"I've seen her," said Noer. "She is ugly, as you'd expect, but only from age and a life outdoors, no worse."

"We should of brang clothes," I realized. "If it works and she frees us, I don't want to be wearing these foul things, however loose they are. They might stick again."

"Ha, how much did we wish for them, eh?" said Noer. "And now they are our curse."

"Shh!" says Filip, and we all looked at the door.

'Twas not a horrible face at all that showed in the opening.

'Twas a fair one, if foreign. 'Twas a *very* fair one, with bold eyes that took the three of us in—blink, blink, blink!—and then the fair face laughed! My gracious, had she not been so pretty I might have been mortal angry, but I were prepared, with her prettiness, to hear kindness in that laugh, to hear sympathy.

"Oh," she said, "I have heard of you!" She opened the door wider for us and, still smiling, ushered us in. "Oh my goodness, look at you," she said, almost to herself. "Come in here, sirs."

She put us in a kind of parlor, to which she let in some light by pushing back drapes even richer and heavier than those in Keller's bestroom. She was a fine figure. Was this the mudwife herself, spelled up young, very young, and beautiful? She had something of a witchlike way about her, I thought. She was very sure of herself.

"Please," she said, "take your ease. I will let the lady know you are here."

We sat in delicate plushed and gilded seats that had our furry knees up to the height of our nipples, and we looked about at the chandelier, at the heavy gold picture-frames, at the carpet like a blood-colored cloud underfoot.

"Gawd," said Noer softly. "And us dressed for the occasion."

With all the richery around, we were not inclined to talk much more than that, and so we sat trapped in our pretty chairs until slipperish steps outside and a croaky voice muttering set us struggling up to standing, and straightening ourselves.

The witch, the tiny witch, rustled in in a brocaded house-gown and matching cap, and just an ordinary grumma face, all wrinkles and nose.

"Good morning, gentlemens," she says.

"Morning, mum," says Filip, all humble, and tells our names. "We of come to ask for your help."

241

"Yes, I have heard of your perdicament," she says. She wore rings on her clasped hands that were like great polished extra knuckles. Her hair was plaited white and tight, the tail of it over her shoulder like some animal were crawling down her back.

"Let me see how the skin is joined to you." She had a fine set of ivory teeth in there, the very best that money could buy.

"You show, Bullock," Noer startled me by saying. "You are not so cut about with experiments."

Filip unlaced me, and then I turned my back to the window-light and pulled the bearskin aside as far as it would go.

The leddy disengaged a hand from her ring-tangle with a heavy clicking. Then her fingertip moved on my skin from the top of the join to the bottom. It was all I could do not to shudder. Was she fixing it now? Was it undoing? Was that magic shivering through me?

No, it was not.

"Hmm," she says. "What were you doing when this happened?"

"Sleeping," said Noer. "Sleeping in Keller's bestroom at the Whistle. The Whistle Inn, mum. Up by Garner's Lantern there, you know."

"Had you taken food or drink?"

"We had feasted at the mayor-hall, mum," said Filip. "For Bear Day, you know. We had shared from platters and jugs with many others, none of whom were so afflicted."

"There were a fourth bear there with us," I said, "what et the same as we did and could still undress at the end. His bear-suit came off just as normal. Just as it ought." I remembered enviously Dench swinging himself in the window-light at Keller's.

"So," says the widder. "When was it you were just you three together and no one else?"

We looked at each other. "Why, never," said Filip. "From the moment we met up, when Bullock herded them girls toord us in the twitten, to the time we discovered the skins could not be removed, there were always someone with us, mostly no less than six or seven."

"That's it!" I said, sudden enough to make everyone jump. "That's where it happened. In the twitten."

"Where *what* happened?" said Filip.

"How would *you* know?" said Noer to me.

"I remember. You shouted, too, both of you. We went through this thing, this . . . There was like a flash, like a *pop!* I went through it twice. I dint know what had happened to me, but then I forgot, in all the rush. I remember, because I took off my hat and wet my head just before that at the well, but from then until the time I tried to take it off in the night, I didn't attempt it again, so I didn't discover. But that were when—I swear it, dint you notice?" Because they were looking at me as if I had cracked.

"What are we supposed to have noticed, Bullock?" said Noer gently, dangerously.

"The both of you, you shouted. *Yowp!* you went, one after another."

"How could you tell one shout from another in that melly, you donkey?" He was angry now.

"Because it had just happened to me and there was a tone to it of . . . of . . ." Noer was looking as if he'd like to tear the bearskins off me and my man-skin with them, and then pour a barrel of lye over me. "Of fear," I finished. "All the other shouting were teasing the girls and encouragement one bear to another. This was different, and surprised, like you had been slapped of a sudden, or stung by a bee."

"And why is none of the girls stuck in their dresses, then—

unless they are, and are just keeping very quiet about it?" Noer looked his most withering, but at his elbow Filip was frowning, thinking. I was sure he almost remembered.

"I think . . . because they were not dressed up as bears."

Now Noer were uncertain. And Filip squinted at me hopefully. I was not trying any tricks on; I was just letting the knowledge bubble out as I thought it, with no calculation of its effect. They could hear that in my voice, my own surprise in the face of it. Their eyes searched around me, fast and flickery as if a cloud of flies were circling me.

There was a rattle outside and in came the pretty again, with a tray of flower-tea makings so fragile and fine, I almost said, *We're bears, remember.*

"Please, will you sit and take some teas," she says, and we girt fools folded ourselves again into the girl-furniture. With much grace and amusement, she juggled the infusing and giving. The weak sun shone on the cups and pots and strainers and the pouring, so it was as if she were arranging the very light and the shine. She nestled two morsel-cakes on every little salver against the cup before she handed it across. Was she in mourning? Certainly she were dressed very dark. Dark and shapely. A fine figure, as I said.

"Thank you, Urdda," says the widder.

Miss Foreign—Urdda—had brought a cup for herself too, and she poured it and drank from it, her eyes laughing at us over the rim, or so I thought. Well, we made a picture, did we not? We were cleaned of soot, at least, but we were still three growed lumps of men in bear-hats and filthy bear-furs, Filip in his boots, too, for the warmth. But it were not Bear Day, so the sense of the costume was somehow lost, and we were not rampaging about the streets but visiting a lady in a parlor. In our big hands, the silver cups-and-salvers were like dollware, with the tiniest ornamentations engraved upon them—was there ever an incising tool so small? Had she given us teas to make us more ridiculous? I would not put it past her, the bold miss.

"In the twitten, you say," said the widder to her teacup. "Which twitten would that be?"

"The one that cuts behind Hogback's," said Filip. "From Murther Lane down to the laundresses."

She pussed her mouth and blinked at that. "Hmm. And were you doing owt improper at the time, or lawless?"

"Well, mum, the whole of Bear Day is for lawlessness," said Filip. "We had been being improper on girls and women many hours by then; it were expected."

"Netherless," she says, "there must have been some type of infraction occurred." She looked around beadily at us. "And where there is infractions, there must also be appeasements, I am thinking."

"We were only doing what was arksed of us," sulked Noer. "What every other Bear have ever done."

"Appeasements?" said Filip. "Appeasements is things we can do, isn't they?"

"That's right," said the leddy. "They make right what is done wrong toords the powers that be. I am thinking some kind of sacrifice is in order here. And as this is all bear-related, it stands to reason a bear be slain, and the right words said, and the right parts consumed and offered up."

And that is how we came to find ourselves, early next day, high in the forest on Olafred's Mount. Noer had his bow, and with us also walked Sollem Archer and his son Jem; Filip and I, poor marksmen both, brought only knives for the skinning and removing of the pieces. The widder had told us we were to eat this and burn that, and boil the bones up so, and bury them white with the skull uppermost by Olafred's Tree—that pine, lightninged into a claw, where the story said the saint had sat in amity with all the animals, chief among them that famous bear, what is on all our pennants and insignias through the town.

Girt fools we looked, and I was glad we had left Wolfhunt and the other men in that lower camp, where the boiling would happen, and only had the Archers, for they were taciturn as we could wish, and seemed to find none of this amusing—even the thought of the bear-bounty this would earn them of the town. They had such eyes and ears, such noses—they were more limbs or extensions of the mountain, stepping silent upon it, than stumpers and grumblers like us townsmen, out of our place and longing for comfort and civilization.

A long, hard, dreary climb it had been behind the hunters, half in the dark and then less stumblingly in the dawn. As we neared the place of the caves, the air tightened with the Archers' attention, and I began to worry, and see shadows looming among the trees, and push thoughts out of my head about the size of grown bears and their ferocity in the early spring.

Cave-mouth to cave-mouth we went, and Noer and Sollem and Jem performed their examinations, and for a long, tedious while it seemed there were no bears to be had.

Midafternoon, because we were so chafed and tired and complaining, Sollem put us next a spring and took Jem off to search some higher caves that we could not reach comfortably. We sat and took bread and cheese, and drank of the spring, and did not talk much to each other in our disheartenment.

"We will be Bears forever," says Filip gloomily, stretching out on the needly ground.

"Sometimes it is days, when the real hunt is on," Noer

pointed out. "They go back at night to camp and cauldron, then out next day to stalk again, and next day and next, living on rabbits and brought provisions."

"That is no kind of life," said Filip.

Miserably we lay, in the bits of late sunshine we could find, and one by one fell asleep.

I woke, and the light slanted differently. A scent filled my head, filled my body, filled the clearing, that was all the green and brown of the world—all the blood, all the bone, all the wild water. I sat up. "Filip! Noer!" I whispered, for there was the creature we were after, a full-grown she-bear drinking at the spring. The scent rushed off her, poured from her fur and her lungs and richly from her hindparts, billowed out.

"Noer!" I whispered again. "You must shoot her!" How would he do that, close as she were, huge as she were, a moving mountain herself? I took another noseful of her, fresh as the first cider of autumn, clean as the first good snow untrod by man or beast.

"Craw Mighty." Filip had woken, and sat staring. "What a creature."

She swung her head to look at us, her muzzle all diamonded from the spring, drops in her eyebrows and frosting the edges of her ears. Her face was big as a hanch-platter. I tried to remember there was teeth in it, and a brain behind, and behind that who knew how hungry a stomach this early in the spring, after her long time in the underworld with only hell-moss and hell-fungus to eat? But I could not care. All I wanted was to see her closer, to bury my face and fingers in her fur, to have her enfold me.

Noer woke and saw her and shrieked up the slope there. Though I could not take my eyes from the jeweled face, from the breathing muzzle, from the amber eyes, at my sight's very edge I registered the foolish boy swarming up a tree. She can climb, you know, I thought, hoping all the while she would stay near me, seeing all the while how his shout had attracted her, and her face was turning toords him and I was losing her. "Stay," I think I even said.

"No," I heard Filip breathe.

But she was moving now, the bulk of her, the darkness. New suggestions and flourishments of her scent flowed over me as her limbs and folds opened and closed passing near. I put out my hand, and the brush of her passing flank was coarse fur only, but it left on my fingertips some oil or paint of enchantment, and I did not know—Should I put it to my mouth? Or rub it on my skin? Which would be the more delicious?

Noer clutched his tree-trunk as if it were a lady-love. He made very similar sounds to a lady-love himself.

"It's all right," Filip called out to him, all dazed. "'Tis a magic bear, Noer, and no risk to us." Which I was not at all sure of, for she had took some of the smell with her, and now I could see her gray feet, and remember her teeth and likely appetite.

Filip went after her, but I walked slower in my uncertainty. The three of them assembled themselves like holy statues in a grotto: the masked bear-boy crouched in the tree-fork; the hatted man and the bear in their furs below.

"Come down, Noer. She'll not harm you," says Filip happily.

But the cloud of her had already risen. Noer lay along the tree-limb and hung his arm down; his fingertips almost reached the nosing nose below. The bear upheaved herself against the tree-trunk, and he cooed and stroked her as if he were huntmaster and she his best hound. And Filip's hand was a pale star in the fur of her back.

Part of me felt great alarm, and part said to myself, Of course! This is the way it *should* be between man and beast. Certainly between man and bear, for we are twins in being separate from the general run of creation, she in her size and magnificence and us in the power of our intelligence to apprehend and to tame them. "Come now, Noer," says I weakly.

"Come now *what?*" He gazed into the huffing hanch-platter that was her face below him. And Filip, too, looked at me as if he were two year old and I were calling him from play to wash himself and sit through prayers.

The fear croaked in my voice. "Come away, the both of ye. There is magic at work here, and I don't like the feel of it."

"Well, *I* like its feel," Noer chuckled. "I like its feel *very* much." And Filip had both hands in the bear's fur now and was kneading, as if he could not fill himself full enough of the feel of it.

"Come along," I said, stepping back, frightened. I wanted to run at them and free them as I were free, but at the same time I longed to be trapped like them. But two are enchanted already, I managed to think, and the third must keep his head. "We have a *task*," I said, to myself as much as them. "We have an *object*. I tell you, if we did not have these skins on, we would be filling our trews at the sight o' this bear. You would be climbing out the top o' that tree and into the clouds in your terror."

Noer's face filled with the sweetest amusement I had ever seen on him. "Ah, but we do, we *do* have these skins. We are bear like her. We are the same creature now."

And Filip looked out too, blindly and dumbly at me, his fingers working in the fur.

I turned from them to catch me a big breath of plain forest

air untainted by this enchantment. Then I ran towards them and caught Filip by the arm, and I pulled on him. I am bigger than him, but he stood like one of the stones on Hallow Top, fast in the bear's spell. The air of the she-bear were stars and pepper and exploding dew on my skin; the little breath of her that I gasped as I dodged past Filip dizzied me like a wine, clarified me like a slap to my face.

I ran at Filip bodily, at the height of his hip so that he would be knocked away from her but not necessarily to the ground and requiring lifting. He gave a shout of disappointed rage, staggered, and fought me all the way, but I had surprised him, and once he were disengaged from her she had not quite such power, and I managed to force him well away from her and hold him down until he wept like a babby. I stood over him and gasped in the flat air—the tedious normal breath of the world, with no magic in it, no taste and no sensation but boring ongoing life, in-out like a water pump. I kept my back to the bear, knowing that if I saw her I would run to her in the longing for those other sensations, those greater.

"We must get Noer away," I says frightenedly to Filip.

"Yes," said he. "He should not have her while I cannot." So he were still under her power. I gave him a bit of a kick there, rolled him farther away from her. He squirmed and wailed.

"Let me c'llect myself," I said. "How can I knock him out that tree?"

"Ah," says Filip into the dirt. "I see it. I see it. She had magicked us. What were I thinking? Oh—" And he gave her a fixed look. "I can feel them both at once. Bullock, I am in love with her! In love with a bear! And yet not in love, yet I can see, at the same instant—" He put his hands to his face and tried to shake the thoughts out of his head.

"A branch." I cast about for one. "Big enough to poke him

down. Whereupon the two of us might—" But Filip was look-ing very mazed and useless there. I might have to do this all myself.

I found a branch long enough, but it was too heavy, even for me and Filip both, even supposing he came to his senses. "Curse it," I said. "With that one we might of stood right out-side the magic and dislodged him."

Filip was sitting up now, smearing dirty tears off his cheeks, taking deep breaths.

"Are you nearly back to me?" I said to him. "Because I am going to need you."

The she-bear's voice tingled the back of my skull and twan-gled my loins. Noer murmured back. Oh, it was horrible; worms of envy were crawling all over my skin. But the anger of that, I thought, might help me propel him out of this, propel all of us. Oh, where was the right stick? I was mad among the bushes, stomping and flinging about.

"I think . . . I think . . ."

"I don't care what you think, Filip! Find us a branch. Two branches: one to prod him out the tree, the other to whack the bear should she come after us."

"*Hit* her? With a *stick?*"

"I know it sounds outrageous, but the outrage is not real, Filip! It is enchantment, I tell you. Just pick up a good stick and let us have at the both of them. You *do* want to save Noer, don't you? Or shall we let her take him?"

He upped and helped me then, and we found the requisites.

"Now, take a good breath of the clean air," I says, "and we will run in. You poke him; I will beat the bear, for I do not love her as much."

"Very well," he answers me, all unwilling.

"Are you with me?" I say. "Because we must get on and

251

have Noer shoot her, and pull these skins off ourselves, and everything that goes with them, such as the love of bears."

"I don't know." Filip looked at her, half in horror and half in longing. "It sounds so daft when you say it, but the love of *this* bear, and only this one, to whom I would gladly . . . wed myself?"

I pushed him and pounded him. "You wet-shirt!" I screamed in his face. "Hear what you said! You are mad with this! Believe me, do just as I say! Take that stick there and save your friend with it, your friend who has been your friend since you was babs together, not just these last few instincts! Poke him down and drag him out of there, away from her. Do you hear? Do you hear? Will you do that?" All this I shouted over the sounds of her and Noer charming each other, which was like rats gnawing on my liver.

Then there came a thud, and Filip *oh'd* as if someone had punched him, someone stronger than me. He gave out at the knees, and his eyes shone disbelieving at me and then empty, and he fell at my feet, dead as a stone, with a crossbow bolt in his back buried up to the fletching.

"Sollem!" I screamed at the man-shadows running the slope.

"Nice work, boy!" I heard from Sollem as the two hunters broke from the trees.

"What are you at?" I shouted. "You have killed Filip dead!"

Jem stopped short of us, and gasped, and threw away his bow as if it were afire and burning him. Sollem ran right down, though—he had to see the deed close; he had to feel Filip's face, Filip's neck where the blood should beat, to believe it.

"Oh my gracious!" wept Jem. "Oh my lords and ladies. I thought he was a bear. Leddy help me, I have killed a man! I thought he were a bear going you, Bullock; I thought I were saving your life. Oh, but he looked *just* like a bear!"

Rage from the old unmagicked Bullock welled up in me. "How could he," I shouted, "with that girt bonnet sticking up off his head? There is the bear, *there!*"

But the she-bear was gone—and Noer with her.

"Noer! Noer!" And I ran after them. But I only had the one glimpse, far off in the forest, as they passed through the last freckles of sunlight before dusk. She carried Noer as a mam does her child, and he were wound around her tight as paint-stripes on a Maypole. They were gone in a moment, and only me left, with Jem wailing behind me and his da too distracted by the murdering to give the bear chase.

We brought Filip back to St. Olafred's that night, the Archers and the rest of the party not having the heart to continue the hunt, and I did not like to say, now that there was only the one of me, that weren't the unspelling of me still important? For indeed it hardly seemed so with one man dead and another abducted.

"We have probly lost the two of them; let us not fool ourselves," Wolfhunt says along the way.

I did not think so myself, having heard Noer and his lady crooning at each other, but I could hardly say, could I?—*No, he have eloped with her. It is love.* For no one who had not breathed the stars and the dew of that woman-bear would believe me, and I had had enough of people's scorn by then.

So I went to my home. Wolfhunt came with me to see me safe and spread the word about Filip, but I could not stand to hear him tell my mam and da. I went straight to my bed and there sought peace unconscious.

Mam woke me late next day with a bowl of bread-milk. "Here, Bullock, it's time to rise—you must go to the constable

253

and give him your account of the events. And Filip's mam and da too. They are eager to speak to you— Oh!"

The bowl thudded to the mat and she stepped back, wide-eyed.

"What is it?" Dozily I took in the spillage, and her face.

"You have gone . . . *furred* in the night, my son."

And it were true. My arms were much thicker-haired than yesterday, my fingers shorter, and my fingernails a little longer. And my face—such as I could feel it with these coarser fingertips—more than bearded, it was coated cheeks and chin, forehead and all, with short, soft hair.

While I felt it, shakingly Mam darted forward and gathered up the bowl. The milk were all gone, but the sodden bread lay there. I saw her look at it; I *heard* her think, as clear as if she said it, *Well, that's good enough for a bear.* But then she caught my horrified eye.

"I will make it afresh," she said, and hurried away.

I lay down again; I turned to the wall; I did not want to face this day.

Mam brought me more breakfast, and took the soiled mat, and cleaned the floor and laid a fresh mat down. "There," she said. "All's nice now. You sit up and eat, Bullock." But I would not turn my face and appall her further.

When she had gone, I ate, but I resolved to stay hidden, and so all the day I lay abed. But my misadventures got out all over town, of course, and the house filled up with the mutterings of people talking about my plight, and I must indeed face the constable and also Filip's da, who came to collect my story, though his mam was too grief-struck and frightened to look upon me.

"Ah," said the da, peering at me and patting my furry cheek. "You are in the same state as our boy. And we still cannot get the costume off him, to wash and funeral him properly. He will have to be buried a Bear."

I hung my misshaped head. It would be easier to have taken the quarrel myself, I thought, than to sit here onlooking Filip's da's suffering.

Teasel Wurledge came, and my, that were a disturbing visit. At first I did not want to see him, but then he sent in with Mam a message that something similar had happened to him when he were Bear last year, and in my hopefulness of knowing he were no longer furry-faced I allowed her to admit him.

Well, straightaway he started to laughing at me, quietly but most cruel, I thought. He tugged at my bonnet and laughed the more; he tweaked the fur of my forehead and cheek and went to swaying and soundless mirth.

"So how did you begone of this, Teasel?" says I, desperate enough to overlook the cruelty. "What did you do, to be back to a man?"

"Oh, I were much further along with it," he says. "I had fur all over me, and claws and teeth and extra size and— Big! I overtopped the head of a standing cart horse, I would say."

"I heard nothing of this," I said.

"I were magicked away," he says. "And in Magic Land I was this bear, three year and more, so no one saw me here; I had no such embarrassment as you. And when I magicked back, I were myself again, not stuck in my skins like you lads."

"Magic Land," I said. I was not inclined to believe him, but why would he come and spin me such a tale?

"Aye, and Davit Ramstrong have been there too, if you think I am pulling your leg-end. Ask him next time you see him. Aah," he says, grinning and shaking his head over me, taking in my sorry state like some old codger under the Square Ash who thought he knew so much better than me. "I had me such a grand time there. King o' the Forest, I were. And there was queens for me! Yes, 'tis true! As well as all the other, I were accoutred with a good big bear-pole, I tell you." He measures it out from himself with his hand, an improbable length as all such measurements are. "Which I put to good use, yes I did. I have to warn you, Bullock; bury yourself to your bull-sack in leddy-bear, you will never be satisfied with what you can get back here."

He were looking off dreamy, but now he checked to see how impressed I was—which was, to blankness, more or less. He had run away with all my sense, and I did not know what to think. I were trying very hard not to think of Noer and *his* lady-bear up there on St. Olafred's Mount.

"With their narrow arses, you know, and only that scrap o' fur, ha-ha-ha. 'Tis nothing like the real thing."

"So you cannot give me methods, then," I says, "to save me from this bearness? There is no trick to it?" For I did not want him to continue in that line of talk.

"No, I am surprised it is so partial. I were tekkin right away and made fully a bear. Then I come back, all man again, and here I have been since," he says with his hands out presenting himself, as if to say, *And what a man I am, don't you think?*

"Well," I said with difficulty through the jealousy—for the man-ness of him, not for his adventures up the queen-bears—"I am glad to see it is undoable, Teasel, so I thank you for coming and showing me that, at least."

He looked me up and down, pitying. "Were I you, I would rather go the other way, and be the full bear awhile." And he makes two fists and shows his teeth.

There was a knocking then, at the front door. I stopped him speaking more, signing that I wanted to hear who it was, though truth to tell I were deep fed up with peerers and gossips at me, and only wanted him to stop that smut-talk.

"I heared of some misadventure," croaks a voice, and a stick clacks on the doorstep.

" 'Tis Leddy Bywell!" I murmured, and it was a mark of how bad Teasel Wurledge had soiled the air that I found the thought of the woman kind and wholesome by comparison. "I must send you away, Teasel, and discuss the night's events with the leddy."

"For what?" he says. "Is there a tea she makes, melts the hairs offer you?" He bent around so as he could see up to the door, then shuddered at me. "She's a-tappin her way down here, and that Urdda-girl with her, the foreign one that thinks so much of herself. I'll be moving on." And he clapped my bear-sleeve, spared me a last snort at my costume, and were gone. "Mileddy," I heard him say, and "Miss Urdda," and the maid said "Mister Wurledge" most dutifully, but I could *hear* the leddy's wordless stare at him, and that made me chuckle deep inside myself. She knows a thing or two, that oul mud-wife, what's worth a greeting and what's not.

I was so glad to see her and be rid of that discomfiting Wurledge that in spite of my embarrassment of having her pretty maid see me, I sat up and suffered the oul witch to examine me, the state of my coat, and I told her as best I could how we had been so strong enchanted, me and my friends, that we would fall enamored of bears if they approached us.

"To kill one," I said, "I don't see how that is possible, the glamour they cast upon our minds. I know I could not have done what you bid us, had we caught her: eat the parts of her, boil the bones. You might as well ask me to eat my own mother. Or my wife, if I had one, would be closer." And I pushed away the thought of Noer in the she-bear's arms, for still I did not know how to regard that.

The widder stood thoughtful and unhappy-looking, the foreign miss attentive beside her. "I am loath to meddle any further in this," the old woman said, "and make things possibly worser still."

"Oh, please," I begged, "if you can help me in any way at all—" And pitifully I groped for her hand and held it in my awful paw-likes.

"I do not mean to say I will abandon you, Mister Oxman." She squeezed my paws and patted them. "I only mean, let me consider what has happened now. Give me time. Let me think what we might resort to."

"You *know* what to resort to," said Urdda to Lady Annie as they walked up the town.

"I do?" The widow arranged her teeth belligerently.

"You must summon that Miss Prancy, the sorceress from Rockerly."

"And why must I do that, Little Miss Know-all?"

"Because this is all to do with that hole in the lane behind Eelsisters' that Dought made through to my old world."

"Is it, now."

"And for which you are responsible, having put him through to that other place the first time."

The widow walked on, making great play with placing her walking stick at the precise centers of the cobbles. "Nobody has gone anywhere, in this instance," she eventually said. "Nobody has come from anywhere, as you did. I do not see that it has to be similar."

"It is all bear-magic, Annie. And it is exactly the spot—you know that. And what's more—"

"Stop bludgeoning me with your reasons, girl!"

"What's more, you naughty woman, there is only one cof-fer, a quarter full, left in your cellar, of enchanted riches."

"What, you are saying it is time to go through and fetch more?"

"You know I am not." Urdda nodded a greeting at a passing marketwoman. "You can afford, now, to undo what you did. That's what I'm saying. Ramstrong and I, we have exchanged your false wealth for true, and passed it out of town bounds as far as we could. One quarter-coffer, more or less, makes little difference to your well-being, now or in years to come."

Annie strode ahead.

Urdda caught her up without difficulty. "I know you are afraid."

"She will be so *angry*," said the widow under her breath. "I wonder, can I engineer it so as I do not actually *meet* the woman again?"

12

*I*n her great generosity—or perhaps in her pity for my furred condition, and her guilt at having sent Filip to his death and Noer to worse enchantment—the Widow Bywell arranged for me to travel, in her own carriage, with her own coachman, all the way to Rockerly town, where there was a woman called Miss Prancy who to her mind could help me. She also arranged for me to be escorted there, knowing how I would dislike to show my face outside of carriage or inn.

"Davit Ramstrong would be best," she told me, "but he cannot be spared. But his goodwife, Todda, has agreed to come and negotiate for you, and I think she will be most suitable."

"Will not I frighten her little ones, though, the hairy face of me?"

"Oh, they will not be coming. Urdda and I will share them with Davit and Wife Thomas the while."

It seemed to me a very peculiar arrangement, but Wife Ramstrong when I met her was entirely calm, both as to sharing a carriage with a monster and to leaving her bonny sons partly in the care of two witches.

The evening before we left, Filip's family buried him, which I felt uncomfortable either to attend or to avoid. So I lay in my bed while the bell tolled. The mourners carried Filip up the street outside, his mam and her women wailing and shrieking at the head of his procession. Every sound and thought was torture to me. Filip died in front of me again—fell to his knees, fell to his face. Over and over again he died, until the memory were burnt into my bones.

I woke, exhausted, to my mam's coaxing and lamp, with hardly the energy to cover my face with a cloth as I passed from the house to the carriage outside.

The journey to Rockerly was long, with two laborious patches of bog, one between Olafred's and High Oaks Cross and another deep in the forest outside of Rockerly. Wife Ramstrong did not talk overmuch, but she attended very closely to the passing landscape, having never traveled this far before either, and when we passed through the villages and I drew the curtains to cover myself, she kept me apprised of what was happening outside. She was the best sort of company, kind and thoughtful and comfortable in herself. I counted Davit Ramstrong a lucky man to have her, and those two sons lucky lads.

Rockerly was a dizzying big place, I saw from the hill approaching the town. At this time of evening, St. Olafred's would be a patch of shadow and sparkle on the side of the Mount; this town covered all of its hill and half the hill beyond, and had many more lanterns, regular disposed about its streets as well as in its windows.

It worried me to see them, thinking how many curious pairs of eyes each spark I could see represented. When we reached the gate, I hid in the carriage while Wife Ramstrong made inquiries of the guard, and it came out that there was no such person as a Miss Prancy, but only a much-respected doctress called Miss Dance, who lived at the top of the town. They gave Leddy Annie's coachman the directions, and up we went, past lane-ends very much like the lower parts of my own town, only busier for this dark hour, and then up among houses of more substance, past an alehouse where there was a fiddle-player and a piper and dancing, past a grandish house through the curtains of which I saw a man raising a wine-cup to a table of guests, past a chapel where Rockerly citizens milled and spilled down the steps from the candle-bright doorway.

Then the streets quietened and the houses grew even larger and straighter and better trimmed, and finally the carriage stopped. The goodwife alighted; I stayed skulking inside while she consulted with the coachman, knocked on the house door, was admitted, and disappeared inside.

She were gone a long time; it must of taken her a while to explain our business to this Miss Dance. Now and again I drew the carriage-curtain aside to look at the fine house, at the fern-fronds carved across the lintel and the blade of lamp-light angling between the red curtains in that front room. Nothing changed except, perhaps the third time I looked, I noticed a cat had come to one of the other windows, a dark one. It were not much more than a soft shadow, as still as an ornament there; but the eyes on it, catching the street light, glowed eerie-bright, glowed down at *me*, it seemed, though surely my twitch of the curtain had been hardly enough to catch its attention?

I didn't want to be looked at by cats any more than by people, so I did not peep out again. Eventually, with the quiet, and the tiredness from the long journey, and my longing for my own bed, I slipped into a doze, only to start awake, not knowing where or when I was—a whole night and day might have passed, I had been gone so utterly into sleep—when the good-wife rattled the carriage door opening it, and spoke through the crack.

"She says you're to come in, Bullock," she said. "Wait a moment, though; there's a rider passing. But no one else to see you."

She took me inside. The hall was cold, and empty except for the cloak-hooks and their burdens, and some dark wood chests either side with red cushioning upon them, where people might wait to be attended by the witch, I supposed.

We did not sit there, though. Wife Ramstrong calmly led me into a firelit room that was parlor and library both, with a table scattered with papers and packages, chairs of varying degrees of comfort before and behind it, at the fireside and nearer the curtained window, and only a few items of decoration about, and none of them ladylike: a dark painting of what looked like an assemblage of dead dogs; some kind of scarred battle-helmet on a stand; a mounted stag's head gazing across an imagined moor; and a vase of what looked like funeral flowers, which, when I looked closer, were made of silk only, and quite dusty.

"Miss Dance is very busy," whispered the goodwife. "She is cooking up some medicine in the kitchen and bossing a maid about papers. Sit here, Bullock, and we'll wait."

Miss Dance, when she came, was a tall spike of a woman, dressed darkly, fierce of face—though handsome with it—and swift of movement. The cat came with her, and was no less unnerving and attentive in this parlor than it had been at the upstairs window.

Miss Dance took one look at me and said, "I see. It is exactly as you told me, Wife Ramstrong. I could not credit it until I saw it. Forgive me."

"It is an improbable tale," said the goodwife.

Miss Dance came unnerving close and examined me, my furred parts and my skinned, and particularly the joins of bearskin to man-skin. She tutted and sighed, and her face grew ever more fierce. Finally she straightened, and walked away to the table, where a writing-desk lay open, the cat beside it being an ornament again. Miss Dance sat down there and tapped her fingers, frowning at me. Then she said, "Tell me, Mister Oxman, what you can recall of how you came to be in this condition."

This I did. I had never spoke to a woman like this before, who had no apologies for herself yet were not laundress nor night-girl nor gypsy. It felt very like talking to a man, except with a man there is always them little jousts going on and those little assessments, yourself against him. There were none of that with this person; now that she had the sense of my predicament, she were bent only on the matter of what I said.

She wrote it all down, very fast and scratchy, holding up her hand to pause me whenever she took more ink. At certain points of my tale she nodded, as if, yes, a shoe-hammer to the brain were only to be expected, or to see your friend carried off like a bab, like a cub, by a she-bear. Nothing in my tale seemed to surprise the woman. The cat, on the other hand, seemed not to find a word of it credible.

When I had finished, she set to thinking, and I waited, feeling offended in some way but not knowing how, with Wife Ramstrong beside me, hopeful in the silence. The papers-maid appeared at the door and was waved away. The kitchen-woman came, and was told, "Take it off the heat for now,

Marchpane." And after some more thinking, Miss Dance came and seated herself in the big winged armchair opposite us.

"I am not at all happy at this," she said.

"No," said Wife Ramstrong. "It is terrible events, one on another, for these Bears this year."

"And they smell, all these events," said Miss Dance, "of someone practicing outside their abilities."

Oh? I was all ready to be further annoyed, that she did not think me worthy to be Bear—which truth be told, I had to agree, for recent Bears is not of the quality the old ones maintained, anyone in St. Olafred's will tell you. But then I realized she did not mean *our* practicing—neither mine nor Noer's nor poor Filip's. Do not speak, I warned myself, and show how tired you are, or how dim-witted.

"They do?" said the goodwife.

"Indeed. It could be this Widow Bywell you have told me of. As I said, she is not known to me. There are several practitioners in that part of the country; it could be some wild-worker in the hills there. Someone who has not been instructed properly and is working against the natural interests, to gratify or advance herself. This is how it looks to me—though I see it only secondhand, and at some distance. I must look closer, to be sure, and speak to these others you have mentioned, goodwife: Misters Ramstrong and Wurledge, and the Bywell woman and her girl. And I must act quickly, before that boy—Noer?— meets with misadventure in the forest. And before you lose yourself entirely in bearness, Mister Oxman." Her face cleared. "St. Olafred's—I can ride there in a night." And abruptly she stood.

"Tonight, you are thinking of going?" I said, surprised, for it were night already.

"I will set out directly. You must rest here from your travels, under my roof. But do not show your face abroad in the town—my servants will tend to you, and to the widow's coach and drivers. And, again, when you take your carriage back to St. Olafred's tomorrow, Mister Oxman, allow no one to see you, if you please."

"Very well," I said.

But she was already gone. "Wife Marchpane?" she called in the hall. "Hilda? Have Gadbolt saddled up for me. Marchpane, we must leave our preparations for the moment." And her voice died away as she strode through the house, still issuing commands. The cat jumped down from the table, and with a last look behind and a meow of scorn, followed her out.

"Now, there is a woman," Wife Ramstrong said, patting my hand and laughing with the surprise, "who knows, and *exactly*, what is what."

In the autumn of her twenty-fifth year, Branza and Wolf walked up to Hallow Top, where the stones lay every which way in the heather. The wind was cold, but the walking warmed her, and she stretched her fingers and swung her arms to uncramp them after her morning's work embroidering under the window. Liga was still there, sewing; she never seemed to tire of it, never seemed to hunger for air and movement.

When she reached the Top, Branza climbed up to sit on one of the stones. The wolf leaped up too, and settled beside her, his head raised like a lion's on a crest, blinking into the wind.

With her heels kicking the stone's side high above the ground, Branza was a girl again, though she was full-grown long ago; though the years had accumulated behind her in their great pointless pile.

The wind was fitful, like an irritated hand scratching and slapping her. It hissed in the tall, dry grasses and hummed on and off in Branza's ears. It moved the grass unpredictably, tugging Branza's glance to here and to there with the illusion of things arriving, or darting about. She expected at any moment for that little crotchety girl with the basket, her dark sister, to round a rock before her and stamp into sight, her eyes full of thoughts and rebellion. She would be muttering, *Of all the daft things! When we could be in town by now. Always dallying and dreaming.* And then she would look up, and push her hair out of her eyes, and call, *What are you up there for, goose girl? Let us go!*

Urdda. Urdda. How long it had been since the name had sounded in Branza's mouth! How sorely she still missed her: the underlying fact of all her days was that she was absent a sister; that her three-corner family was broken, one of its corners lost, cracked off like the edges of just such stones as these by the ices of many winters. *How* many winters had Urdda been gone? Would it be ten this year, or eleven? 'Twas a hopelessly long time, whichever. And Branza was no wiser as to why than she had been that day, when Urdda had risen early and walked out of the house, and not returned for breakfast, or for the evening meal, or to sleep.

Things came, things went, and there was no sense to it. First-Bear had arrived, and then flown away to the moon. That littlee-man, he had popped up and stamped himself away as he pleased. And then Bear—that second bear, the one that Mam had not trusted so much—he had gone too, run away to nowhere, out through the back of his cave.

Wolf laid his head between his paws, and Branza dug her fingers into the ruff of fur at his neck to make his eyes close in bliss. Kick, kick, went her heels against the stone. It was all so long ago, but these were the last important things to happen to her, so she remembered them clearly, remembered them often.

Had Urdda stayed, the loss of second-Bear would not have seemed such a blow—he was not, after all, so noble an animal as first-Bear; Mam had been right in that. But he had been Branza's last connection with her sister. The day before Urdda left, while Branza had dug the littlee-man's grave, her sister had stood among the trees imploring that bear for something, plaguing him with her curiosity. Bear had arrived; Urdda had bothered him; and next day Urdda was gone. Had he answered her pleading, somehow? Had he told her where he came from, and how to reach that place?—for that was surely what she had wanted him to tell her. And had she got there, or had she wandered afar and lost herself—or died!—in the trying? If she had not died, where was she that was so much better than home that she could stay away ten years, or eleven, without visit or word?

These were the thoughts that always revolved in her mind. If she spoke to Mam about the lost Bears, or Urdda, or the nature of the world, Mam moved very quickly on to other matters. Ada Keller, and other women in the town, grew glazed-eyed or worried-looking if she asked them. Everyone seemed to want Branza to know exactly the little she did know, and no more.

Kick, kick, her heels went, like a tiny child's against a window seat. Dig, dig, went her fingertips into the warm depths of the wolf's fur.

"What would I do if *you* decided to go, little brother?" she said. "To one of those other worlds?"

He blinked vaguely and lifted his chin to her scratching.

Worse, what if Mam were to go—to walk into a cave one

morning and never come out again, to stamp her foot behind a rock and disappear? Or if Branza were to find herself in one of those places, with no Mam or Wolf, no Urdda or Bear—with only nasty littlee-sorts on all sides, laughing and cursing at her, swinging from her hair?

There seemed no reason why such things would not happen. This was the awfulness she met at the edges of her nightmares, the night going on and on all around her, the worlds and the possibilities multiplying, with nothing in place to limit their fearsomeness and hostility. From this locked terror she would reach out, her blind hand moving stiffly down the darkness between the tapis and the bed-paneling, to touch Wolf's warmth and constancy; to move her fingers in his fur, which was as good as lighting a lamp; to hear him half wake, and mouth the ordinary night, and resettle with a croon and a sigh to his untroubled sleep.

The moment she saw the woman at the door, Urdda knew life was about to toss her up from its blanket again, and who knew where she would come down this time?

"Is this the house of the Widow Bywell?" The woman was white-faced, with eyes bruised from exhaustion, but alert for all that, and determined.

"It is," said Urdda. She turned to the boy in the hall behind her. "Anders, run for Mister Deeth," she told him, and turned back. "You have ridden a long way, mum—our Mister Deeth will care for your horse. And how might I introduce you, mum, to my mistress?"

"Miss Dance, tell her. I am come from Rockerly."

"Horse!" said Ousel, wandering from his breakfast into the hall to see the goings-on.

"Just so, Ousel!" Urdda scooped him up. "You have ridden all the night, then, mum? Are you hungry? Will you join us at our meal?"

"I will not, though I thank you."

When Miss Dance had instructed Mister Deeth in her horse's care, she followed Urdda upstairs—for Urdda had seen at a glance that she was not to be put in the parlor to await the widow's leisure.

"Lady Annie?" Urdda poked her head around the widow's chamber door. "There is a Miss Dance here, come all the way from Rockerly to see you."

The widow's teacup rattled to the saucer. She looked as if she would rather leap from the window than face this meeting. But she only nodded, fearfully, for Urdda to show the lady in.

Miss Dance wore costly riding clothing, odd, severe, dark, and absolutely silent in its movements. Her authority clothed her in another layer of darkness and mystery. Lady Annie quailed at the sight. "Stay by me, Urdda," she said. Suddenly she seemed a child, her own clothing fussy and overorna-mented. "You have no objection?" she said to the visitor.

Miss Dance glanced quick and fiercely at Urdda and Ousel. "Of course not," she said. She crossed the room and sat down uninvited. She scrutinized Lady Annie as if she had just forked her out of a stewpot to check whether she was tender yet. "But you and I have met before!"

"I believe we have, miss. Many a year ago it were, miss, but I do recall you, yes I do. At High Oaks Cross, it were, at the market there, by Wife Matchett's powders-stall . . ." She fin-ished in a whisper, her gaze on the knot of ring-stones in her lap.

"High Oaks Cross, was it? Maybe so. I seem to recall our

270

having words, yes. You were not so well placed in society at that time, I think."

"No, miss. I were but a little hedge-doctress, and no more." The widow made herself littler in her seat.

The silence was charged with the forceful woman's thinking. Urdda looked up from occupying Ousel with his wooden animals on the floor. Miss Dance was so handsome, so serious! Her strange dress must be exactly correct for the exotic place she hailed from. Rockerly! She, Urdda, must see that place someday, where women dressed so beautifully yet so plain, and rode about alone. No one would dare spit upon this woman, or call out at her. She had a different kind of boldness, a strength that did not defy that of men so much as ignore it, or take its place without question beside it—Urdda wanted some of that boldness.

Miss Dance released an impatient breath. "Judging from other information I have gathered this morning, you have done what I expressly told you not to do."

Annie's forehead drooped an inch towards the rings.

"You have given someone their heaven. Or tried to. And maybe half succeeded. That is the feeling I gain from this, from what I have seen."

Lower still sank Annie's head. "Please, miss," she said, "what is it you *have* seen?"

"A furred lad, that cannot shed the bearskins he put on for your Bear Day feast," said the lady. "This wealth around you, very suddenly got, so people say. And two men, I have heard, who stumbled on a heaven in error and languished there, not knowing how to return."

The mudwife now was panting, her whole small frame atremble. Ousel looked up at her curiously, a wooden sheep in each hand. Urdda sat forward with her hands stretched out to distract him, and promptly he handed her a sheep. "Seeps," he whispered, then handed her the other. "Nudder seeps."

"I did send him there," the widow said in a low, frantic voice. "And he died there and was et."

"Who was et?" said Miss Dance, as if this were the most sensible conversation in the world.

"My friend Collaby Dought. My old friend from Onion's days, my fellow orphan." She looked up at Miss Dance with tear-bobbled eyes, and her ring-bobbled hand groped out towards Urdda, who dropped one sheep in her lap and clasped it. "Honest, I meant no harm, only to rescue him from his troubles."

Slowly, Miss Dance sat forward in her chair and fixed a gaze on the widow. Then she murmured, thrilling Urdda with the sound, "Who did you think I was, Annie, when I told you not to meddle there? Some busy-biddy like yourself?"

"I did not know, I did not know, miss. I can—" A gulp interrupted Annie. "I can see now that you are a person of consid'rable power. Honest, though, when I first met you, I were but a foolish maid—"

On the floor, Ousel took up a wooden chicken and clucked softly.

"It was this Collaby Dought's heaven, then?" said Miss Dance now, more sharply. "But how can a man die in his own heaven?"

"Oh no, miss! Dought's heart's desire was all stumpets like himself. The place he went, he never met a single littlee. Only girt lumps, he said, same as here."

Miss Dance sat silent, an expectant thundercloud.

"That place," said the widow unwillingly. "That is, Urdda

and I have discussed it, haven't we, Urdda? And we think, perhaps, though we cannot be sure . . ." But in the face of Miss Dance's disapproval, she could not go on.

"We think it is my mother's place," said Urdda. Her voice was a surprise to both ladies—and to Ousel, who in a moment of doubt held the chicken to his chest. Annie let go of Urdda's hand and watched her nervously.

"My mother, Liga Longfield," Urdda said, with some satisfaction at knowing the name. "It is the world as my mother would have wanted it, for us all to be safe in, her and Branza and me—Branza is my sister." She accepted Ousel's chicken and looked up at the two ladies. "It is quite like here, only simpler, with all the cruel people taken out, all the rudeness and suddenness, and much of the noise and bustle. Ale and spirits also. And the coin and jewels, and much of the commerce involving them, too—though Lord Dought seemed to find plenty there, when he visited."

"You have been there too?" said Miss Dance.

"I lived there all my life, until a year ago, when I came here."

"All your life? But you cannot have been *born* there. Well, you cannot have been *conceived* there, to travel here as more than a phantasm."

"I cannot?" I knew it! Urdda thought. I knew I belonged here, even before I properly knew this place existed. "Then my mother must have taken us there—me and Branza—when we were but babbies."

Miss Dance touched fingertips to her temple and forehead, and closed her eyes a moment, resting Urdda and the mudwife from the sight of her intelligence. "So your friend Mister Dought, Annie—he has died in this girl's mother's heaven?"

273

"Indeed," whispered the widow stringily.

Miss Dance glared. "Was it *you* that sent the mother there?"

"No!" The little old woman reached out again, and Urdda spared her a hand to clutch. "It were not me! I never met the girl! I only ever sent Collaby through—and since then I've done nothing of actual spelling, not even looking at fortunes. I only herb and heal now; Urdda will confirm it. I took up those harmless things again, close on her arrival here."

"Do you know the sorcerer who did send the mother?"

"I do not, Miss Dance. I don't know of anyone with powers but myself and you. And Gypsy Tross, what taught me all my herbing—but she's long dead."

"Very well. Now, you say the man Dought was eaten in that heaven?"

"I believe so. Urdda saw it. Et by a bear."

"Et by Teasel Wurledge as a bear," said Urdda, handing a sheep back to Ousel, "as went from here to there on Bear Day, a year back last February—that is, in this world's time. Three winters ago and more, by home's time—if you believe Teasel, which you may not want to."

Miss Dance nodded, closing her eyes again. "So you destroyed the key-joint, mudwife."

"I'm sorry?" whispered the widow.

"The factor, the mechanism, the *piece*," said Miss Dance in a voice that positively crackled with frost, "that keeps the times aligned between here and a heaven."

"I did?" The widow's voice was a dry squeak.

"Have any remains been retrieved?" snapped Miss Dance.

"Pardon, mum?" said Annie.

"Bones, hair, clothing—has any part of the dead man been brought back?"

274

"Nothing, mum," muttered the widow.

"Although . . ." Urdda glanced at the women and then at her lapful of animals. "Although quite a lot of him would have come back absorbed into Teasel, I suppose."

Miss Dance cleared her throat. "And before he died, am I right, Mister Dought brought back jewels from Liga's place?"

"Yes, stones such as these." Annie let go of Urdda's hand to turn her rings in the window-light. "And coin, coin in abundance—gold and silver. As much as he could carry, every time."

"How *many* times did he pass across?" Something like dread inflected Miss Dance's voice.

"I would not know," admitted Annie, "for I think he did not always tell me. He knew I were worried about the effects—"

"Approximately, though?"

"Four? Or five—that I knew of, as I say."

"Always by the same perforation?"

Lady Annie sank back ashamed again. "I don't believe so," she said softly. "I believe he made several . . . puff'rations."

Miss Dance abruptly stood and went to the window. "You have set me quite a task, mudwife," she said with studied gentleness, to the glass, to the street outside.

"Puss!" said Ousel joyfully, and held a wooden cat out towards the sorceress.

"I told him he ought not," said Annie. "I only really authorized that first puff—the first time he went through."

Miss Dance turned at the window, but the other side of her was no less focused and terrifying. "I would have you tell me, Widow Bywell, *exactly* how you achieved that first perforation, if you please."

"Puss!"

"Show me the puss, Ousel," whispered Urdda, and put out her hand. Doubtfully he placed the wooden cat in it.

"It were a long time ago," murmured Lady Annie, "to go remembering everything."

"Nevertheless, I must have all the details, if I am to undo this mess you have made. Here, this will take some time." From the saddlebag she had left in a chair by the bedchamber door, she fetched writing kitment and a small canister, which she handed to Urdda. "Would you brew up three goodly pinches of this to a wine-cup of water for me? Don't fear," she added at Lady Annie's gasp. "There is no power in it—it is only to keep me alert, for I have had no sleep, and I've much to do today. I can trust you, can I not, to give me a full account of your activities in this matter without my using potions or powders on you?"

"Indeed you can," the mudwife said humbly.

"Then we will begin." Miss Dance sat at the table by the window and began unpacking the kitment.

Urdda took the canister, swept up Ousel and his cat, and withdrew.

Anders was on the stairs. "Who is that lady?" he whispered as soon as the door was closed.

"That is a wise-woman, and a very powerful one, I am hoping," said Urdda. "Come, we must make her her special tea so that she can continue to be wise."

"She has a fine mare," said the boy, words he had borrowed from Mister Deeth.

"Oh," said Urdda, beaming at him as he followed her down, "she has a fine *everything*!"

"You would not think it so exhausting, would you," I says to Wife Ramstrong, "to sit in a carriage all day and watch the country pass?"

"Oh, there were a hill-climb or two," she said. She looked as fresh as if just woken. *I've two babs and am cooking up a third,* she'd laughed to me earlier. *This is like a resting-cure to me.* "And a spot of clambering around the muddy parts. And just the excitement, of strangers and strange places—that tires a person, two days of it."

"All that way," I said, looking out at the streets of St. Olafred's, which shone with drizzle and lamplight in the dusk, "for how long a conversation? And now the woman is right here anyway. We might have just summoned her with a message on paper."

"Oh, that would not have compared with the sight of you in your predicament."

" 'Tis true," I glummed, "I am an inspiring object."

"You are." She laughed kindly.

The goodwife came with me to my father's house, and saw me in, and told my mam and da the gist of what had happened, the good woman. When she were gone, though, there was no disguising the looks of my family as they inspected my beastishness.

"I thought she would magic it all off of you," says my brother Millwheel.

"I am hoping indeed that she will," I says, testy in my own disappointment, which I had not really felt until then, so strong had been my faith in Miss Dance from the effect of her personality. "But it is not a simple thing."

"Why, what's she up to, that witch? Did she want money off you? Is that it?"

"Hush, Mill," says Mam, but Mill went on expecting an answer.

"She is finding out the story in its entirety," I told him. "Ramstrong is in it, and Teasel Wurledge, and the widder, and she have to speak to each to get the fixings."

"Just like a woman—all gab and no go." Mill yawned noisily. He's enjoyed my being gone, I realized, and now he is cross with me for returning. He might be rather glad were I never released from this fur and these skins, leaving him the eldest able son, lording it over Hamble and the others.

"Are you hungry, Bullock?" says Mam, covering her own feelings with kindness.

"No," says I. "I will only wash and sleep, I think. I et well these two days courtesy the widow, Mam, don't you worry. And that Wife Ramstrong, she looked after me near as good as you would of."

I would have gone and kissed her had I not been worried she'd shrink from me, from my furry face. It was good to see her littleness, and my da's blustery look, and my lounging brothers. Home is home, no?—whatever layabouts you live with, whatever tempers and timidities. I was glad to glimpse them, and glad to go to my own bed among them, with the right smell and the right hollows holding me, and no more carriage-noise rumbling through my head. I tried not to think beyond that, but only to rest and be hopeful.

"Well, this is as close as we can be without drowning," said Lady Annie beside the swift-running stream. "But it were summer then, and the water were just idling down the middle there. That messiest willow there, the one most hung about with offerings and wish-cloths—we were in the stones below that."

Miss Dance, clearer-eyed from her night's sleep, stood, hands on hips, and surveyed the wide stream. "Very well," she said, and examined the bank around her as if hunting out a good flat stone to skim. "It would be best if you all stood quite well back from the bank," she said absently.

"You have no herbage?" said the widow. "Shouldn't we build a fire?"

Miss Dance returned from a distant place in her mind to raise her eyebrows and then—wonders!—to laugh. "Oh, you are a wicked woman, mudwife," she said.

"Why is she wicked?" said Urdda.

Miss Dance shook her head. "Using matter for such matters. No wonder the key-joint cracked. No wonder the times have slid out of place."

"Well, I weren't to know," said the widow.

"Had you asked, I would have been pleased to tell you," said Miss Dance, "rather than have you cause such damages. Back," she said, and pushed her strong slender hands at the little group around her.

They stood back in a row: Todda and Ramstrong, each with a son in their arms; and the widow beside Urdda, her expression a strange cross between alert and offended.

"How will she do it, then," Urdda whispered to her, "without all your preparations?"

"The way it ought be done, I persoom. I've no idea."

Miss Dance stood very still and straight, facing the water, seeming deep in thought. After a time, Anders whispered to Ramstrong and was reassured that soon something would happen, but the rest of them watched motionless, trying to listen through waking-forest sounds and the stream's rushing, and to see through the predawn dimness to that other place, to that sunny place or that snowy.

Urdda sensed it begin, just in front of Miss Dance. There was nothing to see, but—just as when Urdda herself had pushed through the cave wall into the twitten—a strong, sharp smell obtruded of something catching fire, fur or moss or rotten wood or feathers. And everything loosened and swarmed. Now

279

Urdda could not see clearly what was stream-shine and what air-shiver, at the forwardest reach of Miss Dance's arms.

The sorceress spoke, but Urdda could not hear the words. She went to the waterside, where she could read Miss Dance's lips without impeding her work.

"Time is *racing* by in there," said the woman. "This will take strong intervention. Can I maintain any kind of form, I wonder, as well as realign the times?"

Miss Dance watched the movement of things Urdda could not see—although she thought she could almost—*almost*—sense them, in the movement of the air near the woman, in the fine skin near the corners of her eyes and mouth.

Then Miss Dance pushed her hands into the instability so that they became unstable also, like hands viewed through misted window glass. She commenced whispering, and she continued to whisper, with a fixed look and with tremendous tension accumulating in her frame. The shape of her skull began to show through the flesh of her face, as if a strong wind were pressing on it. The stink of sorcery built steadily; they would all soon catch fire with it, Urdda thought.

Whispering, whispering, Miss Dance took the slowest forward step imaginable. Her face blurred, and the front of her body smoked darkly.

The wolf woke Branza, touching his cold nose to hers.

"What is it, my beauty?"

He whined very slightly.

She sat up and swung her feet to the cold floor, and he made way for her and stood watching, stepping from paw to paw.

"Ah, the impatience!"

She went to the door and opened it. The cold autumn air flowed in. The wolf ran out, paused, then looked back for her.

"But the sun is barely up!" Not even the very tips of the highest trees were yet sparkling. The shadowy wolf loped away a few paces, back a few paces, and whined again.

"Truly? Wait, then, while I make myself seemly." She returned to her bedside and there quickly dressed, and combed out her pale hair. Liga slept on behind her curtain, breathing steady and warm.

"Where are we going?" Branza said to the wolf, closing the door behind her. She followed him under the lightening sky into the forest, replaiting her hair as she went. "What have you heard or smelt or sensed in your bones, wild lad?"

The wolf kept on very intent and steady. He did not come back for her, but sometimes he waited while she caught him up. "Where now, beautiful? Around the rise, eh? Very well."

Through the forest towards the heath wolf and woman passed, in the first quiet of the morning, while all the birds stirred and questioned in their nests and roosts. The branch-work above and around them was black with the night's rain, and the remaining unfallen leaves lit the canopy yellow and rust before opening it up to the twig-laced sky. Branza loved all seasons, and each one's creatures and weathers and actions, whether of blossoming or rot, of flaring or fading color. She could not be happier than she was now, following her friend—almost her child, she had found him so young, and attended him so long—through the trees on his animal mission.

He paused again and did not run out onto Hallow Top as he usually did. Branza came up beside him, and stood silently there. Out in the pre-dawn, in the rabbit-nibbled grass there, something shone, and the wolf gazed at and was stilled by it, and did not want to approach.

"What is it?" Branza stepped out of the forest's cover and walked forward slowly.

A silver pail shone there, like a milk-pail, only there had never been a milk-pail so new and bright, mirroring everything around it. Some tool's handle, also silver, leaned inside it against its rim, and in the grass nearby—was it an insect-swarm, a cloud's shadow? No, it moved too sprightly. Something *danced* there, teasing Branza's eye.

She crouched a short distance from the pail, focused hard on the movement. She was almost sure that it was a shadowy cat. But was it a tiny kitten, leaping and darting at its whim, or an older cat, more sinuous and sly?

She stood again; the cat-thing did not retreat. Inside the silver pail leaned a silver trowel, the most inviting thing. Its handle would exactly fit Branza's hand. And the shadow-cat pawed the ground, drew the same circle with its undulations, patted the ground again.

"Oh, this is where . . ." Branza glanced around at the forest frowning over her, at a fallen standing stone slumbering on the hilltop. This was where they had first met second-Bear, she and Urdda. This was where Bear had torn that nasty manlet to pieces and eaten him.

She took up the trowel. Its edge gleamed fine as a fresh-honed cleaver's. *Pat, pat*, went the kitten-cat's dark paw on the ground. Branza knelt and began to dig while the shadow frolicked and purred around her hands.

Liga was crouched by the garden when she was overtaken. Whatever it was, it lifted every hair on her body, goosefleshing her almost to painfulness. She half stood. What is happening; am I turning into a bear? she wondered.

And she was poised there, bent all unnaturally, when she saw the gleam of Branza's hair in a shaft of morning sun among the trees. She is a witch! Liga thought, because the fear, because the goosefleshing, seemed to flow from her daughter's figure, rendering her movement sinister. What will she do to me? She will question me, and force it all out—she will ruin everything, undo all I have worked for.

Liga found herself in the warm, bready air inside the cottage, the door gaping dangerous behind her. Her hand was on the chimneypiece, as if she would climb up inside it as she had done the other time.

But that was impossible now: the fire was strong in the hearth, and the bread was baking there in the oven. And her skin was crawling, rippling—it would lift right off her bones! She must not entrap herself again. She had time—*just* enough, she thought—to slip out the door and run for the trees behind the house, before Branza arrived, and whoever, *whatever*, was with her.

She hurried out of the house again. Branza was not yet in full sight, but under the arbor a beast waited—a big dark cat, was it?—its shoulders eager and its head low, a fire-stink flowing from its fur.

Liga slipped along the front of the house and ran across the grass. The cat would thud into her back, with its claws and its fur; it would only need to take one leap, the great vicious thing.

She reached the trees, but they would not have her. There were more springy branches than first appeared, and gently they threw her back into the house-clearing. She staggered, but did not cry out. She glanced back, and could see neither arbor nor cat, but only the slim candle flame of Branza emerging from the forest's edge, carrying some awful, shining thing, bending to put it down, to conceal its shine and its awfulness behind a tree there.

"Mam?" Her tall, fair daughter came sunlit towards her.

Beyond Branza, at the house-corner, the cat-thing loomed and lurked, its head there, its shoulder, its hideous looping tail.

"What has it done to you? You are in its pay, daughter, under its beguilement."

"Mam, Mam, hush!" Branza came to her, carrying nothing; reached for her and drew her from among the branchlets; held her against her familiar frame.

Through wisps of her daughter's white-gold hair, Liga watched the cat approach, and nothing was reliable—neither her skin's sensations nor her sight's impressions, nor even the movements of her mind. Her thoughts would not travel in a line, but flashed terror, reassurance, the threat of Da, the chimney-smoke, the sun in the last leaves, the crawling crawling of her flesh, of her stomach, the animal crossing the grass like a black flame, the awful object Branza had hidden like a wound throbbing unpleasantness out into the forest-scape.

"Make it go, Branza!" She hid her face in Branza's shoulder, feeling the animal flow past into the trees.

"Look, Mam—it wants us to follow!"

Now, behind Branza, Wolf moved doubtfully towards them in the grass. Ahead, the cat—for a moment it was only a cat, and Liga saw what her daughter saw: the intelligent glance, the fine white teeth as it summoned them with a meow, the alluring tail. Then it bulked larger, though, and the meow turned to a baying in its throat, and it must crouch and force its way along the path under the trees.

Branza took Liga's hand and followed the cat, and Liga could feel her daughter's excitement and determination through her fingers. "Only because an animal is leading you," she said, glancing behind. The wolf was trailing them; she met his mild gaze. "Make her see sense," she commanded him, not knowing anymore what could be commanded and what must be yielded to.

They reached the stream. The vast-cat, swelling and shrinking, sometimes as solid as a horse or cow, sometimes as faint as mist or zephyr, led them along the path, down past the rapids to the flatter ground. There it bounded away and back again, and now the awful thing—a highly polished pail full of dirty bones, and the two jewels—*her* jewels, Liga's! The monster must have uprooted the bushes at her door—was momentarily in its jaws. Then the cat was on the streambank, beaming out danger. Liga backed away from it, crying out to Branza. Water swirled around her ankles. A rushing blotted out all other sounds; a burning stink obscured the forest smells, the water smells. The cat curled its tail—which was part of the rushing stream now, part of the smell—around its tree-trunk legs, across its tree-root paws. It nodded, satisfied, and Branza's wolf was tiny in its branches, between its ears; he was no longer a wolf but a tiny, brittle bird, blue, white, and unlikely, piping on the cat's head. And then all was darkness, and rushing, and stinging heat, and only Branza's hand kept Liga from flying to pieces.

13

$\mathcal{J}$ woke to the groaning of a distant cart at the bottom of the town. It was still dark, but the air was all wakeful, and when one of them Strap children ran frantic along the lane— "Come, Mam! Look a' this!"—Mill raised his head, and Hamble and I caught each other's glances, and we were up and out too.

People came out of their houses all over, into the before-dawn dimness, their eyes soft and swollen from sleeping, their hairs pushed this way and that, and stumbled along the lane with us. And when we reached the open street at the bottom of the hill, there labored a blackness that was the biggest of Marks's big cart horses, pulling not just a wagon but the festival-wagon of oak, with the carved and painted shafts and wheel-rims of ash. Wolfhunt was sitting beside Marks on the seat, and all those hunters were ranged around the insides.

The load bulked dark. "Oh my," says I. "Can it be?" My legs felt likely to go from under me; I pushed to the back of the people and leaned against the house-wall there.

The cart crept up the cobbled hill. Huge, dark, wild, dead, the she-bear hulked upon it like rubbished cloth, like furs thrown off a full council-room of lords. One of her forepaws hung off the back edge of the cart, the claws shaking almost alive when the cart bumped over the cobbles. The big blind head gaped, as if she were luxuriously asleep. They had bound her eyes with a rag—as you must, to keep the beast from seeing and magicking you—and blood was issuing from her mouth, as dark and slow as treacle. As the hill steepened, the horse's slow heavings and the cobble-tremors set the blood-puddle moving, and a long drip of it dropped off the back of the cart-floor, heavy as honey, leaving a string on the air behind it as sticky and wandering as the first thrown thread of a spider's web.

I snatched my hat from my head. I stood straight now, and steady as rock. Noer, where was Noer? Had they killed him too, like they did Filip? *This* might kill him, if the hunters had not. This was like to his *wife* being shot and carried up the street in public view.

My mam were coming through the people. "Bullock!" she says, and her face was bright as if she hadn't just seen me the night before.

"Run up to them," I say. "Ask whether Noer—"

But she was weeping, throwing herself on me. "My own boy!" She stood back; she slapped my cheeks. "Look at you! Oh, throw away this filthy thing!" She took the bear-bonnet from me—from my hands!—and flung it out in the road, where it skidded in the bear-blood.

"Mam!"

"Quickly!" She pushed at me. "Let me at the lacings. Take *all* of these off, Bullock, before the wind changes or whatever, and you are stuck again."

"I have my own hands back!"

"Bullock, my boy!" Here came Da now, Hamble at his shoulder.

"Mam, you can't unclothe me out here in everyone's view!"

"I can and I will. Oh, the *stink* of it!" And she threw the shirt after the hat.

"The stink of *him*," said Hamble, falling back from me. "You smell like a rotten cheese, you do, Bullock. I'll wait'll you bathe before I embrace you!" He held his nose with one hand and clapped my arm—my man-skin arm, with only the man-amount of hairs on it—with the other.

"Ma-am!"

"Take them off! Take them off!" She was laughing a bit mad now. "Get them off him, Oxman! Our grandparenthood depends on it!"

"Run for his trewsers, Hamble. Tek them bear ones off, Bull, and hold 'em up front for your modesty."

"But not touching, not touching!" hooted Mam. "For if they stick again— Oh!" And *she* didn't care about the cheese-smell of me—she was all over me, checking no bear-bits were left and kissing me. "Thank the Leddy, the curse is lifted! It must have been the killing of that bear!" she says. "Just like that oul witch said. You make the sacrifice and everything's set right, no?"

"Well, I dinnit . . ." The cart was near out of sight now, a ripple of Strap children running along beside, the hunters standing tall with spear and bow around the lump of the she-bear. "I dinnit eat the heart of her like the widow wanted. Din-nit boil the bones," I said, "or nothing." It wasn't even properly light; we were all milling and laughing in a dimness like un-derwater, with no color yet except that streak of rose-and-lemon cloud in the eastern sky.

"'Tweren't required!" Mam danced all glee around me.

"Look at him!" she said to the grinning neighbors, to the round-mouthed just-woke children brought out for the hunters' spectacle. "The bear have let him go!"

I did not think she had it right. We'd not done half of what the widder reckoned we ought; nothing could have been appeased by our poor effort. Some other's work were in this, and I were willing to put good coin on its being that fierce Miss Dance.

Daylight returned to Liga's eyes, as after a slow blink, and here was the forest again, but flushed green with leaf-buds and the nip gone from the air. The cat-creature was gone; as for the pail with the bones—why, that woman held it, the stranger in the dark, well-cut gown, and it was awful no longer, though it still had the same shine, and held the same remains, the same jewels.

Liga's flesh was her own now, and firmly wedded to her bones. Whatever had been happening was ended, and birdsong and stream-rush gentled her ears, and in the space vacated by her fear and unbalancement, she had time to examine the figures on the bank, all mysterious to her except for that little woman, whom she knew from somewhere.

"Bless my arse and whiskers!" the little woman said, and held her hands out from herself as if she were startled that she had them.

Liga would have exclaimed too, had she the courage, for all the many-colored stones of the rings that weighed down the small woman's fingers now squirmed in their settings, and their polished surfaces brightened to quite different kinds of iridescences. They crowded and bristled, and next she knew they had lifted off the woman's hands, and flown as a flock out over the bank, chirp-and-twittering, clearly small birds, until they vanished, faded to nothing in the air between Liga and another person, fine-dressed, aghast, ruining her shoes in the shallows.

Examining this face—older than she recalled, but younger by far than it ought to be—Liga felt to the deeps of her body the untapping of ten years' sorrows, untouched heretofore and unacknowledged, like the breaching of a dam wall, the bursting of a water-barrel or wine-keg. What kind of a mother am I, she thought, appalled, that I never felt the loss of this child? What kind, that I should not *want* to feel it, should not want to *feel* at all? What kind of a person? And she waded towards Urdda, stretching out her arms to the girl, who faltered there; who ought to have been brave and laughing, but instead swayed weakly; who had always been full to bursting with chatter but now could hardly bring the single word to her lips: "Mam!"

"Mam!" Urdda staggered forward and let Liga take her—Branza, too, that tall Branza grown to womanhood in little more than a year. For quite a time, the three did not see beyond each other, but only wept and laughed, and stabbed at what had happened with half-sentences and exclamations.

When finally they realized the dampness and inconvenience of their location, they waded out, laughing, and walked up the bank to grassier ground, and Urdda presented Liga and Branza to the Ramstrongs and Annie. Liga held on to Urdda's arm, clearly disliking to meet so many strangers at once—and not her usual strangers, all similar-faced and inclined to smile and avert their eyes.

"These are all friends, Mam," Urdda said. "And friends who know our circumstance and where we came from."

"Where *did* we come from?" Branza said. "And if we are no

290

longer there, where indeed are we, with you and . . . these friends?"

Miss Dance stood in the shallows, where she had been moving from crouch to crouch, examining things beyond anyone else's seeing and making careful smoothing motions with her hands. She eyed Branza, clearly assessing how the bringing was to be explained.

"May I say, mum?" almost-whispered Liga.

"Why, of course, Liga, if you can see a way."

"This lady has . . . has woken us, Branza, from something like a dream, that was our life before. And now we are in the waking life. I once lived here, a long time ago, but you were only a bab here, and will not remember. It is shaped much as our dream-life was, but there are more . . . it is more . . ."

"Populous," suggested Ramstrong. "And varied."

"And there is commerce," said Urdda. "And alehouses have ale in them, which men get drunk on. There are a lot more men altogether here, and . . ." She tried to remember back to her early days here, and what had bemused her most.

"But there are no bears?" said Branza. "Or . . . or wolves?" She glanced around at the new acquaintances, not sure if they would know of wolves.

"Oh, yes, there are all kinds of wild creatures here," said Liga.

"Good," said Branza, and nodded. She seemed very tall and tentative, even gentler than Urdda remembered her.

"The animals are not quite so tame here, though," she warned her sister, "and nor are the people."

"Are there many littlee-people?" Branza said nervously.

"I have not seen a one, not here nor in Broadharbour," Urdda said.

"You have been to Broadharbour, daughter!"

"I have! Oh, Mam, I have so much to tell you! A year and more's adventures!"

"A year and more?" said Branza. "Much more than that."

"Let us sit in the sunshine." Miss Dance bent to squeeze water from her hems onto the shore. "There are many things I need to explain, and to have explained to me." She straightened. Her face was entirely without color, except for the stains of exhaustion about her eyes.

"Miss Dance, are you injured with what you have done?" said Todda.

"Only very tired. I did not expect my resources to be taxed so far." She sat where a stone formed a step in the streambank, and spread out her skirts to dry. "Very well," she said, watching the rest of the company settle on the sunny grass. "This is what I have seen and done."

This lady, Miss Dance, intimidated Liga. She hardly smiled, and she was frighteningly clever; much of what she said, Liga could not grasp or follow. All that business about time, and keys, and joints, and right process—it fragmented as it passed into Liga's ears. It flew off in pieces, connecting with nothing, telling her nothing. The most she could gather was what Miss Dance had first said: that the times had slipped out of place and no longer matched between this real world and what Miss Dance called the "false" one; that the ten years that had passed since Urdda left were but one year in the real world; and that Liga and Branza were that decade older than they ought to be, and nothing could be done about it.

The sun grew strong and their hems dried, and still the talking went on. Liga's spirits sank yet lower. They had taken a great shock when the cat had appeared—she was somehow to believe that Miss Dance was that cat, and that the man Ramstrong had been the first Bear, and some absent man, a nogood, name of Teasel, the second. Then she had been terrified by the movement from that world to this—the darkness, the rushing, the sense of strain; the fact that the dreadful cat was leading them. And then the joy of seeing Urdda had been almost spoiled by the other strong emotions—My daughter! My daughters! As if she had not realized before that she had daughters—the significance of that, the intensity.

And then she gathered that she herself had been at fault, all those years, all her girls' lives. *I can understand, to a point,* Miss Dance had said, *that you were allowed to take two tiny children there. But how you managed to keep them there for so long, as they grew, is more of a mystery, for they did not belong there. Urdda did the natural thing and returned to life in search of her true future; Branza ought to have done the same. It is a great misshapement of things that she stayed so long—until the age of twenty-five! She has not had enough of a true life to even conceive of her own heart's desire. To spend her whole life within yours—tut! That is no kind of existence.*

So Liga was to understand, just on the point where the full import of their existing at all had come home to her, that she had failed her daughters. For all her work, she had given them *no kind of existence.* Miss Dance seemed to think she should at least have visited the real world now and again—Liga had not known this was possible!—so that the heart's-desire world adjusted itself to meet her later wants, her woman's wants beyond her girl's. But worse than holding her heaven in the mold she had made at fifteen (but *had* she made it? What of that moonbabby's part?) was that by doing the only thing she had known for certain was right, holding her daughters to her and caring for them in that safe world instead of relinquishing them to this "true" one of alehouses and gossips and jeering town boys, Liga had done very wrong by them, Miss Dance was saying.

Did Miss Dance have children? Liga could not imagine it. Would she know what was right or wrong for them? But she spoke with such certainty; she spoke as if she knew. Liga had never heard a woman speak so.

And then Liga's own daughters, both of them, and for years!—and this pained Liga deeper than anything, and seemed proof of Miss Dance's accusation—had not *betrayed* her, exactly, but they had kept things from her; they had had secrets! This business of the man, Mister Collaby, Mister Dought—Liga could see, clear as day, that he had been the source of Branza's nightmares. It was not the ghost of Da that had haunted her—how could it be?—but this little quarrelsome beastie, who had made what Miss Dance called "incurgeons" into the place of Liga's heart's desire. The woman with the rings-that-had-turned-into-birds had sent him there, repeatedly—or at least made it possible for him to return and return again—and it was his being there, and his dying there and remaining there as bones, that had somehow pushed the times so badly out of alignment. Liga did not even pretend to understand how this had happened. She was only glad to see the woman looking appropriately ashamed as Miss Dance described what she had done. She was only glad that Liga Longfield was not the only person here who had done wrong.

Now they were talking about what should be done with Liga and Branza, where they were to live in the real world. There was no cottage anymore, Urdda had said; it was all fallen to ruin; they would have to live in the town. In the town! A shudder ran up Liga's spine.

On top of which-all, in this amiable scene, as the gray-faced Miss Dance laid matters out—the woman had them so clear in her own mind, and was explaining and repeating things, with more patience than her fierce looks would have led Liga to expect—in this scene sat the family with the two little sons. Anders was the older boy, Ousel the bab; the mam with the reassuring smile was Todda; the da was Davit Ramstrong, and Davit Ramstrong had been Bear, the Bear Liga had known in her young womanhood, when she had had girl-children; the Bear she had leaned against and scratched the head of and addressed so freely—how much of it had he understood? Her face grew warm at the thought. How much had he told that wife?

Liga snapped off grass-stalks at her side. She would rather he had been a part of that other world and disappeared, as Miss Dance had said their cottage, and Branza's Wolf, and the St. Olafred's with the missing houses had disappeared when Liga passed back into the real world. To have him here without his guise of speechless Bear, without his animal lumbering that she could laugh at, but instead unmistakably a man, and fine-looking, and respected as her da had never been . . . Liga could not sort one emotion from the other about him; it was all a muddle of discomforts.

"Are you happy with all this, Mam?" Urdda now said, and all of them—man and wife and daughters and cat-woman and the little ringless one they called "the widow," or Annie—all of them were turned to her with their different degrees of smiling and concern, all with their different minds behind their faces.

"I'm very sorry," she said. "I'm so tired. What last you said—"

"That we stay with Annie for the moment, until we establish some customers for our sewing?"

Annie twinkled across the grass at Liga and gave her an encouraging nod. Liga did not remember her quite so aged, or nearly so smiling. She was finely dressed, though; where had that lace at her collar come from?

"I am very happy for that," Liga ventured, "if you all think it is for the best." The sewing—of course! She had her trade now, and her two daughters as assistants. She was not the poacher's girl anymore. But what if people should recognize her? What if true-world people—a stab of sick horror shook her—should recognize in Branza and Urdda not only their mam but their different fathers? Liga might be unworldly, but she knew, by Da's anxiety for concealment all that time ago as well as by the wrongness written deep in her body, that a bab got by one's da was not a thing the true world would forgive. As for Urdda, if any of those five men recalled Liga and their deeds upon her, and then noticed what to Liga were the Hogback boy's unmistakable lineaments and color-ing in Urdda's face—well, just the thought of them *thinking* made Liga's heart run fast with fear, let alone what they might begin to *say*, to each other, to the town. But perhaps—it dawned on her as Miss Dance went on to explain, again, to that Mister Ramstrong's wife Todda, how the times between the two worlds had gone mismatched—perhaps that very mismatchment would afford Liga's little family some conceal-ment. For while Urdda was roughly the age she ought to be here, Liga and Branza, being a good decade older, were likely to throw off the calculations of any town person musing on their pasts. And if she only had a credible tale to distract that person—

"But one thing," she said.

The faces had all been turning away to Urdda and Miss Dance, but now Liga had them again. She felt as if she had no breath, might laugh or faint or weep or any wild thing, so her voice, when she found it, came out very low and controlled. "I was married," she said.

None of the faces winced or changed at the lie.

"None knew of it," she went on, "and it was not for long. I was widowed by the man before Urdda was born. Name of Cotting."

Todda and Annie and Davit Ramstrong searched their memories for the name; Branza looked astonished, and Urdda delighted.

"And you were Longfield before!" Urdda said. "Ramstrong and I have found that much out."

The name, unheard for so many years, hit Liga's chest hard enough to dizzy her. "Yes," she said. "But the less said of that, the better. We will go by the name of Cotting."

"Urdda Cotting," said Urdda enchantedly. Liga suppressed a pang of guilt as the false name took hold of the girl's imagination. "Branza Cotting—I like that, Branza!"

"I did wonder," said Davit Ramstrong, looking relieved, "that I never saw nor heard mention of a man."

"I never heard of a Cotting," said Annie, and Todda stopped frowning and shook her head in agreement.

"He was from the Millets," said Liga.

"Ah," said Annie, as if that explained everything.

"He had fallen out with his family—I never went there. I never met them."

"And it was on your widowing that you left this world for the other?" said Miss Dance.

"It was," said Liga quickly. Then her eyes met Miss Dance's intelligent ones, and a fierce heat rushed up her face.

Miss Dance watched it thoughtfully. "We are all very weary," she said. "I am thinking we should rest, us twixt-world travelers, before we talk further."

"We have rooms ready," said Annie, springing up. "And fine linens all purchased of heaven-money, thanks to your canny daughter, Widow Cotting."

"I should not take such pride in that, Bywell," Miss Dance said, rising.

Bywell! Liga felt another jolt in her chest. Annie Bywell! Muddy Annie!

"Oh, you must sleep in them before you make your judgment, mum," Annie said cheekily.

That muddy old hag, Liga's da had said, and the sound of his voice, and the sight of the mudwife all transformed, and the look that had been in Miss Dance's eye just then—the look that said, *Cotting, eh? I will have the truth out of you soon enough*—all these combined to make Liga tremble as she rose from the grass with the others, and prepared to face the real St. Olafred's for the first time since Branza was born, nigh on a score and five years ago.

Mam washed the bear-mank off me, singing and laughing and calling in any passing person from the laneway as would come, to see me and marvel and share her good cheer.

"There is a bigger crowd for you than for any newborn," said Ivo Strap.

"Craw, yoodn't want to've birthed that great lummock, goodwife," someone added, and people laughed.

"But I did, but I did!" Mam said, and kissed my wet cheek.

"Have anyone found what happened to Noer?" I says when she next were sudsing me.

"He is alive, they say," says Da. "That is all the hunters would tell, though."

"Alive, and un-beared too?" says Mam. "We'll see him at the feast tonight, if he is."

At the feast. She meant the feast of bear-meat, of hunted she-bear meat. She meant the whole custom and fol-droll of the bear-feast that must happen, the whole town present, and the gypsies waiting outside for the leavings. Oh goodness, how could we ever join in that? Ever again, unspelled or no?

Mam came to me more sober when the bath-show was over and most the people were gone. "Mab Woolscar come up," she says. "Noer is brought home to his mam, is the word. But they say he is quite mad, from being in the clutches of that bear so long. Near a week she've been toying with him, like a cat with a mouse. I did not think bears did that; I thought they ate something direct on catching it. Anyway, that is where they found him, between her paws, preparing to be torn from limb to limb."

Between her paws. I shivered. He is mad from having been *between her paws* and being there no longer. He is mad of being "rescued." He is mad of grief and rage, of breathing town-air and house-air, people-farts and the breath of bedding and cold ashes. Yesterday he were in the forest, with the sky and leaves overhead and greenness all around, the tree-trunks holding up the canopy so that bird and breeze might be free to fly through. Yesterday he were *between her paws*, spelled by her amber eyes, and now she is dead, and she have taken his mind with her.

"I will go and see him," I says.

"You think you ought?" says Mam.

"Why not, ever?"

"Only I don't want you catching it off of him, if he is still enchanted."

"You daft-mam," I said, and patted her worried cheek.

I walked out through the busy lanes. Many a man shook my hand as I made my way along and down to Noer's da's house. People told me on the way that his family had prisoned Noer in the hut in their backyard there, as being not fit for human company and distressing his mam and his brothers and sisters, so I went around and I let myself in their yard, and there was Oswest, sitting carving by the backhouse door.

"Bullock," he says. "Look at you, man, in your own skin. I heard o' that. That is some relief."

"How is Noer?" I says to the door. "Have his furs fallen off him too, like mine?"

"His bonnet is gone. If the rest is loose, still he will not cast it off. And can no one get near him to tek it off him. He have been wild. I thought he would knock the structure down, chains or no chains."

"Chains?"

"Nowt else will hold him, poor nonny. He is strong as a bear, just as he's dressed like one."

As if he had heard us, Noer inside sent up a loud, weird wail, and the backhouse shuddered and thudded as he wrestled his bonds inside.

"Let me go in to him," I said to Oswest next time I could be heard above the noise.

"Oh, you don't want to," he said. "He will tear you up; he is quite wild, and angry at everyone."

Almost I shouted, *They have crossbowed his wife, man! Who would not be wild at that?* But I did not say it. "Let me see him, Oswest, and him me. My poor friend!" Noer wailed within; the back of my neck crawled at the sound, so much more mournful than threatening.

"Very well, I will chance it," says Oswest eventually, putting down his knife and wood. He stood and went to the shuttered window. "Noer? 'Tis your friend Bullock has come to see you. Bullock? You remember? What was Bear with you?"

The wailing faltered and stopped. I held my breath, thinking Noer would explode again.

Oswest listened too awhile. He made a thoughtful face and opened the shutter, peered inside. A low, awful growl shook the wooden wall. Oswest waved me up urgently. "See?" he said nervously to Noer.

I could see nothing inside. I was afraid a bear-claw would swipe out the opening and take off my face. "Noer?" I says, even nervouser than Oswest.

A thick black silence maintained in there for several moments, and then a voice came out. "Bullock?" And in pronouncing that name, so precise and so piteous, he showed himself to be still himself, still my poor friend and fellow fool Noer.

He commenced to sobbing. A powerful familiar smell of sweaty skin-dirt pushed me back from the window. "How can he breathe in there?"

"Can none of us get in there to clean him," says Oswest. "I tell you, he has never been like this, just crying. Either he fights or is asleep—that has been the way of him since they brought him back this morning, all bound up for his own safety."

"Bullock," came Noer's voice from inside. "Bullock, are you still there?" There was a stir, and the rattle and thunk of chains pulled tight.

"I'm here, Noer. I'm not goin anywheres." I went again to the window so he could see me.

"You have lost your hat off too."

"I have, Noer. Let me in to him, Oswest."

"Are you certain?" Oswest whispered. "He is as best he's ever been, but I don't know he'll stay that way."

I trembled not to hit Oswest—he could not help his

ignorance. "I am certain. Open the door. Please, Oswest, before my heart cracks wide."

Shaking his head and frightened, Oswest took out the key and unlocked the backhouse door. The smell spilled out and filled the yard as he stood back. "Stay beyond the reach o' the chain," he whispered as I passed.

But I went right straight in and gathered Noer up, his filthy bearness into my fresh-washed arms of person-skin, against my clean, thin clothes of cloth. I stood and rocked him, and he wept on me a long time, a long time. The only things he could speak of to me were too great horrors for words, and the only comfort I could offer was understanding them, without him having to tell them.

Words we did find, though, eventually. We sat side by side against the wall, and every now and again one of us would attempt some halting thing, and after time the haltingness eased somewhat.

Oswest peered in the window at us, and brought family, and they observed us too, and ventured inquiries as to Noer's health and sanity.

"I am more or less myself," he says to them. "But I am not at all sure who that is, to be true with you. Bullock here is helping me remember."

"Will you not come and eat with us?" says his mam. "And take off them awful furs, and wash the madness off you? When was the last time you ate, boy?"

"Don't worry, Mam. I'll come out presently. Leave us be, for now, while we catch ourselves up."

His da undid his chains and then the family left us to our commiserating. All that morning and afternoon we sat, and while we sat, the bearmeat-feast were assembled. The mayor-hall up the hill from Noer's had the only kitchen big enough, and the only pots, and we could not help but hear the shouts and chats of cook-wives and meat-hands and trestle-men, the tumbles of cut logs delivering for the kitchen.

"Is Filip up there, then?" Noer said bitterly, "putting up tables and such?"

"Filip? What are you— Oh, but of course, how would you know it?"

"Know what?" says Noer, full of dread.

"Filip is not there, nor at any feast again, Noer."

"What happened to him?"

I searched my neat-trewsered knees for the way to tell him.

"He is imprisoned too?" says Noer. "Or worse? He is not *dead*!" But he confirmed it from my face, and clapped his filthy sleeve-ends to his mouth.

"He were shot for a real bear by mistake."

"No!" he whispers into his fur. "When? How?" he says, tears catching in his throat.

So there was that unhappy accident to tell, on top of all the other improbables.

His family brought us bread, and smoke-meat, and ale, and when they heard that we would not be coming to the bear-feast, so scandalized were they that they brang more ale. Os-west, poor fool, even offered to convey some bear-meat to us when it were done, though he stumbled and stopped half through offering it when he saw me shake and shake my head, and Noer's cold stare.

There were nothing I could do to keep the smell of her out, though, the hall and its chimneys were so close. She hung over the place in a cloud, strong and rich; we might not eat her, but we could not help but breathe her.

"Mebbe we should get out this town," I said. "Go out in the fields. You could wash yourself in the river. I could fetch some trews and shirt for you from your mam."

He thought on that, but were unable to bring himself to leave the little malodorous refuge we had there. So we stayed, and every little while someone would come and replenish our food and ale, but mostly they let us alone, under instructions from Noer's mam.

For a while that evening there was quiet as they said the prayers up at the mayor-hall, honoring all beasts but in particular the sizable races and the fierce, such as wolves and bears.

"At least there is some reverence there," I said to Noer, who were quite drunk by then and falling to weeping. "This is the closest we are likely ever to come to appropriate ceremony. We ought be grateful."

But then the mayor shouted and there was a cheer from all the men, and the lady mayoress cried out, and so then did all the women, and the feasting began; and for me it was bad enough, but for Noer the noise must of been like hundreds of biting spiders under his skins. For a time there he could not keep still, pacing out into the yard and back again in the heavy, savory air, the *mouthwatering* air, however hard we tried not to find it enticing. Terrible moans came out of him, but it were only ale that made them sound so animal, not any returning bearness of him.

All night I stayed with him in that hut and yard, holding him back from losing himself in his own mind, making him talk proper when he were done with each spell of weeping and raving.

"I do not want to know this," I asked him as we sat out under the stars in the deep of that night, the both of us very full. The singing had started up at the hall, and the thunders of dancing. "But it is eating me up so as I cannot think of anythin else." And I breathed beer-air across his dazed face.

"I know what it is, my friend. I know what it is," he said.

"You do?"

"I do. You're wanting to know exackly how. The exack degree of . . . you know, as we were as husband and wife. Whether we had congroonce like you do between man and wife—as man does, as people do. Whether we lay abed together."

"I do not want to know it."

He sat up straight, preparing himself to answer. Some pocket of beer-bubbles trickled tunefully up the back of his throat.

"Ah," says I. "Even in the belches you can tell the quality of Keller's ale, the superior nature."

"Erp. Indeed." And like it takes a cart horse something of a winding-up and a goading to get a laden wagon moving, he initiated himself forwards again, throwing his arm around my shoulders. "Which I was about to say, Bullock. I am very happy to be able to tell you, if you do not want to know, that I cannot say."

"Iss too private," I agreed.

"No, I just cannot . . . not *not remember*, exackly." He frowned up at the sky and the drifting smoke. "I may well have, but I could not say definivvely. I coonot give you instances: moves nor locales nor how the flirting nor the seducing went, you know? It is all lost in one big bearish wonderland, her fur and the smell of her and her weight and splendence and . . . We companioned each other, Bullock, and were all that the other needed. Your question—even though you have not asked it!—forgive me, but it is a chile's question, a smutty-minded peerer-into-bushes' question, peerer-into-barns'. Though I understand you asking and I realize you did not mean it so." He squeezed my shoulders.

"I dinnit even want to know that much," says I gloomily. "Every word you say about her is like a stab to me, is like a smack and a laugh in my face, I was so spelled by her in that short time."

He put his other arm around my front and held me hard.

"Easy. I'll be sick," I said.

He released me only a little. "You *know*," he said, grinning in pain. "You know something of what I am enduring, Bullock, my friend. You are the only man in the world who can intimate this."

"Well, it is no pleasure," I told him.

"Oh, no. But at least I am not quite utterly alone in this. At least someone has a whisker of understanding."

"Not much more than that," I says unhappily. Through the ale and sleepiness I were beginning to see somewhat more clearly how us three Bears—well, the two of us surviving—how our lives had been tumbled like a half-keg of salt-herring rolled down a hill, and now we lay unpacked and dizzied at the bottom.

"I were worried," says my Todda, "when Miss Dance said she ought to bring them back."

It was the middle of the night; she had just brought Ousel in with us; he was busy and breathing in his nest between us, and above him she watched me, the thoughts pouring out her eyes in the dark.

"Why is that?"

"Well," she says unwillingly, "I thought perhaps the mother had . . . a place in your heart, Davit."

"Oh, she does, and she did," I said. There is something about talking in the night, with the shreds of sleep around your ears, with the silences between one remark and another, the town dark and dreaming beyond your own walls. It draws the truth out of you, straight from its little dark pool down there, where usually you guard it so careful, and wave your hands over it and hum and haw to protect people's feelings, to protect your own.

"The way you spoke of her, when we first talked about it."

"Yes," I said. I thought about her at the stream there in her prime, much the age of Todda now; I mused upon the sensations and the muddied impressions that come to a man through his bear-fur, through his bear-mind.

Then I realized she was waiting, listening to me muse, not knowing what I were about. "You've no need to worry," I said, and reached across and rested my hand on her hip. "So much has come between, so much more: you and these babs. I married *you*, remember?"

"I should not like to think it were a duty now, and you preferred another," she said low.

See? You can bring out the jaggedest feelings—if you are my wife and know how to state them calm—into the night quiet. They will float there for consideration, harming no one.

"It is no duty, Todda, but a joy and a revelation to me every day. Had I the choice now, I would not go back to that place, don't you fear."

"No?" she says.

I put it before my mind's eye again. "No."

Ousel made a small, greedy noise. Todda's doubt floated over us between the grains of darkness.

"I said no, Tod," I moved my hand on her hip.

"When she came through, though," she murmured. "When first she stepped out of that other land; when first you saw her, Davit?"

"Relief," I realized, with a little laugh.

"I were relieved too," she chimes. "Why were you, though?"

"That she had not the same spell over me. That all I felt was worry that she and Branza should be comfortable here, not be too frightened."

"I were glad, and this is not admirable of me . . ."

I gave her hip a little shake. "Go on. You were glad because?"

"Because she was older. At first I thought Branza was the one, and that made me think, *Oh, she is beautiful. I am lost. Maybe I am!* How do you feel for Branza?"

"Todda, I knew the girl as a bab, almost! 'Tis indecent to do more than think, *Well, haven't she grown up fine from that little sprite?* But go on: then you realized?"

"Then I realized it were the older woman and . . . I were glad she were older, that's all. I were glad she were old enough to be a grumma. Not that she is at all ugly or careworn—she is beautiful. But . . ."

"But no longer the girl I met."

"Yes. But then I also thought, *Well, where am I bound, if not for that age too? Do I want women like me, young mams, to be so relieved? Do I want my man to look at me when I am twoscore and more, and feel no desire for me?*"

"I promise I will not."

She laughed at how earnest I said it, and how fast.

I hoisted up on an elbow and listened over Ousel. He sucked a little, half woke by my movement, then slipped back into his milky dreams.

"Here," I whispered, "give me that bab and I will put him

out the way of our husband-and-wifing. Before you is too wizened and ugly for my consideration, eh?"

"Oh, yes," she laughed up at me. "We had better move right smartly, I think."

Towards dawn, I roused myself and shook Noer, who had fallen to weeping and then sleeping on my lap on the hut floor. "I must go. They'll be doing the bones soon," I says to him. "Do you want to be there for that?"

He sat half up and squinted about, stupid as if he'd been blonked with the constable's cosh. "Whather?"

"Like her funeral," I says.

He looked at me and dragged his answer out from behind some drunken dream. "No, Bullock. I coonent. You go for me, though. You pay my respecks."

So up I went to the hall and joined the procession of the hunters, carrying the she-bear among them—her peeled bones, her scraped and her boiled, her broken for the marrow, her giant skull, her knuckles and backbones in rattling bags—out of the town and up onto the Mount, where they buried her, and rolled a stone onto her that would be rolled off again next spring to set her free, and Wolfhunt said the long prayer that was all about the bear-strength they had eaten, and the threateningness and the savagery of bears. It were awful—I felt the awfulness of it on behalf of Noer-who-had-been-*between-her-paws*, and it seemed hardly dulled at all by the amount of ale I had taken.

When it was done, we went down the hill again and the town rose opposite. I knew that place should be my home, but after my night in Noer's mind it seemed a peculiar pile, its streets a maze, needlessly crowded, where we slender people, so naked of fur we must make extra skins for ourselves, muddled and ambled and skipped in our dance of alliances and enmities, offenses and fancies. We thought too much; we calculated too hard. I would rather have wandered among trees, with their more meaningful conversation. I would rather have been solitary and unharried, never required to speak nor account for myself, to do anything else but what come natural.

But I could not make for the forest now. My friend needed me. He was in that pile, in that town somewhere, sleeping and suffering. I would go and wake him—now was the right time for that. I would see him cleaned and set aright. And then I would go to my own home and sleep myself, and perhaps when I woke, all this stirred-up anger and magic would have gone back to its resting-place, and life would not seem such a strange and sad affair.

Miss Dance tied her bag to the saddle and briskly turned back to them. There was still something skull-like about her handsome face. She had had no more than an hour or two's rest last night, answering all their questions, and asking many of her own, and spending time aside with both Liga and Lady Annie.

What did she want of you? Urdda had asked Liga first thing that morning.

Liga had looked patient and sad, and so much older than Urdda remembered her. *Nothing important,* she said.

She wanted to rap me *over the knuckles,* Annie had laughed, sweeping by with one of Urdda's white bread-loaves. *And I've no rings to protect me no more—ooch, it stung!*

"I am pleased to have set this right, as well as it could be set," Miss Dance now said to the assembled women. Ramstrong had hied himself to his wool-merchants, so it was only Annie, and Todda and the boys, and Liga and Branza and Urdda.

"I wish you would rest a day," said Annie. "Tea or no brightening tea, you will doze as you ride and fall from that beauteous mount of yours. Even spelling things improper tires a person."

Miss Dance smiled down and took both of Annie's ringless hands. "Well, I hope you will not tire yourself that way in the future, Lady Bywell."

"Oh, I think I had already learnt my lesson, mum," said Annie. "'Tis years since I done more than brew up herb-messes and shoo the odd wife or child from death's doorstep."

"Keep an eye on this woman, Urdda," said Miss Dance. "She has more talent than schooling, and a soft heart—and that is always a dangerous combination."

Urdda was still afizz with the adventure of it all, Ousel on her hip as if he weighed no more than a twitter-will. She bobbed a curtsey. "It has been an honor and adventure meeting you, Miss Dance."

"And you, my dear." Miss Dance seemed about to say something else, but Ousel waggled his hand at her. "Bye-bye," he commanded.

The sorceress chucked his cheek. "Bye-bye, little man," she said, and turned to Liga and Branza, who stood together, somewhat faded from yesterday's excitement and a lack of sleep. "Go carefully, Liga, Branza," she said. "Be kind to yourselves. Much is different here, and you must expect some shocks and confusions."

"I wish you would stay a little, as the lady says," said Branza impulsively. "And . . . instruct us."

"Instruct you in what, my dear?"

"Oh! I don't know. In the ways of this world, and how to be comfortable in it."

"Comfort is not the *aim*, Branza," said Urdda with a laugh. "Comfort is what we *had*. Here we have . . . Well, Miss Dance calls this the true world. Here we have truth!"

Branza looked chastened and fragile, and Miss Dance took her elbow. Did she do magic on her? Urdda wondered, watching Branza straighten at her touch and risk something of a smile through her uncertainties.

"Rest and observe, Branza," the sorceress said. "Things will come clearer with time and thought, I'm sure you will find. Liga, you also. Take matters slowly—as you may, from your vantage point under Annie's roof."

"I will be very careful," said Liga, hanging on Branza's other arm, and Urdda jogged Ousel on her hip and made faces for him rather than look at her mother and sister, for their extra ten years were all too evident in their faces, which strove for politeness through fear.

"Journey well, mum," said Todda to Miss Dance, and Miss Dance mounted the mare in a single efficient movement. She looked down at them, a fine-cut figure against the cloudy sky. Oh, we are so motley, Urdda thought, with all our doubts and frights—how wonderful to be this woman, and know everything!

"Bye-bye," said Ousel. "Bye-bye." And he wagged and wagged his hand as Miss Dance brought the fine mare round.

"Good day, ladies," said the sorceress. It was clear from her eyes that her mind had already gone from them to whatever duties awaited her in Rockerly.

"Bye-bye," said Ousel again.

"And gentlemen." Miss Dance flashed him a brief smile. "And little gentlemen." She released the mare into a walk and, with an arm raised in farewell, rode away from them, down the street.

Liga and Branza slept away the morning. A cracked voice singing outside, warbling from growl to trill, woke Liga around noon, and she lay abed unmoving for a while, listening and waiting for her situation, her surroundings, to come comprehensible to her. In her hand, under her pillow, was the cloth with the two jewels wrapped in it—or the two *seeds*, or whatever they were, from which the red-flowered and the white-flowered bushes had grown and perhaps the entirety of Liga's heaven-place with them. Miss Dance had given them to Liga last night.

They are yours by right, she had said. *And by the fact that they retain their form in the true world, I would dare to say that that other world might remain somehow accessible to you. But beware!* And here the sorceress had glanced out of her thoughts and her exhaustion with a flash of feeling. *Should you be inclined to return to it, come to me in Rockerly, rather than appealing to any mudwife to help you reach there. There is a good chance, with these gems in hand, of my conveying you to that place, but who knows how Annie might imperil you, imperil us all, meddling with the things?*

Liga climbed out of the comfortable bed and went to the window. Annie was at her fire place on the paved area beyond the kitchen garden, singing as she cooked up a brew in a big black medicine pot. She did not have her teeth in—Liga could see that even from the upper window—and she wore a soft old dress, somewhere between green and brown, and a filthy apron.

Quietly, so as not to wake Branza, who was soundly asleep in the other bed, Liga crossed the room, took her dress from the chair-back, and put it on. Quietly she let herself out of the chamber, and slowly she walked to the stairs, and down, glancing into rooms where she could. Good; Urdda was nowhere to be seen. She walked through the wafts of fume and song to which the widow had left the house open.

My, look what she has achieved! Liga thought, eyeing Urdda's kitchen garden. A little raw and new yet, but yes, my wild girl has laid it out almost exactly the same. Perhaps she is not so wild after all.

She walked down the path between the rows. "Annie?" she called, so as not to startle the woman.

"You're up!" Annie said. A gust of air off the brew floated across the bean trellises and stung Liga's nostrils.

"I've placed you now, Annie." Liga crouched at the edge of the garden closest to the fire, pretending to be interested in weeding there.

"Whassat, my dear?" Annie stirred on with gusto, pausing every few strokes to lift hot mucks and lumps out and admire their blackness and variety. Her tune murmured in her throat, but did not burst forth as before.

"You used to be Muddy Annie, I think. We were almost neighbors a long time ago."

The widow's music died away entirely. Her face was all lips and scowl, as if she had caught sight of something unpredicted lurking in her pottage. "Lo-ong time," she said softly.

Liga reached in among the rhubarb stalks and plucked a tiny weed—two first-leaves only, a white thread of a stem, a fine hair of a root. "You would remember, though, my father, Gerten Longfield."

Now the stirring-stick was moving very slowly in the mixture. "I do, at that."

"He came to you three times, for very particular things."

Annie gazed awhile into the mess. Then she leaned her pole

on the rim of the pot, wiped her hands on her grubby apron, and stepped down from the stone slab she stood on for stirring.

Liga searched among the cool red stalks, bending them this way and that, until she felt the breeze and breath of the old woman squatting beside her. Then she stopped pretending to weed. "There was a horrible tea, first, and then he bought from you some herbs and powders to burn, and the third time he brought home two packets, because . . . because I was already six months on with Branza."

The words disappeared out of the air, as if inconsequential, as if they had never been said. The rhubarb leaned and nodded its improbably green leaves, veined with improbable pink.

Annie leaned forward and turned Liga's face to her gently, with both hands. "From him?" she said. Her hands were cool-skinned but warm within, shiny-wrinkled, and smelled strongly of aniseed. "From your da?"

"All three," said Liga.

Annie nodded. For several moments, hers was the most beautiful face Liga had ever seen, every whisker and pouch and glisten of it. Liga's head felt unsteady, as if a small whirlwind spun inside.

Then the older woman put her hands to her own face and said painfully to the paving between her knees, "But not Urdda. The cocky bugger were dead by then. She was of this Cotting?"

"No," said Liga. "There was no Cotting. Cotting is only a name I chose, for sake of respectability. Urdda was . . ." She tried out in her mind various ways of saying it, but all were too gross for this sunny garden, too harsh to bring out before this kind woman. Finally she said, "Town boys," and the words came out as little more than a spit, a hiss.

Annie covered her eyes and crouched lower. "Reg'lar?" she said in a muffled voice.

"Only once," said Liga. "But there were five of them."

"Five? Greshus. Greshus the feckin Leddy," said Annie through her hands to the paving. Then she waddled sideways until she reached Liga, and she put her arm, hardly longer than that little lad Anders', around Liga's waist and, with her eyes still covered, held on to her with the full force of her tiny wizened sympathy.

"Oh." Annie wiped her eyes on her apron; she looked around as if trying to see just a garden before her; she coughed some, from a passing ribbon of pottage-fume. "But Urdda come from it," she said when she recovered. "And Branza from the other. That don't turn it around, but at least there *is* them. At least there *is* them." She took a ragged breath and scrubbed at her nose with the apron again.

Liga nodded. "There is," she said brokenly, again overtaken by those emotions she had discovered on the streambank at the first sight of Urdda. How could Branza sleep, she wondered, how could Urdda run her errands in the town, and not be aware how their mam was being attacked, beaten, crushed, by her own loving fear for them? She hardly knew what to do, it had been so long since such strong feelings had borne down on her. It was like carrying another creature inside her, and nothing so benign and natural as a baby. Undamped, untamed, the pain and exultation of her attachment to them blew through Liga like a storm-wind carrying sharp leaves and struggling birds. How long she had known her daughters, and how well, and in what extraordinary vividness and detail! How blithely she had done the work of rearing them—it seemed to her now that she had had cause for towering, disabling anxieties about them; that what had seemed little plaints and sorrows in their childhoods were in fact off-drawings from much greater tragedies, from which she had tried to keep them but could not. And the joys she had had of them, too, their embraces and laughter—it was all too intense to be endured, this connection with them, which was a miniature of the connection with the forces that drove planet and season—the relentlessness of them, the randomness, the susceptibility to glory, to accident, to disaster. How soft had been her life in that other place, how safe and mild! And here she was, back where terrors could immobilize her, and wonders too; where life might become gulps of strong ale rather than sips of bloom-tea. She did not know whether she was capable of lifting the cup, let alone drinking the contents.

She cleared the tears from her eyes and tried to collect herself. "I only thought I should tell you," she said, "what kind of people you were sheltering. For though I intend to keep quiet myself about it, I saw the brother of one of the men as we walked up the town yesterday, and I thought, what if it should come out? And I thought you ought get it from me first."

With a mop of her face and a hoot of laughter, Annie sat to the paving, and waggled Liga's knee that she should do the same. "Well, you ought know what manner of lumpling is your landleddy, too, girl," she said ruefully, clasping her ringless hands in her lap, little worn yellow-brown instruments that they were. "I cannot entirely be sure, but I think I may have killed him."

"Killed . . ."

"Your da that day," said the mudwife. "I think I may have ill-willed him under them carriage wheels."

"You may?" Liga was astonished. "But what did he do to you?"

"Them were my thoughts exactly, on that day, after he come and seen me for the makings of moving that bab out of you. Good silver, he guv me, and there likely would be more— why should he ever stop? *A tidy one of these purchases every several moons*, I thought, *and I could be quite comfortable*. I tried to think that, Liga Longfield. I would have you know, I did try. For I were not wealthy then, and that is the way the poor must think, no?—looking all the time to their next meal, and perhaps to another wool blanket to see them alive to winter's end."

"Oh, I understand it, Annie. I remember that."

"But then I thunk, *Every several moons?* And—well, I am orphanage rubbish, as you know, and quite oft acquainted with men tekkin what they will from me without my say-so. But the thing with orphans, you see, is: mams and das is great mysterious things; they is everything we've missed out on and that lucky people have. That your mam should leave you in his care, and you be lucky enough to still have a da, and then for that da to—to use you that way! That is the horriblest insult, Liga-girl, worse than having no da at all; oh, so much worse. How is you supposed to know what you are and what's natural?—"

It was too much, Annie's witchy face, its concavities and its glittering eyes. The sight confused Liga. Had she not always wanted someone else, some woman, to know and understand and join her in her anger? Yet here was Annie growling and distorted with it, and all Liga felt was dread at the widow's—at *anyone's*—having turned and seen what no one had ever been supposed to see. Sickened, frightened, she knew she had disobeyed her father in the worst way possible. From across the years, his eyes widened, his words assembled themselves for the roaring, and the air pressed in, unbreathable, all around her—

"He always called me by her name, in those nights," Liga

burst out over Annie's spitting. "He was almost asleep often, when he— Or he would come home drunk—" And then the wretchedness and the dirt of it all stopped her, and she sat over the tear-dotted lap of her skirt, with memories fondling her and hissing in her ear.

Annie's wrinkled hand touched Liga's chin, lifted her face. "He might o' been drunk, Liga Cotting-that-was-Longfield, but he were not that addled. He never mistook the two of you. He knew what he were doing, from first fumble to last thrust and drizzle. Don't you mistake me."

"I asked for it," Liga said, almost soundless. "He told me I did. By my ways of moving, of standing. By my shape. Sometimes I think I did ask for it."

"No girl asks for that, to be poked by her da—no girl. Let me tell you."

"I was stupid—"

Annie took Liga's head in her hands with some urgency. "Oh, we are all *stupid*, girl. That is none of the man's excuse."

And then Liga could not think of any further let-outs or mitigations for him, and the bald, cruel truth of what he had done to her and repeated on her, time after time, bab after bab—the two of them stupid in the night together—fell in on her like the roof of a cottage whose pinnings have slumped just a little too far. She crouched there, small and tight as she could possibly hold herself, and while the wormy rafters and the rotted thatch crushed her and threw up their dust and vermin around her, she sobbed rage and grief in the little old lady's arms.

So Liga and Branza joined Urdda at the Widow Bywell's house. Lady Annie provided them a sum of money—she would have given it freely, but Liga insisted that they would repay it when

319

their profits allowed—to equip a room downstairs that might have been a dining room, had the household ever had guests to dine. This they made a workroom, and at its broad table the three Cotting women plied their shears and needles. They began modestly, with table linens and children's garments that they sold at market, and then they progressed to dressing the grown women of the town, beginning with Todda and Lady Annie, who were pleased to become the first and best advertisements for their work.

"Wherever did you learn this style of stitchery?" said none other than Sukie Taylor, frowningly fingering the leafwork edging a fine linen tablecloth.

"Why, inland," said Liga, with the smiling heavenly version of Sukie's mother in her mind.

"It's so pretty, but quite unusual. How much did you say it was?"

And because the Cotting women were fair of face and figure, and diligent about their work, and guests of a wealthy household, and visited regularly by the Ramstrong family, the women of St. Olafred's allowed themselves to purchase the goods they offered at market, and even to be drawn into conversation with them at the market stall, or up at the house, did they happen by there for one of Annie's cures.

In Annie the three women had found the best companion they could have wished for in their adjustment or readjustment to the true world. And she, in them, had the means and motivation to step out into a town she had found unapproachable despite and because of her wealth, and without the assistance of Lord Dought. Together they could begin to accomplish what none of them were able to do alone, consoling each other for their worldly ignorance and devising ways to overcome it that were not too terrifying to enact.

When they worked thus, affairs generally went well. And Urdda, having been in the true world for a year, seldom made such errors of judgment or impulsive decisions as would redound on her unpleasantly. But Liga had been away a long time, and Branza sometimes forgot that she was not at home anymore, and there were times when they conducted themselves quite strangely according to the customs of the true town. Branza would greet any person she saw, and be upset if they tut-tutted, stared at her, or ignored her. She did not understand the purpose of guard dogs, and several times was badly frightened, and once nearly bitten, by the savage things.

The worst misunderstanding began when Urdda and Branza, returning from the market one afternoon, happened on Vivius Strap flogging one of those near-broken-down donkeys of his outside the fetid stables he kept in the alley off the ash-tree square.

Branza flew at him and hauled at his arm, trying to take the switch from him; it took all Urdda's strength to detach her and move her along, with Strap fouling the echoing lane with his language after them, and calling them spinsters and witches and busy-biddies.

"How could he treat an animal so?" wept Branza.

"Do not *speak*, Branza. Do not *utter* until we are back home safe!" Urdda spoke so savagely that Branza's tears stopped in surprise. Urdda propelled her on up the hill, forcing a smile at a goodwife whom she half knew, who had paused and would have asked for explanation had the two women not swept past her so determinedly.

"You are not the sister you were, Urdda," Branza said tremblingly as they entered Widow Bywell's street, which thankfully was empty of people, with only Larra Kitchener's canary pouring its caged heart out in the window there.

"Well, you, *you*, are *exactly* the sister you were." Urdda released her. "And you *cannot* be, Branza; it will bring you nothing but trouble. Everything is different, and you must learn a different behavior to match it."

"That little animal, that starven. Did you see how miserably it stood? And is standing now, no doubt," insisted Branza, "as he beats it, with not the energy to obey him, so poorly has he fed the creature."

Urdda opened the door of Annie's house. "He's thrashing it twice as bad because of your interference. Did you think of that? You did not succeed in stopping him—you only made it worse for the beast."

"But I could not just walk *by*!" Branza passed her sister in the doorway.

Urdda shut the door behind them. "Why not? He told you true: it is his beast and he has rights over it, to treat or mistreat as he will."

"Who gave them to him?" wept Branza. "Who gave him rights to injure something so? They are as great criminals as himself!"

"Oh, shush-shush! There is nothing you can do." Exasperated, Urdda embraced her sister, who was taller than her, and so much older, and so intent, it seemed, on not seeing things as they were. "You must watch and wait, Branza, to see what powers you have and don't have. It is not like home. We ruled there. Everything fell into place around what *we* wanted. Here, we are not the only ones wanting, and we must make room for other people's desires."

"But other people's desires are so *wrong* and so *cruel*, Urdda!"

"Not always, sister. And when they are, one girl, or even two, can often do nothing more than take their own displeasure and walk by. You cannot set everything aright as you used to, keeping secrets, burying littlee-men—"

"What ails her?" Liga had come to the workroom door at the noise. "Urdda, what has happened?"

"Go in with Mam, Branza—give me your basket. I will put these in the pantry and bring us a dandwin-and-water to steady us."

And she ushered Branza into Liga's arms, where she would find consolation telling her unfortunate story to another recent outcast of heaven.

Beside the cottage step, Branza attacked the ground with a stick. Liga had dug holes for the two jewels using only her hands, but this weed-field had been garden then; now it was wasteland, the ground hard as stone.

"Aach!" She stabbed with her stick, and a mean lump of earth cracked upward. "Cruel stuff," she muttered. "Have you been magicked against me?" She was hot from walking, and clumsy from the excitement she had carried here, from the secret, from the goodbyes-that-must-not-seem-like-goodbyes with which she had left the house.

Alone? Urdda had said. *That is not wise.*

I will go straight down to market, she said. *There are plenty of women there. I need to stretch my legs and walk straight, and look at something more distant than my needlework. My very eyeballs are cramped.* With those words she had cleared the suspicion from Urdda's face.

More small, hard chunks of earth broke away. "You are the *same earth,*" Branza said. "How can you be so stubborn?" She fought some more loose with the stick. "Mam dug you in her *sleep,* almost." She tried again with her fingertips, and loosened a stone the size of a pea, and a few grains of earth with it.

323

How deep, Mam? Did the moon-bab say? Branza had asked the other day. *As in the stories, you know: "Dig you an arm's length; there will the treasure lie." Or "A hole the size of your own head, and lay the charm-stone in it."*

No particular depth, Mam had said. *Just to cover them.*

Foolish girl, Branza told herself. You should not have asked and drawn Mam's attention. Now she has only to remember that conversation and she will know exactly where to look for you.

Perhaps she should have wetted the ground—brought some bowl or bucket and filled it from the stream, and soaked and softened and made the earth diggable that way. Perhaps there was a bowl in the wreckage of the house, for surely Mam would have used such? Branza sat back on her heels and eyed the gray thatch rotting in the doorway, glued flat there by the years' many weathers, the weathers of all Branza's life span— well, the shrunken version of it that had passed in this world. No, she would not even begin to lift that roof-edge. Surely town people or gypsies would have come by and taken anything useful long before the roof fell in.

Just to cover them. That was not so deep. She returned to her task, and after some dogged work had a hole big enough, she thought. She took the cloth from her belt and untied the red jewel. Ought she to say something, to beg those powers- that-be that Annie spoke of? No, Mam had been too tired to beg, she was sure; Mam had only dug and buried.

She had been there herself, baby Branza! "Why did you not *look?*" she told her infant self across the years. "Why did you not lift your babby head from your wrappings and take note for me what she did?"

She held the heavy jewel and banished frivolous thoughts

from her mind. She ought to be solemn at least, about this. Part of the success of this came from single-minded wanting— or wanting *not*; wanting escape. She thought of the town in her mother's heaven: of the peaceful streets, of the green squares that brought sunshine in among the house-rows; she held Wolf in her mind, the feeling of his fur, his cold lick on her hands, on her cheek; she cast imaginary bread onto the path, and the birds came flocking, and she named them, aloud, while Mam wove rushes by the window.

Please, she thought as she reached down into the warm, dry earth and placed the ruby there. "Please let me go there," she said aloud, in case the moon-bab was listening just outside the skin of this world, as Mam had said, waiting for a woman's distress to activate it, or a falling Bear's, or a stamping littleeman's.

Now she filled the hole, businesslike, and crossed to the other end of the step, and began again. She should be doing this at night, maybe at midnight; that was always a propitious time, Annie said. Not in the glare of afternoon, when things were emphatically not magical, but bald, and hard, and too clear-lit, with no mystery about them, no power. But she could not have got away in the night. There was her inquisitive sister; her anxious mam; and Annie, who noticed everything, though she did not always say; then there was the town guard, who might in that other place permit her to pass, with only a reminder to be home before dawn so that Mam would not worry—and not even that, these last years; only a nod these last years. But here they would step up smartly and require her to state her business, and were she to say, "I am walking to my mam's old house, whence I hope to convey myself magically to the land of her heart's desire," would take her in hand, she was sure, and smiling to each other would lead her kindly home, perhaps calling for a physic along the way.

So it must be done now. She brought her dig-stick down on the hard dirt at the southern end of the doorstep. The blow jarred her knuckles, her elbows, her shoulders, and made her teeth clack together. Oh, it was hopeless.

But hopeless or not, she must persist. For she might discover it to be quite easy, once this part was done. Why, Mam had slept away the passage there—Branza herself had slept her bab-sleep, and woken in that other place. Coming the other way, Ramstrong had simply run up into the air and flown. Urdda had pushed her way through with the force of her wanting. And that Teasel boy, from what Urdda said, had fallen through, in the excitement of fleeing—fleeing from Branza, that lucky Branza who had not known how lucky she was. That happy Branza, whom nobody disapproved of or stared at, who never had to concern herself with town opinion.

So Branza dug, and with what felt like appropriate words laid the clear jewel in the bottom of the cavity, and filled it in.

Then sleep, child, the moon-babby had said to Mam.

And that is all you did? Branza had asked her, affecting to be only curious, sewing, sewing—she could see the very flower, a fanciful crimson and rose-pink thing, on which she had been working as she spoke.

I was capable of no more, Mam had said, and laughed. *I slept the way a stone sleeps, or a fallen log on the forest floor. And when I woke, I was there.*

And Branza had watched her, all ordinary there, diligently hemming, and Mam had raised her head from the hemming and given Branza a distracted smile.

To sleep on the doorstep, with her head to the east—that would be the most magical thing to do, Branza thought. But the sun was strong there; she would not be able to sleep in that heat. So she lay among the weeds along the wall, and a fine soft bed they made, and a consistent, if thin, shadow, and she pillowed her head on her earthy-smelling hands, and she quelled her racing thoughts—of Mam, of Urdda, of their realizing she was gone—and convinced herself that the warm wall behind her was the bulk of Wolf, lain down with a whine behind her, and guarding her as she slept.

Urdda and Liga strode about St. Olafred's. The light was almost gone, but still they peered into every alley and doorway they came to that might conceal Branza, every chink and corner.

"She will not be in the *water*," said Urdda, turning back to find Liga still on the bridge she herself had just crossed.

But Liga searched the stream below, and eyed the culvert into which it was rushing. Then, slowly, she walked down the bridge, seeming to age further with every step.

"We must go back to Ramstrong's," said Urdda. "We will tell them we have had no luck. He will organize a search. He will have her found in no time."

Liga took the arm she offered, but would not adopt the stride Urdda wanted. All her briskness and purpose, all the anxiety that had driven her out of the house and around the town, seemed now to have flown.

They reached the corner and Urdda would have had them go Ramstrong's way, but Liga stopped, silent, her head down.

"What is it?" said Urdda. "Come, Mother. While there is this last bit of light."

"I must go home and see if something . . ." She raised her face to Urdda almost pleadingly. "Before we tell anyone."

"See what?"

"Well, see if she has come home, even. While we searched for her, no? And then . . ."

"Then what?" Urdda tried to set a stronger pace in the direction Liga wanted, but although Liga moved, she seemed still reluctant.

Urdda felt a flare of impatience, but she adjusted herself to Liga's creeping, and bent to where Liga almost cowered under the press of her thoughts. "What is it, Mam? What are you thinking that's worrying you so?"

"She was asking me about the—about how I came to be in that heart's desire of mine, that place . . ."

"Ah," said Urdda. "So she's gone hunting that moon-bab, you think?"

"I think maybe that. I have a terrible feeling."

"To the cliff-top, then?"

"Yes, and what if she casts herself off it, and the bab does not save her, and she dies falling? Or, just as bad, what if the bab saves her and takes her utterly away from us?"

Even in the dusk, Urdda could see Liga's eyes brimming. "And what if she only walks back and forth, begging into the night? I have done that often enough myself. Or what if she finds the little moss-patch we found before, and sleeps there, and wakes saner in the morning? Always your mind goes to the worst, Mam, and the worst very seldom happens. She will not throw herself off that cliff, don't you worry. She would not do that to us. Only *I* would, when I was younger and sillier."

"And I did not think she would *attack* a man, either," said Mam tremorously, "for beating his own donkey. But she did that. She is not herself."

Urdda tried yet again to remember Branza's goodbye that afternoon. *I will go straight down to market,* she had said. There had been nothing special in her bearing, had there, particularly? Urdda remembered her own annoyance. *Annie and I are in the middle of a batch,* she had said, *or I could come with you. Can Mam go?* Now she could not recall whether Branza had looked secretive or sly at all—she *thought* she would be able to tell, were Branza trying to hide something, but she was less sure of this grown sister than she had been of the one she had left behind with the Teasel-Bear.

"I failed that girl," Liga muttered at Urdda's elbow. "I did her a great wrong, just as Miss Dance said."

Urdda sniffed. "Yes, you failed her so badly, all she wants to do is go back to the world you gave her, ungrateful girl! To the time that you were failing her. How she must hate you!"

"I should not have said it was stories, when I was telling you both about here. Only, it relieved her so to hear it, and I wanted her to be at peace."

"Of course you did, Mam! When she is not at peace, she's most irritating. Such as lately. Such as tonight."

"Oh, do not say that—it is not night yet!" And Liga glanced up anxiously at the first few undeniable stars.

When they reached Annie's house, Liga had the energy to establish quickly that Branza had not returned, and then to hurry upstairs, but when Urdda had reported on their search to Annie and followed her mother up, she was sitting against her bed-edge in the dark, and her window seat was opened and its contents half emptied onto the floor.

"She has taken the jewels," Liga said.

"The jewels?" Urdda pictured Annie's coffer as she had last seen it, a quarter full of glitter and gleam.

"The stones the moon-bab gave me. The red and white. I shall never see her, my golden girl, no more," Liga said piteously.

Urdda went and wrapped her in her arms. "She will come

329

back, Mam. She knows what Miss Dance said. She knows she must come back, not stay forever as you tried."

"She will try, too," wept Liga. "She takes so much after me, she will stay forever, I know. She will be perfect happy there. I should be glad for her, I suppose, but—"

"So selfish!" Urdda whispered angrily into Liga's hair. "How dare she run away and hurt you so!" *What am I saying?* Urdda thought. *Who am I to talk, that ran away a full year, which multiplied to ten for my poor mam? If this is how she suffers for a night's loss, what kind of a state did I put her in?*

But Liga's mind did not go the same way; she did not even seem to hear Urdda's words. She must be too deep in this present distress.

"I will go to Ramstrong's now," said Urdda. "We will start everyone looking. Out to the cliff, out to the cottage, everywhere. Don't you worry, Mam—"

"No," said Liga, holding her tighter. "I cannot stand that her name be bandied about in the town so. If she is found by some gang of townsmen, even Ramstrong himself, she will be so embarrassed. Tomorrow, you and I will go out to look. We will be the ones to find her wandering, or her body, or her gone altogether."

Branza paused and drank at Marta's Font. When she straightened, Teasel Wurledge was in the road ahead, and the air around fairly thrummed with Branza's aloneness, Branza's impropriety.

"Such free spirits, you Cotting girls," he said.

"Good morning," she said stiffly. Should she call him "Mister Wurledge"? But she was so much older than him.

He stood aside, then fell into step with her. "What are you at, out here on your ownsome at crackerdawn?"

330

She did not like him so close to her elbow. Or like at all the set of him, with his hint of stooping and secrecy. She walked a little faster, but he kept pace easily, and the noise of her hurrying skirts made her slow again.

"I remember you young and fair, Branza, as no one else here does."

"My mother does, and Urdda, and Ramstrong—"

"As no man. No St. Olafred's man remembers you as marriageable as I do. I seen you just blossoming, in your perfection."

She walked on, watching the stones before her feet. She did not understand. He was describing some other sort of woman.

"I seen you—"

"You should not talk to me like this." She hurried again— let her skirts panic as they may.

"Why not? I am free to walk here. And you've no guardian, so we've privacy, whatever I might want to say."

"I do not like it."

Several more steps passed.

"You still have a full figure, though your face might be flagging," said Wurledge.

Branza had no clue how to answer this.

"What have you been doing in the woods all alone, with the leaves in your hair?" He reached, impertinent man, and plucked one out. She veered away from him. "Rolling on the ground, is it? Imadging you were a lady bear?"

There was the memory: the mounted bear and the mounting, and all the zinging strangeness that engendered. And a stab of fear—the forest flashing, him crashing behind. Her throat made an unbidden, realizing sound. He heard it and knew she remembered; he saw her face, and it made him grin.

"You know what I like," he hissed close behind her ear. "You seen me with her."

"No," she said, meaning, *No, that is not what my face meant, my surprise*. This was too dreadful—this man, this misunderstanding, her crawling away from her night's disappointment, from her gray drear dawn against the wall of the ruined cottage, only to find this embarrassment waiting for her, making of her something and someone she was surely not, affecting to know her but completely mistaking her, and then forcing his mistake on her, demanding that she answer to it.

You must not go out alone here, little Urdda had said, so smooth-faced and sure of herself, the day they had arrived here. *It is not the same in this world. It isn't safe, a woman alone. Just tell me, and I will go with you. Or Mam.* Mam, Urdda—both so unreachable now.

"And I seen you watching, Branza. You dint run away nor blush; you looked me straight on, me and my big rod. Don't you tell me it did not excite you."

He walked sideways beside her. What would she do if he stopped and blocked her way? And if he showed her again—for his trousers were all malformed over himself, she could see from the corner of her averted eyes—whatever would she do?

"You wanted of me, just like that lady-bear did. I seen it in your face."

"You did not," she said shakingly, "for it was not there." She stepped aside as if to go around him. The bend was just ahead; soon they would come in sight of the town gate, and maybe a guard.

He was terribly close. He had hold of her arm. His breath was in her eyes. "Oh, I seen it, all right. How long had you stood there, watching? For we had been going there a good long time, that time, I remember it. How could you watch it and not want some?"

She twisted from his grip and ran from him, and was around the bend. There were people: a cart coming out the town gate, and a woman talking over the fence of the pig farm. Branza did sob then, with gratitude, though they were too far away to hear.

Wurledge rounded the bend behind her and stopped; she heard him as she hurried on. "Never mind, you will have me, Branza Cotting." His voice diminished behind her. "I have had your titty out your bodice before. I will again. You will lay down with me again like you used to."

She ran a few steps, then slowed to a hurrying walk. She trusted to glance behind her. He was making for the trees at the road-edge, in his stooping, sneaking way.

She composed herself to pass the carters, and then to walk up into the town. Such a long way, it was, up there to Lady Annie's! She would never leave there again, not without Mam or someone. What a hideous person, that Teasel Wurledge! How could she have guessed—

But she could, she could have guessed. The bear showing himself off, the man boasting of that—that *rod*; of course they were the same. And all his playfulness as Bear, all his company and comfort, had been in order to push himself up close to her, and fumble with her skirts and clothing. And she, so stupid, stupid—Mam had known, Mam had known exactly. Mam had always been looking dark, and pressing her lips together about him. Why had she not *said* out-and-out, directly? Why had Mam not warned her?

She passed the end of the laundry lane. Two of those red-armed girls looked up from slapping wet laundry on a wash-rock. Sunlit water sprayed and shone in the lane behind them; steam billowed across and girls turned ghostly within it, and men pushed barrows there of sodden cloth and stacked clean. Their talk was brazen tones, with no words or feelings in it, with no meaning; a kind of garbled, harsh music.

"Someone have been a-wandering in the forest," fluted one of these closest girls to the other.

"Such luxury, to amble about and lose one's senses." These words came, quite clear, like small, evil people, across the cobbles to Branza's ankles, where they stood and smirked up at her.

She made herself walk on.

". . . and then to lie back on my pillows, no? And call for a glass of Franitch wine . . ."

"Watch the visions sporting in my bed-curtains . . ."

"Oh, visions, is it? Well, that would make a change." More slapping sounded, and laughter.

Branza picked two curled dead leaves from her hair and dropped them on the damp cobbles. In my town, she thought, your lane was dry and empty. My sister and I thought those stones were there for us to climb on. Mam must not have liked you either, to have wiped you so cleanly from the world. It cannot only be me, then, who feels this fear and out-of-placeness.

Someone hawked above her, and a white spit hit the cobble just before her skirt passed over it. It is that Tallow boy at his window, she thought. I will not look up and encourage him.

"Here she is, the donkey's savior."

Young men—six of them, or seven—crowded in the mouth of a lane, all ready to laugh at her. Branza's twig-teased hair wisped across her eyes. She tried not to falter in her walking.

"I hear she did not manage to save the poor old beast."

"Bone-arse Bobby? Oh, no, he is dogmeat now. Whipped into slices, neat as a cleaver done it."

As if a single mind moved them, they made of themselves a curved wall of chests, an arm's length around Branza. She turned and tried to walk around the end of their line, but the curve of them moved with her, cupping her, and her progress became a horrible dance, with Branza leading and all the more ridiculous for doing so.

"Ooh, do not beat him, Mister Strap!" one cooed. "I pray you!"

"Leave his poor, lazy bone-arse be!" said another.

"Or I will take the ribbon from my hair and stripe your own flanks with it, so I will!"

"How could you be so cruel?"

"Oh, Mister Strap!"

"Mister Strap, how *could* you?"

They moved rapidly with her up the street. They had a smell, collectively, so strong it stopped her thinking. Their feet sounded harder than her shoe-soles on the cobbles. When she tried to see her way, the rows of their teeth and eyes bobbed below the rooves and the window-shutters.

She stopped, and closed her eyes. Maybe she was still asleep, still adream on the cottage doorstep. Maybe she'd only to pass through this nightmare and there she would be, with the garden-rows spreading out at her feet, with Wolf trotting up the path to say his good-mornings.

She breathed the boys' smell. Their noises swarmed in her head: bumpings of bodies and cooing voices and slapping feet. If only Wolf were beside her now! His growl bubbled in her throat.

"I shall whip and whip you, Mister Strap!" sang a boy.

"I shall whip you and worse, I shall!"

Branza bared her teeth.

"I shall bring the law down on you!"

She barked, sudden and deep. She bit at the air, right close to the ones in front of her.

"What the buggery!"

Surprise knocked one of them to the ground, and others, more agile, leaped back.

"We have druv her mad! We have broke her brain!"

One of them crouched up the hill, in her path. "Come, doggy-doggy-dog!" he crooned.

She walked to him. She was full of wolf-teeth, wolf-love of herself, wolf-rage on her behalf. She took the boy's head in her two hands and bent to him among the others' hoots and whistles, and she bit his cheek hard—which was salt, which gave, meat under her teeth, the scratch of his reddish beard on her lower lip.

It did not matter what happened thereafter. They encircled her, but none touched her. She tasted the boy's blood on her teeth. They held the bitten boy back from her, and none would come near her. With conviction that felt like magic, she reached for another boy's head. He shrank before her, and she walked through their circle and up the hill, past a stunned matron here, a wide-eyed child there, doors opening, and windows, past the end of the lane where the donkey had been whipped to death, and on upward.

Finally Liga had slept, after most of the night staring at her own fears playing themselves out against the ceiling. In her exhaustion, in her body's relief at her mind's ceasing to strain it with onerous thoughts, she had slept well beyond first light, and Urdda must have decided to let her sleep, and told Annie to do the same, for neither of them had disturbed her.

What woke her was commotion outside, down in the street and coming closer. Young men's voices, a group of them, overexcited—the frighteningest sound in the world.

She was at the window before she came properly awake, knowing in an instant they had come for her, for her babies, to commit whatever outrage they could. She clawed the drapes aside, clawed the lace. There they were. There, there! was her bab, all-grown-up Branza, in their midst, tall and fair and besieged. What were they about, with their rage and taunting? How dare they even look at her, let alone speak, let alone speak in those tones!

"Oh, my poor child!" Liga fumbled with the window-catch. It resisted her frightened fingers, She stood imprisoned at the glass.

Look at the girl! Look at her hair, all wisping and leaf-littered; Urdda would be appalled! Urdda would be appalled at Liga herself, all bed-clothed and frantic, displaying herself at the window. But look at her elder girl there—what gave her cause to walk so firmly, so straight-backed? She might be Miss Dance, she had such purpose in her step. And she glanced around at the lads with a face Liga had never seen on her daughter before: a taunting smile, bright ready eyes, almost *greedy* for trouble! And could that be a smudge of *blood* on Branza's chin? What on earth had she done?

Whatever it was, whether she had torn someone's throat out with her teeth or only bitten her own lip in some scuffle against these boys, a warm wave of purest relief, foaming at the fringes with pride, now washed through Liga, to see her daughter so. Look how they circled her, not daring to touch! In some way, she had bested them; they were *afraid* of her, look! It was marvelous that she, Liga, so frightened herself, had made a girl who could claim a path ahead from a pack of hostile lads! She wished she could fling open the window and cheer—how angry Urdda would be if she did! She had to laugh at the thought, even as she drew the lace across and continued her watching through it.

Gracious, there was Whinney, the constable, hurrying up

337

the street from behind, two young men running with him, chattering wide-eyed, waving their arms. Shutters were flinging open now, on other houses, at the noise below; the Kitcheners, across the way, were coming out onto their doorstep to watch.

"Oh, *good*," said Liga, pleased that people should see Branza so calm and sure and strangely happy; that they should see how she held her own among those shouting, skittering boys; pleased too that they would disapprove it, that Urdda would disapprove too, yet here went Branza like the queen of a spring parade, bestowing her smile, her *wicked* smile—she must have some witch in her!—on her tormenters. But how could they be tormenters if Branza refused to be tormented by them? They became just jumping children, scared of this tall, beautiful, smiling girl with her madwoman's hair.

Liga heard the front door open, although nobody had knocked. She could not see Branza clearly at that angle; she only knew that the constable had reached her, heard his firm voice under the lads' noise. Urdda, too, spoke, and *her* voice was clearly audible: "What have you done, Branza?"

Liga laughed again—two of them! That both her daughters could face such a mob of men—a constable among them!—and keep their voices, and their posture, and their spirit, astounded her, delighted her.

Now they were babbling at Urdda, those lads. Some were angry, some laughed in their excitement, and others joined forces to drag forward one of their number—oh, look at his face there, the flap of flesh, the stripe of blood down his front! *That* was the deed, *that* was Branza's crime! Oh!

Liga was caught between covering her face with fright and clapping her hands. What would Da have done if she'd bitten him so; what would those boys? And yet she wished she had;

she wished she had had some blood from them, as they had had from her.

Out of the confusion below, the constable very determinedly led Branza by the arm; she did not resist, but appeared to be just as happy to be led by him as she had been to conduct herself up the hill.

"How *dare* he!" And Liga pushed aside the lace, wanting to open the window and shout at the man like a laundry-woman.

But even as she loosened the catch, she saw the cloaked figure of Urdda pushing forward through the rabble, taking Branza's other arm. That smaller, more fiery figure turned then, and, as if she had read Liga's mind, she *shot* her a look, even as Liga pulled the lace around her face like an Eelsister's wimple—a warning look if ever Liga saw one—before walking on, as straight-backed and certain as her sister among the milling men.

"What the blazes?" Annie flung back the bedchamber door.

"My Branza appears to have been arrested," said Liga.

"For biting that Hopman lad, who'd-a-thought!" Annie joined her at the window, and they both stood there laceless, in clear view of curious neighbors and of trailing lads who might turn to look. "Not that someone oughtn't to've bit him a long time ago. But I'm not sure that that Whinney-man has my same sense of justice. Look at him, loving the fuss. Look at them all."

"Look at Branza and Urdda—are they not brave?" breathed Liga.

Annie peered and grinned. "Heh-heh. There is nothing like upbringing in a heaven to give a girl false confidence."

"False, you think?" said Liga anxiously, dropping the lace back across the window.

"The size o' that mob, Liga? I say false. Get yourself dressed, girl, in your very best; we will need to summon all the menfolk and all the respectability we can, if she's not to be whipped in the street."

Branza slept in perfect peace. The world echoed empty around her. Her bed was stone; she must have moved from the weedy wall sometime in the night. The light was dim yet; before long, the sun would come up over the trees and warm the cottage step as it always did. That dream where she became a wolf and bit the man attacking her, where she was paraded like a prize and like a naughty child through the town, where she sat in that cold room with the bloodied boy and the boy's raging mother and the constable shaking his head and the clerk staring and scribbling by turns—that would all be burned away. Wolf would come from the forest and greet her; Mam would start to move about in the house; and another peaceful day would lift out of night and begin its slow arc over her.

The sounds of rubbing metal and thudding wood woke her into the cell: to the glistening stone walls, to the stone bed like a sarcophagus, to the cool light spilling in from the barred window. The door was opening, the heavy door, and there in the cool light, improbable, stood Mam and Urdda, with the constable hovering warily behind them, his key in his hand.

Branza sat up. "So it was not a dream," she said. "The constable, and all those people shouting."

"Leave us a moment, please, Mister Whinney," said Liga loftily, without looking over her shoulder at him. "While we explain to her."

"Very well," he said. "Make sure she is quite clear, though, as to what's required."

Liga nodded and waved him away, again not dignifying him with a glance. "He is angry," she whispered across to

Branza. "Ramstrong has just given him a right talking-to. And on top of a nagging from Wife Hopman, I believe. Poor man is beset, all sides."

They stepped in, Urdda pausing to shudder, Liga coming straight to Branza. She took up her hands and clasped them, and looked straight into Branza's heart—it felt to Liga as if she stabbed her daughter with a sword, but at the same time it opened her own eyes so that all the pain and worriment she had had since Branza took the jewels and left the house last night shone there, ached there. All the certainty and humor Liga had had at the cell door vanished, and these other emotions—Branza saw them coming like unlocked water down a mill-channel. Then up they welled and down they spilled, and Branza rose from the bed-stone and took hold of her, and mother and daughter wept on each other's shoulders.

"Come, come," said Urdda. "But it is all *fixed* now, and well."

"No, it is not; no, it is not!" said Liga, and wept so hard that Branza made her sit down beside her on the stone in case she collapsed to the floor.

When she calmed enough to speak, Liga said, "How did you think life would *be* here, if you were not with us?"

"Why, much as it was without Urdda, I would say, for ten years."

"No, no!" Liga sprang fresh tears. "That was in my heaven! I felt nothing there, nothing unpleasant! Here I feel everything, and fears and sadnesses the worst, because I am so out of the habit of them, after all my years of serenity."

"So why may I not go where *I* am free of those bad feelings, Mam? You wanted to go—why should I not?"

"But I did not have a mam who wanted me to stay!"

"Or a sister!" said Urdda.

341

"No!" said Liga. "Or good work, or fine friends such as Ramstrong and Lady Annie, and all these others we are meeting and making dresses for! Or prospects of marriage, and making a happy old grumma out of your mam! I went because I was so unhappy; had I stayed, I would have died of it, *died* of it. I came to that cliff, and I was *determined* to die of it, all on a sudden, and I held you out, and I—and I—"

Branza gathered Liga up and held her tightly. "Stop, Mam, stop! I did not mean to have you so distressed. Of course, of *course* I do not want to be dead; of *course* I am not as unhappy as that! Hush, now!"

But Liga would not hush; she sobbed and groaned and rocked in Branza's arms as if the memories were blows, cuffing her this way and that. Urdda sat the other side of Liga, to contain her misery that way.

"I'm sorry, Mam!" Branza wept. "I'm sorry! Forgive me! I won't talk of it again, Mam, I promise! I won't try, I won't run away. I'll stay with you, I will! Morning till night," she sobbed, "just as you want it!"

Liga shook her head, and could not speak for a while.

"I will not go, Mam," said Branza. "Or even try to go, I promise, if it upsets you so—"

Liga's hand over her mouth interrupted her. "Hush that," she said, and now she recovered herself, and in a few moments it was as if she had not shed a single tear, so suddenly steady were her voice and figure. "This," she said, "is entirely my own doing. I should not be surprised, not the tiniest bit, at any of it. Miss Dance told me I ought not to have kept you—you, nor Urdda neither—in that place for so long. Hush, let me finish, Branza-girl! No, it was *my* world, as she said; *my* idea of what the world should be like, conceived when I was fifteen and in miserable times. It was no place for a girl to grow up in. I should have let you grow in the true world, and make your decision, on truth, what life you wanted to lead. And now—she is right—I have spoiled you for the true world. I have grown you up believing that things are one way when they really are another. I have *deceived* you, is what it is. I have practiced a cruelty upon you just as bad as those—as they did—as bad as any cruelty that was *ever* done me." She pushed away a memory with her hands.

"What cruelty, Mam? What cruelty was done to you, that you wanted to go away forever?" She leaned close and laughed a little through her remaining tears. "Tell me who did it to you, Mam—I will go and *bite* him!"

The three of them had to laugh at that. "You have got away with it the once," Urdda said, "but I do not think Whinney will stand for you biting anyone else."

"Indeed, you must promise him you will not," said Liga, wiping tear-traces from her cheeks with her fingers. "That is one of his conditions of releasing you."

"And you must promise you will never go out unaccompanied," said Urdda, "by me or Mam or Todda or some other respectable person."

Branza rolled her eyes. "He sounds just like Urdda, doesn't he, Mam, with all his rules and warnings?"

But Liga was off in her thoughts and did not answer. She took a hand of each daughter into her lap. "You must forgive me, the both of you, hiding you away in my heaven so long. I thought I was preserving all our happinesses, keeping us there."

"Of course you were!" said Urdda.

"We were *so* happy there," said Branza in consternation. "How can you think we might not have been?"

"You shall go, Branza," Mam said.

Branza blinked at her.

"She shall?" said Urdda. "But I thought you didn't want—"

"I shall ask Annie to lend us of her carriage," said Mam. "And you shall go to Rockerly and have Miss Dance do the necessary magics to send you to *your* heaven."

"Miss Dance?" said Branza fearfully. "She would do that?"

"She said to me, if I ever wanted to go back I should come to her." She sat back and smiled—smiled determinedly, and with not much natural joy.

Branza could not muster a smile in return. She ought to feel glad, she knew, that Mam had stopped distressing, and would help her in her quest. Instead, she was bewildered. The change had been too sudden. How had it come about? Also—though she knew it was foolish to feel this way—Mam's agreeing upset her as if it were a banishment. There was a difference between Branza achieving her heaven in secret and being sent by Mam to Rockerly to gain it.

"Are we ready, then," said Urdda, "to face the constable, and Annie, and Ramstrong, and the rest of St. Olafred's? We are keeping Ramstrong from his work, I think."

They were both waiting for Branza's answer: for her permission, for her readiness. How could she want to leave them, she wondered, to go to a world where they existed, if at all, as ever-pleasant facsimiles of themselves? Did she not want to know them truly, in all their tempers and moods, too, in their storms of weeping?

But they were keeping Ramstrong. Branza stood up from the stone bed. "We are ready," she said. Urdda stood too, and they pulled Mam to standing, and all hand-held together, they left the cell.

14

" 'Tis a pity Ramstrong could not come," said Branza at the carriage window. "And Todda. And Anders would have loved this too. He would have been full of questions that would knot our brains."

"There are many things for Ousel to count, too," said Urdda. "But they are too busy readying the house for the new bab."

Branza said nothing. Would she even see that bab? Perhaps not, if this mission to Rockerly was successful.

"You know," said Urdda confidingly, "Ramstrong told me he was hoping for a daughter."

"Todda says he has wanted girls all along, since meeting you and me, Urdda."

"Truly? How nice to think that! Although he could not wish for better children than Anders and Ousel."

"Oh, there's no doubt he loves them dear, too. As we all do."

The light flitted and fluttered on Branza's face as the

carriage passed among trees. The tearful goodbyes were long behind them, but Urdda remembered them all, particularly how sweetly Ousel and Anders had put their faces up to Branza to be kissed.

"You should have children of your own, Branza!"

Branza looked at her in surprise. "I am nearing *thirty*, Urdda!"

"A score and five years is *not* near thirty! And plenty of women older than thirty have babies. And you are still beautiful! All you need do is show an interest, and I should think you would have your choice of suitors."

Branza's face was grave and closed, holding back some thought.

"What is it? You have a secret! Had you someone in mind? Oh, tell me! Who? Who was he? Who would you have?" And she bounded up out of her seat and plumped down next to Branza.

"No, no." The sunlight slanting in on Branza's hands, which were clasped in her lap, showed the texture of the skin: tiny pleats, like the finest, supplest leather. "When you went," said Branza. A shaft of guilt passed through Urdda, and closed her mouth, and made her cease bouncing in her seat. "When you went, Urdda," said Branza very measuredly. "I thought I was being punished, for turning my gaze from our childhood together to Rollo Gruen."

"Oh, Branza, how could you be anything of the sort!" Urdda took Branza's hand in both of hers. "When I went, it was my own whim and adventure alone! How could I know time would run on there without me as it did? It was an accident, Miss Dance said, caused by Lord Dought's incursions. It had nothing to do with you or me or anything we decided."

"Maybe not, but I told myself, *If I have done this, perhaps I can undo it. If I lost her for a boy, I can perhaps bring her back for lack of one. And if it can bring Urdda back, I will not so much as glance at a boy.* And so I ceased to glance, or to think of Rollo or any other boy there."

"Oh, Branza!" Urdda swayed, horrified. "But now you know it was no such punishment, don't you? And—and you have me back, and you need not think that anymore. You can glance again, and consider—"

"And I have not looked at a man these many long years, and now men are more foreign a creature than toads or eels to me. If my wolf could walk out of our old place as a man, as Mam's bear did, I might consider him, but these *men* men here—they are so rough with each other—and the way they speak to women, or about us when they think we cannot hear! They despise us so, Urdda!" She retrieved her hand.

"Not *all* of them." Urdda eyed the hand, but did not reach for it again. "And not all of *us*, Branza. Look at Ramstrong! All his family—none of those men despise us. Mister Deeth, he is always perfect charming and gentle with us. That is one reason I had Annie hire him. And Bakester and his sons, down the market—"

But Branza only looked out at the fields: at the darkening late-spring leafage tumbling past the window, the flying dust.

"Please, Branza." Urdda hardly knew what she was begging for. "I would hate to think of you in a lonely old age."

"I had a lonely youth," said her sister. "This feels quite natural to me."

"Don't say that!" Stung, Urdda leaped from her side to the seat opposite and sat staring.

"Why not? It is true. And you are the one of us that prefers things true."

Urdda stared more, then slumped against the seat-back. "You hate me," she said. "You hate me for being happy here, and for taking you away from those boring kind people and your birds and rabbits and your precious *wolf*!" she finished in something like triumph. With pleasure, she saw the tears rise in her sister's eyes.

But Branza blinked them back, and turned to the window again.

"You used to *fight* me!" Urdda cried in frustration. "Now it is like kicking a sack of . . . of wet sand! You used to have so much more spirit than this!"

Branza took several deep breaths, her eyes flickering with the view. "I do not hate you, Urdda," she finally said. "Only, we want different things, you and I. Quite different. We always have. I can marvel at what you do, and how fearless you are, and how you throw yourself into life just like those two little ones of Ramstrong's, but what I want is peace, and safety, and nothing unexpected to happen. I am not one for adventuring like you."

The carriage rumbled on awhile, and it seemed there was nothing left to say—the two of them looking out at the landscape, Urdda stonily, Branza resigned.

Then Urdda picked herself up and sat next to Branza again, close again but less insistent this time. "You say it was me who left," she said low.

"But it was!"

"But you left me just as badly, Branza."

Branza turned her clear eyes, her fine-featured face, to Urdda.

"Look how tall you are!" said Urdda up at her. "Look how old!"

"But—"

"You became *twenty-five*, Branza, from *fifteen*, while I turned barely a year! *You* it was, left *me* behind! I know you did not mean it—even as *I* did not mean it, to put ten years between us. But it has happened, and they are there, those years. And it is hard to speak across them, with you a woman and me still a girl, when we might have grown up together, finding out things in their same order, and at much the same time."

The brown eyes appealed to the blue, and the blue considered the brown. Urdda leaned against her sister, as she had always done when they sat together ever since they were tinies, Urdda always the tinier.

Finally Branza reached the end of her thoughts. She picked up Urdda's hand and held it firmly in her own lap. "Let us *not* speak, then, for a little while, if it hurts us," she said.

And Urdda leaned in deeper, and laid her head on Branza's shoulder, and the carriage thundered on towards Rockerly town.

"Branza, wake up!"

Urdda tapped her sister's arm and they both straightened in Miss Dance's parlor chairs. Branza glanced at the clock—it had ticked away nearly to midnight!

But now Miss Dance was home. "You cannot be serious," she said sharply from out in the hall. "At this hour?"

Miss Dance herself opened the parlor door as the housekeeper's softer voice explained. A large black cat circled both women's ankles.

Urdda sprang up and curtseyed. "Good evening, Miss Dance!" Branza rose more slowly.

"Evening? It is dead of night, girl! What has happened?" The sorceress took two steps into the room and the cat followed

349

and then preceded her, eyeing Urdda and slowly waving its tail. "What has that naughty drudge done now? The Bywell woman?"

"Why, nothing, mum," said Urdda. "Only, my sister has a request of you."

Miss Dance stripped off her gloves. She turned her fierce, exhausted face upon Branza.

"Perhaps it can wait until morning," said Branza. "I had not realized the hour. I dozed—"

"I will be busy tomorrow. There are fevers in Rockerly lanes that are taking all my attentions lately. Tell me now. What is it that you want?"

"My—I—" Still shaking sleep out of her mind, Branza cast Urdda a confused look, then fixed her gaze on the carpet. From the corner of her eye, she saw Miss Dance look from sister to sister, keen as a hawk.

"Come to my study, girl. It will be cold, but it will be private." She took up one of the lamps.

Urdda's face was a picture of disappointment as Branza went after Miss Dance. Branza had told her, though: *I will speak to her alone*, she had said.

But I want to hear what she has to say!

I will tell you, when it is done.

But you won't remember everything! I just know.

Then you will have to do with a partial story. I cannot have you there, Urdda. This is my business and no one else's. I'm embarrassed about the whole matter.

Up the cold stairs Branza followed Miss Dance. The very swish of the woman's skirt was frightening—how was Branza to state her wish without sounding like a selfish child, to this woman who had been out doctoring folk all night instead of sleeping?

She hurried along the hall and caught up with Miss Dance at the study door.

The sorceress unlocked it and opened it onto a room such as Branza had never seen, where bookshelves stretched from the floor to the ceiling, higgledy-piggledy with books and papers and scrolls and canisters, and an ebony bust or two, and *bones* here and there, they looked like. A large desk filled half the room, and it was piled with more books, and papers too, and writing equipment, and two candlesticks so thick with wax drippings that Branza could not see if they were silver or brass. The cat pressed warm against her skirt hems, then insinuated itself past her into the room.

Miss Dance set the lamp on the desk, returned to the door, and closed it. "What seems to be troubling you, then? To have brought you all the way from St. Olafred's, I am assuming it is not some frivolous problem of romance."

"It may well seem frivolous, mum."

"Sit." Miss Dance indicated which chair. "You look as tired as I feel. It is Branza, is it not?"

"Yes, you brought me and my mother back—"

"I know you. 'Twas only the name escaped me, for a moment." And she sat too, with her soft gloves over one knee and her fine hands like pale spiders glowing in her lap, and waited for whatever words would fall from Branza's lips.

"I was hoping you would help me to return there."

"Return there. Return to the place of your mother's heart's desire, do you mean?"

Branza nodded, all hope knocked out of her heart by the blows of this woman's sharp voice.

"That is impossible," said Miss Dance.

Branza sat there in the silence of the books, in the hiss of the lamp, in the dull shock of the brutal words.

"You know it is impossible, I think. You know that when your mother came back to the true world, the false one ceased to exist."

"Yes, I did."

"Why did you come, then?" Then the sharpness and the disbelief left her voice, and were replaced by real curiosity. "All this way, to ask the impossible?" She picked up the gloves and put them on a corner of the desk. "What were you thinking?" she asked, almost gently.

Branza tried to remember back to when she had set out on this foolish journey. "Well, Mam said you had told her, if she ever wanted to return, she should come to you."

"That is true. And you thought that I could engineer you there too? That is a fair supposition."

Branza looked up. Ought she to feel hope, then?

"I cannot," said Miss Dance, "but I can see how it would seem I might, from your point of view, from your mother's."

"And then, I thought . . ." But Branza was suddenly too tired to continue. "Never mind," she said. "It is impossible, as you say. I will not waste any more of your time." And she pushed herself up from her seat.

"No, no—sit down, girl! Tell me all!"

"But you say— But it is all—" She turned away from the lamp so that this strong, fearsome woman would not see her first tears fall.

The expensive swish of Miss Dance's skirts rose behind her, and the sorceress's hands were firm on her upper arms. "Come," she said matter-of-factly. "Sit down over here, more comfortably. I will build us a fire, and you will tell me what you thought, and I will explain what I can explain."

By the time the fire had been lit, and begun to crackle and converse like a third and more cheerful person among them,

Branza was somewhat recovered. The cat came from wherever it had been hiding and leaped up to sit on the arm of Miss Dance's chair.

"When you first brought us back, me and Mam," she said, "I remember, on the bank of that stream"—Miss Dance nodded from the hearth where she knelt—"I remember you said that ten years was as close as you could come to pulling the two times back together."

"I did. I was working at the very limits of my powers to achieve that much, too."

"Well, that made me think. It sounded to me as if, *before* you had got it back to ten years, the times between the two places had run on very much *further* than ten years."

Miss Dance nodded, and leaned forward to give the burgeoning fire a good shaking-up with the poker.

When she had sat back, Branza ventured, "And so it seemed to me that what you had to do, to bring the times as close as you did, was to *undo* quite a number of years. The way a person unpicks a seam, so as to let out a dress."

Miss Dance raised her firelit eyebrows, but nodded again.

"So that you had to un-happen I-don't-know-how-long of Mam's and my lives that had already happened. Which, I thought, we *did happen* that other way—we did stay, and you did not come through from this world and fetch us until much later in our lives, if you had not managed to pull the differences back, back to ten years." She covered her face, leaving only her mouth clear. "Am I talking nonsense? I am so tired!"

"You are making perfect sense, my dear. Let me see, and you were hoping that I could lift you from this world, where your life is running one way, and place you back on that seam that I unpicked, there to live out your life with your mother."

Branza nodded.

"And without your sister."

Branza swallowed. "If that was the price, yes."

Miss Dance looked to the fire again, but it was burning most spiritedly now, and did not require her attention. She hung the poker on its nail and rose, weariness evident along her every limb, and sat in the armchair opposite Branza.

"I only thought," said Branza hopelessly, "that if you had so much powers over time, and over people moving between worlds, you might be able to do all sorts of things that seem impossible when I first look at them."

Miss Dance laughed low, her teeth glinting in the firelight, and nodded.

"Perhaps to send me there," Branza went on, "or even, only, to bring my friend Wolf into this world. I would not mind that he was of dream-matter. He was real enough for me."

"Either of those is, strictly speaking, within my powers," Miss Dance said to the fire. "But what one *can* do and what one *ought*—those are often two different things. Annie Bywell will be able to tell you that. In all one's movements and transformations, one should be working *with* the directions of nature, not against them."

"But nature gave my mother her heart's desire," said Branza, not hotly, but puzzled still.

"Nature did, and I do not question that it was of benefit, in terms of her safety and your own."

Branza met Miss Dance's gaze. "What was she keeping us safe from? Has she told you? Wild animals, was it? And improper things that men do?" She pushed the memory of Teasel Wurledge from her mind.

"If your mother has not told you, I will not tell it you either; I will not breach her protection of you."

"I am a grown woman."

"Then go like a grown woman and ask her. She may tell you; she may not; but it is her story to tell, not mine."

"And you will not send me back to that place of safety—or to whatever world is mine? To my own heaven?"

She heard it in her own voice: her last bit of hope and longing, the appeal she was making to this mysterious lady's pity.

The lady looked upon her a long time. Then the fire crackled and spat sparks out onto the hearthstone, and she turned away to take the little broom there and sweep them back.

"A heart's desire," she said, sitting back when she was done, "it sounds like a fine thing. And your mother's was, as she wished, the best place to raise her babies in: a kind world with no enemies, gentle upon children and full of natural wonders and pleasant society. Having walked there, I can vouch for your mother's good heart; I have been to other heavens that were nowhere near so sweetly made. I do understand, Branza"—here she reached across the space between the chairs, and her white hand, surprisingly warm, rested momentarily on Branza's—"I do understand your sadness in being here, in the true world. I took you away from your home most abruptly because I was under such strain, and your grief will be greater for it, for the suddenness with which you have had to adjust to a world without your wolf, without all those littler wild things that you loved and that seemed to love you back, without all the kind people. You are enduring a great loss."

Branza sat silent, stiff with disappointment, seeing those animals, that house, those brown-haired people, all too clearly.

"But heart's desires? My dear, I see by your misery—by this very request you are making—that you know more of true men's and women's hearts than once you did, than your mother's world permitted you to see. Such chipped and cracked and outright broken things they are, are they not? They have their illnesses too, and their impulses. And hearts are not always connected well to minds, and even if they are, minds are not always clear and commonsensical. A heart may desire a thing powerfully indeed, but that heart's desire might be what a person *least* needs, for her health, for her continuing happiness."

Branza hardly heard the words—these would be the parts of the conversation she would be unable to relate to Urdda later, for she was listening only for the tone, the gentleness, the understanding coming from this woman, who had seen inside her to her raw, sore soul and was taking such care not to damage her further.

"My mother," she managed to say. "Mam was healthy and happy there—and so were we! Well, I was. Urdda always yearned for the true world, even before she knew of it, I think."

"In your mother's case . . ." Miss Dance's eyes looked blind, reflecting the fire's orange. "She had suffered so greatly, you see—but that is her story to tell you. But I think she was in such deathly pain—and none of it deserved—that when she came to that place, the precipice there . . ."

"The moon-babby took pity on her, are you saying?"

Miss Dance took up the poker and stabbed the fire slowly, thoughtfully. "Something like that. I will not pretend to know exactly what happened."

"And I am not so sad as Mam? Or not so undeserving of my pain?"

Miss Dance sat back, a smile on her face that Branza could never have imagined there when they first sat to talking—all the tiredness of the world was in it, and yet all the warmth, too, and the humor, and the generosity. "You are pure-hearted, Branza, and lovely, and you have never done a moment's wrong. But you are a living creature, born to make a real life, however it cracks your heart. However sweet that other place was, it was not real. It was an artifact of your mam's imagination; it was a dream of hers and a desire; you could not have stayed there forever and called yourself alive. Now you are in the true world, and a great deal more is required of you. Here you must befriend real wolves, and lure real birds down from the sky. Here you must endure real people around you, and we are not uniformly kind; we are damaged and impulsive, each in our own way. It is harder. It is not safe. But it is what you were born to."

They sat awhile; the fire popped and whispered as Miss Dance's words sank into Branza's mind, and spine, and grieving heart.

Miss Dance regarded her, her face in the firelight sparely fleshed, strong-boned, decisive of nose and chin. Her eyes, and the cat's beside her, seemed to glitter with equal intelligence. "You may never be entirely happy; few people are. You may never achieve your heart's desire in this world, for people seldom do. Sit by enough deathbeds, Branza, and you will hear your fill of stories of missed chances, and wrong turnings, and spurned opportunities for love. It is required of you only to *be* here, not to be *happy*. But believe me, you will have a better life here than in the other world, where your mother's happiness was the ruling principle—and the idea of happiness she held at *fifteen*, no less! She never refreshed or nurtured it by exposing herself to any truth, or hardship, or personality more complex than her own daughters'. And while I can understand why she did not, given the strength of her fears and the distresses of her past, I cannot—almost—" She laughed a little. "Were it up to me to forgive or no, I could not forgive her, I do not think, for depriving herself so, and you and Urdda with her."

It was not as if Miss Dance had been talking; it was as if she had been reaching into the clear stream that was Branza's life and one by one turning over the rounded stones at the bottom. Deeper and deeper she had gone, until she was unsticking stones that had been fast in the stream-bed, turning them and rubbing them with her long white witch-fingers so that the mud broke off them and was carried away. And now she was done, and the last, deepest, stone was excavated and washed clean, and the water ran clear among them, and all their surfaces, all their colors and veins and smoothness and imperfections, could be seen afresh.

"Miss Dance?" Branza said, but then her mouth would not pronounce such formal words as came to her mind. "Forgive me," she said, and pushed herself up out of her chair again, and bent and kissed Miss Dance's high, smooth forehead, and then both hollows of her cheeks. "I will let you sleep," she said. "I have stolen so much of your time."

Miss Dance laughed, low and quite as a witch should. "Better you should steal my hours, my dear—my days, even—than that you should stoop to hedge-witchery to achieve your heaven."

"So," said Urdda as the two sisters followed the footman's lamp down the quiet streets of Rockerly to their night's accommodations. She had been asleep when Branza returned to the parlor, and even with the goodbyes and the sharp outside air, she did not feel properly awake. "Will you be coming home with me? Or will you go home to Mister Wolf? You are so sprightly in your step, I think the second." Even in her sleepy voice there chimed a little sadness, and even with her sleepy ears she heard it.

"Oh, no," said Branza cheerfully. "You will not have to travel alone."

"I won't?"

"No, no. I am coming with you." She glanced at her startled sister, then reached through the slit of her cloak to take Urdda's hand and tuck it into the crook of her own elbow. Then she laughed, and the laugh echoed back from the walls of Rockerly's houses. "I may not be happy," she said, "but I will *be*."

"You *seem* very happy," said Urdda crossly.

"Do you wish I were not?" said Branza. "Do you wish I would glum and gloom for you, as you're used to?"

"Of course not. Only—" Only she did not know what. She felt three-quarters asleep; she could not be sure she was not walking in a dream.

Well, in a dream it hardly matters what one says, does it? "I don't know what you are talking about, Branza. I think Miss Dance has magicked you a little bit mad." But she squeezed Branza's arm hard, and she leaned against her sister as well as she could while they walked so that Branza might know how glad she was to hear it, to know that she was staying, to keep her in the same world.

When Urdda and Branza returned to St. Olafred's, all went well for a time. Much of Liga's anxiety faded once she knew that not only would Branza stay by her in this world, but that she would do so willingly, in response to whatever Miss Dance had explained to her. And the two daughters were not so cross-purposed as before; instead of seeming to blame Urdda for the way the town life operated and the thicket of customs and prohibitions she must negotiate, Branza, with many a roll of her eyes and an exasperated sigh, would consult her younger sister as to the manners to employ with different people and the shades of signification given off by garments and gestures,

359

glances and tones of voice. The two of them still squabbled, but the fear had gone from Branza's side of their arguments and the frustration from Urdda's, so that often Liga would find herself smiling as she listened as ghosts of her littler, less troubled daughters flashed and chattered in the air between the two young women.

Their business began to prosper too. The wedding of the ale-man Keller's daughter Ada in early June was really the making of them. It was a fine occasion, with Keller laying on a feast for the greater part of the town to come to, for Ada was his only daughter and he wanted all his customers to celebrate with him. And the bride looked so well in the raiment Liga and her daughters had made, both father and groom were brought to tears at the sight of her there in the dappled sunlight under the wedding-laurels, and several matrons of the town decided then and there that when the time came, their daughters would be clothed by those Cotting women.

Midsummer came. Liga had only vague memories of these celebrations: of hanging at the edges with her mam, too shy to join in the dancing and games. Urdda and Branza, from about nine years of age, had gone up to town to join in, but Liga never quite assembled the courage, preferring to sit out the long evening at home, with the town bonfire a distant flare, a distant scatter of flying sparks, and the shouts and music gusting partial and insubstantial on the warm breeze.

This year Branza and Urdda would not hear of her staying indoors; they gathered a group of Ramstrongs and Threadgoulds in the middle of which Liga could be comfortably swept along through the masked and garlanded town and out onto the Mount, and deposited near the bonfire. And there, seated on a blanket next to Todda, who was big and beautiful with child now, Liga hugged her knees and watched and watched, the dancing on one side and the games on the other. Everyone, from infants just walking to old grummas and grumpas, raced and threw at marks, and balanced eggs on their noses, and everyone danced. Liga had never seen—had never allowed herself to see, at home—husbands and wives, and men and women of marriageable age, dancing together, though she and her mam had danced, and she and her girls, a little. She saw the girls' hands in the boys', the men's hands on the women's hips as they spun and promenaded them, and—she hugged her knees tightly—she hardly knew how to feel, that this was public and permissible, that no harm was meant by it. How blithely the girls moved, her own daughters among them! They talked as they danced, and they laughed, with the men and across to one another—they stumbled and missed steps sometimes and scrambled to catch up, and still they laughed! Girls danced with their fathers—she had not seen this, had not known this—gloriously carefree, with no fear of beatings or bedtime. Such lives they had! Such lives she had given her daughters, she reminded herself—look at them! beautiful, the both of them!

Here was Ramstrong, damp-shirted and pretending exhaustion after the loopings and passings of the clover waltz. "Liga, you've not yet danced a step!" he cried, approaching her and putting out his hand.

"Yes, have a dance, Liga," said Todda. "I cannot partner him; 'twould be like his dancing with a fatted goose!"

Liga resisted at first, but Ramstrong urged her: "Come, 'tis a simple enough step, the simplest"; and Todda: "Go on, Liga; I promise he will not trip over your feet," and the music was very easy-rhythmed and enticing, and before she knew it, her hand was in a man's and she was being led, heart pounding, in among the couples.

Oh my gracious, she thought, but the music and the chatter and fire's roar and crackle hid that whimper she gave, that gasp. And Ramstrong turned to her, all kindness and relaxment, the most reassuring face in the world, and caught her other hand, and then she was dancing with a man for the first time, held by a man for the first time in her life without any force or evil intention. The fire made the faces around them glow and the eyes sparkle; she knew she must be as kindly lit, and she knew her hair, dressed and beribboned by her excited daughters that afternoon, was more becoming than it had ever been. Terrified, dazzled, and elated that she could dance in company and no one could discern that she did not belong, did not deserve this, she followed the steps she had learnt with her mam; danced with her giant mam; danced with her tiny girls on the grass around the cottage, on the matting on the cottage floor, but which were meant—didn't she know? couldn't she see now?—for nights such as this: warm, dark, and sparkling and glowing with bonfire light, with music all around like a spell, like a magical cordial, to be drunk in deep drafts from the air. With people all around: their voices one over the other; their smells—now sharp sweat, now the cedar and lavender of gowns stored yearlong just for this dancing.

"You do not dance like a bear," she ventured to Ramstrong, with a laugh.

"I do not," he said, smiling back. "But you and I know, Liga, how much of a bear I am at heart."

This delighted her, that he would confess to that bulk and clumsiness when here he was, as tall and strong as a man could wish to be, and yet so slender and fine-made in contrast to that beast.

She danced two dances with him, but then a round dance was called and she could not bring herself to be passed from stranger to stranger, especially as she felt herself to be too over-wrought, and the light too patched and poor, to identify whether any of *those* men, Cleavers or Foxes or such, were among the partners assembling. Ramstrong returned her to Todda's side, and took up Branza and was gone again.

"He have not shamed me and crushed your toes?" Todda said, passing Liga a water-cup, and she drank gratefully.

"I did not use my toes, I think, but only floated above the ground!"

And she sat to calm herself and watch Branza turn and greet the others and move through the stately dance. Perhaps I have not spoiled her life utterly, she thought to herself, by keeping her so sheltered for so long. Perhaps Miss Dance has brought us back in time for the girl to devise her own joys and desires. And look at Urdda there, talking to Widow Tems and making her laugh so. Need I be anxious on either of them, really?

Not on a night like this, she decided, surrounded by kind friends and with all the townfolk aglow and celebrating before her, with Anders running up to his great-uncle to plead for something and Ousel curled in a nest of blankets beside his mother. On Midsummer Night, I may put my worries aside, I think. I may have as much pleasure from Midsummer Night as the next woman.

"Ah. I see."

Lady Annie watched for a while as Branza went at the ground with a stick. She made as if to sit on the cottage step and enjoy the morning sun, and rest after her walk here, but then she changed her mind and went to the far end of the stone, and poked at the ground there with her walking stick until she found the soft place. "I see what you have been up to."

She wandered off to find a better tool than her walking stick. Branza stayed, diligently digging, her jaw set. Rainshowers had sealed over the surface and compacted the dug dirt a little, but they were only six weeks' rainshowers, not a decade and more's interspersed with baking sun.

Annie returned and began to dig. And to hum, the warbling wandering song she always sang when she was busy. It was an awful sound, hardly music at all, but still it was a comfort for Branza to hear it, and to have the old woman working beside her.

They dug on, and Annie hummed, and also cursed occasionally. "Nawp, a little farther," she said, drawing a dusty hand out of her excavation. "You've wedged it in well, girl." She wore a town dress, which she now cheerfully wiped her hands on, leaving pale paw-prints. She flashed Branza a neat ivory smile and went on working.

A little later, as Branza sat on the end of the step wiping the dust from the ruby's splendor, Annie cried, "Ah, there she is!" And she held up the clear jewel.

"Can you feel any magic in the thing?" said Branza. "Or was it all drained quite away by Mam's desirings?"

"Oh, I would not know how to use such a thing, or even assess its powers." Annie stood and turned the crystal in her dusty hands. "All I can tell you is that it is of improbably good quality, for a stone its size. If that makes it magic, then it is magic." She laughed. "Of course, that it were guv your mam by a sprite would indicate too!" And she brought it and gave it to Branza.

"Could you speak to that sprite, Annie, if you had need?"

"Might be, my love. I have seen one or two creatures similar. Moody things, they are, though; hard to make 'em take substance. They must decide for theirselves. And my need have never been as great as your mam's that time."

"Why, what was her plight? 'I was very unhappy' is how she puts it to me; no more than that."

Annie wiped her hands on her dress again and sat close behind Branza on the step. "Ah, 'taint for me to tell you, poppet. You will have to press her."

"I don't like to. It might distress her, the telling."

"It might well," said Annie blandly.

Branza looked sidelong at her. "Are you telling me to press her, or telling me not?"

"I am telling you to do whatever you will do, my sweet. 'Tis your business and hers, between you."

"But it will distress her."

"Ah." The little witch wagged a crooked finger. "But you ain't in her heaven now. Things are *allowed* to distress her here."

"But I do not *like* to distress her."

"Then, you silly, you have to weigh up, don't you, which is the better: to not distress and never know, or to know and mebbe set her a-weeping." And she tipped to one side and then the other, under the weight of the two imaginings.

"Make Mam weep! What a terrible thing!"

"Oh, 'tis not so terrible, a tear dropped here and there. 'Tis all part o' the match-and-mix of life. There are mams have told me that babs were *put on earth* to make mams cry! If that is true, I would say you have been failing in your function some." She looked up at Branza through her eyebrows.

Branza laughed at her.

"Far too good a girl, you have been. You need to kick up your skirts and kiss a boy or two, I'm thinking."

"Oh, I am too old for that, I think."

"Old! You with your golden hair and that skin, that skin! Why, I would not say no to a man's lips if they were offered me. I would rather they were not age-withered, though, nor surrounded by gray beard." She looked thoughtful. "But then, I cannot expect much, guv the state of my own mouth." And she cackled ivorily.

"Enough of this silliness." Branza smiled down at the glowing jewels in her hands. "Tell me, Annie: if you wanted to, could you send me back there, the way you sent Lord Dought?"

"Back to your mam's heart's desire, my darling?"

"Yes, or to my own, where everything would be just as pleasant, that being how I wanted it?"

"I might be able to," said Annie with a shrug. "But very likely I would bugger things up again, and mightier than I done before. I tell you, it near split my brain athwart just *remembering* what I done for Dought, when Miss Dance come along and tried spooning it out of my head. All the intricacies and the work-arounds. If you have powers, you've got to find help in your youth; someone with stronger magic and practice have to advise you, someone who knows their ears from their onions. And I never did. I just blundered along in the dark with a few thumb-rules from that gypsy, and look what happened. I broke that thing, that time key, and Miss Dance had to practically kill herself pulling things as back to rights as she could get 'em. And your mam and you lost ten years out of my doings—or gained them, if you think of it that way."

She searched the weeds next to Branza's feet for the insect that was shrilling there. "What's more," she said, "I promised the woman I wouldn't. Time was, I would of gone against that promise for convenience or silver, or *copper* if enough had been offered me. But nowadays I am a woman of my word."

Branza smiled at her glum tone. "That is a great pity, Annie."

"It is, int it?" said the mudwife, and cackled again. "You need to find yourself a fresh-sprouted witch, just crossing from girl to woman, and have her use her more-power-than-sense on your behalf. I know an orph'nage where you might start your looking." She stood up in the weeds and laughed down at Branza. "You'll want money, enough for the makings and to lure the girl, but I can help you wi' that. You won't require much—just enough for a pair of blue satin shoon for dancing, I should think, and a sugar-fig or two."

"Who knows where I would end up, Annie, with that girl's help?" Branza got up too, tying the jewels to her belt by their cloth.

"Some wastrel's heaven, or some murderer's." Annie pushed through the weeds towards the path, throwing the words back cheerfully over her shoulder. "Much the same as this world, really. Hardly worth your while, sweet girl!"

The household had retired to bed. Liga was at her window, nightgowned, drowsy, not wanting to leave the slight wafting of the breeze for the stifling comfort of bed.

A soft knock at her chamber door gladdened her that she need not sacrifice the one for the other just yet. Rather than calling out, she crossed to the door and opened it herself.

There stood Branza, still dressed, and looking a strange combination of secretive, embarrassed, and amused. "Here, Mam," she whispered. "I've something of yours I must return."

She put into Liga's hands the cloth bag Liga had sewn during their first days here, of green linen embroidered with an approximation of the red flowers and the white, and the foliage of the bushes that bore them on either side of the cottage door in the place of Liga's heart's desire. Inside that familiar cloth, the shapes of the two jewels were softened by the wrappings that kept them from clinking together and damaging each other.

Liga held them and examined her own embroidery. "I never could quite capture those blooms," she said.

"No? I do not think they could be any other kind of flower."

"Oh, no. I did not quite catch the . . . the *force* of them, though you can see me trying and trying." She turned the bag over and laughed softly at her efforts on the other side.

Then she covered the bag with her hand; she could not talk about nothing forever. "I am glad you are giving these back, Branza. Does it mean that you no longer are trying, or yearning so much, to go home? I had thought you seemed happier since you went to Rockerly, although Miss Dance disappointed you."

"I know—it is unexpected, no? I'm surprised myself, how much happier I feel, how much more sensible things seem. And, you know, I don't think I could tell you what Miss Dance said that changed everything, the words she used, but I do know that they were exactly the right words. I could feel her setting things to rights inside me. Perhaps it was magic, but I don't think so. I think that she is just such a clever, kind woman, if she says I am to stay, it must be true and I am happy to take her word for it."

"She *is* kind," said Liga, surprised, "although she seems so fierce at first. She is careful with people's feelings. But she will stand no nonsense, no falsehood. She wants everyone to look at things very straightly, very clearly lit."

"Yes, and there are not many people who want to do that," said Branza eagerly, but quietly, in the dark hallway with its chamber doors like watchmen in a row. "I suppose because it is not comfortable."

"Oh, it is not." Liga had spent long hours the night she arrived here from that place, telling Miss Dance the whole truth of her meeting the moon-bab and the events that preceded that, all the way back to her own mam's death. She remembered it well; she had shed barely a tear in the telling, Miss Dance had sat so upright and alert to listen. The things that had been done to her by Da, by the town boys, while they had seemed just as great injustices as they did next day when she wept floods onto Annie—to Miss Dance they were elements in a calculation more significant than Liga felt she could comprehend; she felt as if, with her own information, as full as she could make it, and Miss Dance's experience and intelligence, the two of them were piecing together some part of creation Miss Dance had never managed to delineate before, as if the story of her small self were a lens through which Miss Dance was able to see the movements of some much larger mechanism, some tidal, or volcanic, or planetary movement from which her considerable powers derived, and to which they were also destined to contribute.

"But," Branza went on, "as Urdda said, though I did not really understand it at the time, comfort is not what we are here for, or not necessarily."

Hearing her daughter say so, so bravely, and seeing Branza's face so full of thought and the effort to understand and make things right, and feeling the weight of the jewels in her hands, the jewels that had bought them so many peaceable, comfortable years away from here, Liga felt like a piece of shot silk, shining proudly one way, regretful when a different light struck her. "That only makes me want to comfort you," she said rather desolately, stepping into the hallway and taking Branza in her arms.

"Of course it does," said Branza, laughing softly at her ear. "You're my mam. That is what mams are for, to comfort us when other things disappoint us."

"Oh, no," said Liga, eyes tightly shut, holding Branza close. "That is what *daughters* are for, angel child."

15

$\mathcal{A}$ few days after Midsummer, Todda was brought to bed, and very easily, of the daughter she and Ramstrong had hoped for.

He brought the news up to Annie's house, where the two boys had been lodged while Todda labored.

"I am the happiest man alive," he said, "the happiest father." And he looked it, tired but unable to keep the smile from his face. He clinked cider-cups with Lady Annie and smiled upon the world as represented by that lady's garden, Liga and Branza under the arbor with them, and Urdda being chased in and out the house by his two wild sons, Ousel having to stop sometimes to get breath for more laughing.

"Oh, there is nothing like daughters," said Liga. *A man wants sons, a man wants sons*, said Da in her memory, but look, it was not true. Ramstrong wanted daughters, and the fathers at the Midsummer bonfire, dancing with their girls—none of their faces held the scorn and impatience Da had shown at the sight of her.

"Daughters and sons is both grand," asserted Lady Annie. "But a mix makes a nice rounded family, 'tis true." And she sipped her cider so satisfied, she might well have forgotten her own orphanhood, and the absence of any family at all, her whole life.

But they did not drink sufficiently to the health of mother and child that day. The baby stayed well, but something went amiss for Todda Ramstrong. Two nights and a day she lay abed, sleeping only when she exhausted herself with the delirium of her fever. She could not nurse her daughter after the first night, and by the second she could no longer recognize her husband, nor anyone who came to her aid, whether it be cousins or sisters with fever-food, or Annie with her herbs and mutter-spells. Just before dawn, she came clear and it seemed the fever had broken and the worst was over, but all the woman had strength for was to instruct Davit Ramstrong to tell the children, when they were old enough to understand, that she was sorry to leave them, that she loved them more than anything in the world, that her heart was breaking of it. And then she was gone.

People could scarcely believe that a woman of such goodness and diligence would be taken. Liga could not believe it; she reeled at the news, and then fell into something of a stupor. "Once and for all it is proved to me," she said to Annie as they sat in the dark kitchen, trying to bestir themselves sufficiently to make a breakfast, "that no one gets what they deserve. People walk around St. Olafred's today, unpunished for evils they did, yet Todda Ramstrong, blameless wife and faultless mother and kind, kind heart—" Here her voice began to fail her. "And the daughter, babby Bedella, who will never know her, not even the little I knew my mam!"

"'Tis cruel," admitted Annie, house-gowned, bed-bonneted, and toothless. She looked a hundred years old, a shadowy crone in the cold predawn light from the window.

Ramstrong was a strong man, but he did break a little, he did break for a time. He was a wise man, but for a time after Todda died, he did not know how to care for himself or his sons and daughter, or of any worldly matter.

Liga felt she knew nothing useful for this time and situation; she could help Ramstrong in no way—bring him all the meals she and her daughters might, distract the boys for however many hours, befriend little Bedella's nurse however closely. She could do all these things and yet know that she was not addressing the central part of the problem, and never could. It was within no one's power to remove the cause of the grief that afflicted them all, but Ramstrong and his sons the worst.

Through this wretchedness occasionally intruded memories of Midsummer, and Ramstrong dancing with her in the bonfire light. *You and I know, Liga,* he had said, and she had often repeated the words to herself, to evoke again the pleasure she had felt. Now she repeated them and was horrified by the thought that she had somehow, with the repetition, precipitated Todda's going. I did not mean *that,* she told herself. I did not mean to claim him, or to take him from her.

But seeing how he mourned, how he must be taken in hand by his brothers if he was even, in those first days, to wash and to change out of the clothing he had worn when Todda died— as well as fellow-suffering, Liga felt a certain enchantment. I wish Todda could see this, how he is useless without her! The strength of the attachment that, broken, produced this wreckage of a man—she had felt something like it, perhaps, with regard to her daughters, but to feel it for a man! To have a man feel it for you! She had not known it was possible before; now she watched it in wonder. Could she ever dare, she thought, to want it for herself?

I remember when Anders were born, how all on a sudden I was joined to everything. When, as a bear, I flew across the country and I saw the pattern we all belong to, well, that was a momentary thing, and the sight faded behind my later adventures; but when my first son were handed me—I remember, I thought I had never held linen so clean, nor been in a morning so absolutely new—the pattern came clear again, but this time, rather than flying above it and seeing it whole, I fit into it and was right down here on the hearth and against the beat of it, my face in the warmth. I felt the house of it all around me.

The atmosphere, the mood of a place, is different between a little cot and a house like Annie Bywell's or Hogback's, knowing how far the rooms, the grounds, the outbuildings extend. This house I now occupied went on and on, out and out, farther than any other house I had ever been in. And in each room a family lived, and in each family a da had held his first bab, son or daughter of his blood, of his wife's line and his own, and had shaken with the echoes of this house that we were all in, extending forever out in space, forever back and forth across the ages. I remember how, exhausted and frightened, I marveled at the enormousness, and at the same time how it spun in like the pattern on a snail-house or a seashell, all towards this little face, red, near-blind, and mystified, these two soft flowers of hands not knowing what to do with themselves, to crumple closed or spread wide and waver on their stalks.

And I thought that was all, you know? I was blissful and ignorant and I thought that was the whole pattern—even I thought I could see how my mam's dying and my da's fit in there, although I wished too that they could be here to enjoy the sight of Anders and to meet what a grand wife I had got myself in Todda Threadgould.

But when she died—that wife, that grand wife, who had done nothing but grow in grandness and constancy, who had become that entire other person as well, the mother to our sons—I saw there was this other wing to the house I had not sensed before, even though 'twere true I had been bereaved. Da had lived there; Uncle lived there now; and I was wandering its halls for the first time and hearing the rooms echo beyond their swung-open doors, and the shuffle of the listless feet and footling activities of the left-behinds. I did remember shrugging off people's embraces and pities when Mam died; I had been at the age where I wanted to think myself a man who had no need of others' pity. But now that I was a father and a family man and joined that closely into the pattern, other men seemed to feel they could come to me, other widowers, and there was a look in their eyes—those first days I only had to meet it and my tears would flow and they would take me in their embrace, and I began to recognize that there were some bereaved who knew that part of the pattern, and others who had lost and lost—several wives sometimes; both parents, several children—who still did not know, or see, or understand that it was there.

The most surprising of the former men were those two lads who had been so misfortunate last Bear Day. Who would have thought? For they both of them came from families quite intact, and neither was married, although I knew the boy Noer were courting the sister of Filip Dearborn, that died by accidental shot of Jem Archer at that time, mistaken for a true bear.

Anyway, they both came, together, to the burial and back to the house afterwards, where the Cotting women, the Widow

Bywell, and my cousins and cousins-by-marriage had prepared a fine board, busy women, while I sat in my stupor or wept upon any who came near.

And when I had drunk a little and fuzzed and furred the edges of that hard blood-black pain dragging through me like I had swallowed a spiked boulder, they came and sat with me awhile, those two unexpecteds, so young beside all the widowers condoling me. They did not try to talk or understand or assert their fellow feeling. They sat either side of me, and Bullock chatted to Noer about his brother, almost as if I were not there, and Ousel came crying from something and climbed into my lap, and then Noer—Noer, who was almost a stranger to me, about whom I only knew that he had been caught up in that mysteriousness of the skins on Bear Day that Miss Dance said Widow Bywell were accountable for, along with so much else—he started up to singing, the exact right song—"The Seven Swans," which had neither loss nor woman in it nor tried to counter the grief with unwanted jollity, but instead brought some mood, beautiful and healing, to the room. You could see with what relief people joined in, reaching for the familiar words. Many times in the days afterwards I would sing that song when it were just Anders and Ousel and me and the darkness threatened, so that we all would recapture the relief that prevailed for that short time in the room, that little warmth, that little lifting of us—not quite as high as a flying bear, so that all the world was visible and made sense, but high enough so that we could breathe, and see a little beyond our sorrows, before we had to sink again and continue our enduring.

They said to put the little one with the nurse: "Make it easy on yourself, Davit, and then she may sup whenever is required." But I could not endure to put her there permanent, I had lost so much already. So back and forth I went, all hours of night and day, with Bedella wrapped up, a little warm scrap of bleating treasure in my arms, between Lissel's house and mine. Sometimes Ousel would wake up and come with me in the night—and that was pleasant, to have a companion—and Lissel would often meet us at her door: "I heared the littlun ordering my milk to start," she would laugh.

Sometimes I was able to leave Bedella there until the morning. If not, I waited at Lissel's, stretched out on a bench in her kitchen with Ousel on top of me like a partial blanket, or sitting up sometimes, my arms a pillow on her table while at the other end Bedella sucked and grunted and settled, or Lissel took her upstairs to bed and caught a little more sleep as she fed.

"Here you go, Mister Ramstrong." She would wake me and hand the bab, all tight-wrapped and peaceable, back to me. "She's full as a well-fit boot now." And off we would go into the night town, which was quite a different place from the day, cooler and more restful, with the stars and running clouds, and no people to bother us and be solicitous towards us, only Ousel stumbling and rubbing his eyes at my side.

"Leave her with the girl," says my brother. "It will cost ye no more and you will rest better."

"Oh, 'tis not so, Aran," I say to him. "I cannot do without the littlun in my house. She is my last hold on Todda, and so much the image of her."

But, to be true, the bab was the seat of more confusion than that, and it was as much rage as missing that made me keep her. 'Twas a terrible switch-potch of feelings sometimes I got, looking into her sleeping face or her woken one, bleary, frowning and grimacing at the world. For it was her being here that killed my wife, there was no getting around that. Yet she was so

377

much what we wanted. It was as if that were too much happiness for one man to deserve, too neat a family. *No,* said the fates, *this is Davit Ramstrong we're speaking of; he is only allowed the one good woman in his life at a time, a mam or a Todda or a daughter. Should he gain one of these, another must go.*

So it seemed to me in my grief, these thoughts working to enrage me sufficiently to wake me from my first uselessness I fell into when my darling died. You can see how nature works, and how practically, even as you are lost, lost to yourself in the swilling and buffeting of all of the emotions. *Let us get this man up out of his madness,* says nature, *make him walk and work, for there are three littluns needing his care, no? He cannot be allowed to languish too long. Here, I will put into his head Jannes Mazer, who has his mam and his wife's mam in the house with him, as well as his wife, that cheerful soul, and those two daughters, along with the four sons. All set about with women, the man is, and always complaining, but complaining the way a rich man complains how heavy are his sacks of gold, gratified to bear the weight. Yes, look at Mazer, Ramstrong, and feel how meanly I have doled out the women to your life. There, see Ramstrong now, shaking as he puts the bab in the cradle, walking away to keep from harming her. He's awake now, isn't he? He's alive. That is the main thing, to keep the man alive, tending the babs so that they may grow old enough to submit to the miseries I have in store for them.*

It was not even true, and I could see this when the day arrived and my little misters clambered into the bed with me for the morning stories and chat we had used to have with them, me and Todda. Still their same sweet faces, bemused by dreamings, turned up at my bedside, and their little arms not caring yet about manliness went around me, and I thought, Just as Aran said, there is a dozen women in this town is free for my choosing and would love to take these on, these three fine children, and give me more besides. There were men who with their very condolences mentioned their cousins or daughters— *Not now, I realize, Ramstrong, but when time comes for you to look about again.* And maybe that time would come; maybe it would. But for now I was in the cesspit, and it took all my work just to keep my own head above the cess and my little men from sinking, and the babby girl Bedella milk-full and tidy and breathing on.

After Todda's burial came a terrible time, where life kept going and kept going and the dead woman still was dead, and all Annie's household felt it, though they tried not to dwell upon it—only bend to their work, which was, as seemed only appropriate, a strange mix of bride and funeral dress, with costumes for the harvest festival soon to come. Straight after Midsummer the daylight had changed, softening and goldening towards autumn. Now the air cooled slowly and then began to chill, mornings and evenings, and Liga, Branza, and Urdda had to save the simpler stitching and assembly for the poorer light of evening and only do their finework in the middle of the day, and close by the window at that.

"It is something to do with Mister Cotting, isn't it?" thought Urdda aloud one of those middays, into a quiet stretch of stitchery.

"What is?" said Liga.

Branza and Annie were gone out this afternoon, to market and to Ramstrong's; there would likely be no interruptions for a while. "What you will not tell us. What you always send us away for, talking to Leddy Annie, or when Miss Dance were here. It's about our father, isn't it? Why? Are you ashamed of him? Was he a no-good?"

"He was a no-body," Liga said dryly.

"What, he had no standing? Why, what did he do? What was his work?"

Liga cast her a long look—a rather hopeless one, Urdda thought. "Why, should I not be curious, about my own father?" Urdda tried to put some amusement into her voice, to charm Liga out, but her smile went unanswered.

Stitch, stitch, went Liga, and the question hung there. "Cotting is a story of mine," she said eventually. "Miss Dance saw through me immediately, but no one else has questioned it, so I have persisted with him. And very tired of him I am, too— it strains a mam to keep things from her daughters."

"Who is it, then, if not Cotting? Is it someone we know?"

Liga gave a kind of shrug and a kind of headshaking, both at once.

Urdda tried a little laughter again; again Liga did not brighten. Urdda made an exasperated sound.

"There are nice ways for babbies to be got, and less nice," said Liga with a warning glance. "Yours and your sister's are not such pretty tales, my love."

Urdda rolled her eyes. "Pretty! Time and again you have given me pretty, Mam, when all I wanted was the truth, as straight as you knew it. Come along!"

"Well, this truth is not straight, however much you may think you want it." She bit off her thread-end, and spread and examined the seam over her knee. "You cannot jest me into telling you, for it is not something that is pleasant for me to remember."

"'Tis who I am, Mam!" said Urdda. "'Tis what I may become. You know how it is here. Everyone's whole life depends on the man who sired them."

"Not yours, my girl. And not Branza's. You'd not be as well off as you are, if that were so."

"Oh, he must be a very low sort." Urdda watched and waited. "You are moving all sharp and quick," she said. "You must hate the man terribly. Why, did he betray you? Beat you? Leave you penniless?"

Liga sagged her work to her lap, the heavy black funeral robe she was sewing for the God-man. "Branza is happy not knowing."

"Branza? Forgive me, but I am not Branza."

"No indeed." A smile crossed Liga's face like a wisp of steam touching a windowpane. She picked up her work again and went industriously at it.

Urdda did not resume her own, a white taffeta gown for a bride's younger sister.

She waited. Liga noticed her waiting. She went on working, and Urdda waited on pointedly.

"Shall I tell you, then?" Liga's voice was so heavy with doubt, it seemed to come from somewhere behind her, about the level of her chest.

"You shall!" said Urdda, victorious and fearful both at once.

Liga looked about, seeming hunted. "Close the door, then, daughter. I should not want Mister Deeth, say, to overhear any of this."

With alacrity and a little trepidation, Urdda shut the door. She returned to her seat. She did not take up her work again; she would not proceed with it until she had heard what she wanted to hear.

Liga's face above her finework was complicated with age and thought; opposite her, Urdda felt smooth-skinned and innocent—*Too* innocent! she told herself fiercely. She felt as if she stood, straight and unflinching, in the path of a carriage that thundered towards her. She was brave enough for anything, she thought; brave enough for the worst that her mother might tell her.

Liga looked up one more time, clearly bracing herself for a distasteful task. Then she went at the funeral vestment, and without lifting her eyes again, she began, softly and slowly and with much thoughtfulness and gravity, to tell about the day that Urdda had been conceived.

She told it well; she had always been a good storyteller. Urdda felt herself disappearing—all but her breath, which became less steady the longer the story went on, and her heartbeat, which grew firmer and faster. She felt the weight of baby Branza in her arms, the resistance of the cottage door in her spine; she smelled the chimney ash and clung to the cold, scratchy stones.

Beyond a certain point, Liga could stitch no more as she spoke, but still she held the stuff ready for the stitch in one hand and the needle's little shining dart in the other, and she spoke over these towards Urdda. She explained everything: she described how the thing was done, all the small acts that contributed to the larger, the differences of one act from another; she spared neither herself nor her daughter a single jeer or bruise, indignity or panic-thought of the entire business. Yet she told it all without her lip curling once, without her emotions disrupting the story at any point. She reported it as if she were a messenger bringing news of an enemy's movements to his commander, the value of whose report consisted in its completeness and its dispassion.

Now Urdda herself could no longer watch the words issue from that calm, beloved mouth. She wanted to hear no more, but she had prompted this telling, and now that it was in train, it would only be further indignity on her mother to stop it half told. So she took up the shears, and some scraps of funeral velvet and bride-sister white that had been pushed by her mother's work to her side of the table, and she snipped away small pieces, some of them so small that the snippings fell as little more than dust to her lap. The snipping stopped her hands from shaking. The *slish-slish* of the blades through the cloth was a calm, mechanical sound behind the other—her mother's voice, building a tower, a tower of unspeakable creatures, like loathsome toads that had agreed somehow to fit together, to balance and cling to each other and become this structure, however much their instinct was to slide, to ooze, to clamber and spring away. Urdda's face was sore from staying as expressionless as Liga's; her throat ached with restraining the exclamations that leaped up, demanding to be uttered.

When the story was told, both women sat, the one with her cloth and needle, the other with the shears clutched closed in her lap, their faces turned from each other as if each wished most heartily that the other were not in the room.

"Then . . ."—Urdda's voice felt rough in her throat, sounded hollow in the air—"how was Branza got, if that was me?"

"That is Branza's business, and my own."

"But Branza won't ask you!"

"Then I will not tell her."

"Is hers any better a story than mine?" said Urdda.

"It is no better, no."

"Is it similar?"

"No, it is quite another thing again from yours."

They regarded each other across the broad table. Though Urdda's face felt as if it were flaming, the rest of her, inside and out, felt cold, drained of blood and life by Liga's tale. As for Liga, she had not just told the tale but endured the events in it; had had the whole thing, in all its details, enacted on her.

Urdda had not known that such cruelties, such violations, could be practiced on a person, yet Mam had undergone them—Mam, who sang over the bread-making, who looked so pleased smoothing a fresh-completed piece of embroidery, Mam, whom Urdda had so delighted in making to laugh, making to join in play; Mam, who had made that garden and kept that cottage and raised the two daughters. And one of them, this ungrateful daughter herself, had hauled Mam back from the place where she sang and hummed in perfect safety to this world, where these men—Urdda had *seen* Hogback Younger, and people talked of him all the time!—where these men moved and lived, entirely free, who had done *that* upon her mother, her gentle mam, while baby Branza slept silent, hidden, in the same room.

Urdda bowed her head. Before her along the table-edge lay five small figures, the largest—snipped from the funeral black—in the middle, with two of the bride-white on either side. Men, they were, all five; trousered men standing legs apart and arms wide, taking up as much space as they could. Her mind struggled like a bogged cow in all she had learnt. She took a pin from the paper lying near, and anchored the black cloth man to the table by his privates. She took another pin, and fixed a white man by his. Three more pins she took; three more figures she fastened down.

She stood and walked around the table. She took the heavy cloth from Liga's hands and lap and lifted it to the table. She knelt in front of her, laid her own head in place of the work, and encircled Liga's waist with her arms. She held on tightly, pushing as if she would push through Liga's stomach wall and back into her womb if she could.

Liga's hands were in her curls, and stroking her face. "Look what came out of it all, though, out of such a dire event: my

Urdda! How many good years of Urdda I would have missed, had it never happened. Think of that."

"How can you walk!" Urdda whispered fiercely. "How can you *smile*—I have seen you—you *smile* at Widow Fox in the market! How can you stop yourself saying, *Your son—your precious son—did this to me when he was younger!*"

"Widow Fox is not to blame. And her boy himself I have seen, him and Thurrow Cleaver and— They are none of them the same lads as they were. They are never two of them to-gether, for one. I think they do not like to remind themselves what they goaded each other on to do."

Goaded each other on. Urdda would be sick with loathing them so much. "But—"

"And neither will you speak to any of them, while I live— or any wife, or any relative of theirs. Or to Branza, or Annie, or anyone, of this. I forbid it, Urdda, do you hear? It is *I* have been sinned against, and I say, leave the thing. It is old news and gone, and I will not have it stirred up again and chattered about by all St. Olafred's. Promise me."

Urdda blurted some form of agreement into the cloth at Liga's hip. By now she had all but crawled behind her mother on the chair. Should she scream or should she weep? Should she beat Mam with her fists or should she forbid her ever to move outside this *room*, outside Urdda's own arms, for her own safety?

"Girl, girl!" Liga retrieved her from her crawling, hoisted her up. Urdda remembered being held so in the passionate rages of her childhood, her hot face twisting with emotion, curls straying down into her eyes, her mother's hands cool and dry against her cheeks, her mother's kisses solving nothing, mending nothing.

"It is over, Urdda," Liga said now. "It was over and gone

long ago, my sweet. It was dreadful when it happened, to be sure, but the years have been so many and so kind since then, they have more than made up for my hurts. And I would never choose life without my wild girl over life without what happened that day."

"That is . . . an *impossible* choice!" Urdda burst out. "How can you *not*? How can you not want to *kill*—"

But Liga covered Urdda's mouth and kissed her again, and shushed her, and said her name, and would not stop shushing. Urdda fell to bitter weeping, there in her mother's skirts, while Liga murmured and stroked her.

Branza and Lady Annie brought their laden baskets up the hill, Branza laughing at some rude remark Annie had made for her entertainment. Up ahead, her sister stepped out the widow's door into the street. "Urdda," cried Branza, "what is it?" For there was something urgent and furtive about her sister's movements. "Where are you off to alone?"

"Walking," said Urdda, fending off their approach with her shoulder. Then she strode away.

"But I will come with you!" Branza thrust her basket blindly towards Lady Annie.

"Leave her go," said the old lady, taking the basket and Branza's hand with it.

"But what can have happened?" Branza tried to go, but the widow held her firmly, and Branza did not want to pull the lady over by insisting. "She *knows* not to walk out by herself. She has told *me* often enough."

"If she wanted to tell you, she would of flang herself upon your neck right then, child," Annie said. "Let us take ourselves inside and see how is your mam. Open the door, now."

"Mam?" called Branza as soon as they were inside, and in

her worriment she left Annie to manage both baskets while she hurried to the sewing-room door.

Her mother lifted a serene face to her, although there was something hard-won about the serenity: some weariness about the eyelids, some dutifulness about the smile.

"What has happened," cried Branza, "that Urdda is rushing out by herself, and all red-eyed from crying?"

"We have been talking."

Annie came to Branza's elbow. A look passed between her and Liga, and Branza felt a flash of annoyance at her that she knew, that Mam knew she knew, that they were conspiring to keep whatever it was from Branza.

"And both of us became upset," said Liga. "That is all."

"Why? What were you talking about?"

The striving of Liga's face intensified, but she remained calm. "Nothing you need worry about, angel girl. I do not wish to talk about it more. How was Ramstrong today, and his little ones?"

Then Liga rose and put aside her work, and patted Branza's arm where she stood ready to embrace and console and evince more anxiety. "Annie, you will be ready for a cool drink," Liga said. And with studied cheerfulness, she passed into the hall, ready to admire and discuss their baskets full of purchases.

Urdda strode alone up the town. These were the quieter streets; but even had she walked downhill, straight through the market, her swift step would have kept her safe from interference—and her unreadable face, and the impression she gave of being quite uncaring as to anyone's disapproval or poor opinion, she was so intent on such vital business.

Uphill, though, there were sloping cobbles to pit herself against. Steep flights of steps felt even better; grimly, she hoisted her own weight from foot to foot. She came to the castle, passed into the courtyard, and started up the steps of a tower. She could have climbed a long time up the darkness, wearing herself out, forcing herself on to no particular where.

But then she burst out onto the tower-top. It was empty of courting couples. The cloudy light glared all around. There was no other place to go but to the wall, to fling herself off, maybe, or throw down a handful of these tiny gravel-stones here, or shout oaths at passersby below.

She went to the wall, breathing hard and shaking. She stood with her fists on the battlement, all her muscles tight as fiddle-strings. Her teeth ached from clenching. She watched smoke trail up from Gypsy Siding. Treetops moved, thick and dark green and oblivious, around her riveted sight, and the town—though it seemed motionless under its gray, under its damp slate and its lichens and behind its stones—seethed like one of Annie's terrible brews: opaque, acrid of fume, abubble with lumpish and stringish ingredients, vegetable, animal, unidentifiable. If this crime against Mam had gone unpunished, who knew what else had been done? If no one spoke of this, from guilt among the men themselves, from distaste and fear on Mam's part, who knew what other secrets bubbled here? The whole town, the whole *world*, was fouled by this, was made unclean, to Urdda's mind.

Bastard daughter of Hogback Younger. Her iron gaze lowered to fix on his roof—purple-gray slate like the roofs of other houses of substance, but pointed and pinnacled and cupola'd like no other structure, so that Hogback might stand and enjoy his own elevation in the town. But from now on, Urdda hoped, he would feel, as he admired his elaborate gardens, the hatred of his daughter-by-force beating down on the back of his neck from the castle wall. She hated him to the point of shaking there, braced against the battlement by her digging, paining fists.

Yet look at the color of her fist on the stone. He was in her skin; he was in her very blood. At the thought, her blood thickened, crawling and choking in her veins, requiring hard, painful heart-thumps to drive it along. To hate him was to hate herself, for she was half Hogback.

And why him, particularly? It might have been any one of those boys; as Mam said, Hogback had treated her no worse or better than the others. Lycett Fox, Thurrow Cleaver, Joseph Woodman, Ivo Strap—she might have been half sister to that whole crowd of Strap children that ran about town like wind-gusts, like bird-flocks!

Cotting—ah, why couldn't there have been a Cotting truly? And some small tale of betrayal or bad luck for which Urdda could have consoled Mam. This was too great a pain, too monstrous a series of injuries. It lumped in the past like . . . like a bear on a hearthrug, impossible to ignore. But the lump was not as big as a bear; it was only as big as an Urdda. Had she not existed, Mam might have had a chance of forgetting, of putting the injuries behind her; of pretending, if she wished to, that they had not happened. Instead, the very face of one of the men, the very *skin*, had been before her every day of her life. The ten years they had had in Mam's heaven without Urdda—perhaps they had not been such a trial after all, if Mam had been free at last of the sight of the ghost of her attackers, had been able to rest awhile from being reminded.

Urdda's face flushed hot in the wind across the tower-top; she blinked her wind-stung eyes. She was a fool; she was a fool. Why had she badgered Mam to tell her? Could she not see how unwilling Mam had been? Had she no heart? Why had she been unable to endure admitting that sometimes grown women *did know better* than ungrown? They already knew what anguish they were sparing those younger ones, because they carried it with them everywhere, pushing away its memories every waking hour, every living moment, to make space where they might sew, or prepare meals, or enjoy the small flowers and birds in the hedgerows, or pass the time of day with the Widow Foxes of the world in the marketplace? How was Urdda ever going to put what she had learnt out of her mind? How had Mam managed to go on, who had hidden her bab there in the cottage, and hauled the door closed, and clambered up the chimney and been *dragged down again*—

Urdda was in the dark stairway again, running, falling against the walls. She could not go home to Annie's; she could not face Mam again; she could not go back to that blissful, blessed state of not knowing. It was insufferable, the knowledge she must live with now, and yet she was only the daughter of it! The whole business of Mam's going to her heaven, and the boredom and the tedious, unadventurous, unrelenting *safety* of the place, all of a sudden was cruelly clear to her. Of course, what a kindness, how absolute a necessity that other place had been! Yet she, Urdda—ignorant, frivolous, disrespectful, interfering *fool* that she was—had forced her way out of that place, and worse, had nagged Annie to bring Miss Dance, to have her undo the protection Mam had been granted. *I want my mam here,* she had as good as stamped her foot and demanded. *I want my sister!* And look how unhappy Branza had been! And look what Mam must now endure, every day—the passing of Hogback's carriage, the greetings of Widow Fox, the shrieks and smudges of ragged Strap children.

Back out into the town Urdda walked, with an air of purpose that quite belied her horrid confusion. She walked through almost every avenue and laneway of St. Olafred's. She would have walked out the gate, too—she wished she could walk out and disappear into nothingness, as Mam must have seemed to do all those years ago. But she also—practical, true-worldly Urdda—knew how late it was. She did not want the town gate closed on her, to come back in the chill of night and have to explain to the watch where she had been, and have people talking about why she might walk out alone, about whom she might be hoping to meet in her wanderings.

She returned to Annie's tired in body and numbed in mind, just after lamp-lighting time.

"Where have you been, Urdda! We were worried," said Branza in the door.

"Walking, only walking. I met no one and did nothing un-toward." Urdda submitted to Branza's embrace and looks of concern. "Is there supper?" she said, to put an end to them.

"There is. Give me your cloak and go through."

Liga and Lady Annie were there in the kitchen's warmth. The three women examined each other, and each thought the other two looked very tired and lost.

"You of been up to something," said Lady Annie. "Were I not so slumped, I would scrutinize you proper, for that glitter in your eye, and your general air."

"I have done nothing but walk off my feelings," said Urdda, and went to the scullery to wash her hands and face.

"Don't you think there is something of an air around that girl?" she heard Lady Annie say behind her.

"An air?" Liga said. "I am very tired too—perhaps too tired to distinguish airs."

Then Branza bustled into the kitchen, relieved and anx-ious. Supper happened—a fine supper, but a subdued one. Urdda heard Branza attempt several bright beginnings of conversation, but nobody else could sustain them very long, and she herself was torn between pitying Branza and envying her her ignorance of the truths, of the histories, that seemed to hang above the table in a leaden cloud, threatening storms and tears. Did Annie feel that cloud? Urdda was almost certain she did, and as they ate, she examined various times when in Annie's presence, Annie's and Mam's, certain people had passed, or certain names been uttered, and some small silence had occurred, or some change of subject or other evasive maneuver had been performed, unimportant to Urdda until now. And now—oh, it was intolerable to be trapped in the now and to see all this! How was Urdda ever going to forgive herself for having had Mam and Branza dragged back to this world, for making Mam remember all the details she had related today—every word and bruise; every button and torn dress-seam; every drop of spittle; every flutter and leap and throe of terror and revulsion? How would she ever make things right?

When a girl of fifteen, hovering on the point of entering womanhood, wants a thing, there is only so much she can do, and for most, *most* such girls, the wanting itself—even with all the hope and will and power they can muster—will not be sufficient to gain them that thing.

But Urdda was not most girls, and there lurked within her—pressed tight and in-crinkled as a closed flower bud, mysterious as a seed or egg, invisible as an unborn in the mound of its mother—abilities most girls do not have. Whether they came direct from some powerful great-granddam of Liga's or less straightly down a sire-line, from home blood or from foreign—well, such matters are never clear. But there they were, and until that afternoon they had been all-but-formless potential, unable to be wielded in any directed or specific way.

Strong feelings were required to arouse them, and many varied and well-honed skills to manipulate them. Few stronger feelings exist than those Urdda had undergone that day on behalf of her mother, and these emotions had brought the potentialities to a state of alertness as she wept in Liga's lap. Whatever filament had kept the bud closed, it was now released, and though still tight-folded, the flower held among the sprung-apart tips of its outermost petals the "air" that Annie had sensed and spoken of. This air was responsive and interested, and engaged itself immediately in considering Urdda's distress and rage, insofar as it had intelligence.

There is power everywhere in the true world, and Lady Annie's house was no exception. The mudwife herself, for one, had considerable ability, though it had never been more than partially and poorly employed. Liga's energy existed mainly in her bitterness and anger, so deep in her bones now that she thought she did not feel them anymore. The strength with which she had forced them below, to protect herself from their derangements, was a positive force on its own. As well, there was the miraculous stuff that runs like sheet-opal through the matter of all people—Branza had it, and Mister Deeth, and every passerby. Unaware of anything more than her own distress and anger, Urdda had that afternoon drawn these stuffs from the people near around her and those beyond Lady Annie's walls, so that the core of her rage and sadness had been surrounded by appropriated abilities, as a bonfire is surrounded by the wavering air of its own heat, or an emerging flower by the first waftings of its soon-to-be-irresistible scent.

And as she had walked that evening, Urdda had passed many powerful people: children touched with charm, clueless that it was within them; maids whose frivolous fortune-telling always held a germ of truth; mothers and wives whose soups were as good as medicines in times of illness; and men who simply attracted luck, or women who sped healing, with a touch or a word. And those inner scales or sheets of power in us all, so slight and fine that we deny them or never notice; the wisp-flames of happy-chance that touch us, sting, and then flicker away before we can calculate how they were conjured, how they might be kept—Urdda had all unknowingly drawn these out of every person, every house, every plant and creature she passed. Through the town she had moved like a boatlet being poled across a mirror lake. Powers had pleated and arrowed and rippled behind her like melting glass—but gathered in *towards* her, not spread out in her wake. The town had dulled and lost energy as she passed; people had become somewhat aimless, needing to remind themselves what they had just been doing; people had shaken themselves and blinked and propelled themselves with newly necessary effort about their duties and businesses.

Annie had sensed these accumulations on Urdda's return, but because of her own diminished powers, she could not properly see, or bring herself to care very greatly, what had happened. Had she pursued her first questioning of the girl, she might well have detected what was emerging, undisciplined, and been able to confine its effects to some degree; but she did not. She only supped as the rest did, and when Branza, frustrated by the women's moodiness, dismissed them from the table, she only climbed the stairs, with Urdda plodding ahead of her and Liga trailing behind. While Branza clashed and scrubbed and sang in the kitchen below, the three women bade each other good-night and retired to their rooms.

When Branza, too, had gone to bed; when the whole house slept; when the whole town, unaccountably tired, had gone early to its rest and lay drained and dreamless on its pallets and pillows and piles of straw, the accumulated forces and feelings of that day tendriled from Urdda's body and memory down through the house like curling, inquisitive rootlets. Through the floorboards and the laths and plaster and the ceiling beams they sank—soundless, sightless, odorless, persistent—and into the workroom, where events—or the *telling* of events—had first evoked them.

The man-figures Urdda had snipped from the black cloth and the white—at first they stayed cloth, and moved only slightly, as if a draft had caught them. The pins that held them to the table glowed dully—only as much as you would expect from moon- and starlight gathered from the uncovered window—but the first real sign of Urdda's coming into her powers was the pins' brightening to red, and further, in time, to orange. One by one, the cloth-men ceased their now energetic rippling and noticed their shining pins, and pushed themselves with their blunt cloth hands up to sitting, and tried with those hands to quench the pins' heat. They spoke to each other, at first in sounds that would have been inaudible to normal ears; and then in dry whispering like the rubbings of cloth throats; and then more slipperily, like scissor-blades snipping—*slish-slish*.

They plumped out, flat cloth no longer, and stretched up, growing from doll-sized to the size of the men they matched in true life. Their feet met the floor.

"Oh, cold!" said one under his breath.

"Do not worry," said another. "We will hot things up." He stroked his swollen pin, which stood out from him, orange-hot, with yellow sparks winking and hissing on the pinhead.

Clothes appeared on the men, though vaguely—maybe only chalked, or tattooed, or embroidered on the white skins and the black. Their faces came into being, as uncertain in their features as the clothes were, fading and sharpening on their heads as their different hairs glimmered around. Younger versions, they were, of their matching men, twelve-years-ago versions of the boy Woodman, and Thurrow Cleaver, and Ivo Strap, and Fox, and Hogback Younger, son of the foreigner, Blackman.

"Where will we start?" said the littlest one.

"Fox was the first to sin upon her," muttered another. "We should follow history."

"But young Hogback's shaming will be the greater. He is closest to a gentleman." The black figure's hands hissed on his white-hot pinhead, which stood out like a constable's cudgel from his velvet-seeming trousers.

"Let us save him till the last, then. Let us work upward, from lowest to highest standing in the town."

"Yes, and for each we will follow the original order, with Fox first, then Woodman, then me, and so on."

"A grand plan!" The Fox figure clapped his hands. Flashes as of lightning lit the room.

Murmurous and flickering, the five cloth-men moved beyond the walls.

Thurrow Cleaver they found in the Thatchlanes, in the arms of his favorite laundress. At the touch of their clothy hands, she leaped from the bed. She snatched up her kirtle to cover her nakedness and stood against the wall, screaming loud the full time, bringing the household down. Each visitor had his way with Thurrow: the Fox-man, the Woodman, the Cleaver, the Strap, and the Hogback-man. The laundresses crowded in the doorway, exclaiming or staring or laughing helplessly, each according to her nature and past relations with Thurrow.

Ivo Strap was cozy in his cot with the second Mistress Strap and seven of his twelve children. Nobody saw the cloth-men walk in through the front wall. They pulled Strap from the bed by his ankles, and the children and the wife spilled everywhere with his clawing. They were still complaining of his stealing the blanket when the Hogback bared Strap's bottom and offered it to the little Fox-man. "Here, Fox, and don't spare him. This one were partic'lar rough, as I recall."

The others stood round and kept the shouting wife and the screaming sons out of the way, flicking them back like flat-beetles, while Strap was dealt with. Piteously he cried, until he went insensible from the treatment they dealt him.

"He suffered nicely, that one," said a cloth-man, wiping his hands on his coat-ends as they stepped out through Strap's door into the crowd of woken neighbors.

"He made good noise, to be sure," agreed the Hogback. "My oath, but it doesn't last long, though, the relief. Look, I am orange again already."

"How it itches and it burns!" said the Fox-magic. *Zzzt-zzzt-zzzt*, went his hands upon his pin.

Joseph Woodman was a good way away, out in the forest in the cutters' camp. All of his brothers were there with him, and two of their wives to keep the woodmen fed.

"Teller? Jock?" said Joseph mazily as the cloth-men pulled him from his lean-to. "What muckinbout is this? Lemme sleep."

The Woodman-magic tore off the man's trousers. "Look at him," he said. "Bright as two moons. This is the one what instigated it, boys. Make sure he remembers." And they went at him, each with his great glowing pin. The whole camp woke, and watched or fled, according to their stomachs. A man or two tried to go to Joseph's aid, but the cloth-men proved difficult to grasp ahold of, and then frightening in their difference from human textures, so that no man held to them for long. Then the deeds were done, and the cloth-men threw him out of the pack like a dog-chewed rag-a-doll, and they muttered and moiled away among the trees, with a flash of shirt there and a gleam of velvet here.

Ah, Lycett Fox, so small and smart. Only his mam was there to see what he underwent, but that proved quite humiliating enough for the both of them.

"Mmm." The Fox-magic smacked his lips as he climbed out the chamber window onto the roof. "He were good and tight. He almost quenched me. He almost done the job."

"Save yourself," growled the Hogback, folding himself after him. "The best is yet to come. Enflame your pin for this last one; he will quench you well and truly."

So finally to Hogback's they repaired. There they found the gentleman at cards and tobacco with a large party of his closest confreres, frittering away the fortune and reputation his father had spent his life acquiring.

Hogback leaped up at the sight of the motley men stepping into the drawing room. But then he espied his own self—only strangely clothed, and brightly pinned, and giving off a strong incendiary stink, and his "How dare you!" died on his lips.

"Ooh, this is a fine, upstanding feller," cooed the Fox-man.

"He is no better than the others," said the Hogback-man, striding forward. "Only his fine clothing takes more negotiation. Let's have at him."

They descended on him, all five, and there before the merchants of the town, and the most respectable, and such of their ladies as ran from the adjoining parlor at the hubbub and did not faint dead away at the sight, they stripped away Hogback's fine pantaloons and visited on him exactly the measure of degradation and damage he had dealt out to Liga that afternoon in her father's cottage, those many years ago.

"Well, we are done," said the last cloth-man, withdrawing from Hogback's bottom and letting him fall limp and bloodied to the fine Turkitch rug. All around them, the gentlemen expostulated and broke candlesticks on the cloth-men's heads, and the ladies shrieked and malaised and ran about. Unperturbed, the five figures tucked what was left of their dulled pins away into the matter of their clothing, or their flesh, or whatever it was they were made of. They stepped out through wall and window, descended to the street, and strode, too fast to follow, up the town. In the morning, some onlookers would say they had fled downhill; others would swear on the Eelmother's chastity that they had tripped off all five in different directions; still others would insist that they had flown into the air on bat-wings, or caught fire and burnt themselves up to nothing and nowhere.

However they reached there, when they arrived at Lady Annie Bywell's house they walked straight in, and across her front parlor, and smoothly through the back wall of that and into the workroom. By then they had shrunk to the size of children, and were more clothy than fleshly, and they slipped and slithered, clambering up to the bench and thence to the worktable.

"That were so gratifying," said the Hogback-man sleepily, his voice risen to a child's chirp.

"It were," screeked another one, drawing a loose pin out of his pants and fixing himself to the table with it. "Goo'night, brothers."

And anything else they said, it sounded like scissoring and

snipping and no more, as they arranged themselves and flattened and shrank further, and pinned themselves by their privates to the tabletop, and lay down to rest, until they were just as they had been when Urdda put them there: five cloth shapes, flat and silent in the empty room, their pins gleamless in the dark.

16

Liga and Branza stepped out the next morning, to walk down to the dairy for milk and fresh-cheese.

"There is a smell about," said Branza as Liga closed the door behind them.

"There is." Liga sniffed it. A Strap cousin ran across from one lane-end to another, and down in the market square there was a general busy-ness not usual at this hour. "Someone's house has burnt down in the night?"

They walked on, examining the sky for smoke and listening for hints in the conversations all around. "Constable," they heard, and "attacks," and "even into Hogback's place!" A crowd of men huddled outside the locksmith's house, muttering, but these fell silent at the approach of the women. Some passersby hurried frightened; others whispered and suppressed laughter.

"Liga, good morning! And Branza too!" This was Widow Tems, for whom Liga had made that good linen dress she was wearing.

Liga drew her aside. "What has happened, Widow?" she said, and Branza stepped closer to listen. "Everyone is running about like ants in a stirred nest, and so early!"

"You heard nothing in the night?"

"I ought to've?"

"Why, even I was woken, with the events up the road at Hogback's."

"I gather someone has attacked him?"

"Him and many others. Everyone I speak to has a new name. The butcher's boy, Cleaver, is one, and one of those scoundrel Straps—Vivius, I think, or maybe his brother Ivo."

"Oh. Why those three, does anyone know?" Liga's voice was curiously dead.

"Oh, there is others as well. But barring Hogback, they were all very much a lower type of person."

Liga moved her basket to her other arm, looking flustered. "Dear oh dear, what a terrible thing. Is there any idea who attacked them?"

"A gang of them, it was: ten or twenty of the brutes. They broke into people's houses and tore the husbands from their beds. Of course, Hogback were not sleeping. He had guests, but that did not stop these men. They walked straight in, the brazen fellows, and there, in front of everybody—" The widow glanced at Branza's bright eyes, tut-tutted, and shook her head.

"Are they—are they very much injured?" said Liga.

"No one knows of Hogback—he is under the care of his physician, though, so it must be quite bad. Of the others, I have heard—I will not *say* what I have heard, before a maiden," said the widow, with another sidelong glance at Branza, "but none of them were let off lightly, it sounds."

"Whatever for, was this done?" said Branza.

"No one can ascertain!"

"Oh, why does *anyone* gang in and do violences!" Liga gave a brittle laugh. "Come, Branza, we must to the dairy, and then sewing awaits. Good day, Widow Tems."

"It has the whole town terrified," said the widow after them. "Every man-jack. Good day to you."

Branza sped after her mother. "Why are you hurrying so? You are not especial friends of the Straps and Cleavers, are you?"

"I am not." Liga hurried on.

"And Hogback Younger—well, Annie says of him, *Great wealth does not a gentleman make.*"

"None of it is good," said Liga, still hurrying. "None of it."

Here came Ada Gilly-that-was-Keller. "Liga, Branza, have you heard it all?"

"We have," said Liga, and would have walked briskly on.

But Branza slowed. "Some of it," she said. "A group of men have attacked three households, is how much we have."

"Five it is, now that I've straightened everyone's story." Ada closed her eyes to remember. "Foxes and Cleavers and Straps—and out at Woodman's camp, for they brought him in this morning, Joseph Woodman. He was hurt the worst of them."

"And Hogback Younger, of course."

"Oh, Hogback! It is all over town about Hogback, what they done to him."

"Which is what?" said Branza.

"Oh, maid, I cannot dirty my mouth with it. But it were most indecent. I don't know how he will look in anyone's eye—"

"Come, Branza," said Liga.

"Widow Cotting, are you feeling quite well?"

"I am very well, thank you, Ada. Only, work is pressing. Good day to you."

"Good day, ladies."

"Mam? Mam!"

"Don't call out on the street, Branza."

"But why does this upset you so? You've no work pressing, particularly; why did you tell Ada otherwise?"

But Liga only hurried them on.

Out at the dairy, she would not dally and talk with the other widows and wives, and Branza could overhear nothing, so watchful was everyone of her maidenly sensibilities. They bought their fresh-cheese and had their milk-pail filled, and then Liga wanted only to hurry back home. Branza followed, lagging when they drew near a huddled group, and in the ash-tree square; hurrying a few steps, disgruntled, when Liga urged her on. That smell! But had there been any fire? Hogback's house looked intact, and Ivo Strap's, down that lane next to where Vivius kept his poor donkeys. Whatever had upset Mam, that she was so incurious about these events?

When they reached Lady Annie's, Liga went straight into the sewing room without removing her cloak, and Branza heard her say—it must be to Urdda, for she would not use that sharp tone with Annie—"Did you cook this up?" And her basket thumped onto the table.

"Cook what up?" Urdda said.

"Did you put Lady Annie up to it?"

Annie? Why would Annie have anything to do with this? Branza hung up her cloak and went to the sewing-room door. Mam looked like a hawk perched on a rock, sighting a kill down in the grass. Urdda sat with the yoke of the bride-sister dress over her knee, surprised from her stitching by Mam's fierceness.

"The two of you are tight as thieves sometimes," said Mam. "I would not put it past you."

"Put *what* past us?"

"This business with Hogback Younger. And the others. The attacks in the night."

"What attacks? And what others?"

Mam took an impatient breath.

"Cleaver, was his name?" said Branza. "One of the Misters Strap? What would she have to do with such as those, Mam?"

"Cleaver and Strap, and each one I told you about yesterday, Urdda. You bothered so little to conceal your choices—could you not have added a few innocents, just to throw me off the scent? Or fallen one down a well one month, and have another bit by a mad-dog the next? All in the one night, *last* night, and all some terrible, brutal, indecent thing—I am not magic myself, Urdda, but I can smell the stuff, all right. And I am not stupid, though you may think me so."

Urdda blinked. "What's gone on, Branza? *You* tell me, if I cannot get sense out of Mam."

Branza told, and as she uttered each of the men's names who had been assaulted, Urdda's face changed just as Mam's had, realizing, afraid, and very still.

"Some indecent thing was done, says Ada Gilly," Branza finished. "To Hogback Younger, at least. I don't know about all the others."

"None were let off lightly." Liga sank to the bench, opposite Urdda. "It must be Annie, then."

"Why?" said Branza. "What possible—"

"Swear to me it was not you, Urdda," said Liga, as if Branza was not there, had not spoken.

"I *do* swear!" cried Urdda. "I have been in this house since you told me—except when I walked last evening, and then I neither stopped nor spoke to a soul. I don't even know where Lycett Fox lives! How would I—"

And then Urdda jolted back, as if a mouse had run out from the cloth on the table in front of her.

"Mam!" she whispered.

"What is it?"

Urdda stared at the mouse, or whatever it was. She gave a tiny tilt of her head to beckon Liga.

"What, child?" Liga sprang from her seat and hurried around the table. Branza approached more slowly from the other side.

"Where did those come from?" Liga said, frightened.

"I made them," said Urdda very softly. "While you told me your story yesterday." Still she leaned away from the table, and Liga stood behind her and laid her hands on her shoulders.

Branza saw the cloth figures now. "Five little men," she said. "What have they to do with— Oh!" Liga and Urdda were still transfixed. "Hogback Younger, in the middle there," said Branza. "And . . . four more. What is this? Did you *mark* these men, somehow, to be attacked?"

Shakingly, Urdda reached out, and one by one pulled out the pins and laid them on the table. "I don't know what I did."

"But why? What-for those five, particularly?" said Branza. "We know none of them, do we?"

"They hurt our mam. That is why we don't know them; she kept them out of her heaven."

"Why, what did they do, Mam?"

But Liga only stared at the little men, as if they might

indeed up and attack her. "Maybe you have caught it off Annie," she whispered to Urdda. "Maybe it is a disease, like coin-sores. But maybe it was Annie herself done this!" She sat on the bench next to Urdda and gazed hopefully into her face. "Annie knows. I told her soon after Miss Dance brought us here, before it could come out otherwise."

Urdda shook her head. "It was me," she said. "I know it. I was so angry, beyond . . . beyond *anything*, last night, but this morning I woke so fresh of it all, every memory of what you told me gone, until you accused me now—and even now, thinking about it . . . Yesterday I thought I would burn with that rage for the rest of my life. Today—well, I have no particular feelings about it at all. That is not natural."

Branza tried to read what went between them, but their expressions would not resolve themselves, Urdda's into fear or delight, Liga's into pride or dismay.

"I did it. I did *something*," Urdda said calmly.

Liga stood up. "I will speak to Annie. Has she woken?"

"I have just taken her up her bloom-tea."

Still in her cloak, Liga hurried out. Her swift feet sounded on the stairs.

Branza sat next to Urdda, and exchanged with her that look that sisters exchange when one of them has just married, or birthed, or been injured, and the world changes shape around them.

"These—" Branza tapped the nearest man of cloth. "Are these the reason that Mam went away? Are these what she was running from, when she met the moon-babby?"

"These, among others. But these are quite bad enough, I would think."

"Why, what did they do?"

Urdda tried to find ways to say, but only shook her head.

407

"Come," said Branza. "I have some idea what town boys do, get them together in a bunch."

"Oh, no, Branza," murmured her sister. "They are *so* much worse than I ever thought."

A peal of laughter rang down the stairs then, from Lady Annie's throat.

"What is she laughing at?" said Branza. "Has she gone mad? Should we go up there and rescue Mam, maybe?"

There was a flurry of thuds upstairs. Annie croaked and Liga protested. Then Annie's walking stick *tack-tack-tack*ed along the upstairs hall. "Let me see the girl!" she cried.

"Urdda?" called Liga, not entirely happily.

Branza followed Urdda out into the hall. At the top of the stairs, Liga was wringing her hands. Lady Annie hobbled energetically into view, her gleaming house-gown trailing.

"Little witchlet!" she cried out when she saw Urdda, and laughed delightedly, showing the full glory of her ivory teeth. She came to the stairhead and held the rail and waved her stick. "Greater love no daughter has, than to shaft the buggers what shafted her mam!"

"Annie, please! Branza knows nothing of this."

"All you need to know, Branza, is that justice have been done this day. Come up here and let me kiss you, Urdda-girl—don't make me break my scrawny neck upon them stairs!"

I woke up feeling as if I'd put in a good night in Keller's alehouse. Anders was shaking my shoulder, and Ousel stood by the crib, out of which Bedella's wail rose, thin as twine, miserable as a kitten down a well.

"Bab wants her nurse, Da," says the little man.

"I think I hear that, Anders-lad. Which one of you dropped that anvil on my head i' the night?"

They both of them eyed the bed for it, which made me laugh. "Come along, then, my lads, let us go and put her at Lissel's."

The moment we stepped out the door, I thought: Annie. The air stank of twitten-magic and streambank-magic and all that stuff of those Cotting women and that widow. What's she been up to?

It did not take long to find someone who wanted to tell me. A little longer and I had several tellings, which, when put one beside the other, the true tale began to emerge. Further on, my cousin-in-law Arth Barrens gave me a good accounting. What have Annie got against those five? I had to wonder.

I left Bedella with Lissel; she were now crying full and lustily, convinced she would die milkless. Then up my boys and I went to Annie-Urdda's, as they called it. They fair danced up the town, and despite my thumping head I felt the cheer in my own step, and the burnt air had the same effect, I felt, as the clean air at the summit of the Mount when the first snow has fallen.

The Widow Cotting opened the door, and straightaway, by her pallor and her nervous manner, I knew I had come to the right place. She embraced the boys, distracted, and stood back as they ran on into the hall. "Come in, Davit," she says.

"Good morning to you. Is that leddy at home, or is she still flying about, spelling people?" I said jovial, walking in.

"Oh, Davit." She shook her head and shut the door. " 'Tis not Annie! Come in the workroom; we are all huddled there."

My, they were a picture, the three faces that met me from around the table.

"Davit!" cried Annie happily. "You will never guess how this has come about!"

"I think I will," I said, because Urdda had flushed red as soon as she saw me, and Branza was giving her that look, part awestruck and part glad it was not herself that was at fault. Anders and Ousel were sat along the bench with them already; they loved this room, but were seldom allowed to enter it. "But perhaps you had better tell me, rather than me waste your time guessing."

"Ooh, little mens!" Ousel danced a white figure cut of cloth upon the tabletop. I saw both Branza and Urdda restrain themselves from snatching it from him, and all the women stiffened, or tried to disguise that they were stiffening.

"How many is there, Ousel?" I said.

He counted them up from the bench beside him. "*Five* mens!"

"That's fine counting," I said. "Five, eh? And what would Miss Urdda Cotting have against those five particular men?"

She were gazing down the table, away from me, but Branza was not so embarrassed. "They hurt Mam," she said, "once upon a time."

Now Liga reddened, and Annie was no longer so amused. And it all thunderclapped together in my mind: the word "hurt" and what it could mean, coming from Branza's mouth; the sudden seriousness; the extent of what had been done to the five townsmen. Then, with a littler concussion, the black figure Ousel was making to walk along the table: of the five, that must be Hogback Younger. No one but Branza and Anders would meet my eye.

"How long have you been witching, Urdda-girl?" I said, to move myself off such thoughts.

"A single night," she said with a bitter laugh. She looked

410

up, and clear as a clanging bell Hogback's lineaments marked her face. I felt as if I were seeing her for the first time as her mam must see her. *They hurt Mam.* That would be Hogback's way; he would never do anything without assistance, without an audience.

"And even then, I did not know I was doing it," Urdda went on. "I did not know I *could*!"

"She have just come into it," said Annie with quiet pride. "She have just reached the right age, for her, and the right pitch of feeling."

"That must be quite some feeling," I said. "Widow Fox, it's said, has lost her senses, seeing its effects upon her son." Urdda hung her head. "Hogback has sent for his physician at High Millet." I spoke gentler, seeing how she sank under my words. "And there are fears for Joseph Woodman's life, he is bleeding so badly."

Urdda's nose was no more than a finger-width from the tabletop. Ousel walked the black cloth-figure and a white one up to her head. "This is a big rock, fallen in the road," he made the white one say, and then he laid the black one down and had the white man scratch his head. "What are we going to do?"

"What *are* we going to do, Ousel?" I said.

"We are going to have some breddamolk," he said decisively. "Because we are *too hungry* to lift it now."

"I think we have done enough," said Liga; she had sat forward so that her face were hidden from me by little Annie. "Are you saying we should go and *tell*, Davit? Admit what Urdda has done, and have the constable up here again? Explain to *him*? Go through the whole . . . Go over all the reasons, past and present?"

"Of course not," said Annie. " 'Tis too late for that. Urdda

411

have took matters quite into her own hands and accomplished them. I say we should keep our heads well down."

I thought of Constable Whinney's laborious face, the embarrassment it would show as he was being explained to. Crimes against women he had no sense at all of; powers other than fists and blades he did not want to acknowledge. "I think you are probably right, Annie, for your own peace's sake. But what are we to do with our new sorceress here, to keep her feelings running off from her again?"

"I think there is nothing else in the world," said Urdda to the tabletop, "that would make me as angry as what Mam told me yesterday."

"Ah, but you will not always require that degree of feeling," Annie said, "now that you are woken. Much slighter annoyances will set you off. I had to move out of town to that mudhole of mine, I had tripped up so many people here or made them fall in fires, just for being born luckier than I was, or speaking harsh to their wife or child. You will call down who knows what for some fleeting irritation—*unless!*" Here Annie slapped the table, making us all jump, making Urdda lift her head and look hopefully across, making Liga sit up and lose some of her worried look.

"Unless what, Annie?" said Branza, for Annie would only sit there with her eyes flicking back and forth, watching her own thoughts, a smile showing more and more of her fine teeth.

"Why, unless she is proper instructed, of course," she said, beaming. "And there is no need for her to manage on gypsy scraps and dares-and-do's as I did, and made such trouble. We know exactly where to send the girl for teaching—and very gladly she'll be taken on, to keep her away from my dangerous urgings and influence!"

412

And she rocked and cackled there in her seat, like a little black hen so pleased with itself for having at last, and after much struggle, squozen out its first egg.

The carriage stood in the road outside St. Olafred's gate, dark and glossy and stern as the woman who owned it; the horses, the black and the dapple-gray, tossed their heads and stamped and made rich sounds with their harnesses; the coachman waited, dapper and solemn in his seat; the footman stood neat at the door. Miss Dance's house-woman, Goodwife Marchpane, who would companion Urdda on her journey to Rockerly, strolled in the roadway, somewhat apart from everyone so as not to intrude on the goodbyes.

"Here he comes at last!" said Liga, and there indeed was Ramstrong, carrying little Bedella down from the town gate. Anders and Ousel ran ahead.

"Oh, is this *your* coach, Urdda?" Anders marveled.

"It's splendid, isn't it?" Urdda was glad to be distracted from the thought of bidding everyone goodbye.

"Horse!" Ousel skidded up behind. "One horse, two horse!"

Urdda caught him up and kissed his soft face. "Oh, I shall miss you!" she said, and she could not help it; the tears started to come. "Who shall do my counting for me?"

"Bedella were in the middle of her breakfast," Ramstrong explained to those waiting. And as if to prove it, the baby hiccuped a posset of milk onto her chest and looked aggrieved.

"Now I must go," said Urdda fiercely, putting Ousel down. "Goodbye, Anders; come and hug me. Look after your family for me, won't you?"

Ramstrong twinkled, standing by Branza and Liga. Urdda kissed the baby, and tears for Todda were all mixed in with

413

goodbye tears, and she could not tell one pain in her chest from the other. "Bear!" she said to Ramstrong, and they embraced as well as they could, with the bab held to one side. Urdda could not speak to Ramstrong's kind face beaming down on her.

"You are off to such adventures, Urdda!" he said. "Just as you always wished! Don't worry, I will watch your mam and sister."

"Please do!"

"They will not come to harm."

Before her whole frame should start to dissolve with misery, Urdda turned to Lady Annie.

"Ah, you big sop-wet," Annie said unsteadily, and reached up out of her tininess to hang on Urdda's neck. "Do me proud, Urdda. Mebbe you can make up somehow for the poor kind of witch I was."

"You were a wonderful witch, a *wonderful* witch!" Urdda wept into the mudwife's silk-and-lace collar. "'Tweren't for you, I would never have known this true world existed!"

"You ask Miss Dance how wonderful I am," laughed Annie, tears creeping back and forth down her wrinkles. "I am sure she will tell you exackly." And she kissed Urdda on both cheeks, very wet and firmly. "Goorn, now, before your mam goes to pieces."

But Liga had already gone; she and Urdda could neither of them speak, but held to each other tightly. "My little . . . wild girl," Mam managed to get out into Urdda's ear, through sobbing. "Of the forest." And Urdda could not release her.

"Come, Urdda, come," said Branza, but all Urdda did was reach out and enfold her with them.

"Oh!" Urdda wailed into the middle of them. "I cannot go! How could I think—"

"Of course you can," said Liga brokenly.

"You *must*," said Branza. "You must make proper use of this gift of yours."

"She's right, you must." Lady Annie patted Urdda's back. "Else whenever you take a temper, all St. Olafred's must watch its arse, ha-ha!"

"Annie!" said Liga, and now Urdda had laughter to contend with as well as tears and sobbing.

"We ought to make our start, Miss Cotting," said Wife Marchpane quietly, to one side.

Urdda released Liga and turned upon Branza the full force of her emotions. "I shall miss you so!"

"And I you, daft sister. You must send word when you can, whenever anyone is coming this way from Rockerly."

Urdda stood back. "Take care of Annie," she said earnestly. Both their faces were warped with the crying. "And of our mam."

"You know I will," said Branza.

It was terrible, holding Mam for the last time, and then pulling away, feeling as if, yes, she were truly tearing her own heart into two pieces, with all the pain and mess you would expect. Up into the carriage people organized her, almost by force, she was so disabled by her grief. She tried to dry her eyes and look seemly out the carriage window, but the faces out there, some distraught and all beloved, undid her again. Then the coachman's tongue clicked and his whip flicked, and Urdda leaned out and clung to the sill, and wept her family and her friends out of sight.

Wife Marchpane did not try to console Urdda, but only patted her knee every now and again, and before long—now that the goodbyes were done, the faces gone—Urdda breathed somewhat freer, and her tears slowed, and she could lower her handkerchief more often to let the fresh breeze cool her face.

415

It was early autumn, all the light and the forest leaves proclaiming the end of things, even as Urdda's life, her *own* life, shaped and impelled solely by her own powers, was just beginning. Outside was a festival of warm colors: the dark branches bore past their lading of brass and rust, of gold and startling red. The sky was clear blue through them, with a white puff here and there of cloud. Past Marta's Font, with the glint of always falling water and the battered cup on its chain, the carriage rushed, and the coachman slowed the horses only slightly for the narrow place, just above the dell where the ruined cottage continued to crumble away.

I used to sit in that house, Mam said in Urdda's memory, her voice fine and chill through the scraping and squeaking of branches against the carriage, through the coachman's muttering outside. *My da would not let me go up and look, but I would listen, when a coach came by. Where was it going? And who was in it, I would wonder, flying by me so fast, rich enough for a coach, and free enough to go where they pleased? And now look at me, in a house in town myself, a reputable sempstress and a mam, a mam of two grown girls!*

It was me, Mam, Urdda said now, in her memory. *It was me, Urdda, off to learn my magic properly. There was some accident of time, maybe, and it was this carriage, and me rich and free inside, that passed above you, that you heard.*

She could feel the magic there, in some other level of the world, the wellspring and the whirlwind of it. She had used a little drib of it only, scotching Anders' fever the other night, under Lady Annie's instructions. (*This I caint get wrong,* the mudwife had said. *This I've been doing correct since I first come to womanhood, no doubt of it.*) Now Urdda fairly tingled with all her unused powers. She was going to Rockerly, to live and to work with Miss Dance, the person she most admired in the world! She was apprenticed to a real magic-worker—and she was a sorceress herself! Who knows, she thought, what I might find it in myself to do?

She wrapped her shawl closer around herself and sat back in her seat. At the coach window, out in the fine autumn day, the trees flung past their sunlit leaves of red and gold, like brightest jewels thrown and thrown again from a treasure-box, which, itself being magic, would never be exhausted, never emptied, never spent.

17

$\mathcal{W}$inter came, and Liga was grateful to be kept indoors by the weather so that she need not meet and greet and converse with complicated true-world people so much, who were always unnerving her with unexpected remarks, and requiring her to devise suitable responses. But she was charmed, too, by the pleasantries and efforts people made at Midwinter, to sing and bring light to the town, if only by torches and lanterns; to bring greenery from the pines on the Mount and warm it to sweet-scentedness in firelit rooms; and to enliven the plainer winter fare with this pie and that preserve, this taste of summer and that, brought carefully through to winter's depths in wax-sealed pots.

February arrived, and the world lifted slowly to wakefulness again, the streets unmuffling themselves of snow and becoming first grim and treacherous, with ice between the cobbles, then drying, surprised, in the gentler air that came rushing along them, promising nestlings and flower buds and greenery.

Liga and Branza and Annie spent the Day of the Bear as

guests of Widow Tems, whose house was on the market square, where every Bear must pass at least once during the chase. From an upper window they could gain a fine sense of the madness and festivities, and see clearly the wild, roaring Bears in their flapping skin costumes and the maids screaming away ahead of them.

"How can they *stand* it?" said Branza, clutching Liga's arm, shocked to laughter by the sights below. "How terrifying! And then to be caught so roughly, and dirtied so! I would think it would feel so shaming, somehow."

"Shaming? Never! 'Tis grand fun!" Lady Annie hung over the window railing and shook her little fist. "Show me your cheeks, Tossy Strap!"

And the girl turned up her laughing face, slime-striped by Bear fingers. "Come and run with us, Leddy Annie! I'll bet you could put on a turn of speed if you wanted!"

The year warmed and flowered and warmed some more. Midsummer came and St. Olafred's bonfire burned high, the sparks spinning off among the stars as the townspeople danced below.

Liga danced with Ramstrong. *You do not dance like a bear,* she thought, and remembered his answer: *But you and I know, Liga . . .*

Todda had been dead a year, and of course Liga had not been responsible for her dying—how could she ever have thought that of herself?—and the whole town was saying, *Who is he going to take to him, to look after those three children?*

They were part of each other's lives now, the Ramstrongs and the Cottings and Annie. And they were balanced out in what they owed each other, with Ramstrong's and Todda's kindness to Urdda paid for by all the women's assistance after Todda's death. Liga, Branza, and Urdda were like extra aunts to the children, Annie like an extra grumma, so comfortable were the little ones with them.

And here she was, dancing with him, in the couple-dances and, more bravely, in the round dances this year. Around the circle she went, from hand to hand, and all the men greeted her most politely, and some with that courtly care that made her think, Oh . . . you? And she felt she was beginning to see how matters were organized, how attractions made themselves known, how people sought each other out and entertained the thought of each other as courting couples, as married ones.

Then she arrived back at Ramstrong and the final part of the dance began, the reunited pairs in procession up the middle. Imagine, always to have this arm at your waist, the arm of a good man and kind, who had been to your heaven and loved it too; who had seen your daughters in their childhoods there and begun wanting daughters himself.

That hand there—as a paw it had once rested against her cheek. If that was a man-gesture, and a man looked into you the way Bear had looked, or spoke to you and abased himself as Bear had rumbled and bowed, that would be a man who felt some attachment, no? That would be a man who had some hopes towards you.

The fiddlers played on and the bonfire roared in the midst of the dancing and games, in the midst of the town in its finery and feasting. I do belong here, Liga told herself at the edge of the field, among friends, and with a daughter nearby. It is where I began, after all, before Mam died, before Da spoiled me. I ought to feel I have come home, and that the life of these goodwives, whirling in their husbands' arms, is mine to claim too. Surely I have worked hard enough to prove myself deserving? Surely I have raised my daughters happy and healthy enough for their origins not to matter? Her eyes sought out

Branza, who was with Sella over there, helping Aran into a woolsack for the men's race. *She* feels at home, that is clear; she has no need to inquire after how she was begot, but takes her place quite calm and confident now, in this world. Perhaps I should follow her lead and put past pains behind me, scrub away their last traces and look outward from my workroom somewhat more, and try not to resist whatever joyous events await me, that the true world has in store?

He came to her in the early autumn, almost a year to the day after Urdda left.

"May I speak with you private?" he said softly at the door, and all seemed so right and clear that her heart did not even quicken, as it had tended to lately when he was near.

"Come into the workroom," she said. "Branza and Annie are out visiting."

"I saw them near the Ash. I thought I would take the opportunity."

She went around the table to her work. "Look, the town have given me bear-pennants to make; the old ones are going to tatters. Six portraits of Ramstrong, they want, all sewn onto yellow silk." She laughed and sat in the engoldening afternoon light.

"Oh, no," he said, his eyes on the bear-face that she had embroidered with eye-whites and teeth and a pink pillow of tongue. "Bearness is bigger than only me."

"Bear of Bears, I have heard them call you," Liga said. "Should we not give the young men of this town something to aspire to?" She laughed again—she was laughing too much. She should get her chatter out of his way so that he could say what he had come for, and make her life in this true world all right and complete.

421

He waited until she had sewn a few stitches. "I have come to ask you, Liga."

The sunshine was warm on her back and shoulder; the yellow silk shone it out, making all corners of the room glow, making Davit's face glow. There was much in his eyes, but now he had a man's mouth to speak it; he need not nudge her with his great furred head, or snuff and grunt and cry out, voicelike but inarticulate. "Yes?" she said, and smiled up at him, his face always so kind and thoughtful, so familiar now—the face that anchored her in the true world, that told her she had returned, and why. Then she looked to her stitching hands again, because he was finding words difficult and she wanted to give him peace and time to phrase it however he wanted, without her looking expectant.

"I have come to ask you for Branza's hand."

Her needle stopped in the cloth. Everything stopped—all sound, all movement, life. Just for a moment it stopped, while her hope, while her illusions, detached themselves from the cliff-face of what was real, what was likely, and collapsed around her. And upon her, crushing her, deafening her, raising a suffocating dust.

Bruised, breathing very carefully, she made another stitch—a poor one that she must undo directly, a black thread straying out into the yellow like a spider's leg, like a loose hair of the bear who, though wild, must be heraldic, must be better-groomed, less shaggy, than . . . than bears Liga had known.

"Branza's hand," she said wonderingly, slowly drawing out the errant stitch.

She had not thought Ramstrong could be so cruel. But look at him, speaking there, glowing, his face not a whit less kind than usual. He was *not* cruel; he had no idea what he was—

with that blur of talk from which words darted to stab her: *affection, beautiful, protect her and take the best care, feels the same towards me*—what he was disassembling within her, what he was condemning her to live without. How he was embarrassing her! Because of course! Even Branza was somewhat older than he; in this world, Liga was old enough to have *mothered* him. How could she ever have thought it possible?

But she had. She had thought he would remember their little time together. She had thought that in his recollection of that day at the streamside, of all those days, all those scratchings and strokings, he would somehow—but how would he ever, in this harsh world? why, everyone would laugh at him!— he would somehow overlook the years between them, would be able to see in her, to love in her again, that younger woman she had been—and still was, here inside; still was! She felt she was crying it out to him, in her slow, careful stitching. She still was that girl, the age that he was now, inside this older body. She had had a good life—nothing had broken or embittered her. He had only to accept her as that girl and she would *be* that girl again, full of vigor and laughter. Anders, Ousel, Bedella—they all loved her; they did not think her beyond their consideration. How could he— Why did he not—

Still he was talking. They were thinking of wedding before next Midsummer. *Midsummer.* She nearly choked on the thought of the word, on the thought of the time, on the thought of herself dancing, overexcited by the touch of a man, knowing nothing, stupid as ever, turning her own head with fantasies a woman of twoscore years and more ought be ashamed of. She sewed, slowly and unsteadily, up the bear's cheek towards his ear. She had drunk too much dandwin that night; she had lost her senses. But that did not account for the weeks since, when, cold sober and in the clear light of the softening summer days, she had continued to hope—to *expect*, idiot woman!—that Davit Ramstrong intended to marry her.

"That is," he said now, "if we have your blessing, if you are happy for us to proceed."

"Of course I am, Davit," she said, careful not to speak too coolly, or too sweetly either. "Of course you have my blessing. We are so much like family already, it is . . . it is wonderful that we truly will be." She nodded gravely across the table. It was the most she could do; she could not assemble anything like a smile onto this face of stone.

He thanked her; his voice was uneven from the strength of his feelings, from the strength of his love for her daughter. There was a small silence then, in which everything Liga must not say seemed to clang around the room, ragged and noisy as Strap children: *But I shall be your mother-in-law! You know, of course, that she is my sister as well as my daughter. But did you ever feel for me, there by the stream, or anywhere? Oh, tell me I was not mistaken, not such a great fool!*

She put the bear-pennant on the table. "Oh," she said, "I will fetch us some dandwin, and we shall toast your betrothment."

This they did. Ramstrong's eyes glistened a little. An actual tear fell from Liga's, though had he tasted it—had he licked it from her cheek!—he would have known it to be a bitter one, not a tear of joy. And they sipped their wine and talked of many things, true-worldly things: children, and living arrangements, and the timing of the ceremony, and how the marriage would look to other people. He had given her her part: *You are to be my wife's mother*, he had said. And, always easily directed, Liga slipped straight into what she must do, offering payment for this and for that, keeping always to the practical side of things and away from the subject of her heart, and Branza's, and most of all, Ramstrong's.

They talked so long that Annie and Branza came home and found them still talking, and Liga had the exquisite pain of seeing the news broken to Annie, of seeing Branza radiant with the announcement, bending to kiss Ramstrong's cheek as he sat there, standing behind him with her hands on his shoulders as if claiming him—but of course she was not!—from her mother, a look in her eye that of course was not triumph, but only happiness spilling over, soured and spoiled into something else only in Liga's jaundiced eye. And of course Ramstrong did not mean by that smile, by that laugh at Annie's teasing, to say *Ha! I have escaped you, old-woman Liga!*—it only struck that wrong note and distorted itself because Liga's ears, along with the rest of her, had stiffened with the nightmare she was enduring, and everything was being misshapen on its way into her.

It was misshapen all along! she thought, grief-stricken, remembering so many sweet smiles of Branza's to Ramstrong that had been to her own mind only daughterly, so many fond glances of his towards Branza that Liga had taken for fatherly, or shyly bear-like, so many instances of Branza's urging that they go to the Ramstrongs' house, which Liga had taken for solicitude towards the motherless children. Now all these came clear, as steps towards this betrothal, where before they had been pleasant gestures somewhat to one side of Liga's own hopeful purposings.

But *had* she been utterly wrong? Could she have misread so badly his bear-eyes, his bear-gestures, his bear-paw against her cheek, his green breath? She longed to know for certain; she yearned for him to tell her—but only that he *had* loved her, and only in company with his *still* loving her, loving her now, and wanting to wed her. She did not want to hear him say, *Oh, yes, Liga, I did, I loved you dearly. But that was in the past. It faded as soon as I saw you step aged from that other world, no longer the young mam I fell for.*

She would not ask him. She could not stand his saying *no*, the misery of it. And if it were *yes*, she could not endure his embarrassment, to have once loved the woman who was now to be his mother-in-law. She must keep smiling, this quiet, re-tiring smile that seemed to have fixed itself to her face so that no one would bother her for her opinion, her reaction. She must think, now and always, of Branza, and of Branza's happiness—had not her main care, however misdirected, al-ways been for her daughters' happiness?—and keep smiling, with her wise lips closed upon that aching question.

The day before the wedding of Davit Ramstrong to Branza Cotting, the bride's sister Urdda, seventeen summers now, rode her own bay mare from Rockerly. A fine figure she cut, coming up St. Olafred's main street on the splendid, sweating animal, in dark Rockerly riding garb and a hat from which two black silk ribbons flowed out behind her. She was not yet quite so awe-inspiring in the gravity of her bearing as Miss Dance, but she drew the eye nonetheless with her straight posture, her gaze bright-inquisitive as ever, the smile tweaking her lips and lighting her face.

That evening, the Cotting women and Lady Annie had their supper at Ramstrong's house. Urdda had let it be known that she had brought a gift for Branza that she wanted them all to see, and after the meal and the clearing-away of it, Liga and Urdda joined Lady Annie and Ramstrong in the sitting room, to wait for Branza to come down from putting the children to bed.

426

Urdda could not keep still.

"Stop *rustling*, you, in your fancy silks," Lady Annie said, laughing across at her. "You cannot hurry them babs."

"Indeed, no," said Ramstrong from the window. "Bedella will want the full song cycle tonight, with Branza here, and guests, and the wedding tomorrow. She will take some settling."

"Tell me more about your lessons, though, Urdda-girl," said Annie. "What is that fearsome Rockerly witch learning you in the way of transmoggerfercations?"

"Oh, so much I hardly know where to start telling it! This, that I've made Branza—why, it's just like one of those broidery samples Mam made us do—you remember, Mam?—before we moved on to real linens and dresses. 'Tis a piece of busywork Miss Dance gave me, to practice directing my energies without doing harm to anyone."

"And is that lady satisfied with it?" said Liga. "I would hate to think you were shaming me with your broidery. My, the tussles we had over those samplers, Urdda! I remember your first one—it was all blood-spots and tears. Much like my own first efforts, only with more anger brought to the task, I think." She smiled, and fondly, at the memory of her daughter's rages.

"Miss Dance thinks this is very fine," said Urdda, pinking slightly. She had it in her hand now, a small satin drawstring bag containing some smooth, stonelike thing.

"Show us!" hissed Annie. "Before she comes down!"

"I shall not." Urdda closed her hand around the bag. "It is for Branza, and no one should see it before she does."

Down the stairs through the house, which was all opened to catch any movement that could be had of the stifling air, Branza's singing floated, like a spell itself, like ribbons of gentle sorcery looping and floating.

❖ ❖ ❖

"At last!" Annie roused herself as Branza came into the sitting room. "We are near gone mad with guessing what is in that bag of Urdda's."

Davit patted the back of the guest chair. "Here, my love, best you have the seat of honor, I think."

"Is this gift not for the both of us, Urdda?" Branza crossed the room and sat.

"Oh, no. I've a wedding gift you both shall have tomorrow. This one is just Branza's—but I wanted all to see it, so you can know what I am capable of now."

"This will lift the hairs off our heads." Annie sat forward, perching on the edge of her armchair with her gaze fixed on the bag.

But Urdda did not give it over straightaway. Holding it tightly, she leaned towards her sister. "Do you remember, Branza," she said very low, "a dream that you had maybe two months ago, about your wolf?"

"Yes!" The word jolted out. "However did you know of that?" For though the dream had been extraordinarily vivid and the warmth and wistfulness of it had lingered several days, she had spoken of it to no one, not even Davit.

Urdda chuckled. "I know of it because I made it, sister. I engineered that you would have it, for the purposes of my gift."

"Can you do such? How powerful you are!"

Lady Annie nodded in satisfaction.

Warily, Branza accepted the bag from Urdda. She was not at all sure she wanted to feel again what she had felt from that dream.

But there was Davit, kneeling beside her. What harm could come to her while he was there? What could spoil the fact that they were to be married tomorrow, that she was to be loved and protected by Davit for the rest of her life?

She pulled open the bag's soft mouth. "This purse itself is a beautiful thing," she murmured. "Like all things from Rockerly town—including my sister!" She glanced again at Urdda's radiant face before shaking out onto her hand an oval silver locket, on a chain. Urdda reached across and turned it over, and Branza gasped, for into the front was set a lozenge of polished cannel coal, on which was mounted a fine mother-of-pearl likeness of a wolf's head.

"Oh, it is exactly him!" Branza breathed. "Who made this, that knew him so well? Did you make him yourself, by magic?"

" 'Tis a Rockerly man; he carves all kinds of animal likenesses. I gave him a description. 'Like this one,' I said to him, for he had a wolf there in talc-stone, 'only with the head higher, and an altogether more cheerful aspect to him.' Hasn't he done well?"

"Oh, beautifully, Urdda. Look at him, Mam! Isn't it exactly Wolf? Lovely!" And tears came to Branza's eyes at his loveliness—almost she saw his fur moving in the wind on Hallow Top—and she put a hand to her heart to calm herself.

"It is a fine piece of carving," said Liga. "And set off just so by that black."

Urdda watched Branza admire him for a while. "That is not all," she whispered.

"It is not?" Branza looked up, frightened. Davit laid his hand on the arm of her chair at the tone in her voice.

"Open it, open it!" Lady Annie whispered excitedly. "For a locket must *hold* something, must it not?"

"Must it?" Branza examined the locket's catch. "What is in there? What have you put? *Should* I look now? Should I open it?"

"You should, so that I can watch you. And so that everyone can see."

Branza laughed softly at her sister's proud smile, at her bright eyes familiar from earliest memory, even with the maturity of their extra year since last she had seen them, even framed by the face refined by that year, by the glossy, pinned-up hair sophisticated by life in that other town. How could Urdda be so familiar, yet such a stranger? How could she be such a foreigner, riding into town on her fine mare, yet still be the little sister of Branza's childhood, fretting and pouting and talk-talk-talking?

"Come on, Branza," said Annie. "I am growing older every minute; I should not like to die and miss this!"

Her fingers unsteady, Branza pressed the catch and opened the lovely thing.

The dream rushed out, changing, cooling, coloring everything. They were gone—Branza's family, Annie, Davit, the furniture and the room, incorporated into and become forest, the home forest. Speech became bird-exclamations and the creakings of branches in the wind. The arbor framed her, the rose-vine clambering over, choked with pale blooms and buds. The cottage was behind her; she did not need to look there to know it was restored, fresh-whitewashed, with the two bushes by the door in bloom, laden with their fullest red, their whitest white flowers, with not a bruise or ragged petal among them.

She walked forth expectantly, happily. She knew he was approaching even before she glimpsed his bounding back, the flash of an ear, out there in the forest.

He leaped from the cover towards her. She knew the stride and rhythm of his every mood, and could tell he was overjoyed. His coat rippled around him, white with gray smoke through it; his face laughed, from ears to pink tongue-tip, the pupils of his eyes pinpricks in perfect-rimmed discs of sky blue.

When he reached her, he stood and laid his forepaws on Branza's shoulders. His weight pressed through their pads and claw-tips. He smiled into Branza's face, and breathed warm and licked her.

She held him as she had held him in the dream, grass damp and stones sharp against her bare feet and her arms full of his warmth, his ribs, his heartbeat, and his spine; her ears full of his voice and breath.

My beauty! she said to him. *My friend through those long days, those years!* She held him tightly, digging her fingers deep in his neck-fur and hearing his squeal-growl against her ear. He had been all the consolation she had had: his beauty and simplicity, the constancy of his presence by her side, to reach to and to touch. In her first months here, how she had missed him! Just the memory of that old aching misery made her weep into his beautiful mane. It was dream-weeping, the purest form, springing straight from stirred emotions to pour copiously out into the bright fur. They were dream-tears, invisible; they wet nothing and assuaged nothing.

Then the tears were over, and Wolf was gone from her arms. He sprang about her, aglow in the evening light. He danced away towards the trees, ran back to lick her hand, and then was off again, impatient, along the path the two of them knew every turn and hillock of, the path away to whatever dell or waterside, rock-form or high meadow Branza would choose today.

With the last glimpse of Wolf's pointed ears, the forest began to flicker and spill. As Branza watched, it transformed itself most logically and wondrously into chair-leg and mantelpiece, room-corner and windowframe, shoes and skirt-drapes and Lady Annie's walking stick, thumping with the mudwife's delight on the hearthrug.

"My dear! My girl!" Annie sprang up and flung her arms around Urdda. "Such wonders! Such . . ." Pride in Urdda prevented her from speaking more, and she buried a tearful face in Urdda's shoulder.

Urdda smiled out of the embrace at her sister, not wanting to miss a moment of Branza's reaction. "Whenever you open it, you will have that dream," she said. "Whenever you want to, you can see him for that little while, and hold him."

"Oh, Urdda."

Branza bowed her head. The open locket was lined with black velvet, and several white wolf-hairs were held into the back piece with fine white silk thread. The thought of Urdda bent over the locket-back, knotting that thread, fixing the dream to make a gift for her sister— With a shaking fingertip Branza stroked Wolf's hairs, which felt as real as ever, as ordinary.

Davit touched her arm, consoling, reassuring—whatever it was that she required in whatever state her emotions had put her. Yes, she thought, calming herself. Wolf is gone. All that world is gone, the way childhoods go, the way everyone's childhood goes. But then there is womanhood, is there not? And wifehood awaits me tomorrow, and for some there is witch-hood and widowhood, and other states I do not know of.

Slowly Branza closed the locket. The mother-of-pearl Wolf was almost more than she could stand to look at, so static and carven when she had just felt his pulse, his breath. That dream Wolf, the life in him, the absolutely convincing impression of life—well, she did not know whether she could ever open the locket again. It wrenched her heart to have seen him, though she loved him. It pained her to think of herself in the times when he had been her only companion, when Urdda had gone and it was only herself and Mam and the dream-world around them. No Davit! No children! Only that strange, bland town! She could hardly imagine it now. How poor she had been, and how empty her life!

She enclosed the locket in her hand; it was too powerful a gift—a piece of her soul handed to her, dressed in the kindest, keenest part of her sister's feelings. Still unable to speak, she lifted it by its silver chain and put it over her head. There, now it rested against her chest; she need not see it and grieve over it. She tucked it into her bodice, where it lay private and no one would ask about it.

"A sampler, you say, Urdda, yet you have near broke my heart with it." Still vibrating from all the strong feelings, she took her sister's hands. "It frightens me what else you might do, with the main part of your magic."

"Oh, no such damage as naughty Annie did, in her time."

Annie let go of her and cackled through her tears. "Oh, I never made anything like that beauteous beast! And how'd you transmoggerfy the room so? Greshus, my skin is still all a-creeping with the amazement!"

"Do you like it?" said Urdda to Branza.

"I love it. I shall treasure him." Branza held the locket through her bodice-cloth. "What a gift! What a power!"

"That is two extraordinary women you have reared there, Liga," said Davit.

"Indeed," said Annie. "You can take all the credit for that."

They all looked to Liga, seated by the window with her face to the light, to the faint midsummer air, which moved the tendrils of hair at her temples. She turned and slightly smiled at them all, and tilted her head most graciously, accepting the witch's and the woolman's compliments, and her daughters' pleasure in them, as no more than she deserved.

acknowledgments

I'm very grateful to the Literature Board of the Australia Council for the Arts for the two-year fellowship that bought me the time to write *Tender Morsels*.

The Tasmanian wRiters On the Rise workshop of 2007 gave the first draft a good kick along: thank you to Tansy Rayner Roberts for organizing the weekend, and to Marianne de Pierres, Rowena Cory Lindquist, Maxine McArthur, Richard Harland, Launz Birch, and again Tansy for the useful critiques and the support.

Jan Cornall's monthly Draft Buster workshops also provided essential support. Thanks to Jennifer Moore for the beautiful setting, and to Jan, Jennifer, Sunny Grace, Tom Thompson, Lyn Berggren, Helen Chambers, Cecile Bower, Lee Lamming, Belinda Bourke, Wendy Fitzgerald, Narelle Scotford, Jinks Dulhunty and Barbara Pheloung, and everyone else who came by, creating the climate in which this impossible thing became not only possible but inevitable.

For sustained and valuable editorial input, I'm deeply

indebted to Rosalind Price at Allen & Unwin, Nancy Siscoe at Knopf, and Bella Pearson at David Fickling Books. For making the whole four-way arrangement happen, many thanks to Jill Grinberg of Jill Grinberg Literary Management.

For the title, I thank Jack Zipes for his translation of the Grimm brothers' "Snow White and Rose Red" in *The Great Fairy Tale Tradition: From Straparola and Basile to the Brothers Grimm* (Norton, New York, 2001) and the anonymous translator of the same story in Jacob and Wilhelm Grimm, *Complete Fairy Tales* (Routledge Classics, London and New York, 2002).

The basis of the St. Olafred's bear ritual is the *journée de l'ours*, held every February in the Catalonian town of Prats de Mollo la Preste, which I first saw on SBS's documentary program *Global Village*. A good description and background can be found online at www.anglophone-direct.com/Fete-de-l-Ours-Prats-de-Mollo.